GW01418673

JUSTIZIA

Hi Andrew
Hope you like it!

Tim

TIM BRADY & MELANIE WILLEMS

JUSTIZIA

LIES AND PREJUDICE

First published in Great Britain 2017

Copyright © 2017 Tim Brady and Melanie Willems

First published by Tim Brady and Melanie Willems

Also by the authors:
"Big Ben – law and disorder" published 2011
"Beaux, Belles – grind and punishment" published 2013

Paperback ISBN 978-0-9567919-4-8

No part of this book may be used or reproduced in any manner
whatsoever without written permission from the authors except in
the case of brief quotations embodied in critical articles or reviews

1 3 5 7 9 10 8 6 4 2

Printed and bound by CPI Group (UK) Ltd, Croydon, CR0 4YY
Typeset by Alison Padley

This is a work of fiction. Names, characters, places,
incidents and dialogues are products of the authors' imagination
or are used fictitiously. Any resemblance to actual people,
living or dead, events or locales is entirely coincidental.

www.melandtimbooks.com

For Adam and Mounir and Tim WJ

"Morning, noon & bloody night,
Seven sodding days a week,
I slave at filthy WORK, that might
Be done by any book-drunk freak.
This goes on until I kick the bucket.
FUCK IT FUCK IT FUCK IT FUCK IT"

Philip Larkin

For Adam and Madeleine ("M")

1

Opportunity knocks

Polina wandered through Warsaw city centre. She held a polystyrene cup of hot wine. It smelled of cinnamon and brandy.

It was a bright winter's day but the sun's performance was a disappointment nonetheless – all mouth and no trousers. The celestial orb was not quite up to dealing with the open refrigerator feel of the day. The sun gamely provided an illustration of what warmth might look like. Golden fingers of light did the best they could. They touched the remodelled features of the oft-destroyed city with the cheerfulness of a professional smile. It was still cold, though. The air bit cheeks and chafed lips. The sun's rays were beaten, the cold weather had won.

Polina, having been let down by Edgar again, was dreaming yet again of escape.

She was not supposed to be wandering alone on this Sunday afternoon. Edgar had promised to be there. They were supposed to be in love. They should have been making plans, and executing them. Implementation was everything. Nothing happened, unless you made it happen. You can't just sit there and expect things to happen. Dreaming? Dreaming was like drowning in ideas. Dreaming was a waste of time.

She sighed unhappily. Edgar was often supposed to be there, and he generally failed to meet that aim.

Of course, he was an artist – a musician, no less. Once upon a time Polina had found this compelling and exciting. Sometimes she still felt the sense of pride that had once burned in her. Reality had doused those flames. Pianists lived the life of writers: hours spent on their own, sweating compulsively over expression and meaning, before suffering the glare of attention. She rather thought musicians had the worst of it, because public performance was unforgiving. Edgar got himself into such a lather over performance. He was a melancholy sort. He was skinny, and permanently ruffled. His brown eyes always seemed a little hurt, and he needed Polina. This used to be endearing. Now it felt like a heavy chain. This was why Polina's dreams of escape were getting more intense.

She was training hard in her limited spare time to become a dancer. To fund the lessons and the costumes, she temped in offices. It was dull work. Warsaw was booming, even if not for Polina. It seemed at times to overflow with property speculators and stag parties. She wished that it weren't so. It was like watching a teenager run blindly in completely the wrong direction. She hoped for change, but suspected that the only change within reach was moving from one firm of professionals to another. For something to change properly, someone had to make the first move. Whatever that might be.

Being alone, even with hot wine, was dismal. She was a beautiful girl, with pale clear skin, and the golden hair of fairy tales. How was she reduced to wandering aimlessly on a Sunday afternoon?

She saw a bench, and sat down. It was cold. Her bottom felt cold. This was rock bottom, the pits.

A voice stirred her.

"May I sit?"

The man wore a beautiful leather jacket. She noticed that right away. Polina recognised good material when she saw it. It was rough-looking leather, but it was superbly cut. It made you want to touch it, and follow its lines. The stranger was rough-looking too – but in that devil-may-care way that inspired excitement and wariness. He was slightly stocky, broad-shouldered – yet clean-shaven and neat. Like the boss of a successful removal company, thought Polina.

She moved a strand of her golden hair and smiled tentatively at him.

"Yes of course. You may sit. It's a public bench."

"With you sitting on it, it is more like a throne."

He said this quite seriously. Polina saw straight through the manoeuvre. However, she was feeling downcast, and in that situation you may find yourself taking whatever is on offer. Polina felt pleased that someone had plucked her from invisibility.

She shrugged.

"I don't know about that. Make it your own throne, if you wish."

"You sound as if you have a case of the Sunday blues."

Polina sighed.

"Not really. My boyfriend gave up a stroll in favour of practising the piano. I just feel that I am wasting my time. Maybe I should take up piano playing too."

He considered this before turning towards her:

"If you could do anything at all in the world, what would you do right now?"

She felt a little thrill. Her answer came readily.

"Escape. I would escape. There must be more to life than this reconstructed town centre."

"There is."

She looked at him curiously.

"Such as?"

He shrugged.

"Well, it all depends on how much you really want to leave."

"Oh? Really?"

She rolled her eyes.

He did not smile. He leant forwards and stared intently ahead.

"It's a serious business, moving on. You need to think about things never being the same again. You also need to think about offering what is not already on offer where you are going. Tell me – can you dance?"

Polina sat up. She was uncertain as to where this was going, but it felt very much how she imagined a conversation with fate would feel.

She weighed her words carefully.

"I dance. But I do realise that it is a passion, and not a steady career… "

"Steady career? You should forget a steady career.

4

There is no such thing anymore – hadn't you heard? At best you'll get an unsteady one. Anyway, I don't want to trouble you. I wish you all the best."

He pulled his jacket tighter, and stood up.

"No, wait." said Polina. "You are not troubling me. I'd like to hear your ideas."

"I'm getting cold," he said.

"There is a bar just over the way. Just to talk, mind you."

"Okay, if we can be quick. My name is Janusz."

"I'm Polina."

They shook hands awkwardly and moved on to warmer surroundings.

An hour later, things did not seem so bad. Janusz had explained with some intensity to Polina how he had set up a business relationship with a dance venue in London, and how they were always looking for talented employees. Polina felt that this could be the unexpected breakthrough that she had been looking for: an opportunity to dance, as a principal occupation, in London, the creative centre of the world. The pay sounded impressive, and there was plenty of spare time.

Polina had been reading a number of books to guide her in her decision making. They were often American, and told her to move the cheese, or not to move it, and to seize the day, or to live for it, and how dreams do come true if you just act now and buy a ticket to a conference. Part of her snorted in derision at such simplicity, but part of her wanted to believe it. It must be true that for many people, they simply got lucky one day and then bang! Off they went to an easy, happy life. They worked at things they truly loved. They got paid well for it.

I mean, she thought, how hard can it be? Why not me?

She placed her hands on the table.

"Janusz, if I told you I was interested, what would be the next step?"

Janusz looked at her pensively.

"I don't know if you could take it. You see, you would have to trust me about everything. For example, I can't give you any written contract. This is an artist's agreement. For this reason, I don't think that this is a suitable opportunity for you."

"Surely that is for me to make my mind up about?"

Janusz shrugged.

"What about your family? They will have reservations. Families always do. And what about your boyfriend?"

Polina sighed.

"May I speak to you frankly?"

Janusz nodded.

"My boyfriend, Edgar, is a dreamer. He is very good – a pianist, as I think I told you. He is the embodiment of a pianist. You should see him. He is wiry, and tousled – and he has very long fingers. But it's not going the way I would like. He is wrapped up in himself. He thinks that he is the only sensitive soul on earth. He questions everything. He thinks that he is the first person to have formulated any question he stumbles upon, and that he is the only person in the world who could figure out the answer to his latest preoccupation. I also think that he knows that, in truth, he is not very good looking. He is too slight, too perturbed. So, being with Edgar has not been easy. And now that he proves again that he is not even reliable… "

"So why are you with him?"

"I feel quite sorry for him most of the time – and the rest of the time he is playing music. The music is very, very beautiful. He is gifted. It is something special. But maybe now even that something special is no longer enough."

Janusz stared at her.

"These are all very big decisions. I think you need time to consider this."

Polina laughed a little wildly.

"Time is flying by Janusz! I am twenty-four already. Twenty-four! Almost a quarter of a century. I do not have time to waste."

Janusz nodded again. He produced a card.

"If you are serious, then call me tomorrow. I can sort it all out. But you are going to have to trust me, and I want no complaining. This is your chance. If you take it, you take it."

He took her hand, and squeezed it.

"Please do not waste my time."

With that, he rose and left her.

Polina squared her shoulders. Several drinks had filled her with a wild warmth. She would do it. She was no time waster. Seize the wintry day, throw out the pianist with the bathwater and move to London to be an artist.

This was it.

"Hello, Slava?"

Slava flicked his blond hair back and scowled slightly.

"Yes, Janusz. What is it?"

"I have another package for you. Usual terms. Does this work for you?"

Slava stubbed out a cigarette.

"Only if it works out. When is the arrival?"

"It could be by the end of the month. I'll move fast. Make sure everything is ready?"

Slava smiled.

"Have I ever not been ready? Let me know more in the next day or so."

"OK. Bye."

Slava rested on his sofa, which was new. His ex-council flat in Hackney was looking better now that everything was falling into place. Business was good, but he did need the fuel to keep it growing. Human resources – you need to keep finding them, and using them. Living off the hopes and dreams of others was hard work.

In contrast to Poland, London was warm in the early evening sun. The weather was so unlikely, and so perfect, that the Outrageous Fortune bar had thrown caution to the wind and set up four tables outside. Each table was decorated with a sprig of spring flowers in little glass urns. Rubens, the bar manager, had splashed colour over the iron chairs. They now sat there, freshly painted, picked out in green and pink and blue, like metal chameleons. Ben and Kelly sat outside, resembling a couple in a magazine. Ben, in an Italian suit, was wearing sunglasses. Kelly sported an electric blue dress.

Ben stole a glance at Kelly. She was people-watching with glee. Her eyes darted around the busy Soho street, taking in the edgy, the fun and the downright eccentric. Leaving work on time always felt like a mini-holiday. Kelly and Ben did this so rarely these days – and almost never together. This was a moment to savour.

Kelly nursed a ridiculous looking drink. It was a goldfish bowl of a cocktail, an unfeasibly large balloon glass proffering a blue mixture, with an umbrella expertly positioned on its rim. Rubens had also produced some mixed nuts.

"Mixed nuts in the bar, mixed nuts outside the bar!" Rubens clarioned, as he kissed Kelly fiercely, the privilege of the perfect, sweet friend that he was.

Rubens was happy to see Ben and Kelly together. They had suffered a major hiccup in their relationship recently when she had fallen into bed with a beautiful Scandinavian man in Paris. What, though, did anyone expect? thought Rubens. Paris is the city of light. This might turn any Scandinavian's head – and any American's, too. Kelly was from the South of the United States. Her head was all over the place at the best of times.

Paris is also, of course, the city of love, or at least, of what can pass for love and be every bit as good as love. Hell, who needs love, when there is a stunning, humanity-saving Swedish doctor, offering the chance to have a fling before his difficult posting overseas, in one of those ex-and-soon-to-be-again war zones? As for Kelly – well, she had a body made for sin, and she was a little hard-hearted at times, and sometimes quite selfish. Adorable, in Rubens's eyes. Never a dull moment in her confessions. That mattered to Rubens. He could only be a decent gay best friend if there was something to talk about. It could not be the one way street that was sometimes portrayed. Friendship should be bound with juicy secrets – societal duct tape, saving the many from being utterly bored to death by the few.

Relationship-wise, Rubens couldn't fathom how straight people managed. It was a mystery to him. Of course one could be happy and faithful, living in thrall to convention. There seemed to be plenty of people in situations where the only opportunity for intercourse were the local service providers. Some people, too, may really prefer it if very few others saw what was carefully concealed under their clothes. But when – like Kelly and Ben – you could stand and face your body in the mirror, as proud of its imperfections as of its attractions, revelling in your sexuality, then it appeared to be a little more natural to slip and fall into the cracks of the Giant's Causeway of life's relationships, because life *could* be taken to be a crazily paved natural landscape, that one enjoyed, clambered over, saw beauty in, stubbed one's toes on, and ultimately left, having taken a photo or two. It's just one of those things – each to their own. One cannot, and should not, tell people what to do in their personal lives, mused Rubens.

He grinned in approval of his thoughts, stroked Kelly's hair, and moved to serve his other customers.

Ben loved Kelly. He loved her spark, her Southern gumption, her scorn of authority, her delight in tackling things head on, like a buxom bull in a boardroom. He also loved her for having nearly lost her. He could still conjure up a secret gnawing feeling – that he might have blown it, had he not caught himself in time, had he taken a different tack, had he walked away. Even in the arms of passion one might always dream of walking away. Passion gave such power to hurt and betray. Ben knew his own power. He knew that men and women alike lusted over him. He was no stranger to casually indulging his desires. But when Kelly and he clicked, they clicked properly. They fitted. They spoke of everything. They knew what it felt like to think of many tomorrows with confidence.

And yet – was there not more?

Kelly reached out and touched Ben's arm.

"Hey," she said, "Are you all right? You seem a million miles away."

Ben smiled.

"I'm here, all right. I don't want to be arrogant, but I notice that that cute guy opposite hasn't stopped glancing over, and several girls have been checking me out as they pass us."

"Get you," said Kelly cheerfully.

"How did it happen?" asked Ben.

Kelly looked sharply at him.

"What?"

"You and that Swede Morten. How did it first happen? How did you meet?"

She looked puzzled.

"I've told you this already, no?"

"No. We've certainly talked around the subject. But I think I want to know now."

They sat in silence for a moment while Kelly digested the change in subject.

She sighed.

"I do want to talk about everything with you. But is it really good for us to do that? Isn't talking about everything a little overrated? Does it not simply open up cans of worms that we should leave well alone?"

Ben leaned in confidently.

"I think that would be true for many people. But I've been thinking a lot about this. We – you and me – are different. We really are, Kelly – genuinely so. The sum of us is more than many other people add up to. You're a strong-headed woman who went off and dealt with her own sexual needs in Paris. I'm a bisexual man. This used to trouble me. But I'm growing into it now. It's actually brilliant, and I don't mind if nobody understands or agrees. I have more certainty. I don't know how to say this elegantly – but I could show any man a good time, just like you can. So knowing about what has happened will bring us closer. It wouldn't be the same for a guy who viewed Morten as a threat. I did at first. But I'm pretty sure that I can deal with it now."

Kelly looked pensive.

"I don't know," she said, "I sometimes think talking is the root of all evil. Discussions do not follow agendas – least of all personal discussions. They can veer off quickly and inexorably, careering into things that should remain unsaid."

Ben nodded.

"On the other hand," he reasoned, "who wants to be one of those couples, who only talk about the weather, the TV, what they are eating or going to eat – and little else?"

Kelly shuddered.

"You're right. We *are* different. You're my bisexual best friend and my lover, all at once. It is extraordinary. I know how lucky I am. And I know how close we came to throwing it all away."

She took another slug of her drink.

"God, this is good. I may need to have another one."

"Let's take it easy. A drunken talk is definitely not the same thing as a proper one."

Kelly nodded, happily.

"Must pace myself. I was never good at that. Maybe Rubens will bring me some sparkling mineral water?"

Rubens did just that.

Ben stroked Kelly's cheek.

"You know, I have been considering this. It's not about us in isolation. People tie so much into relationships, and sometimes we get lost in them. They make us scream and ache and mad and happy and lonelier than you could ever imagine being, as well as more tightly bonded than a weld. It's only by hanging on in there that one experiences the full spectrum of feeling – the amazement of survival, that deeper love where imperfections become critically important, because it's the very imperfections that distinguish the person you love from everyone else. But all this can only apply if you chance to be with the right person, the true friend, the best accomplice."

Kelly looked surprised, but said nothing.

Ben continued.

"That's why Morten can't hurt us. He never could, unless we let him. And knowing about what happened is simply a way of dealing with it, and actually feeling happy about it."

"Happy about it?"

Ben banged the table.

"Yes. Happy. Happy for you. Don't you see? It's not impossible. Why shouldn't I be happy that you had a great adventure?"

Kelly looked a little confused.

"I'm not sure I follow you entirely – but anyway, if you want to know, by all means I'll tell."

She settled back in her chair and toyed with the stem of her glass.

"I met him in a café. To be honest, he just hit me like a freight train. He was tall, blond, handsome, in great shape, with intelligence shining out of him. Oh my God, Ben, you'd have gone spare too."

Ben snorted, but he looked amused.

Kelly was getting into it.

"It's just strange how on very rare occasions both people feel the same way at the same time."

"Feel what?"

"That mysterious, but *certain* attraction. It's not always instantaneous, is it? You're always told that falling in love takes time. It seems to be able to develop over several meetings. But it's also a thing that can simply hit you. And you always end up wondering: why *that* individual?"

"People say that it's chemistry."

"I think it is chemistry. It's certainly hard to resist. And I suppose that it can become true love. But we do try to be a little all-encompassing around love, don't we? Everything has to be love. That attraction I speak of – it's something a little different. Part of it is probably purely

14

down to appearance – not necessarily conventional beauty tropes, either. For me, it's more of an independence thing – the fact that someone can take care of themselves. At least, that's what it seems to be for me. Also, I do like being entertained. I think I search like a rat for people who are just not being boring."

Ben nodded.

"That all seems fair enough. I always think that there is a parallel with food. Young, it's all there, you want it all, you eat it all. Older, you appreciate what it does to your body. You feel as if you can do with less of it, too. You view it with a little more concern. I feel now with sex that I'm like an austere little cleric sitting before a table heaving with jellies and roasts and sauces and sweets... "

Kelly laughed dryly.

"Oh Ben, not only have *you* pushed right ahead in the buffet queue, but you've also grabbed the last decent portions on the table."

"I think I have," said Ben simply, "That's where my confidence comes from. And if that's true, we can use our trust and love to live life to the full."

Kelly's eyes widened.

"You mean...?"

Ben looked at her steadily.

"If we can't talk about having a proper open relationship – then who on earth can?"

They talked as the evening first cast long shadows, then darkness crept across the table. They repaired indoors, because the anonymous hum and throb of a bar was an ideal backdrop to chat some more. The full gamut of arguments was run. It would never work in practice – discuss. It offends human nature – discuss. They downed another three drinks each – potent cocktails each one – and taxied home to make love with vigour laced with concern. Where might this all lead?

"Ben," said Kelly as she nestled against him, "I'm game. We could try it as a project. Only as a project – and we each must come first, above anyone else, always. But if we can manage that, why not be avant garde? When we're long dead and buried, people will still be wondering about this. We can leave a trace in time, and see if it leads to a different way of living."

Ben kissed her.

"Changing the world? It might be less hassle than ruling it."

Kelly's eyes glinted.

"Let's not go too fast, mind you. We'll keep this under close review. We're not lawyers for nothing. We'll have to hammer out some rules."

"Well, that tofu wasn't properly cooked."

The dog's owner sniffed haughtily.

"Trixie eats it at home and she is perfectly alright on it."

It was difficult for Rubens to smile at the customer, as he looked up from cleaning up a nasty dog accident. Accident? This was no accident, he thought bitterly. This was the revenge of the dog world for all those strays he had booted around Rio. This was no proper dog, either. It was a *poodle* – a snide cotton puff on four legs. Just look at the bastard thing. It had obviously been bred to serve as a Rabelaisian wiping tool – an aid in removing make up, or at a pinch in wiping one's bottom. It was a terrible excuse of a dog.

Rubens had to remind himself that Trixie's owner was a heavy spending regular at the Outrageous Fortune bar. The thought of those extravagant bar bills helped a little, as Rubens mopped the floor. This was a classic customer and provider relationship, he thought grimly – one of gain and pain.

Oh, the mess made by dogs. Who would not love a dog, eh? Such enthusiastic, playful, loving, loyal, *incontinent* beasts! Rubens narrowed his eyes. Can we all stop pretending, he thought, that it behoves a person to be scrabbling around with a plastic bag behind a dog's behind? How is it that, supposedly intelligent as they are, they cannot be trained to go in one secluded place?

Rubens stared at the dog, which stared balefully back at him.

You little shitter, thought Rubens. *You work creator, you breaker of backs. You're a little sack of meat halitosis and muddy paws. Who would have ever wanted to domesticate you? You may as well have fallen for the tarantula.*

The dog yapped.

Perceptive little bastard. Rubens moved on. He would come back later to polish the floor.

When Rubens had moved on from his previous life as a fitness instructor come go-go dancer (and occasional escort) to the heady heights of managing one of London's up and coming cocktail bars, he had thought that all his Christmasses had come at once. It still took his breath away that the bar owners had taken a chance on him in this way. He imagined that this new position would soon bring the feeling of having truly made it in his adopted home.

This came to pass – to a point. Some days, Rubens felt that he was a bright spark, making England's metropolis flame into glorious life every day. On those days, he considered that London simply wouldn't be London without people like him lighting up its leaden skies, creating a glittering enclave of excitement, and dispensing temporary passes to a wonderful world of style, sexiness and, well, the odd organic tofu treat.

Today, however, had not been one of those days. All the understated cool of Outrageous Fortune could do nothing to protect him from the carousel of chores that lined up like groupies for a boy band. The next task awaited him, as inevitable as a rent boy's betrayal. Ray Cousins had arrived for a pint of Stella – *"How much?"* – and a chat. Oh, that regular chat with Ray. The prospect of it shivered Rubens' timbers as he prepared for the steady descent into the gloomy reality of Ray's life.

If only auld acquaintances *could* be forgot, thought Rubens wistfully.

Rubens had first met Ray a decade earlier. Things had been different then. In those days, weekend clubbing was as important as diligently collecting Club Card points was today. At the time, Ray was one of the characters at the centre of a magical parallel world. He was to be found surrounded by glamorous bodies, eager to partake of his potions and pills. These gave Ray the aura and desirability of a card-carrying A-lister. Few were more popular on the party scene – for a while, at least. Sadly, Ray's clubbing friends had proved as ephemeral as the illicit highs Ray's friendship afforded.

"Rubens, how are things?" said Ray.

The greeting was his first and last offering of bonhomie. After this, everything took a nose dive. It always did.

Today's chat proved particularly tedious. Even Rubens' *espiritu brasileiro* was struggling to ward off its debilitating effects. Ray was droning on again about how shallow people were, recalling how he had been unceremoniously dumped by the beautiful people as soon as an unfortunate episode with a sex toy had curtailed his appetite for the excesses of the night, one weekend long ago, in Amsterdam. Now Ray had run out of money, too. He couldn't understand that the prospect of an evening in his council flat off the City Road to watch Britain's Got Talent and enjoy a microwave curry failed to lure in his erstwhile chums. After all he had done for them. The ungrateful bastards.

Ray sipped his beer so slowly that Rubens was convinced he was losing at least half of it to evaporation. On the quieter afternoons that Ray favoured, Rubens was a caged lion, unable to escape the attentions of customers who insisted on hanging around the bar, talking at Rubens, demanding attention. No one had told Rubens that the hardest part of his job would be feigning interest in stories so dull they made matt look glossy. These things were a barman's Herculean labours. It was not a chore that could be avoided, as it seemed even the most crashing bore suddenly rustled up a thousand friends to badmouth a bar on social media when they felt that they had been mistreated by the serving staff. Damn the internet! Worse, Rubens still felt sympathy for Ray. He wasn't a bad man. He had just fallen far from the position to which he had become accustomed straight into the lonely lows of growing old.

When Ray had suddenly looked up brightly, and informed Rubens that he had so enjoyed their little talk that he was considering breaking the bank and having a second pint, the Brazilian had almost lost his cool. Mercifully, West End beer prices not only allowed ridiculous bar rents to be met, but also swiftly tempered Ray's sudden extravagance. He had spent some time further weighing up whether another pint was really worth the price of two ready meals. Rubens finally breathed as Ray's parlous finances came to the rescue and carried him off to look for a bus home.

Time to polish the floor, then.

Rubens had just finished restoring the shine to Outrageous Fortune's floor, and was getting off his hands and knees when Trixie jumped up and gave him a big lick on the face.

"Oh, look how she likes you. Oh, doesn't Trixie like the nice man who cleans the floor after her! Oh, she *does*!"

Rubens contemplated dropping his waxed cloth onto the woman's coiffured head as he headed past her back to the bar. He decided wisely that it wasn't worth it. The woman may be a patronising old trout, but her outsized tips matched her outsized lips, and Rubens had certainly done worse for the money.

Consoling himself as he often did with the thought of the extra cash, Rubens wondered exactly when the highlight of his working day had become the purchase of his acquiescence with money. Tip tip hooray, indeed. He had discussed this state of affairs with his partner, Tarquin. Tarquin, an art dealer, had also become an expert in tolerating the lack of manners which often accompanied a surfeit of money. They both mused on manners more than occasionally. Was this just the way of the modern world? How many of the people one walked past on the way to work were also victims of the unthinking awfulness that customers subjected their suppliers to? *The customer is always right*, they say. Rubens hated that expression. Customers were so frequently, patently, not right – but got away with their unreasonable requests because most people, most of the time, would sell a large part of their soul to ensure they could pay a small part of their mortgage.

God, work is hell, and hell is other people. That Sartre, he got it right.

Rubens was satisfied that his pity party was going with a swing. There were more arrivals expected. He turned over the facts in his mind. Thanks to London's extended licensing laws, some customers also felt they could be right *all night long*. Why, only the night before, Rubens had made a mistake. He'd allowed a pair of well-heeled Germans to order a bottle of champagne at five-to-closing-time. Admittedly, it had been a slow evening. Rubens had therefore leaned back, smiled and thought of the bar's profits. The staff had not been impressed, as the champagne was drunk more slowly than Bowie preparing a come back album. The Germans seemed blissfully unaware, as most West End late night revellers usually are, of how heartily sick of the evening the staff already were. Milo and Dorota couldn't wait to slip their shackles. Having done all the tidying that they could without physically chucking their customers out on the street, they took up positions at the bar, directing hostile glares at those who blocked their escape.

Rubens had felt guilty.

"I am sorry, but they have just parted with almost a hundred pounds – I can't kick them out straight away. Do you two want to leave me to close up?"

Rubens gave his staff what he thought was a generous, managerial look.

Dorota snorted.

"Don't worry, boss, we'll wait with you. By the hungry looks on their faces when you opened their bottle, they want more than just bubbles from you tonight. If we leave now, they'll whip their Weißwursts out and you will be covered in their *kommen Sie hier* before you know it. And how could you go home to poor Tarquin like that?"

Rubens was glad not to be left alone, even though it meant suffering the loud sighing that Milo and Dorota were taking it in turns to indulge in.

Many minutes of stilted bar chat later, Rubens decided he had to take action. With all the charm he could muster, he approached the two men and advised them of the late night options available to them within walking distance. He ignored their come-to-bed looks and courteously escorted them out the door.

Dorota's eyes flashed mischievously.

"Thanks to God for that! Talk about overstaying your

welcome. I was about to offer Milo's services just to get rid of them."

As often happened in Outrageous Fortune once the last customers left the staff alone, the atmosphere picked up. The glimmer of freedom had returned. The long ride home would at least be on one's own terms. Some element of choice had returned to the situation, at least until the next shift. As he exited the bar, Rubens felt his spirits lift further. Homeward bound!

He bent over to lock up.

"Hello again. Heinz and I were wondering if we could offer you a drink."

Rubens turned from locking the door to the bar to see the two Germans eying him up like a couple of mutts who had chanced upon the winners' enclosure at Crufts.

Was he never to escape?

He wondered how he could let the men down gently. They had contributed all they were going to to his bottom line.

Dorota took charge. She strutted over, dragging Milo with her, and linked arms with Rubens.

"Meine Herren, I am so sorry to disappoint you, but my boys have promised me that tonight they are all mine. And although I can get my legs into incredible positions, I don't think I could manage more than two at once. You've got to know your limits. I very much hope that you enjoyed your champagne, though, and do please come again. *Guten nacht.*"

Rubens wasn't quite sure whether it was disappointment that marked the Germans' faces as the threesome sashayed away to safety. He hoped it was. A man has his pride, after all.

Those moments were sometimes amusing in retrospect, thought Rubens, and quite remunerative overall. But he was glad that the Germans had not made an appearance again. It just got so complicated sometimes. He owed Dorota for getting him out of a hole there. He sighed at the woes that studded his working life, and as if on cue, his mobile chirruped from his pocket. It was from the bar owners, Alex and Jamal.

May we see you after you close up? Alex and I need to ask you something. We're in All the World. Jamal xx

How Rubens' life had changed. Not long ago the invitation to join his best friend for a late night drink in Soho on a Friday night would have lightened Rubens' soul. It was always fun, and it offered endless other possibilities. There used to be a real *anything could happen* feel to the whole shebang. That was then – before Rubens had landed in his relationship with Tarquin Henderson Smythe.

Although Tarquin was away on business, Rubens had no desire to do anything naughty. Tarquin had created a bubble that Rubens had little desire to step out of. It could be love, if love were like an invisible hem to Rubens's carefree nature. Was it love that meant that "a drink" would be just that, and nothing more? Rubens felt, too, that he was in a serious relationship with Outrageous Fortune. His best friend was now his boss. How curious was that. He was responsible for their money, and was building a brand. He had an image to maintain, both for the owners' sake and for the customers. *Oh for a quiet night in, bingeing on a box set!* What had happened to him?

All the World was a hardy perennial in Soho's rich garden, and there was the usual queue to get in. The bar was down its own little alleyway, which at least gave the queuing a semblance of having arrived at one's destination. The walls were adorned with lines that the owners obviously thought would be appropriate for warming up the crowd. Not for the first time, the words caught Rubens' eyes as he waited patiently, alone:

All the World's a stage

And all those men are such players

They have their exits and their back entrances

And one man in his time plays with many parts

His acts being seven ages

At first the infant, screaming and pouting in his nurse's arms

Then the preening schoolboy, with designer bag, prancing like peacock, unwillingly to school

Then the out student, alcohol fuelled, and with woeful refrain, for so much unrequited love

Then the gym rat, full of strange chems and muscled beyond his genes. Sudden and quick in quarrel, seeking the bubble butt reputation of bare-chested club

And then mid-life responsibility. In fair, round apartment with luxury lined. With eyes full of judgement, and shirts with sleeves. Full of catty putdowns, and modern cares; and so he plays his part.

The sixth age shifts into the lean and slippery Portaloos of provincial Prides. His youthful photos, well-saved, a world away from his shrunk import, and his big manly chest, turning again towards chicken bone youth

Last scene of all, is second childishness and grateful oblivion; sans clubs, sans gym, sans everything. Except the Internet of course.

Poetry – even mediocre poetry – always intrigued Rubens. He liked words, and understood meanings to text that were not expressed by the words literally, but rather by their juxtaposition, which itself led to quite specific impressions and thoughts. Plain words that meant just what they said were good too, of course. The reference to mid-life responsibility struck a chord. It was not a cheerful one to dwell on. Wasn't mid-life responsibility the flip side of a mid-life crisis? Did one birth the other? It seemed so. Rubens suddenly noted that he was indeed wearing a shirt with sleeves – and had just been wishing that he was returning to the feather-bedded pad he shared with Tarquin. He wondered exactly when he had traded carefree, youthful liberty for the gilded chains of stability. He pushed the door and went in.

Rubens's friends were deep in conversation at a corner table. Were they discussing his performance at the bar? As Rubens caught himself scanning the room for Outrageous Fortune customers that he should greet on the way over, he reflected that he never thought work could encroach so much upon his social life.

There was no getting away from work. His job involved him being friendly to all, including the dull, occasionally unpleasant characters. Tarquin always said one was unable to choose either one's family or one's customers, but Rubens couldn't help but think that most people's clients at least disappeared at the end of the working day. Rubens felt a little like a doctor on call, never knowing when he would need to snap into work mode. Feigning delight when all he felt was ennui became tougher over time than he had thought it would be. Still, Rubens never failed to remain pragmatic. His thoughts remained coloured by the hope that this continual compromising of his soul would at least bring in honest remuneration.

Escorting had not been like this. On the rare occasions that he had run into any of his escorting clients when on Rubens time, they had displayed an admirable amount of consideration for Rubens' privacy. He grinned. Actually, they were probably terrified that he would encroach on theirs.

His friends rose to greet him.

"Here he is. London's finest host!"

Although Rubens wasn't sure he liked that moniker, Jamal's smile always warmed him. They shared history. The two exotic imports to London life had gelled the first time they found themselves realising the value of their assets on adjacent go-go podiums. Jamal had become the brother Rubens had lost – and had made Rubens realise that he had never really known his own brother in the first place. A lot of baggage had boarded the planes from Rio and Algiers with Rubens and Jamal. While taking London clubland for all it had to offer, the two men had helped each other slowly unpack. Painful memories held more creases than even the most carelessly crammed-in linen suit, and had to be teased out before they could be safely discussed. It had not always been easy, but, as Alex would say, it had certainly been *character building*. And fun. Rubens had to make more of an effort these days to remember the importance of pure, simple fun.

Alex smiled.

"How are you, Rubens? How was business tonight?"

Alex's question seemed to be yet another nail in the coffin of irresponsible freedom. It summed up so neatly the reality of this working relationship. Rubens appreciated that he worked for Jamal and Alex. He looked after their investment in the bar. They employed him, in a role which included clearing up flaming poodle accidents.

Rubens squared his shoulders.

"Good. And good. What's up?"Rubens' smile didn't fool Jamal for a second. His husband Alex could be a little insensitive at times. Jamal leant forward.

"I think you should get to the point, Alex. You are always so good at getting to the point, after all."

Now it was Rubens' turn not to be taken in by Jamal's smile. Something was up. What was coming? They hadn't visited often recently, especially not Alex. Were they going to sell up?

A waiter turned up. They ordered drinks. Rubens' thoughts continued apace. He had given almost two years of his life to building up Outrageous Fortune. His life had changed. He had changed. They couldn't just cut him loose now, after all he had given, all the *crap* he had had to deal with. Or maybe – just maybe – it would all be for the best? Thoughts raced against each other. Rubens' Panglossian side whispered that this way he could get his life back. He might be able to start ignoring all those customers he didn't like. There would be freedom to be a soldier of the night again, a return to his bubble butt reputation. With emotions stirring, Rubens did what he did best. He put on his best, utterly opaque, wide Brazilian smile, gazed into

Alex's eyes – and waited.

Alex looked happy.

"Rubens, I don't really know how to say this, but you are doing better than we could have hoped for. We couldn't have managed this without you, and things are going great guns. Jamal and I have been thinking about how to get you more involved. We both think you've earned it, and it will incentivise us all to share more. We've talked it over, and made a decision. We'd like to offer you an ownership stake in the bar. Of course, it comes with chains. We'd want a guarantee that you will stay with us for at least the next three years in the manager role. We need you hands-on. We don't think anyone could run the bar the way you do. We hope that with skin in the game, so to speak, things can only get better. What do you say, gostoso?"

Rubens was stumped. He did not know what to say, so he nodded slowly. He was incredulous. The bottle of champagne that Jamal had ordered arrived.

"Thank God you agree, *habibie*, as tonight we are going out to celebrate. We'll give you five minutes to call Tarquin and tell him, and then you are ours. You need to show me that you can still bring it, baby. It is the weekend, after all."

Rubens grinned happily.

"Tarquin's away, baby. I'm all yours!"

2

Let's open our kimono!

Event organising is like an animated cartoon. A team of people beavers away to make any event happen at all. Its members are the swan of lore, gliding smoothly on the surface while paddling frantically below. Nobody should be able to guess at the struggle on the day.

Within the team, there will always be a struggle. An events team is a battle of wills, a moveable feast, a dance to music that never stops. Sensible members of the team fight to contain and gag the less coherent ones.

The responsibility of organisation often stimulates delusions of grandeur. These delusions emerge like mindless butterflies, flying around meetings with no connection to reality or cost. Delusions like this cannot merely be suffered: they have to be dealt with. The goal remains to procure for the many the answers to the few straightforward but crucial questions – along the lines of what, when, where, and occasionally how, will something happen?

The sensible members of any team have it easier from time to time. Some occasions are less challenging than others. Take a law firm party, for example. A law firm is a simple beast. It will be grateful for a half-decent drink and a palatable canapé. It does not need its head turned by a world-class acrobat hanging from the ceiling in a costume that a child might have created, had she thrown up sequins all over herself.

The newly appointed events team at mega law firm Sagworth Turner Dickerhint knew that it had to understand both its limits, and the limits of the people it served. There were budgets to contend with, and custom and practice to respect. Ultimately, no one was called upon to be too daring. It would never work – not unless people were either very willing, or very drunk.

The events team were acutely aware of the limitations of working with lawyers. It was a road well-travelled: many of them had been working on producing the same event over and over again for a decade or so. Occasionally, this weighed upon them.

It is not as if they had always lacked ambition. Ideally, they would have preferred to organise the Oscars. The fantasy of running an event with the eyes of the world upon one was a distraction that they enjoyed. Imagine planning every last second of spontaneity! The reality, for them, remained serving up an adequate evening of entertainment on budget, then worrying about every last dullard in the room, before disappearing off gratefully as the event drew to a close, leaving a small gaggle of tired and emotional people in a corner, and someone humping someone else in a stairwell.

There was *always* someone doing that. The protagonists seemed to think it counted as wild and unusual. They were mistaken. It was at best the mechanics of reproduction, performed weakly, in a hopeless place. Those indulging in such coquettish behaviour failed to understand that they were the inevitable and the pretty tragic, rather than the racy and the unexpected. This was so, because the next day, the tale of the stairway sex would be an instant firm anecdote. It would be trotted out regularly thereafter, as a companion story to the constantly repeated tale of the senior partner spasming with the receptionist upon the never-since-played piano in the reception area. That happened so long ago that it was surprising there was anyone still alive at the time of the event to recount it, and yet such tales live on, like out-of-date condiments in a store cupboard. The senior partner concerned was last seen looking old and bow-legged. He smelt of old man now. It's a smell as recognisable as wet dog – a sort of musky mould smell, like the earth of the grave, cut with a streak of soap.

Yes, the events team would have liked to organise something bigger. Could they have done a worse job than those in charge of the Oscars, they wondered? Award ceremonies are such bloated and self-congratulatory marathons. The team argued about this from time to time. It would be good to bring something new into play, they pouted. They all dreamed of finding different dimensions to their daily tasks. The team would never in fact progress beyond keeping legal entertainment events humming along exactly as they already were. The reality remains that few people ever transcend the ordinary – and even the Oscars seemed ordinary these days.

Tonight, Sagworth Turner Dickerhint was launching, formally. Created by a merger, it was huge, almost overwhelming in size – too big to fail, and certainly too big to manage. Its partners now scurried around its corridors like cockroaches in walls, reduced by the size of the organisation to numbers on a spreadsheet. To be a partner now was to be threatened, bullied and relieved of power. It had never been less appealing – and yet there was precious little else to aspire to, once you landed on the treadmill of practicing law in an international firm.

In a conference room nearby, a group of partners gathered to talk, ahead of the launch. They were getting to know each other again. Some had already worked together in other guises, at other ventures. There was a sense of history repeating itself.

This was not altogether comfortable. However, any awkwardness or indeed touch of unease were being absorbed efficiently by the ability that lawyers develop of projecting an air of competency, even when entirely at sea. For, metaphorically speaking, lawyers can spend far longer at sea than sailors. In fact, to say that they are sometimes at sea, one needs to picture them *literally* in a small boat, with holes the size of dinner plates in the hull. That's how on top of their briefs they can be. Yet they paddle on, where sailors would have leapt off long ago into the arms of a passing dugong. On a good day, lawyers may joke about this. But it's not much to be proud of.

Nicholas Casterway entered the conference room. He had the air of someone who feared nothing and no one any more. He had not changed in recent years, as if he had frozen time with an icy glance. He remained tall, thin, his bald head gleaming, his small round glasses glinting expensively.

His mood was not good today, but he had it under control.

Bartlett de Vere followed him, so jovial that his very eyes had crinkled up until they look like clenched sphincters. Peregrine Thornton rolled in, breathing heavily. He is getting fatter, thought the others. He had a head like a melted church candle: rippling dripping rolls of flesh fall onto his collar, with no pause for a chin. He may look a mess, but he is kindly, and they like him. They like him all the more as nobody wants to be him. They don't think he will live very long. Not that they expect his immediate demise – just that he will pass away a *seriously* long time before any of them. It makes you feel kindly towards a person.

After a short pause in arrivals, Harry Gumpert appeared in the doorway, handsome still, in good shape – a welcome contrast. Hartmut Glick arrived after that. He moved like a panther, and he was well dressed. He never turned his back to Nicholas.

They all eventually sit down and exchange pleasantries. Each of them feels a small thrill. They do not like each other much, but occasionally, sitting together in a room with some sense of common purpose ignites a temporary spark of collaboration. They haul their intellects into gear and find some common ground. These are the better aspects of working together.

Bartlett is worried. He thinks that no one has really thought the merger through. He does not believe that anyone States-side truly understands the Swiss Verein structure.

"Is this going to work?" he laments, the small boy spying the naked emperor.

"Why wouldn't it?" says Peregrine, as unconcerned as

any ill-advised, lazy protagonist would be.

The others shrug a little. They don't really appear to care.

Bartlett is startled at the breezy indifference. He's been worrying about this for some time. He attempts to explain.

"Being in a firm is no longer as simple as it sounds. I know this sounds basic, but for the organisation to work, you need a common understanding of how things operate. Bang – right there you have a problem. We don't all operate in the same way. Our cousins across the pond don't always appreciate how *we* operate. They don't get what we have put in place. I mean, we've all embraced the concept of managing the structures separately, with a view to progressing towards full financial merger once figures cease to be – er – shall we call them cobblers and massaged fiction? We could only move to full financial merger once those figures actually start to have some relationship with reality. You know – as in, not how much you *fantasise* about earning for the firm, but how much is *actually* hitting the bank account that you have personally earned. Now, if our new colleagues don't buy into this way forward, we're setting off with one hand tied behind our backs. The second problem is more difficult to address. Isn't it simply this: some of them have no idea about working together for the benefit of all. Why not? *Because it's not in their interests to do so.* A very steep pyramid structure where, frankly, most toil for their own benefit, suits them. It fits the remuneration structure, which is, as you know better than me, veering wildly off towards a rip off of the many for the benefit of the few. Come on – we all know that those at the top are paid far more than they deserve – just because they're there. *And, every year, they build on this.* It never fails to amaze me: who *ever* made them the bosses? It's a pure accident of history. This situation is getting worse and worse as time goes on. To merge properly, you need to be tied in together – committed, in a much more *real* sense. Were any of you told that partnership was like a marriage? I was. I bought that, hook, line and sinker. We can't offer that anymore. People get pushed around, pushed out, and asked to leave. Others leave for more money – because hell, life is short – and *this* – this unforgiving, lunatic-attracting occupation – is no match for drinking rosé in the sun. Careers are not that long. So: how do we cater for all that?"

Nicholas looked up.

"Bit late to realise all that, Bartlett."

He enunciates his partner's name clearly. Nicholas is a snake in a pit of mice.

Nicholas knows that Bartlett has summed up the problem well. But Nicholas is at the top of the remuneration structure, and he intends for things to stay exactly as they are. He is sanguine about it: at his age, he can afford to be.

Hartmut Glick is less worried than Bartlett, perhaps because he is less insecure, and neither does he care sufficiently.

He waves an elegant hand.

"There will always be abuse, and there will always be abusers. We should be grateful for this. It brings the rest of us together. We can only try to do things right. We are not properly policed. To some extent this makes us free."

He smiles reassuringly at the others.

Harry Gumpert laughs uneasily.

"I don't feel free. I do worry about the pace of change. These decisions to merge are made by people who have no idea about the legal cultures they are getting into bed with."

Nicholas sucks his teeth thoughtfully.

"Harry, Harry, Harry. You would hope that despite your fears, that homework has in fact been done. By someone."

Bartlett brightened up.

"You would hope that," he agreed.

David Milner stuck his head through the door.

"Am I late?"

They all cheered up. David was an unthreatening and popular man. They called him "Dangerous Dave" behind his back because, well, he wasn't dangerous. He was a perfect partner – hard working, reliable, of a moderately sunny disposition. He blamed himself before he blamed anyone else. He was entirely taken for granted, but it suited him. He could barely spell "nemesis".

"I'm excited," he announced as he sat down. "Tonight is just a marker on a page, but this is a framework for something that could be extraordinary. Tonight we have clients, journalists, and institutions taking note of who we are. Who knows where this is going, really – but it certainly feels like the right way to me."

Nicholas eyed him with amused contempt. *Silly little man*, he thought. *You'll be paying for this development for years to come. My job is to ensure I get the rewards of being a god damned lawyer as soon as possible. That means exploiting the association with this latest bunch of mediocrities as best I can. I've got to stay on top, and watch you all produce the goods. Yes – keep you all in check. No initiative, nothing out of line. The bigger the mortgages you take out,*

the larger your aspirations for your children, the less you will squawk
as things proceed. A few of us at the top reaping the benefits, the rest
of you below producing the benefits. The structure took a long time
honing, and none of you are going to be allowed to upset it.

He smiled.

"Our message tonight is simple. It's all good. Everything has come up roses. For the rest, let's keep our eyes open. This group should meet from time to time. There is a great deal to be said for informal discussion. We can agree on matters that I can share with other members of the management team. For tonight, let's tell these guests that they are in the bowels of the greatest law firm ever made. Say it right and they will buy it. What do they know, after all?"

This was obviously the right move. The partners clucked and guffawed their way out. Peregrine Thornton left last, as this allowed him to snaffle a final Bourbon biscuit. Waste not, want not.

Arriving early at the party, Ben spotted Caspar Steele.

Seeing Caspar made Ben feel very old. This was profoundly irritating. Ben occasionally tried to work out what it was that had Caspar jangling his nerves like a disturbed banjo player. He couldn't figure it out.

Caspar was everything as a trainee solicitor that Ben had not been. Caspar was confident, well dressed, and always alert. It was like working with a besuited meerkat.

Caspar was blissfully unaware of anything controversial in relation to his sexuality. He wasn't aware that being gay could ever be an issue. He believed that no one cared. He knew that there were laws about discrimination. He trusted in these blindly. Ben did not share this trust. He thought Caspar naïve. Caspar thought Ben *impossibly* old fashioned.

They had skirted around these issues in previous, short conversations. Tonight, though, Ben felt stressed about the launch party. So, as he sometimes found himself doing when tense, he geared himself up for confrontation.

When under pressure, go on the attack. Ben knew all too well that this was poor advice, but he also appreciated the relief from stress that some judicious aggression could deliver. He strode over to Caspar, noting with irritation the slight fall in the younger man's face. *How dare you not be pleased to see me?* Ben thought uncharacteristically. He all but cracked his knuckles as he towered over Caspar.

"Caspar. How are you?"

"I'm good. Look at all this! I'm looking forward to tonight. It's so exciting to have everyone in the same room, talking, exchanging ideas."

"Yes indeed," said Ben, "So many opportunities for something to go wrong."

Caspar smiled.

"I think it's wonderful when everyone comes together. It reminds you of the expertise – even brilliance – that this firm offers under one roof."

Ben snorted, but decided not to comment. He did not need to. His thoughts were writ all over his face. *What sort of unquenchable moron holds a view like that? Had Caspar swallowed a PR manual?* They stood there a little stiffly, until Ben decided to cut to the chase.

"Caspar, do you tell everyone you meet that you are gay?"

Ben was clear on the boundaries he set for himself. Just

because the event was termed a social one, it did not mean that one should trust any of the people who were awkwardly making small talk, just because of their shared involvement in Sagworth Turner Dickerhint. Did Caspar not realise that one should navigate these events attentively, giving up only innocuous morsels of personal information, finely tuned so they could never be used as a weapon against one? If Ben strayed from general comments on London, work or the weather, he usually stuck to reliable tales of college rowing days. In doing so, he stuck to a strict script. He never mentioned the thrill of on-going self-discovery sport had provided, as he realised that his rowing mates gave him impossibly great feelings in the pit of his stomach. He would also carefully crop tales of the late night drinking sessions, avoiding entirely the one, which had ended up with Ben waking up as naked as an Olympian's ambition next to Adam Kirby, the impossibly handsome power house of the boat.

Caspar considered his response.

"I do tell them if they ask me if I have a girlfriend, or if they are unoriginal enough to attempt to bond with me by commenting on how hot a woman is, because she has a short skirt on and is younger than my Great Aunt Barbara from Boulder. I think those sum up the general criteria for finding women "hot" around here. But, seriously – why wouldn't I tell them?"

Caspar looked at Ben questioningly. Ben saw incomprehension mingled with pity.

Caspar continued, reasonably.

"We live in a free society and I have nothing to hide. I don't think there is anything to be shy about."

He chuckled lightly:

"Did you know that two men can get married now, Ben?"

It made Ben feel venerable, reflecting on the folly of youth. Caspar thought that because rights were enshrined in the statute books, it meant that everyone embraced their validity and upheld them. Not many things really annoyed Ben, but this was one of them. There were plenty of people undermining minorities – at *every* turn. In Ben's experience, it was often the very person who listened so attentively to the inspiring stories of how it was important to celebrate diversity, or applauded a woman successfully juggling a demanding career with two small children, who would then delicately suggest a more *conventional* lawyer would be more appropriate for the next important task. *The client might feel... uncomfortable.* That meant: give the opportunity to an overweight white man with some grey hair.

Ben had a hot pool of anger that bubbled away resolutely, available for any time this topic came up.

"Quite, Caspar. Two men getting married, hey? That's a turn up. I hear also that the Japanese have invented portable music machines. Gay marriage. You're right. That solves everything. History is finished. The modern world really is a wonder, isn't it?"

He turned to Caspar with some feeling.

"Law remains a *conservative* profession, you know. We may have LGBT societies... "

Caspar interrupted.

"LGBTQ, I believe, is the modern term. A lawyer should never forget the Questioning."

Oh, it would be good to smack this minority representative.

Since when had trainees become so self-assured? What sort of a gay man did Caspar think he could be? Ben wondered why he was bothering to educate the younger man. Ben pressed on:

"We may have LGBTQ societies – but that doesn't mean that your career here is best served by being an open book. Discretion is important."

Caspar failed to stifle a laugh.

"Oh come on, Ben! Hartmut is almost as famous for being an S&M master as he is for his legal nous, and I'd heard about your escapades when I was still at law school. If discretion were that important in this firm, then how the hell are you even still here?"

Ben had to admit that, on the face of it, Caspar had a point. However, there was much that the young know-it-all didn't know. Ben glared at him.

"If you knew the whole story and how close we came to not making it, then you would play your cards much closer to your chest. Work colleagues do not need to know about your life outside of the office. Draw the line at musical theatre or avant-garde art exhibitions, if you really must share. I don't care who tells you otherwise: diversity still scares the hell out of most of them. I mean, even garish ties raise eyebrows round here. Trust me. You will go much further in this industry if you play by the rules."

Ben knew he was overreacting. He forced himself to smile. He decided that he had given as much of a master-class in the softer skills a young gay lawyer needed as he should.

Disturbingly for Ben, Caspar did not seem to see it that way.

"Thank you for your concern. But I don't share your views. You see, I have rarely – if ever – encountered discrimination because of my sexuality, and I believe that familiarising my colleagues with my lifestyle choices advances our cause far more than returning to the closet and quaking would do. That seems self-evident to me. In fact, Ben, are you sure that you are not actually one of the secretly prejudiced legal majority you believe inhabit these corridors of power? Why are you bending my ear with this? I know you're bi, but from where I'm standing, you've retreated to a comfortable life with your girlfriend, abandoning experimentation, and have made yourself a very regular person indeed. Well done, if that's what you want. But I reckon the biggest problem you have is that you have sacrificed a part of who you are to career and normalcy. Do I remind you of all the fun you used to have?"

Ben wondered if Caspar had a point, and the thought alone was enough to make Ben angry. This was personal now. Was it possible that his own pleasantly pedestrian life wasn't really what he wanted? What on earth could one do about that, when stuck in the well-remunerated rut of a profession? It was true that Ben wasn't yet old enough to be hearing about a riotously fun weekend without wishing that he was a protagonist. He had no immediate come back. He'd probably said too much.

Caspar seemed disappointed that Ben didn't fight back. The pity in his eyes was no longer faint. He turned to move away, but he couldn't resist a parting salvo.

"Oh, and Ben, if you really want to get down with the kids you should ditch your Japanese music machine and try

Swedish streaming – if that doesn't sound too alternative for you, of course. We wouldn't want tongues to wag."

Kelly woke up. Unless she was having a nightmare, this was never an instantaneous event. Most days, waking was a slow, sluggish emergence from the clutches of what seemed like dozens of warm arms, entwined around her, forming a tight and unbreakable cocoon, against which struggle was futile.

Like many overactive people, Kelly did not usually sleep well. She often felt exhausted. She drove herself wildly through the days, only to be wide awake in the late evening, and therefore failing to get to sleep on time. After tossing and turning until Morpheus finally welcomed her, she would then awake, bright and ready to go, at four in the morning. That preceded the deepest sleep you could imagine – a veritable black treacle of slumber that clung to her stickily and certainly was unwilling to let her go at dawn the next day.

Work drugged Kelly, and stayed with her. If she wasn't silently arguing the toss with an intransigent colleague, she was dreaming, vividly, fitfully, of catastrophes befalling all around her. Ben suffered terribly in these dreams – if he wasn't being shot by a terrorist group, he was falling into a gorge, or hiding from evil persons determined to kill them both. A recurring dream involved the house collapsing. Kelly always awoke startled and panting from that one, with the eerie sensation of falling several storeys fresh in her mind and in her nerves. It was an uncanny sensation – the rush, the butterflies of fear in the stomach, the sense of speed, the lack of control. And death obviously – the inevitability of it all did not escape her, asleep or awake.

She marvelled at how the body seemed to know certain sensations, even if it had never experienced them. Falling from a great height was a strange, deadening adventure. It all felt very, very real.

The result of all this cataclysmic night time activity was that getting up became a battle of wills.

It started with the alarm. How Kelly hated that tinny music, that tedious sound, and all it represented. It was the first battle with authority and the mundane. Both were truly terrible things, thought Kelly.

She sighed as the dreadful daily ditty rattled off for the third time.

"I need," she mused, "an excellent and plausible reason for not going to work today."

None materialised, so she pushed herself out of bed.

It was Friday. That was the best that one could say for the working hours yawning ahead. But all was not lost. Kelly brightened as she remembered that tonight she was seeing Cornisha and Monique.

Cornisha, the transsexual office manager of the Beaux Aspen law firm, had now moved seamlessly to Sagworth Turner Dickerhint. Kelly felt that she owed Cornisha everything. From the moment Kelly had started work, Cornisha had been there for her, with encouragement, support and experience that counted for something. She was a woman of some substance – and Kelly considered Cornisha one of her dearest friends. In so far as there existed such a position for a grown woman, Kelly's best friend remained Monique, her ex-flatmate.

Monique's life had taken a twist towards the sensational. She once worked in public relations with competency, but also with the dull despair that only promoting a terribly flavoured milkshake drink could engender in a person. That had still been better than promoting law firms, which were less natural still, and offered no flavour at all. In the midst of several soul searching European trips, Monique had met a tousled-haired, handsome man. By a stroke of fate and good conversation, she had found herself the girlfriend of Jake Le Jones, lead singer of the Fondant Furies.

Things had moved fast for Monique. She had stepped cautiously into the relationship, with expectations as low as interest rates. Her reservations offered good cause: it's not hard for anyone to imagine how tiresome it is to have a famous boyfriend, someone whom many others thought they would be happy with, too. Every off day you have, every irrational rage, every petulant thought that clouded your brow might somehow count against you. Meanwhile, the PR machine whirred smoothly to take away your other half's every flaw, like a car mechanic working on a car's scraped wing, rendering it smooth and beautiful again, and the right side of new-looking, as if an accident had never happened.

Jake was in fact non-stick in terms of reputation. He was decent at heart, never happier than when reading or watching good films. He was prone to bury himself in obscure cinema, which informed his knowledge of human nature, not least the inability of most directors, however talented, to offer up a short, crisp film that made a good point in a concise way. Well into the latest dirge on life, the universe, and everything, Jake would still be happy, watching the world express itself, and occasionally reveal something of itself. He liked art house films.

He was somehow a man of taste and personality, and Monique could not fathom what he could possibly have seen in her that many more could not also have offered. She was content to wonder about this privately, and keep her guard up. She did not want to be hurt. But Jake seemed to really love her, and she certainly stuck by him, watching out for him, guiding him, tethering him to earth like the rope on a hot air balloon.

It had all led to them living together in a beautiful flat in London, a vast loft on a discreet Clerkenwell road. Jake was touring, and Monique had asked the girls over.

Cornisha, Kelly and Monique met up fairly regularly, despite their lives diverging more than ever. As it happened, Kelly had not made many friends at work. This was not terribly surprising, given that she held most of her colleagues in healthy contempt. Cornisha was different – genuinely good at her job, and quietly effective. She was, plainly, lovely – and such people transcend the direness of their environment. Kelly's closeness to Monique had not wavered. Monique held in trust many of Kelly's secrets and lies. Now that Monique regularly featured in Sizzle! magazine, their friendship had been given a solid boost. Everyone needs someone to confide in.

Kelly would have been unwilling to admit it, even to herself, but she also felt excited at knowing someone who was now known to a great many more people than she knew herself. Why this was so was hard to fathom. But when Kelly entered restaurants with Monique, people often looked, and looked again. Occasionally photos would be taken. At least, Kelly noticed some of the photos that were taken. Monique thought photos were inevitable and she found it a little draining now. Kelly still loved the feeling – but then she was not the target. She could escape it all at will.

When she stopped to think about it, Kelly wondered what was the conversation that people imagined they might have with those they admired from afar? What would meeting your idols mean to you? Monique knew where she stood on that score: she was not the target, but merely the conduit. People approached her so as to approach Jake. People loved Jake – and it made Monique wary. She felt queasy at the sight of the shiny eyes, the hopeful looks that abounded once she had been recognised. It still made her look curiously at Jake when she was alone with him. All this, just because he had cobbled together some words about growing up in England? She would catch herself: she knew that he was a little more talented than that summary supposed. But it all led Monique to only trusting friends who had known her well before Jake came on the scene. The sudden solicitousness of acquaintances from way back, or welcoming gestures from near strangers made her anxious and cross. It was more than an ordinary person could bear.

No wonder few could make these relationships work. It's not so much that artists are worse than anyone else, it's that they have more opportunities than other people. Monique shared this thought with her friends, who nodded.

This was one of their standard ruminations after the first cocktail had hit home.

"Not that you need to feel sorry for any of these artists," said Monique sternly, as they mixed the next batch in her gleaming kitchen.

Cornisha smiled.

"It can't be easy living out of a suitcase. I have often thought that it would have been tough for me to survive some of the ups and downs of my life without the framework of an office holding me together."

Kelly nodded.

"The office does suck you in. It's like being in a pack in the savannah. It's a place to be. You know what I mean – nothing for ages, only flat earth and shrubs and then – wooosh! – a herd of water buffalo. Or wildebeest. And they're all fidgeting together, and just... being. Making up their lives as they go along."

Cornisha raised an eyebrow.

"Perhaps I envisaged myself as more of a flamingo than a wildebeest, but that's right. It's hard to be obsessing about what people are thinking of you when you are on a deadline getting things done. Working on your own always seemed to be a recipe for going mad. Whereas not working – in the sense of doing nothing truly productive – is an open invitation for your demons to come to tea. And maybe set up a timeshare for other demons who previously could not afford you."

Monique sniggered.

"Well, I'm pretty much your worst nightmare these days, then. I'm a lazy bones, no doubt about it. I'm doing some

49

consultancy, but it's really sweet Fanny Adams compared to what I did before. I do as little as possible. And I really hated every dull minute of being in an office."

Kelly nodded.

"True – but you were in PR. What would anyone expect?"

"Yes," mused Cornisha, "There wasn't exactly – shall we say – an elite around you."

That was the closest Cornisha got to being bitchy, and the other two nudged their chairs closer in appreciation.

"Ooooh, get her," said Monique, "Still, I'd love to agree – were it not for perhaps it being a bit unfair to tar everyone with the same brush?"

"Oh, grab the thick black ex-naval product and spread it all over the PR bastards!" said Kelly cheerfully, "I remember you coming home and telling me all about the hopeless Johnny boys and cute little women in good bras wibbling on about press releases that no one cared about. And the endless meetings. Heavens, we marvelled at those. As war helped progress aviation, so PR is a boon for workers in stationery. Flip boards, white boards, charts, brainstorming, management speak – it was a terrible ordeal for you. I think it's still – and only just – something we have a little less of in law. Still, it passed away some of your life. No wonder you were shagging Harry Gumpert."

"Don't remind me," said Monique, soberly. "What was I thinking?"

"You were desperate," said Cornisha matter-of-factly. "I think it's perfectly cool to have done stupid things while you were desperate. To be shamed should be reserved for unkind and evil people. You are neither of those things.

The Harry thing was tragic, but you are over it. And goodness knows he was lucky to have you."

Monique shifted uncomfortably.

"It gives me the creeps to think about how I might have passed on other chances because of him. He was like an impractical piece of furniture that you somehow don't get around to throwing out."

"Oh enough!" said Kelly as rudely as you can only be with very close friends, "Forget the past! We are in a very fine penthouse, with some bloke's gold discs on the wall, and some gorgeous black and white photographs of some hot men in a band dotted around the place – all while drinking the most delicious gimlets. We should be living in the present and thinking about the future."

She swallowed her gimlet theatrically. It really *was* the most delicious thing.

Cornisha looked at her indulgently.

"Pace yourself, dear. We don't want to carry you home."

Monique laughed.

"It's Friday. You can stay over if it's easier. I'll make sure that you don't go crazy. Enough about me, too – Kelly, you're lucky that you love your job, but if you weren't obsessing about that, you'd be wound up about something else instead. I think you need to split your preoccupations. You need something other than work to get your teeth into."

"Like a terrier," said Cornisha thoughtfully.

"Like a honey badger," said Monique.

"I," said Kelly, "need a cause."

"Oh dear," said Cornisha.

"I mean it. Something worthwhile. Something you need to fight for. Something where a bit of law might help."

"That doesn't narrow it down," said Cornisha.

Monique looked serious.

"It's actually a good idea. It would keep you grounded, and I think doing things for others is really good for the soul."

Kelly was making another round of drinks, using enough limes to ward off scurvy for a millennium.

"I'd like to help women," she announced, "there are quite a few areas where women often come unstuck."

"Female empowerment," said Cornisha approvingly.

Kelly stared at her.

"Yes. Exactly. That's a very good cause, and women suffer the lack of it."

"They would," Monique pointed out, "the clue's in the title."

Kelly was thrilled.

"Raising awareness, educating, giving people a proper chance... it's the opposite of human trafficking!"

Monique raised her glass.

"We'll drink to that. Not to human trafficking, but to the battle against it."

"How the hell does it still happen today?" wondered Kelly.

"We live in a very protected bubble," said Cornisha, "I was sent some information from an organisation recently. I'll still have it in the office – I haven't got around to dealing with it. They were enquiring about pro bono assistance. We could look at it. You could easily get involved."

"That's what I'll do," decided Kelly.

Monique headed back to the kitchen to make croque-monsieurs for them – the ultimate drinking snack. At this stage of the evening, experience dictated that bread, melted cheese with a dash of mustard and ham formed an incomparable sponge for the gin that was ruining all prospective mothers in its path.

"So. Monique. We saw you again in mags this week, at that awards ceremony thing. You looked amazing."

"That's all they worry about, isn't it?" said Monique cheerfully. "I could be on the verge of writing a masterpiece, but no one would care so long as my gown shimmered in the right way."

"Is it really something to complain about?" yawned Kelly, "I mean, darling, it's the life of bleeding Riley."

Monique looked annoyed.

"I know it looks that way, and, granted, it looks that way because it is somewhat that way. But it's also very uncertain. It brings a whole new set of worries and concerns. It's very tempting to be completely caught up in it. Vanity is like a giant leech. It seems to me that it would suck everything out of you, if you let it."

"I don't mean to be too critical, darling. I'm just jealous. How is Jake coping?"

"It helps that the Fondant Furies get on – genuinely so, despite what I've always said is a ridiculous name. I think Jake has a real laugh. He's quite organised and thoughtful. He's got some good people around him. It may be harder in fact to be someone on the fringes of all this nonsense. Jake's in the eye of the storm – the quieter part where people do try to help you, and get agreeably entranced by what you've achieved. No such luck for me or for some of the others. That being said, he may be getting the worst of it, too. He gets to step into the outside world and from what I can see, it can be as if a wave of desperation hits you. People want you – they pin their hopes and aspirations on you, wanting to be you, wanting to be *on* you, thinking they are you, reaching towards you as if you were the last piece of cake on the plate. It's scary and a little bit disgusting. You simply cannot distinguish the people with real talent and backbone from the others. So you recoil from it all. Then of course people find you anyway. You almost have to remind yourself that you have your humanity in common, and that it's not all about you and what you find important – whether that is high art, pseudo-intellectual garbage, a particular style of music, or a life style."

"It's a very confusing way of living," said Kelly, "but I'm still not sure those pressures are any worse than those exerted on others, in different ways and for other reasons. Then again, I suppose that it's not a competition as to who has the hardest time. I'm just glad I can get to see a little of it through you."

Diversity, diversity, diversity.

If there was one thing Amber was irritated by, it was all this endless talk about diversity. Amber had nothing but contempt for all these whiners, who thought they should be allowed to be themselves and have their viewpoints respected. They would get nowhere in the real world, she thought viciously. Little creeps, with their sanctimonious faces and wronged expressions.

This analysis would not have gone down with others as well as Amber would have liked, given her role as Head of Human Resources in the firm. It was, therefore, a private view. But whenever she could, Amber would whisper poison into the ears of those who were easily influenced.

This was not too hard. Partners lapped it up. Deep down inside, they thought they were special, and that others were not.

"The unpalatable truth is that younger people today want the job to be modelled around them. We cannot promise them this," she would purr in confidential executive meetings. "You can't do this job half-heartedly, or part time. It's a competitive world – if you don't work the extra hours, your competitors will."

Senior heads who had long forgotten what it was like to have a life would nod approvingly.

"Amber, it's refreshingly direct and I can't fault your logic," one of them would sigh happily.

"We can't be the parents of these less capable beings," she would add, looking accusingly around the room. "We can't help them if they haven't already helped themselves. If they don't have commercial good sense, and outstanding academics, they should choose other options. Only the very best should join firms like ours. They must be able to hit the ground running. Society has already self-selected the winners and losers amongst us long before they get anywhere near our gates. We have to guard those gates, gentlemen. Only the best shall pass."

She rounded on the meeting, her eyes like daggers.

"And before anyone accuses me of being *heartless*, let me remind you, gentlemen, that I did it. I come from a poor family and I have had to claw my way up. I need not remind you that I have paid my way. I was in prison. I had to reform and grow. I did not waltz into a job because of the colour of my skin. These mewling women, these plaintive minorities – and quite frankly, these *artistic* types... well. They have no place here. We are here to serve our clients, and the only thing that matters *is* those clients. If they might be offended by a cartoon, we drop the cartoon. We give them nothing that stands out or is different – just pure, undiluted quality. And maybe men are best to serve this up. Men like you, gentlemen. I know it cannot be said outside this room – but I want us all to be clear. We are the winners here. It is our ball – and we're not sharing it. Whatever brings the bacon in, that we will do."

The senior partners loved Amber. She made their moustaches quiver with anticipation. She always dressed so well for these meetings, too, her large breasts bursting out of close-fitting silk blouses.

"However," she admitted with no small venom, "we do need to toe the line publicly, so we will continue to serve up the full menu of diversity initiatives. The latest drive comes out this month. It's called All Colours of the Jelly Bean are Good."

One partner put his hand up.

"Loath as I am to play devil's advocate, Amber, my dear, but I have been wondering about something. Given how long we have been promoting this diversity rubbish, and the thankfully limited results we have had on where the balance of power lies – for which we may be grateful, for all the reasons you have so eloquently put – you'd have to think that the clients are pretty thick for buying into this – no?"

"The clients," said Amber confidently, "are complicit. If clients wanted diversity, they could impose it overnight. Guess what: they don't. It's really that simple."

"She's good. A real asset in the fight against mediocrity" muttered the partners approvingly. These meetings lifted their hearts and gave them small erections. It's so good to push off problems to another day.

Amber left the meeting, clear as ever about her purpose. She was masterminding a firm wide diversity project which would see every employee issued with a small tin of coloured jelly beans, to remind them that we are all different, but delicious in our differences. Her secretary had almost been fired for pointing out that all the beans tasted exactly the same.

She got into the lift, confident of being able to thwart anyone trying to effect change she saw no need for. Before the doors had a chance to draw in, Ben stepped into the lift with her.

Her blood boiled. She despised Ben – the shirt-lifting, gender-swapping, pervert that he was.

There was only one thing for it. Reaching her floor, she farted pungently, and turned to him.

"I'll leave that one with you, Ben," she said curtly, as the lift doors closed on the bewildered American.

3

Tome, sweet tome

"I can't work out whether I want to fuck him or I want to tell him to fuck off. I think both," mused Dorota.

Milo looked up from behind the bar at the man to whom Dorota had just served a double Żubrówka on ice. He had wanted a whole bottle but Dorota had told him he wasn't in Krakow any more. The customer had the strong, bison-like body of a man who did much physical labour and then enjoyed his drink afterwards. He was clean-shaven, with neat brown hair. His rough-hewn features wouldn't look out of place on a heavyweight boxer. What Milo sensed most, though, was the confidence that the man exuded. Milo felt, for a moment, that if he were to get close to that man then all his troubles would just melt away.

Milo always enjoyed discussing customers with Dorota. It whiled away the time.

He shrugged.

"Well, I can see why you might want to have sex with him. Anyone would. He's a beast. More interestingly, what did he do to upset you?"

Dorota was an excellent waitress. She could tame even the

most difficult customers. Milo wondered what had needled her. Even now, she kept on glancing over at the stranger, half trying to catch his eye, this despite the presence of his companion, an attractive blonde woman. Milo pursed his lips.

"He didn't pinch your bottom, did he?"

Milo smirked to himself, remembering the last time that had happened. Dorota had delivered a smart push to the drunk in question. *Do you really think I would like a man like you? You're more the type of my brother. He buggers pussies like you before breakfast. Enjoy your drink.*

It was somewhat shy of the process advocated in the staff manual.

Dorota said that she wasn't sure exactly what made her uneasy about the man.

"He didn't do anything. It was just his manner. It was as if he knew he has power over people and just expected me to fall at his feet and compete with that floozy he has with him."

Milo wasn't sure what a floozy was but guessed it probably wasn't a compliment. Dorota enlightened him. Milo told her not to be so hard on other women. He looked over at the couple. The man was now fixing him with steely blue eyes. Milo held the gaze, determined that he would not let the man get to him. Some customers certainly liked their power trips.

Dorota observed the interaction.

"He seems interested in you, my boy. Of course it could be your forbidding good looks and lean machine body. Or it could be that he has heard of the Penis de Milo."

Milo snorted, but was vaguely flattered.

The man did look familiar. Milo wondered if Dorota was right. Had he been one of the men in the crowd when

Milo was doing one of his legendary strips? The thought of the man being interested in him made the Serb come over all tingly. He rarely got attracted to customers in Outrageous Fortune. Milo judged the customers – harshly – to be professional homosexuals, one and all, lacking the masculinity that he prized. But this man was different.

"Looks like he is ready for another drink already. I think he wants you this time, Milo."

The man caught Milo's eye again, picked up his empty glass, and motioned to the bottles behind the bar. Milo reached for the bottle of Żubrówka and gave the man a questioning look. The man nodded his head slightly, and pursed his lips. He gave Milo an almost imperceptible smile.

As Milo headed over to the couple with vodka on a tray, he tried to figure out what the man's story might be. The customer seemed about as interested in his female companion as Milo was. In one sense this came as no surprise. Although attractive, she looked anxious and unhappy. She did not appear to be someone who made their money from their Excel skills, either. It was an uncomfortable contrast with the relaxed vibe emanating from her companion.

"What a wonderful sight." The slight smile tickled the man's lips once more. "Tell me, what is your name, my friend?"

Milo didn't normally take kindly to presumptuous customers. But there seemed to be nothing to do other than to politely introduce himself. He hoped that the man would reciprocate. Milo also hoped that he would regain control of his own senses soon.

The customer nodded.

"I am Janusz. It is a pleasure to meet you. Oh, and this

is Polina."

Polina greeted Milo with a strained smile.

"Where are the Ladies, please?"

He pointed. She picked up her handbag and walked off. Janusz reached over and touched Milo on the arm.

"I apologise for her. Her new job has not turned out as she thought it would. She is in a bit of a bad mood."

Janusz gave Milo a broad grin, and gently squeezed his shoulder, as if to reassure him that Milo shouldn't worry about Janusz's wayward friend.

Milo met the man's gaze. He wasn't the most handsome man to have propositioned Milo in the bar, but there was something about him that made Milo's pulse race. It was pure chemistry. Milo sensed too that something was wrong, but he was sure that he could handle it. It only compounded the feeling that this was forbidden fruit. Like anyone in a fruit-laden orchard, Milo was eager to taste the offerings, and perhaps eat his fill.

Milo cleared his throat.

"So – do you live in London?"

It wasn't quite as bad as asking the man if he came here often. Milo was conscious of the slight tremor in his voice.

Janusz tilted back on his chair, and studied Milo.

"I'm just here on business. But I come to London regularly."

"Well, I am glad to see that you have some time at least for fun."

Milo was philosophical about his less than sparkling small talk. It hadn't held him back. He thought he was at the right level of hypocrisy – because he really didn't think that a drink with an obviously miserable Polina counted as the best time a person could have with their clothes on. However, drinking vodka in Outrageous Fortune certainly ought to compete favourably with the business meetings Milo supposed Janusz had travelled over for.

Milo continued patiently.

"How long are you staying in the city?"

Janusz looked at him.

"I leave tonight."

Milo felt palpable disappointment. He wasn't sure if he managed to keep a neutral expression.

"However, I will be back in a week. Here's my card. My UK number's on there."

In passing the card to Milo, Janusz made sure that their hands touched. They both gripped the card, seemingly not willing to let the moment of contact die too quickly, until Janusz withdrew, as Polina returned from the bathroom.

Janusz smiled steadily at Milo.

"I'll expect your call. I am sure you can show me how to have real fun in this town."

Milo nodded at Polina and headed back to Dorota. Dorota was looking entertained. It had been a classic pick up, and those were always to be celebrated. She was very keen to hear all about it. Milo knew he would be grilled for the details but he did not mind. For the first time in a while, Milo felt excited.

*

Tarquin Henderson-Smythe was pleased with the turnout for "Bacchanalia". The latest art exhibition he had helped the Bolognesi art gallery put together was a manifest success.

There had been a constant stream of people ringing the bell of the understated door in Bond Street. This caused the security guards in the boutique entrances opposite to wonder what on earth their fusty neighbour was up to.

Tarquin had interpreted the theme liberally, granting space to works both ancient and modern, provided they contained a suitably salacious subject matter. Sex sold. This was so even – or perhaps especially – when the wallets and purses that he was intent on picking belonged to the well-heeled middle classes whose daily lives were often sadly devoid of the essential life force in question.

Eroticism. Tarquin planned to profit handsomely by slipping his expert hand under the cloak of respectability that the word afforded. Eroticism magically transformed pornography into art, and hence upped its price considerably. Tarquin wasn't completely sure where the boundary lay between the two. Did art touch one's soul whereas porn would more likely involve touching one's pole? Who could possibly know – or care? Tarquin had quickly discounted reaching a conclusion on the point, as he recalled his glorious intellectual climax in contemplation of the Barberini Faun. He shuddered in delicious recollection.

But *was* erotic art just exceptionally good porn? Tarquin had struggled with the question, as he contemplated Mapplethorpe's outsized members, as if the then avant-garde were deliberately flipping two fingers – and multiple large penises – at the establishment. What would come next? Would Tom of Finland break out of its gay niche and bring moustaches, divorced from hipster beards, back into the mainstream again?

Tarquin doubted things would ever change much. Some questions would never be finally answered. The few oases of open-mindedness still felt marooned in a desert of tabloid chauvinism. Most of the world was still uncomfortable seeing a penis that was not their own or their partner's. Gay sex was the final frontier. The average Briton was fine with the sanitised version of homosexuality that the media liked to portray, as they seemed far more interested in assisting women to dress well rather than getting a bit of cock themselves. The world really didn't seem ready to confront the messy reality of actual man-on-man action.

Thank goodness for the Ancients. Somehow Greek homosexuality was okay as *they turned out all right in the end.* Only the most perfect physical specimens had been recorded for posterity, usually looking particularly noble, even if they were as bare as a new-born. Indeed, Eros himself had been around at the time to ensure that Greek nudity, and its renaissance descendants, was propelled straight into the sphere of art, with nary a whiff of pornography glancing their perfect forms.

Tarquin surveyed the room, expertly divining where the richest pickings lay. The crowd was as esoteric as his exhibition. The theatre crowd predominated, reflecting the older works nestling in gilded frames, while the modern pieces contributed a slightly discordant echo in the room. Tarquin's life had certainly been enriched with some fine specimens since dating Rubens. Funny how the bar had enabled him to extend tentacles into so many different worlds. Tarquin smiled as he took in two modern day

Olympian specimens, in deep conversation. They definitely had the money and the taste to purchase something special from the show.

He glided happily over towards them. Another day, another dollar.

Basking in the excellent turnout, and networking like a commercial trawler, Tarquin looked over fondly at his friends who were enjoying the free sparkling wine.

He may had had a reservation or two, however, if he realised that Ben and Rubens were discussing him.

Rubens looked perplexed when Ben asked him jocularly if he was ready to settle down. He stared at his hands, as if seeing them for the first time.

"I'm not sure if I'm ready for a garden, gostoso. I mean, I like the idea of having outdoor space, but do you really see me spending my free time looking after plant life? Do these thumbs look green to you? Tarquin asked me if I knew what strimming was the other day. *I* thought it was some pervy thing he had seen on Grindr. I was shocked when he told me that we would need to invest in our own *string trimmer* to cut the edges of the lawn. Is this so that the neighbours will not give us disapproving glances? Is this my future? Is this the reality of settling down?"

Ben looked at his companion with a wry smile. A disconcerted Rubens seemed to be a staple of life these days. Ben wondered idly if his own good self actually had something to contribute to this conversation. Should he mention the importance of slug pellets? Bartlett de Vere seemed obsessed with them. Slugs formed the principal topic of conversation during Ben's awkward encounters with Bartlett at the office coffee machine. *Eleven this morning* had been Bartlett's latest satisfied comment. This was the tally of the night before's slimy murders. Bartlett the slug Ripper.

Ben remained intrigued, of course, that Bartlett thought the dissolution of slugs to be a more appropriate topic of conversation rather than, say, the negotiation of the sale and purchase agreement they were working on – but at least it got them through the inconveniently long time they had to wait while the new espresso machine did its work.

"Interesting, Rubens," said Ben, "I guess there are compromises to be made at all stages of life. The key question for you to work out, my friend, is whether what you are gaining is worth more to you than what you are giving up."

Rubens sighed.

"I know. I know. It is of course what I want now, Ben. I have had so much sex with so many beautiful people in London. It has been good – but been there, done that."

Ben reflected that only Rubens could get away with such a comment without deserving a major slap. Rubens wasn't being boastful. He had a point. This was factual. Ben had seen (and been) evidence himself.

"How things change, eh, Ben? It was okay that most guys only saw the stripper, the gym instructor or the smiling Latino with the muscles, when they looked at me. I was like the Village People – something for everyone, and good enough for most. They weren't remotely interested in the person underneath. As long as I lived up to their sexual fantasy of what *I should be*, it all went perfectly."

Rubens sighed again.

Ben had to admit that upon seeing Rubens for the first time, it had not occurred to him to quiz the Brazilian on the finer points of constitutional law, or to glean Rubens' thoughts on the vital contribution to life of Chitty on Contracts.

"Go on, Rubens," said Ben, suspecting that there was more to come.

"Isn't it strange? Being the fantasy of so many was so much more fun than sinking into the humdrum reality of their lives. Most of the time their fantasies really *were* my life. That was a world that was real to me. I could invite them into my world, let the stardust light up their faces and watch them enjoy living inside the kaleidoscope for a while. It was as true to me as the morning alarm shrieking its call to the office was to them. I *was* the party. It was all there, as if it were on a big screen."

Rubens' eyes sparkled. Ben remembered these Technicolor moments, too.

"Being superficial sometimes gets a bad rap," mused Rubens.

Ben nodded.

"It does. I have revelled in the skin-deep on many occasions."

"That's the point, Ben. What good was it to me, to know what the punters thought about politics, or philosophy, or if they had any hobbies? *Meu Deus*, the hobbies were the worst! I mean, if you pick up in a club, there is really one thing you are looking for, and it is not a viewing of their collection of World of Warcraft playing cards. It's more: babes, just show me what you got – and let's see if you can use it."

Ben identified with this. He recalled a one night stand a couple of years ago, when the only way he could stop his bed-mate from ranting on about Britain's relationship with Europe was to unceremoniously stuff his penis in the man's mouth. Ben hadn't been sure whether the man had been quite ready for that stage in the proceedings, but then he didn't give two hoots about the democratic deficit, and it did seem the logical next step towards even closer union. Sadly the man's gnashers had hastened along Ben's personal Brexit moment.

"However… " Rubens stopped, to emphasise his point. He jabbed his finger at Ben.

"I had become so good at being the fantasy that my mask rarely left my face. I ignored the condescending comments. I blotted out all the settled happiness that I saw around me. I convinced myself that was all just boring, and not me at all. Then, when I met Tarquin I felt something shift. It was dramatic, I tell you. Tarquin tore the mask off. It was tectonic."

Rubens shook his head.

"I will never forget the amazing highs from those trips to Ibiza, but I don't want to be one of those guys who are still trying to live the dream when their looks have faded and they are entering the living nightmare of nobody being interested any more. I want to have moved on long before that springs on me. I would like to see – I don't know – the chateaux of the Loire and the villages of Tuscany – and I want someone to share those experiences with. I want to have people over to my apartment for conversation and use my stove for preparing good food, not for cooking up G. I want to go into those shops on Tottenham Court Road, and have an argument with the person I love about which leather sofa will look best in the lounge. Tarquin is the person I want to do those things with, and I want the security of knowing that he will be there, even when, God forbid, I can no longer rely purely on my looks."

The two men looked at each other.

Ben recognised this desire for stability and certainty. He, too, sought this in Kelly's arms. But it was no longer as clear cut for him as Rubens was describing. He recognised, of course, the fear of becoming boring, of becoming those people who until now were a template of what not to be like, who were living illustrations of some cautionary tale about existence without life. The threat of that existence stalked them both like the Dull Reaper.

Ben felt he needed fewer spreadsheets and more bedsheets in his life. He was not ready to settle down. Things might only get worse unless he militantly opposed the useful and sensible. He wanted to be on the side of the lascivious and lurid – at least occasionally.

Ben wasn't sure whether he was comforted by the fact Rubens was struggling with similar issues, or if Rubens was feeling downcast because of the apparent inevitability of a descent into pedestrian pursuits. If even Rubens, the poster boy of decadent glamour, was about to be drawn into the world of garden centres and monogamous monotony, what chance did he, Ben, have of resisting the golden handcuffs?

"Settling down, eh, Rubens." Ben smiled. "What is happening to us?"

"Would I be interrupting something, my dears?"

Hartmut Glick stood next to them, a glass of champagne in his hand, held correctly by its stem. If that stem knew what those hands could do, it would be bending wildly, thought Ben idly. Ben reflected that Hartmut was a man who, even in corporate handcuffs, would always do things on his own terms. There was no danger whatsoever of there being the faintest whiff of dullness or respectability about the proceedings he engaged in. As if to confirm Ben's musings, Hartmut looked pointedly at the nearest canvas.

"Your friend has put on an enjoyable exhibition, Rubens, albeit with few items of genuine piquancy for me. I would classify all that cavorting in the woods with little devils and goats as weakly titillating vanilla."

"Titillating vanilla, my dear? Sounds like an ice cream flavour that is trying too hard."

Hartmut's wife arrived, clad in an expensive cream jumper and leather trousers. Her boots glistened with discreet metal trimmings. Her heels could spear ants. Caroline Napier Jones smiled at the men, as she introduced her mother, Eleanor. Ben hoped that Eleanor had not overheard too much. He wasn't at all sure he could cope speaking frankly with one as stately as the elder Napier Jones. Eleanor seemed relaxed about it all. In such surroundings, and recalling a previous exhibition she had attended with her daughter, Eleanor decided that a spot of Ben-baiting would liven up the proceedings.

"How delightful to see you young gentlemen again."

Eleanor looked Ben straight in the eye.

"Thank goodness for this cold water, as all of these scenes are enough to make one come over quite giddy.

Although I dare say, Mr Barlettano, from what I hear, these depictions are what pass for standard fare in the Castle Lofts. Maybe without the centaurs, mind you?"

"They are certainly horsing around," observed Hartmut.

Eleanor smiled enigmatically.

Why did women like this manage to make Ben feel as if he were an awkward, spotty teenager again?

Caroline chuckled.

"Oh, don't pick on the poor lamb, Mother! He's a reformed character now, living the life of domestic bliss with his adorable Southern belle. Now, we have some news for you all. Hartmut is thinking of writing a book."

A lawyer? Writing a book? Ben supposed it just about counted as news – although the thought of reading and digesting another worthy tome hardly set his toes-a-tingling.

Rubens looked admiringly at Hartmut.

"I wish I was disciplined enough to write a book. Of course, I am not sure a self-help manual on how to run a cocktail bar would meet with the same success as a book about law."

Rubens was one of the few people Ben knew who could make a positive comment about a law manual without even the faintest whiff of irony.

Caroline smiled.

"Oh, it's not a book about the law. Well, not in any conventional sense."

Caroline's eyes twinkled.

Eleanor was feeling the usual dread that her encounters with her daughter and her daughter's spouse eventually engineered.

She attempted to make light of it.

"Pray, enlighten us, Caroline. I shall endeavour to feign the appropriately shocked reaction."

Eleanor had had enough experience of her daughter's delight in setting a course wholly at odds with her own wishes. It had long begun to pale.

Hartmut looked evenly at Ben.

"I have taken my inspiration from you, my dear boy. You displayed an impressive amount of courage when you came out. I thought that honesty and transparency may yet serve me as it served you. I am writing a book about the alter ego of Glick the lawyer. I am not talking about my collection of Franklin Mint Fabergé eggs, either. It is a novel. My novel concerns a lawyer who indulges in unconventional sexual pastimes, and how he balances his private life with all the sadism and masochism inherent in working in a legal practice."

Rubens clapped his hands.

"Now that sounds like the kind of legal book I might enjoy. Can I get a signed copy, Hartmut?"

Ben was thrown. Hartmut was his mentor, and this was plainly career suicide. Hadn't previous scandals been enough? This was *ridiculous*. Ben wondered if it would be disloyal to start looking for another position immediately.

Eleanor pressed her lips together.

"What a *courageous* choice, dear son-in-law."

Eleanor knew she was expected to gag on her canape. Her daughter still seemed to believe that Eleanor had never been a young woman, had never lived, with all the desires that gush in youth. It aggravated Eleanor. She wondered whether Caroline ever thought about how she had herself made it into this world. The young found it so unimaginable that their elders had ever been young themselves. They always thought that they had invented intercourse.

Eleanor straightened.

"It all sounds rather interesting. I may even see a glimpse of the side of my daughter's life that she feels it so incumbent upon herself to protect me from."

Hartmut remained impassive, a faraway look in his eyes. Was he structuring the plot? Was everyone mad here? Ben felt he had to be the voice of reason.

"It's just a thought, Hartmut – but don't you think it is risky? Are you sure that Sagworth Turner Dickerhint is ready for such, er, honesty? And what would our clients think?"

"I was rather hoping that the clients would enjoy it, Ben. I appreciate your concern, my dear boy, but times are changing, and I feel that this is something I must do. One reaches a time in one's life when the considered view presents itself that people can just bugger off if they don't like what you have to say. I have been careful, measured and considerate for the better part of my professional life. All those unuttered words must come out. So, please do not be a worrywart, and raise your glasses to the success of the admittedly as yet unwritten *James Bondage: man at law*."

Kelly found herself in a darkening London street, looking for an office in the gloom of the early evening. It is funny, she thought grimly – London's offices ran the full gamut from bright, light and beautiful to dingy and moth-eaten.

She checked the address on her printed-out email.

Was this really the place where the charity operated? This unloved and functional rent-a-space?

It was. The charity had hired premises in a ten-storey building with large floors, split into individual offices and groups of offices. To Kelly's surprise, their headquarters were just a small group of three rooms crammed around a reception area.

Kelly pushed her hair back from her face and approached the young woman listlessly manning the front desk.

"Hello," she said.

The young woman sat up suddenly and smiled radiantly. The transformation was immediate. But it was not directed at Kelly.

A man had come in: "Suzy, the dinner has been cancelled so I'll finish the presentation on the small projects... "

There was a sudden silence. Kelly's spine was tingling. She turned.

"Morten?"

It was Morten. Her ex-lover. Her piece of passion in Paris. He was looking amazing. He was amazing. Kelly was astonished at how nothing, nothing at all of her feelings for him had changed. In that second of seeing him they all came back, like a perfectly preserved recording.

He was tall and lean, and wearing a polo neck. It made him look like a fisherman who actually caught fish and fed people with them. His tousled hair was still blond and casual. His eyes were wide open in surprise and they were like a sea in which Kelly was already swimming naked, feet occasionally touching warm, soft sand. He came over and enveloped her in a hug. It was just as well as she wanted to bury herself in him. He fitted so well. He felt so right.

It was all she could do to keep calm.

"What are you doing here?" he asked.

"You've beaten me to it," she said. "Never mind me. What are you doing here?"

"I work with this charity," he said simply. "We look into trafficking. We report what we find in the field. We share projects – raising awareness, providing assistance and information. I've just returned for some respite. It's been a tough few months, as you probably know."

"And yet," she said quietly, "I bet you're dying to get back out there. You doctors. It's such an immediate impact that you have, when people lack even basic health information."

He laughed: "You remembered! Yes. It's a curse. It's essential to have a break – but we are so needed out there, and what we do matters, and helps. No one who hasn't been there relates to how you become umbilically attached to doing everything you can for so long as you can. You become attached – no doubt about that. Oh, it's good to see you."

Suzy was looking a little put out.

Morten flashed a smile that threatened the ice cap:

"Over to you. Are you evicting us, or something?"

"More like moving in. I'm from Sagworth Turner Dickerhint – you know, the large international law firm? Have you heard of them? Cornisha Burrows was sent a request for assistance. I'm the meagre cavalry. I'm happy to help in any way I can. It won't be anything like what you do… "

"Suzy, we'll just go next door."

Morten propelled Kelly into a small office, shut the door

and kissed her. She kissed him back urgently.

She put her finger to her lips.

"We shouldn't do this here," she whispered, "it's unprofessional. But we should go somewhere right away."

"I've been lent a rather nice flat. It's on the river. I have some duty free. Would it be awful of me to ask you over?"

"It is essential that you ask me over right away."

"Why are you whispering?"

"Because I am slightly overwhelmed."

"Let's go."

They sped along the Embankment in a helpful black cab, keeping their hands to themselves but both sensing urgency. Kelly adjusted her hair, and took some deep breaths. Morten looked a little uncomfortable, his gaze darkened with lust.

The cab drew into the drive of a block of flats. The doorman greeted Morten with some affection.

"Thanks, Brian. This is my dear friend Kelly, whom I've just bumped into. Isn't the world a small place?"

"Yes it is, Sir. Good evening, Miss."

"Do you have a number for takeaway pizza, Brian?"

"Indeed I do, Sir. This lot are supposed to be quick and good."

"Pizza," said Kelly in the lift, admiringly. "That is an excellent idea. For later."

The flat was charming – bright, airy and warm. Morten lowered blinds over the large windows, and put some music on. Kelly kicked her shoes off, and pulled him onto the sofa.

Kelly felt that it had been a long time coming, but it was everything that she could have wished for, had she known what to wish for. Morten was simply outstanding in bed. She could only sigh as he expertly handled her. Every angle of him pleased her, every glimpse of him during their strenuous coupling, his honey coloured skin smooth on hers, his lean body supple and commanding, his hair dishevelled, his mouth a warm extension of her in which she sought refuge. He was a sprite – here today, gone tomorrow. He belonged to another world that she had no desire to move into. But while he was in her world, he felt perfect, and she came with cries of relief. How she needed the novelty and the lack of the humdrum. How important was Morten to her well being.

"Thankfully, I've cleared this with Ben," she thought as they indulged in a couple of new positions.

As always, she wondered at what passed through one's head during sex.

Once they were sated, true to his word, Morten called for pizza, and found a decent bottle of red wine to consume with it.

"We're good together," he said.

"For this, yes," agreed Kelly. "It felt exactly as it should."

"I'm not going to ask you about anything in your life," said Morten. "You know I'm not here anything other than episodically."

"Don't worry," said Kelly, "everything is fine. Unless you take that slice with the extra mushrooms on it, that is. What we have had is just a cherry on the sundae of existence. We're not together," she added quickly.

"We are, but in our own way," said Morten.

"I'll drink to that."

4

Slava to love

Harry stepped out of the lift in the Castle Lofts and walked to his front door. He stood there for a while, as if waiting for permission to enter his home. These days, opening his own front door felt more and more like an ordeal. It was as if he were a stranger flogging tea towels or a God system, or pleading for some help in recognising terrible abuses of human rights in countries which he could no longer imagine visiting, let alone living in. In short, he felt as if he were imposing, and the weight of it crushed him like a toppling brick wall.

He stood motionless on the edge of his property, staring at the expensive, security-toughened new door – burglar-proof, or so the company had boasted. It was an obstacle, alright – a barrier between the family sanctum and the outside world. But how much more formidable an obstacle than the door was Sarah, Harry's aggrieved wife.

Sarah knew, of course, about Harry's indiscretions. She may have known for a long time. Knowing and acting on knowledge are two different things in the helter skelter barter of life. In this rude market place, things can change determinedly, from one day to the next. It was like death – you might know it was coming but it's always a terrible surprise when it finally closes in on someone. In domestic arrangements, things seemed to bubble along under the surface for a long time before, suddenly, everything happened, all at once, like a chemical reaction in the worst laboratory ever.

Harry had started going off the boil. It had happened so discreetly, the most surreptitious of developments ever. A small paunch now pushed at his belt, like an animal sniffing for truffles. His face, once charmingly crinkly, tanned and carefree, was looking more hang dog. His eyes were a touch droopy, a tad wearier. His eyesight seemed shot to pieces. Harry felt that the diminishing acuity of his vision was nauseating – although this at least had nothing to do with his sexual escapades. He felt that lack of vision abased him in a way that very little else had succeeded in doing.

Sarah now knew about Monique. It was such old history, but Sarah knew and she was thinking about it. It made no difference that Sarah had only known with certainty after the affair had itself died of boredom. Only Monique's laziness and lack of opportunities had kept it going for as long as it lasted.

Sarah was still beautiful. Her neat blonde hair caught the light, and she took care of herself. She had progressed surprisingly well at work. A part time role in events organising had mushroomed into a proper job. She could even claim to be outshining Harry. People may say that they are able to tolerate a lawyer socially. However, an ageing sleazy lawyer is like a cockroach in a pantry: unwelcome, grotesque-looking, and surprisingly difficult to get rid of. Sarah had therefore moved smoothly to create clear blue water between herself (the children included) and her husband. The family had split almost imperceptively, and its members had been living very different lives for some months past.

As Harry entered the penthouse flat a little sheepishly, Sarah found it hard to contain the surge of contempt that the sight of him provoked these days.

Manners, Sarah, she reminded herself sternly. When the divorce comes around, being civil would pay more dividends.

"Good evening, Harry," she said.

She may as well be tipping a gin and tonic over me, thought Harry. He took in the sight of his wife of a lifetime. She was busying herself tidying the children's casual mess, and smoothed down her expensive-looking skirt.

"Good day?" she asked evenly, not really interested in any response.

"What's for supper?" asked Harry.

"I'm not very hungry, I'm afraid. I had a rather enormous lunch – some very jolly clients. So I was going to have some soup. Would that do? There are some cold meats and cheeses. It could be a bit of a picnic. The girls are over at their friends watching a film."

God, this was awful. What was the point of marriage? Shouldn't it be cosy, and warm, and all about decent food, properly cooked, prolonging health and life and well-being, served happily and eaten with joy, while indulging in intelligent conversation about topical matters and future plans, perhaps agreeing on a specific social escapade to light up the next few days? What was the point of this dull nothingness, this relationship of strained tedium, with no sex, and no potential sex, no food, and no potential food, and no intimacy? What was this hell?

Harry sighed.

"Can I get you a glass of wine?"

"No thank you," said Sarah primly. "I'll be fetching the girls back soon, and anyway, we drink far too much. It's as if we positively want to become those middle class people that the papers shake their imaginary heads over."

"Oh fuck them," said Harry, "I'll binge drink if I want to."

"Yes. I think that is rather the point that they are making."

Harry headed over to the cupboard and looked into it. There was a nice burgundy waiting. He grabbed it and opened it with vigour.

Sarah watched him.

"It's not the answer," she said.

He turned to look at her and frowned:

"I'm not sure you realise how much I don't care."

"Oh, I think I know very well how much you don't care. I'm only trying to help you."

"I can see from your expression that you rather think that I'm beyond help," Harry said melodramatically, waving an enormous glass at her. He liked the enormous glasses. They made a third of a bottle seem like a mere splash.

Maybe it was time to turn up the heat, thought Sarah. This was beyond repair. She worried over how little she felt for this man, who had once embodied all of her dreams and aspirations. Divorce no doubt seemed very alien to those who had not experienced this – standing in a well-appointed kitchen, staring at someone who inspired exasperation and pity. I just don't want to be lumbered with him anymore, she thought. I just want to be free.

She eased herself onto a bar stool, and crossed her arms.

"Harry," she said in a reasonable tone of voice, "Is this working?"

Harry slugged some more burgundy.

"I don't know about "it", he said, "I'm certainly working. Days and nights I spend in that damned office, slogging away for this family. I don't know if I have made it look easy, like a dratted figure skater, slithering around, with a big round bum. Have I?"

He pointed a finger at Sarah.

"It's not easy. It's jolly, jolly hard. It's like playing a game of strategy where there is only downside to consider. And I have played it well. I look back in some amazement at the heights to which I have risen. It was never obvious, you know. It isn't a meritocracy! You don't get places by doing well! It's all about whose arse you lick!"

Sarah seethed and considered making a comment about the literal licking of arses or environs that she suspected might have been occurring rather more than would have been strictly necessary for Harry's professional progress.

She chose a more elevated path.

"I am sorry if you've been unhappy. The thing is, we all have been. I think both of us deserve more than simply putting up with each other. And so do the girls."

Harry stared at her. He had sometimes fantasised about having this conversation, but it felt very wrong now that it was actually happening. Whatever progress divorce had made in the league of lessening stigmas, Harry still found it an excruciating concept – mainly because married life suited him rather well, exactly as it was.

"You cannot be serious, Sarah. Are you saying what I think you're saying? Are you throwing our lives away?"

"I'm not saying anything. I'm suggesting that we should think about things. I'm asking if our relationship is working. I want to hear your point of view – because my point of view is that our lives have died. We do not look forward to seeing each other. We bring each other nothing but unhappiness."

"How can you say that?" said Harry, holding his burgundy with care, but waving his free arm like a demented preacher.

That was it. Sarah could not be a paragon of reasonableness for more than an allotted period of time. This had now expired with the finality of a parking meter.

"I can say it because you've been unfaithful! Because you've hurt me very, very much! Because it does matter, and I don't have to put up with wondering which floors your sordid little pants have been found on!"

"My what?"

"You heard! I am tired of this charade! I want to be free and I don't want some long justification about whose fault it is, and who has done most to variously wreck or salvage this existence. I cannot think of anything that could be more *mutual*. We're done, Harry – not least because I do have things I can do with myself, if I'm given the chance to get on with them."

"Can I watch?" mocked Harry.

No. That was not the right approach – although, *why*? What was *wrong* with a bit of banter to lighten the mood? God, she had no sense of humour at all.

Harry served himself more wine, his hand shaking slightly as he poured. The bottle was light in his hand. He had drunk the wine like water. It was very difficult to gauge how much this had affected him. He felt sure that it was for the better. His thinking seemed to be clearer, and he felt very capable.

"Well," he said hazily, standing as straight as he could, "I think this is utter madness. I don't have to put up with this. You are being wholly unreasonable. I'm… disappointed in you. I think we should have some time apart. Let me see – what day is it today? Tuesday? Tuesday it is, today. I'll go and stay in a hotel until Saturday. We can talk again then."

Sarah put her head in her hands.

"Yes," continued Harry, "That's what I'll do. We can talk again then. Tell the girls that I'm away on business unexpectedly."

He wagged a finger at Sarah.

"We can both do some thinking. About the past, and about the future. We can decide everything then."

He moved deliberately towards the bedroom, and packed. On his return, Sarah was sitting in the same place, looking at her nails, with a pinched mouth.

"I will see you Saturday, Sarah. Around 11 am. I'll be on the mobile if anything crops up."

She said nothing.

Harry hoisted his small, handsome leather holdall onto his shoulder and waved.

"I'll be off, then."

Sarah did not move.

"Goodbye for now."

He closed the door behind him.

It wasn't late, but the evening was very dark. Harry felt nervous but also slightly thrilled. He realised that he had just bought himself three whole days of utter freedom. Sarah need never know what he got up to between now and Saturday.

The lift doors closed on him like a coffin lid, and the square metal box jolted and moved towards the ground.

Surely she wasn't serious? They were well off, but the economics of splitting up were not favourable. Some sort of arrangement might be possible, reasoned Harry. She'd probably met some lame man whom she wanted to go and have tea with. Sarah was so proper that she wouldn't breathe on another man while technically still married to Harry.

How would I feel about that, Harry asked himself. If I didn't know about it, would it matter? I don't love Sarah in that way. He sighed as he remembered Monique's lissom lower back swaying under him. She was smooth and sensuous all over. Sarah was so sensible. Sex seemed to hold the same excitement as the washing up for her. Yet, although Harry admitted to himself that the thought of Sarah embracing another man did not exactly fill him with glee, perhaps she was right. Maybe there was no future possible other than a very sensible one of shared parenting. Enough partners in law firms divorced. There was no stigma there.

The lift jolted to a halt. But how would *I* do? wondered Harry. He had caught Monique as she was vulnerable and lonely. Was there a steady stock of vulnerable and lonely women out there? He had failed in his recent attempts to lure models to drinks. He used to be quite good at that. But now there were other men flashing cosmetic dentistry and well-honed seduction routines. The competition had changed.

He was dimly aware that the internet might hold some answers. For now, however, Harry knew exactly where he was going to go.

He hailed a taxi, and was off.

Eve's Garden was a strip joint. It, along with everyone one else, realised that "Gentlemen's Club" was a preferable handle. So it – and everyone else – called itself a Gentlemen's Club instead. But it was a strip joint. Harry had passed its louche door for years in central London, occasionally popping in at the end of long business days. He had heard many of his less discerning acquaintances praise its provision of services.

It wouldn't have been Harry's first choice, but it was very convenient. It was close to a boutique hotel where Harry had once spent a "conference" with Monique. The hotel was comfortable, even stylish – discreetly lit, good, generous beds, and foreign receptionists whom you felt might ignore what was going on under their noses.

Harry checked into the hotel, and booked a room until Monday – just to be sure. He was an organised soul. He factored in the twenty four hour cancellation policy. He felt that, now that he was here, it was worth knowing that he had a roof over his head for the immediate future. After all, Sarah hadn't confirmed Saturday. There were serviced apartments located closer to the office where he might end up thereafter, if things were to move in that direction. But at least he knew where he was for now.

For the time being, this was perfect. He sat on the bed and breathed a sigh of relief. He ordered room service – he remembered that the steak was very acceptable, and he kept himself to half a bottle of a nice Rhone wine. The television offered him the news. Harry would have gone so far as to say that the evening was shaping up.

Harry felt positively cheerful by the end of the meal. He was fed and watered. The hotel was embracing him like an uninhibited relative.

While he was growing up, his parents had always cautioned him about the exorbitant mark up on room service in hospitality establishments. Their warnings against the delights of the mini bar were like war propaganda in their simplicity and effectiveness. Whenever the Gumperts had stayed in hotels as a family, his mother would bring along her own packets of nuts and assorted snacks. She would then read out the price list of the items offered for consumption, experiencing considerable delight in her own growing consternation.

Harry remembered looking at the hotel menus that peeked out of faux leather folders. They promised delicious things. He fantasised about calling for the expensive items to be brought up. How delicious they would be, precisely because of their pillaging of his wealth. Ten pounds for a bowl of soup? Oh, how Harry wanted that soup. That cream of tomato soup, specially warmed for him, and served on a little table, with a tiny steel vase with a flower in it. Instead, sustenance took the form of ageing, cold sandwiches that curled like a seventies' perm. "There is no value in this world," his mother would be telling his father. "It's daylight robbery" his father would concur, as their heads bent closer over the very small box of crackers priced like a precious stone.

Now, Harry enjoyed room service almost too much. He felt safe and confident. In fact, he felt so good that he was wondering whether it was worth wandering out into the unwelcome London cold. The lights in the hotel room cast an agreeable glow from under tasselled light shades. The bed was a pit of crisp softness. The sheets were calling to him – so different from the tired arms of the marital bed, which recorded every toss and turn of two bothered and discontented people, fretting about children and work and chores and money and age, worrying themselves into early onset old age and death. When death came, no doubt the shroud would be a slightly overused marital sheet graced with stains that no number of stock actors waving soap boxes and flashing white teeth could ever hope to shift. A shroud which would show no face, but simply offer up the fingerprints of sweat, make up and dribbles.

Oh God! Marriage was a trap! Marriage was the anchor which chained Harry to the rusty bottomed boat of his life – a boat that even barnacles would have forsaken. Marriage kept him attached, planted, immobile – like a cow in a tiny field, in a state of standing and staring that would positively make you wish to not have any time whatsoever to do that. Sarah, with her endless quest for the ordinary, her zest for the mundane, her vanilla-sexed existence, was poison to all of Harry's hopes, dreams and aspirations.

"Set me free," muttered Harry.

He wanted to drown in his own fantasies.

Still debating whether or not to stay in, he flicked around the pay per view channels, and caught the few seconds of adult films, samplers aimed at procuring the further exercising of credit cards. The glimpses of pink flesh were a pinch to Harry's senses.

He was not really into pornography, as, whatever his failings, he had always been able to procure sex with live and consenting women. Pornography took up time that he would rather dedicate to chasing skirt. With a large selection of gullible women at work and a firm conviction that some form of legal droit de seigneur existed in law firms, he had indulged himself like a dog in a park. But although off the leash, he hadn't quite escaped the leash – and now it felt as if it were sailing towards him like a cat o'nine tails. Divorce would be a painful sting.

Be that as it may, he was free for now. As he squinted at the screen, he felt as if he should do something about this. He should use the freedom, make it work for him. It could not all go Sarah's way. He knew that he should venture out. The best evenings out often seem to be those that demand an effort to get to.

He should banish himself a few doors away to Eve's Garden, like the confident man about town that he was – at ease with his appetites, and in defiance of any consequences.

Maybe the world should march to his drum beat. The future was a dull concept, especially when one twigged that all it could possibly offer was a slow slide down to decay at best, and at worst some hurtlingly fast accident of health or fate or both, that would chop his legs from under him faster than the Grim Reaper could scythe them. Explode the future. Kick it in the teeth. The alternative was to become an old grey man without so much as a struggle, hanging on to some chosen field of activity, like a weed in a neglected garden, desperately hoping for some form of relevance to be noted, or some form of acknowledgment that it was not all in vain. Perhaps an appointment to (oh larks) a committee? Perhaps the chance to wear a president's jewel? It all screamed of an end game that you didn't know that you were playing.

He called room service and asked them to remove his tray. The small, neat bathroom welcomed him as he brushed his teeth and hair. He splashed cold water over his face and examined his teeth more closely. He looked better than he felt. Onwards, and outwards.

The entrance to Eve's Garden was indescribably naff. Even Harry felt embarrassed by the plaster of Paris Grecian goddesses holding snakes aloft. One of the snakes' tongues had half broken off, leaving it looking like a very thin-tongued reptile with an odd kink. But one got the gist. Harry had armed himself with an adequate supply of cash. He knew the form, and he easily peeled off a tenner for the cloakroom, smiling at the staff who sized him up as their perfect customer.

The performance room offered a thick catwalk fringed

by red lights and velour curtains. The tables were small so as to pack people in, whilst allowing space between the seated patrons. The bar mirror reflected a hundred different bottles of liquor. They glittered with the promise of oblivion. The gloom seemed tinged with navy blue, the stage was red, the occasional spot light, a shaft of white – all very patriotic, thought Harry.

He ordered a bottle of red wine. It was excruciatingly expensive but would work out cheaper in the long run. It was drinkable, if ordinary.

This wasn't about the wine.

The customers were predictable – a few groups of men, and some loners like himself. Harry knew not to look furtive. Beginners looked furtive – those who had not yet made their peace with their underlying sense of entitlement to stimulation and whatever might come of it. The women milling around were prettier than one might expect.

Background music played, but it was soon drowned out by the stage speakers, as a strong beat started up, and four women came out to dance.

Tall and tanned and lean and lonely, Nicholas Casterway's face was set like Han Solo in carbonite. Being feared in the office is easy enough if you are blessed with the characteristics of a functioning psychopath – and Nicholas had hewn this state of affairs into something natural and ingrained. It had become normal. Nothing seemed to stick to him. He combined self-interest, greed and obnoxious behaviour with the conviction of a Spanish Inquisitor. Each of these traits was revved up and ready to roll from 8:00 am each day, a time at which he usually sent the first curt email to whomever might have frustrated him overnight. He only got angry at night, seething his way through the small hours, plotting his moves maniacally, insomnia guiding him to terrifying creativity in his political moves. It takes guts to be a real arsehole – guts and persistence. The sense of self-entitlement would overwhelm most folk. Nicholas handled it all like a master. He knew what was right. He did not have to explain, or justify himself. There was no one he was sensitive to.

His favoured tactic was the fait accompli. Do it, or state it, as if you had impunity. It usually worked. People shrank from confrontation like oysters from lemon juice. They let him be, as if the Beatles themselves had gathered in the corridors to implore them to do just that.

Nicholas had long learned all the useful techniques for asserting himself over more cautious colleagues. Eventually they bent to his will – not through deliberate choice, but through apathy, laced with a small but potent dose of fear.

Nicholas soldiered on, the general watching the battle safely from the next hillside along.

With his bald pate and his little round glasses, he strode through the office, causing heads to lower and conversations to shush. He judged everyone, especially where personal behaviour was concerned. This did not, however, apply to himself. He hated and despised most of his fellow partners. He saw them as weak-willed, predictable and compassionate. He thought that no one understood history, or politics, and certainly no one was as ruthless as they ought to be. To the contrary, they all seemed to be full of ruths. Overflowing with the milk of human kindness, incapable of understanding that you had to keep others down in order not to cast shadow on oneself.

He really did not like Hartmut Glick. He had rid a firm of him once before, when Hartmut had moved with Ben – voluntarily, but self-evidently as a result of Nicholas's machinations and whisperings. Now, the merger between law firms had reunited them. How bloody typical was that? It hadn't been as awkward as it might have proved to be. Nicholas could usually ignore Hartmut and Ben. The office was enormous these days, and communication was so poor that he need never cross their path. But today he was headed to catch a colleague unawares so as to better bewilder and frighten him – and suddenly, he heard Hartmut's deep musical voice. Rage clutched at Nicolas' stomach.

Despite himself, Nicholas drew closer to listen.

Hartmut was in full flow.

"Indeed Ben. Indeed. I know, my proclivities must seem extraordinary to many. You don't have very many openly practising sado-masochists in the City of London. But what can I tell you. I am most proud, Ben – most proud of all, after meine liebe Caroline and unsere pain in the arse kids – most proud of all, Ben, of never trying to fit in. The question seemed to me to always be the most simple of Fragen. Why can't I be precisely whom I wish to be – and still draft some of the best sale and purchase agreements in Britain? Does a cock ring stop you doing that? I have the Antwort, Ben, mein Freund – it does not. Not at all. After all, is your brain subject to your senses, or do they in fact cohabit peacefully for most of the time? More intriguingly still – am I not better at what I do for not masking myself under layers of conventions that merely waste time and money? A happy and confident person is not someone who is living a lie, Ben."

Ben rolled his eyes.

"If only it were that easy to be happy and confident. It's always been hellish for me on that score."

Listening, Nicholas' lip curled. What fools. What utter, deluded idiots. Who did they think they were, with their freedom and their depraved indulgences? LGBT be damned. As far as Nicholas's underlings were concerned, LGBT stood for Less Gay Buggering Today.

Hartmut continued.

"We don't need to make this about you, Ben. It is in fact very much about me. If I want to write a book, I am damned well going to write a book – and I will not struggle as they try to tighten the noose around my neck. You know what to do when they do that, Ben? You stand stock still. You do not budge. You do not help them. Ultimately they may realise it matters not one iota."

Ben shook his head.

"They will crucify you for this. It's just not... *serious*! You're not a writer! Why would you do it? Why hand them the means to do your career harm? You're a fine lawyer, Hartmut! That must count for something? This plan is facile and ridiculous! It would cause great unease."

Hartmut smiled languidly.

"Would it, now."

He stood up and walked to his office window. He looked out over the stretch of the City below him. Light was falling. Office windows were illuminated like little stars in the dusk.

"These windows are like little shining lights onto the world, Ben. In each of them humans are clustered. We barely know each other in this life. And then we die. But we underestimate ourselves all the time. We're the wizard inside the machine. We are the people that make the machine whirr, and tick, and hum, and spin. We can do this Ben without losing our individuality. We can do this without losing the ability to reach out. We can connect."

He turned to Ben, his eyes twinkling:

"I want to write. I want to share. Why should I ever worry about fitting into other people's perceptions of me?"

Ben snorted.

"Oh, come off it Hartmut! You haven't exactly broken your back to do that, ever! You've been on the extreme edge of what is tolerable for a law firm for a very long time. And now you are going to take another step away from the norm? They will snap."

Hartmut said nothing.

Ben was frustrated by his inability to persuade his friend. He reasoned on.

"Hartmut, I am bisexual – but I am commonly seen as gay. I am not treated the same as others. I am deliberately kept away from files involving Africa, or the Middle East. No one in this profession is proud of me. Oh, they don't *mind* me so long as I keep things as close as possible to the norm. Is that the meaning of equality? Of course it isn't. They still mutter about Lynn and Pam. Cornisha is buried in middle management. We are here, we are queer but no one but us is proud of it – and we don't get the same push, encouragement or value placed on us that others do. Values! It enrages me when people talk about values. Why do pricks get ahead, so as to get in the way, and then hold me back?"

"And that is why we make stands!" barked Hartmut, rounding on Ben, "Don't you see that the answer is precisely for me to write about this? Don't you see that unless you are unafraid of the moustachioed idiots, not only will they win, but they will justify to themselves that theirs was the correct stance? I'm going to write it – and I will call it Justizia. Did you know that was considered as a name for our firm when we merged?"

Nicholas could not believe it. What was Hartmut saying? A book? A fictional work? Detailing his... disgusting proclivities?

Anger swept Nicholas like a watchtower's beam. It burst and bubbled inside him. Who did Hartmut think he was?

It did not matter that Nicholas was himself depraved. He considered it an acceptable state of affairs, because he was depraved in secret. He kept his sexual appetites buried, along with any acknowledgement that they existed.

He simply could not tolerate anyone who was more at ease than he was with what turned them on. His sexual side was like an inhibited child, saucer-eyed still over what had been drummed into it by a strict religious upbringing. He was taught that the burgeoning feelings of pubescence were"naughty things". Sex simultaneously mortified and excited him. His desires had thus always been something to be crushed. This was why they squirmed out from under him in strange tendrils, to be indulged in bursts, and then padlocked away. They whispered to him in the dark, and at unexpected times, causing him to do things that he chose to forget, for fear of penetrating that darkness too deeply. Nicholas also felt, had he chosen to acknowledge it, a terrible fear that any contravention to his certainty about what one should do or reveal about oneself would be a personal attack both on him, and on civilisation itself as he saw it.

Hartmut had to be stopped. That much Nicholas knew.

Amber knocked on her brother's door, a little impatiently. She stood on the solid concrete corridor outside his flat, hugging the edges of her expensive leather jacket around her.

No sound came from within.

She banged on the door, with growing annoyance. Not again! This was the second – or was it *third?* – time she had been stood up, after dragging herself all the way to Hackney to catch up with her no-good sibling in his unattractive estate.

Amber now lived in Bermondsey, in a chi-chi flat from one window of which one could glimpse the grey ribbon of the Thames. She had certainly come up in the world from less salubrious surroundings. Anything that was now distressed in her flat was deliberately so. Bare brick walls, white ceilings, a hint of chrome and wooden floors throughout – Amber was content that she had escaped from what she perceived to be a lowlier class of surroundings. Despite this, she had a love-hate relationship with neighbourhoods that reminded her of her past.

The umbilical cord was never entirely severed. She felt

at ease in the streets she was used to roaming, and knew how to walk, look, and navigate the environs.

"Oh, for fuck's sake," she said, furrowing her brows. She did not have time to waste.

Slava looked at her sharply as he emerged from the stairwell, weighed down as he was with heavy shopping.

He saw what looked agreeably like a gangster's moll stamping her feet outside his neighbour's flat. Slava assessed people well enough, and his interest was piqued. He liked her leather jacket. Her figure was all manner of alluring, and her visible vexation appealed – an open manifestation of the daily annoyance of life. She looked strong, properly strong, as if she might beat the door down with her fists or with a well aimed kick at the lock. He wondered why she was keen to see his neighbour. The neighbour was a ne'er do well. She on the other hand appeared to be a go-getter. She would have to be, in order to go and get that jacket.

"I don't know where Darren is, but you're welcome to wait in my flat until his return," he drawled, putting down his shopping and patting his pockets for his key.

Amber turned the glare of her eyes upon him.

"Uncanny. That's exactly what the Health and Safety Executive recommends for women waiting outside flats," she snarled.

Slava laughed heartily.

"Oh, come on! You look as if you could defend yourself."

Amber shivered. It was a classic English day, dry but grey, with a light but penetrating breeze that seemed to find its way in through the very seams of her clothes. Temperatures were struggling to hit anything like T shirt weather.

Slava looked at her, amused.

"What's the worst that could happen?"

Amber looked over coldly.

"Ask yourself the question, mate."

He blinked.

"Okay, okay. The offer stands."

His backing off made the decision, as usual. She had to see Darren – she was not going to drag herself over here any more often than she had to. She gave it five minutes, and then knocked on his door.

Slava opened and smiled engagingly.

"What is it regarding?"

"It's regarding the fact that my nipples are like ice cubes." She walked in confidently.

Inside was immeasurably better than outside. Amber looked around with interest and growing appreciation. Slava's flat was a knock out. Amber actually whistled as she took in the main room. It was beautifully decorated, with flair and taste. A large sofa dominated, with deep comfortable cushions. They looked welcoming. Slava had installed what looked like a supremely expensive gas fire, fitted into a wall. Amber had never seen one of those in a council flat before. Tones were muted, save for a few rugs which offered exquisite patterns and vibrant colours.

She turned to look at him with new respect.

"So... what is it you do, exactly?"

"You are a terrible English person. We haven't even been introduced. I'm Slava."

He gripped her hand. She gripped his right back.

"Amber. Amber Bluett. I'm in Human Resources."

Slava smiled widely.

"Well, now, that is a coincidence. So am I."

Amber stared at Slava. He stared confidently back.

"Am I a source of amusement to you?" she asked.

"Not at all. I am intrigued by you. You are not like other girls."

"Women, Slava. Women. You did not learn much on your diversity courses, apparently. Was the English too fast for you?"

He scowled, but unaccountably did not want to fall out with her.

"My English has been good enough to get by in all courses of action."

Amber softened. A man in control of his anger was always an attractive proposition.

"I can see that, Slava. This is a beautiful flat. Human resources, you say... "

She picked up a stunning stone sculpture. It was a small abstract shape, but it looked and felt expensive. She hefted it in her hand.

"Good for a smack in the head, this."

Slava laughed heartily.

"Not what my art dealer said, but yes, I expect so."

"Art dealer? You have an art dealer?"

Amber rolled her eyes, but did not comment further. Slava watched her.

"Would you like a drink?" he finally offered.

"You, my friend, don't need a drink to be seduced," said Amber, loftily.

Slava looked surprised.

"Who said anything... "

She glanced at him.

"I'm an action woman, Slava. I'm not some giggling girl slipping against your cushions. Things in my life are to be on my terms."

His eyes widened slightly.

"That being said, by all means let's drink," said Amber, stripping herself of her leather jacket and settling into the wide sofa. She flexed her arms, stretched her legs and patted the seat next to her.

"Wine would be good. Decent stuff, mind you. I work with wine snobs. It brushes off on you, like pollen off a lily."

"Red, or white?"

"Oh, I think white."

She studied Slava as he left the room.

He was very well built. He also had the most satisfying bulge in his jeans.

Amber was used to indulging the fantasies of men who were not at their peak, physically. Older men collected power, like squirrels collected nuts. Power was a standard replacement for actual sexual fitness – not least as it usually represented money, too. Amber learnt to switch off, and enjoy what one could about such creatures. That sometimes only consisted of such activities as could be indulged in with clothes on.

She knew it was a compromise, but would have argued with anyone that, as far as she was concerned, it was worth it. There was a powerful erotic thrill in feeling as if the world revolved around one, as one floated in the wake of someone with more power, with life becoming a huge path of manageable water through which one could sail without being seasick, ignoring the painfully clashing waves on either side, chucking other people around uncomfortably, whilst one's own every material whim was indulged.

But Amber had not entirely turned off her critical faculties. No one is immune to the tantalising effect of a well-cast human body of the gender of one's personal preference. Slava was looking like someone she felt like feeling.

He came back with a surprisingly decent Burgundy. That all but sealed it for Amber. It's all about timing, she pondered – the right offering at the right time to match the right urge. Slava expertly opened the bottle, setting about matters with some determination. His decisiveness excited Amber. He was taking things a step at a time, but moving along briskly – an appropriate manner to adopt in a world full of dithering idiots. His energy pleased and moved her.

He offered her a glass and sat next to her on the sofa. He was very much at ease. Amber thought he should be – he was on home turf. But having to coax lovers into the right mood and angle, even when they had organised the session, was one of the banes of Amber's life. It annoyed her deeply. Many things did. This was pleasing. She felt more relaxed than she had for days.

She drank slowly, eyeing him up. He reddened very slightly but lent forward.

She leaned over and kissed him.

She really kissed him, not because she liked him, not because it seemed the next move. She kissed him because she hungered for him like a feed or a drink. And it felt as good as she had hoped. He was smooth and experienced and fitted with her like a long standing dance partner.

It took them a while to remove their clothes. They were calmly deliberate about it, almost as if daring each other to out-nonchalance the other.

Slava removed his shirt, revealing a tight, hard torso with several scars and some intricate tattoos. Amber worked her hands over his upper body and down, pausing at his belt, slipping a finger in to feel the base of his erection. He stayed silent but sighed – quietly, in control. Amber removed her blouse quickly, and sprung open her front-fastening bra, a gift from Nicholas Casterway. Slava grasped her large breasts with wonder and greed. Amber enjoyed his look of genuine awe. She knew her breasts were a desirable feature, like a parking space in the centre of town. It was scarcely believable that they could be so luscious and real, given the ever widening gap between reality and aesthetics permitted by enhancements of many origins for the fashion-forward and under-confident. Amber had never had to resort to any such artifices – but the casual observer could never know of this until her naked body was pliant beneath his eager hands. It was a shame that women felt obliged to mould their mammaries into shapes that they supposed that they ought to have – but then again, let the silly fools do just that, if it gave Amber the edge in addictiveness and appeal. She watched Slava coil at her bosom. It was working, yet again.

They kissed more urgently, semi-naked.

This is where a necessary pause occurred – because, whatever the convenience of denim, it's not that easy to peel off in a hurry, unless you happen to be wearing a stripper's velcro version, which neither Slava nor Amber were. So they sprung apart briefly. They stood to take off their jeans after kicking off their shoes, with a wriggle of the hips for Amber and a straight tug for Slava. Then Amber pushed Slava onto the sofa and straddled him. She expertly dressed his genitals with a condom and lowered herself like a docking spaceship. It was her turn to sigh deeply. He was magnificent.

They fucked and drank with abandon.

It didn't take overly long. They were both efficient and selfish enough to get off quickly. But they liked what they experienced.

Slava looked at Amber with some admiration.

"This was good."

She slurped her wine thoughtfully.

"Do you think bloody Darren will have graced his flat with an appearance yet?"

"I don't know. But it would be good for you to grace mine with a few more. I'm thinking too – we may have some options. Would you like to consider some work?"

Jake was back.

A short break in the Fondant Furies' international tour schedule had returned him to London. Monique had been looking forward to this for weeks. It wasn't so much absence making the heart grow fonder, as absence creating distance that became harder and harder to bridge.

Monique knew that so much that was good (and bad) in relationships stemmed from shared experience. Shared experience was the key. It led to people understanding each other – knowing how to make each other happy. Distance was the enemy – not least as touch was one of the things that made most people happiest.

Jake bounded in as if running on stage. Everyone made a communal cry of welcome – a mix between Hey and Hi and Woo Hoo and Yay. Each person felt a little self-conscious, because with every absence Jake grew a little different. His returns were like chord changes – slipping upwards, increasing in intensity, with added orchestration.

As the band's renown grew, Jake too became well known, more recognisable, more in demand. Fame crashed into the room with him. His face was that little bit more familiar for having seen it regularly reproduced in public media. Fame choked and exhilarated people. A little jealousy flickered, a lot of projection happened, and people perked up like watered plants.

The stylists had got at Jake. Cornisha looked him over. Older women can do this more freely. She remembered the sweet youth she had first met, locally admired and already successful, but still rough around the edges. Now every lock of his hair seemed to have been carefully fashioned into place. His clothes had the pristine sheen of the new, and yet gave him a casual air that belied the considerable thought that had gone into assembling them. He wore sharp looking boots and a deep green top that seemed... Japanese? It had the odd asymmetrical fold.

Monique rose to the challenge. Dating a rising star had inspired her to continue pretending not to care, whilst keeping an eye on her own sartorial performance. She was wearing a burnt orange mini dress that flattered her slim figure and long legs. She looked beautiful – and Jake glowed at the sight of her.

Cornisha smoothed her rich green velvet dress. Her series of green velvet outfits were like a second skin to her, and – unaccountably – she suddenly felt glad to be never changing, as she observed these young people spiralling higher and higher. Icarus. One, the other, or both of them were Icarus – although Monique would be the one packing a spare pair of wings.

Kelly was munching on some of the food that Monique had laid out. Kelly was the least well prepared for the visitation. It's not as if she hadn't thought about it, throwing on a half decent dress herself that morning, only to pour coffee down it and sit on a chocolate biscuit during the day. Work clothes collected the most curious and absurd collection of stains, from ballpoint pen all over your breasts to dark marks on the hips that suggested one had collided with a small but deliberately filthy machine. The grease spots over time formed a menu of what had been consumed at lunch, in a rush, while hunched over the desk – chilli con carne from a takeaway van, limp sushi from a local shop, wildly overpriced burritos from a relentlessly over-marketed store, and every type and variety of sandwich on the market – all dripping fillings as if to spell out the range on offer upon papers and garments alike. Here was egg mayonnaise, a firm favourite, the stalwart of the sandwich world. There was bacon and avocado, the guilty and the good. There, too, was chicken, chicken everywhere, festooned with sweetcorn, coloured with paprika, smothered in secret sauces, with a lettuce leaf paying a constant and grimly determined supporting role. The stains left on Kelly's clothes together confirmed one of the many things that she felt very strongly about – that dry cleaning was a rip off, because, obviously, no one cared to do any job properly if not motivated and constantly challenged to do so.

Today's chocolate biscuit incident had been unfortunate – not least as Kelly had been saving it for later. It had involved one of those experiences in a women's bathroom where a person twists and turns to reach and deal with the offending blemish, splashing water and soap over herself like a demented washerwoman with a bad aim, while other women came and went, ignoring the solo twister game played out before them, as if she were but a ghost in the machine. Most of the stain had come out but Kelly looked a little crumpled. And yet she too glowed nonetheless.

She was alive and excited. Jake had nothing on Morten. Kelly was in the throes of the biggest flush of renewed passion that she had ever experienced.

Obviously, Jake's return was interesting – even important – and obviously Kelly was keen to hear from him. But as she ate a particularly delicious vol-au-vent (who even made these anymore?) she was conscious that all she really wanted to do is talk about herself. Surely Cornisha, Monique and Jake would want to guide, inspire and educate her, as she tried – like many others before her – to match her desires to societal norms and expectations?

She was sure that they would be thrilled at her news and thoughts. She ate another vol-au-vent in celebration.

"Oh no no no no no no. No you don't. Not again." Cornisha

was aghast. "What is it with all this nonsense, Kelly? We've done this one to death. Why again?"

Monique looked a little stunned, too.

"It sounds a little risky, and fraught with problems," she offered.

Kelly looked hurt.

"I have discussed this with Ben. I did mention that, didn't I? Don't you see? We're trying to break down the last barriers that prevent society being fulfilled and happy – the restrictions of monogamy."

Monique snorted.

"You've discussed it in the abstract! I am completely sure that you haven't told Ben that it's Morten!"

Jake broke in.

"It's not cool, Kelly. I know Ben – he's a good guy. Am I supposed to keep this secret? I may well see him this week. Not cool, man."

Kelly bit her lip. How was she supposed to discuss anything seriously with someone who used the expression "Not cool, man"?

She would have to be patient. Her friends were not forward-thinking free spirits like Ben and herself.

She decided to change the subject.

"Enough about me!" she said gaily, probably on the only occasion when others had not heard enough about her, "Jake, how is the tour going?"

Jake needed no encouragement to veer off a difficult subject onto more anodyne ground. He also deeply loved touring. It was all still novel and exciting. He was discovering places for the first time, meeting people that he was in awe of. He shared this in a low voice, still conscious that it might sound like bragging – or, worse, that it might be of limited interest to others.

Kelly listened but found her thoughts drifting off to Morten. Love was so selfish, she mused. It possessed one. She was thrilled to feel this way again. It had been some time since she had yearned for someone. You had to live and yearn. Life was awful without a bit of hankering.

She looked over at Monique, who was definitely playing it cool. Such games, thought Kelly, her eyes flitting between Monique and Jake, who were still talking about Kyoto. Even though they love each other, they are playing games. Relationships are one big sports field.

She looked at Cornisha who caught her gaze and held it, pursing her lips. Cornisha did not approve. Kelly sighed. Why were the most unconventional people the most ordinary underneath? Such bourgeoisie!

Cornisha was a good mind reader. She sat by Kelly, smoothing her dress.

"You must think me very square," she said.

Kelly shrugged.

"Not square as such. You've kind of broken that mould. But I did think you would get that a woman can love two men at once."

Cornisha laughed.

"I do hope that that is not meant as a slight. If it is I would have to respond with something like: why don't you take a running jump, you silly Southern cowgirl. But it needn't come to that. I'd be disappointed if we ended up trading insults. However, I find the situation bemusing. I think you are not weighing up sufficiently the great care with which conventions have to be bent. I mean that. Things have to be changed gently. You bend them slowly, and inspire a different approach. You take small steps. You don't snap a convention in two. If you do, you end up with blood on the carpet."

Kelly felt sulky. She was so sure that she was right.

"Conventions don't bleed."

"No, but hearts do." Cornisha leaned in: "You've spoken about it with Ben. But did you agree to just jump into it? Does he know that you've reunited with Morten?"

Kelly rolled her eyes.

"I don't think there is a recipe for how to change things," she grumbled, "I actually needed this, and I'm hoping people would have understood. None of you do. If Ben doesn't, then I'm the one who'll be disappointed. Don't you see, Cornisha? Men are *complementary*. I can't get all that I need from one man."

Cornisha laughed again, softly.

"I think some men have been thinking the same about women for some time. Is this progress? At first blush, it doesn't feel like it. I suppose that it depends on the individuals concerned. You can be the Pollyanna of polyamory if you like. We're your friends. Whatever you do, we'll endeavour to understand. Just make sure that you are not dressing something up as something that it is not. I had surgery to deal with my issue. You can't have surgery for yours."

"Okay, okay," said Kelly, surrendering to her friends. "I'll talk to Ben. Just give me space to do it, all right?"

Jake smiled.

"That seems the right thing to do. I love you guys."

"Loving guys is about the sum of it," said Kelly. "There is a light that goes on when you fall in love. It just keeps burning. It's probably a good thing – but here I am, burning away, and you're looking at me as if I've eaten a baby."

"Well," said Monique, "you've certainly eaten a baby's weight in canapés. May as well go for the larger child's worth."

She offered a tray.

"We won't judge – yet."

While Kelly whiled away the evening with Cornisha and Monique, Ben was keeping a long standing engagement with Cornisha's husband, Arthur Bilks.

This was the kind of plan that Ben made happily well in advance, but always ended up half regretting as the date grew nearer. He supposed it was better than sitting home alone waiting for Kelly to return. The idea threw off a kind of cheerful "Why not?" appeal in the abstract, before he actually had to displace himself. He told himself that it should be interesting to catch up properly with Arthur, the steady, reliable receptionist, concierge and all round invisible, all seeing guardian at the Castle Lofts. It may even prove *instructive* to see Arthur in his own space.

Ben liked to think of himself as a man of the people, and Arthur was – well – a person. Ben's theory about social events was that if you didn't want to do it, it may prove to be a good thing. He hadn't really kept track of the success ratio of this approach, but it still seemed to make sense.

Of course, on the evening, it all felt too groanworthy to be true. He bemoaned his social experimentation – not least as it meant leaving a warm comfortable home and heading out into the wilds of London.

He exited the tube station cautiously, and immediately checked his phone to see which way he needed to go.

He cursed his curiosity about Arthur's neighbourhood. He had stepped into a foreign land of anonymous suburban boxes. He glanced down the quieter roads where a kebab shop seemed to pass for a destination address. The creeping gentrification that was slowly transforming his home in Elephant & Castle – which he had always thought to be about as gritty as one could get – seemed absent here. As far as he could tell, it all blended into an anodyne grey-brown mush. How did anyone ever find their way round this place? Thank heavens for online maps. What did one do before them? He sighed and stared more intently at the map to bolster a feeling of resourcefulness.

It didn't take long for Ben to be ready to give up and phone Arthur. However, asking for directions would obviously be an admission of abject failure. It was very annoying. Ben was sure that Caspar – that dratted representative of the younger generation – would be able to teleport to any destination on the planet using the latest sharing-economy apps in his pocket, arriving in an environmentally-friendly way, at the lowest cost imaginable, and with some appropriate gift under his arm. But Ben was not that youngster anymore.

It wasn't Ben's fault. He *was* part of the digerati – truly he was. He must be. If his stupid map was telling him that he should be right in front of the pub when all there was to be seen was a closed pound shop and a blank wall, then what was he to do?

He felt as doomed as Captain Oates. *I am just going outside central London and may be some time.* Then he had an idea. What about a side or a back entry? He of all people should remember those. He assumed a quietly triumphal demeanour when, upon rounding the corner, he finally espied a dingy-looking establishment displaying a faded sign. This announced he had at last arrived at the Spotted Duck.

As Ben pushed open the double doors, he realised he wasn't in Kansas any more. The place looked as if it had never entertained any friends of Dorothy. The precious few customers who were there communing with their pints raised their eyes to take in the newcomer. They then went back to contemplating whatever it was that they seemed so transfigured with – whatever it was that lay at the bottom of the glasses.

The pub was dimly lit, with a thick red patterned carpet to pad about on. Even in this light, Ben could tell that it had seen better days. Smoking had been banned indoors for years, but the Anaglypta-covered walls remained that deep, brown-tinged yellow. They seemed to ooze decades of smoke slowly back into the rooms.

Ben coughed sympathetically. He took in the heavy wooden tables and generously upholstered, but slightly threadbare armchairs, together with the imitation flame fire. They gave the establishment a comforting feel, like that pair of old jogging pants that you couldn't go out in but were perfect for delicate Sunday mornings indoors.

The landlady came to the rescue.

"They're in the snug, darling."

Ben wasn't sure what a snug was, nor how the cheery landlady could possibly know who he was looking for, but he followed her directions obediently. He pushed open a dark wooden panelled door. It sat in the middle of a wall boasting grimy stained glass windows, fringed by ancient posters advertising a health-giving elixir called stout.

A gruff voice spoke out:

"Ah, Ben. You found us then. Come along in and sit down."

Arthur was seated at a table with two other men. They were John and Bert. They sat in the secluded space beyond the panelled door. It was a simple small room with just two tables, open to a small section of the bar. At the bar stood the landlady, flitting between the serving points. She told him with a wink that she was named Stella.

After some stilted conversation, and two pints later, Ben was wondering exactly why he had agreed to spend the evening with his East-end doorman from the Castle Lofts and his two taciturn companions. The men seemed as content as the solitary drinkers the other side of the wall to sit and gaze into the amber depths of their glasses. Ben couldn't help but contrast their behaviour with the rambunctious affairs that his evenings out with Rubens inevitably became. He berated himself silently for giving up an evening for this social endeavour.

Enough was enough. Ben drained the last of his pint and readied himself for delivering an excuse to leave. He would say he had to check on some emails. He wondered if the old boys would actually know what they were.

"I have to go I'm afraid. Work." Ben thought they would appreciate his word economy.

"Ah. Time waits for no man."

They were the first words, excepting *hello* that John had uttered all evening. Bert nodded thoughtfully. Arthur looked as if he were about to say something, then seemingly thought better of it. However, as Ben stood up, Stella, who had been hopefully polishing glasses the other side of the bar, broke the silence.

"You can't leave just yet. Our gentlemen have been working up to ask you a whole load of questions about your experiences in London."

The gentlemen in question looked briefly as if the only thing they wished to ask was why Stella had made everyone feel so awkward. John cleared his throat ostentatiously and looked straight at Ben.

"Truth be told, Ben, I never would have guessed you were one of them fairy fellas. Just goes to show you. You would never say either that our Cornisha used to be a man. I reckon she must have been a pretty lousy bloke because she is one hell of a woman."

Although not exactly language fit for Sagworth Turner Dickerhint's LGBTQ group, Ben guessed that John was attempting to pay him a compliment. How to respond was quite another thing. Bert already looked as if he were about to have a seizure. Ben wondered if he should just press on with his goodbyes.

John, however, had the bit between his teeth.

"I may not have ever enjoyed the pleasures of man-on-man action, being more of a tits fella myself, but I have wondered what the hell it must be like to be with another man. Before you two swallow your teeth, I don't mean in a physical way. I mean in a relationship way. We've spent all our lives trying to work out how women tick, understand their moods and all those feelings they're so bloody specialised in. Damn sight harder than a City & Guilds, if you ask me. So much easier understanding another bloke. There would be far fewer misunderstandings and arguments. We could enjoy going to the match together. The telly could be constantly set to Sky Sports. No problem farting and burping either. Only problem is, I really haven't got the faintest desire to clamp my gnashers round anyone's cock. And as for my back passage, that's strictly one way. I even feel a bit queasy if I enjoy having a crap a bit too much."

"Well it never rains but it pours."

Stella was evidently the only one who was not feeling aghast about John's little speech.

Arthur remembered the last time John had ventured far from the madding football crowd. It was the night that he had discovered that Cornisha Burrows, the woman he'd lost his heart to, had lost some body parts herself. Rather unexpectedly, John's frank talk way back then had woken him up to the fact that emotions were not an enemy to be held at the gates, and being different was all right. He ordered another round. It was time to talk.

"So, Ben." said Arthur, "You are in the privileged position of knowing what it is like being with a woman, and also being with a bloke. It must be different. Is it just like having a mate you want to shag, or does it get all complicated like for us normal folk?"

Arthur stopped:

"That came out wrong. I didn't mean it like that."

"It's okay, I didn't take it in any bad way."

It was Ben's turn to pause. He felt four pairs of eyes keenly watching him, to see how he would respond. The men's gruff awkwardness seemed to have rubbed off on him, all the more so as they appeared to have overcome their shyness, and were ready to discuss subjects which Ben never thought he would broach in such an environment.

He shrugged. Sometimes you just had to say things, not overthink them.

"I'm the last person you should be discussing the theory of relationships with – but sure, some things are easier. Gay men don't tend to be massively into sport, but some things may be easier. Like... like... " Ben drummed his fingers. "Well, I don't know... er... "

He cast about wildly:

"Take farting in bed. This is funny rather than awkward amongst men."

Ben blushed suddenly, wishing he hadn't said *in bed*, thinking – correctly, as it happened – that the three men would be wondering if a lot more farting took place after what they supposed gay men got up to in bed. What exactly was he trying to say?

He pushed on valiantly.

It's hard to say – really it is – what is properly different. Let's see. What is easier... what is less so... ? Well, you definitely encounter the same jealousy. And you worry a lot more about your looks. Of course, women like a looker too, but in my experience they are unlikely to be as brutal as men are in judging how you look. Your value on the dating scene may be different. Women are less hung up on exactly how big your biceps are, how ripped your muscles are, or how pretty your face is. In both cases, of course, there is always the younger, fresher model to worry about. You may feel that you seem to be working out all the hours of the day to make sure you have done enough to get by, you get horribly aware of how your youth is just slipping away, visibly eroding your value, steadily, incessantly... "

Ben paused as he contemplated the pleasantly plump men in front of him, who had probably never graced a gym in their lives. Not at all awkward, this.

Arthur cleared his throat.

"All the bright precious things fade so fast... and they don't come back."

Ben hadn't expected Arthur to quote The Great Gatsby at him. Of course, those words were as true today as they had been almost a century ago. It put him in mind of a T-Shirt he had seen in a shop in San Francisco. He had found it compelling, but knew he would never have the guts to wear it. It said *Your looks will fade, but my dick will be massive forever.* It seemed to Ben at the time to be a wonderful putdown for the attractive, stuck-up muscle queens who acted as if they ruled the world. Maybe he could wear it, when he was older? Unlikely, on reflection.

Bert harrumphed:

"So. Are you saying that men treat other men the way we treat women?"

This elicited raised eyebrows all round.

Ben grimaced.

"Well, Bert, there can be a lot of pressure on a gay man to constantly look your best, if you decide to join the race. Women might relate to this. For example, I can totally see why some women wear make-up to the gym. I wouldn't want to go to mine on a bad hair day. People judge you all the time on how you look."

Ben paused again, wondering if the men could grasp the concept of a bad hair day. As there was precious little of the matter on any of their heads, it probably wasn't top of the list for them. He laboured on.

"And it's more acute,, actually, because the men who see you stripped off in the changing room at the gym, are often the ones you're trying to simultaneously both impress as competition and potentially attract as a partner."

Ben couldn't quite bring himself to say *sex partner*. He pressed on:

"You can't hide your imperfections when you are standing, momentarily naked, under the unforgiving neon lights, with the harsh eyes of body fascists passing judgement on you. It's great for the ego when you feel you've been elected to the club, but it's *so* precarious."

Ben remembered how he had felt when he finally knew he was one of the chosen ones, with the attendant looks of approval, and the opportunities that opened to him like rosebuds in May.

Bert jumped in.

"It's not that different at Upton Park if you think about it. You're only as good as your last match. Mind you, your team mates and your manager are likely to be judging you on how often you get one in the back of the net, rather than how you look when you reach down to pick up the soap in the shower."

Bert looked round, hoping for a chuckle. Arthur and John paid him little heed, and looked at Ben, waiting for him to continue.

Ben shrugged.

"That's why we have individual cubicles in gyms now, Bert, and liquid soap dispensers. All that bending over must have been a real hazard in the past. Health and Safety closed down all that fun."

The old boys weren't sure whether they should be laughing or not, so they just nodded and said "Bloody Health and Safety" disapprovingly.

Ben sat back:

"It's funny really, because on one level it is a lot simpler when you are all men together. Understanding each other can be easier. However, it's also more complicated."

Looking at the faces staring intently at him, Ben realised he had his audience's attention as if he were giving out secret information on the form of the runners and riders in the three twenty at Doncaster. He was starting to enjoy himself.

"These younger, fresher models we all live in fear of – often visitors to our shores who have been honing their perfect bodies in the darkest depths of Bucharest or Caracas or Wrexham – are not only your competition, but are the very ones who can also be your next shag. They arrive all repressed, with their youth, innocence, and overflowing desire and then burst upon the London scene with all the instant popularity of the latest reality TV star, making yesterday's celebrity old news. I should know. I was one of them once, and I didn't even know it at the time. Now I am one of the old magpies, who feels threatened by these constant newcomers, but still can't help turning his head at the latest shiny new thing I see."

Bert looked enquiringly at Ben.

"So do gay builders wolf-whistle each other when it gets hot?"

"Have you been watching repeats of Little Britain, again, Bert?" John clapped his old friend on the shoulder: "It's a bit of a bugger when all you've learned about gays comes from TV."

John turned to Ben.

"You obviously know what you're talking about, but surely it can't all be superficial like that? You see blokes on the telly who've been shacked up for decades, blokes our age who've been together since they were in their twenties. I saw a programme the other day. It was more about strange hobbies taken to extremes. This bloke was obsessed with Morris Marinas, but it happened he was gay. His husband preferred the Austin Princess. They hadn't even traded in their cars for a younger model, never mind each other."

Ben realised he had focused in rather narrowly on the A-List clubbing scene, and a particular subset of it at that.

"Gay men do stay together, you're right, John. But there is so much temptation around, and sex is so readily available. When you are playing at the top of your game, surrounded by all that flesh for fantasy, it would take a very saintly mind not to indulge. Just imagine what it is like. Men are largely opportunists when it comes to sex. We can be disciplined, but if it's there on a plate, denial has to fight the blind power of biology. And when we are all men together, where is the restraint supposed to come from?"

"So you reckon that us men have about as much class as Slack Alice who used to work the Whelk and Whippet on the sly?"

"Slack Alice. Now that's a blast from the past. That pub closed down when Bruce Forsyth was knee high to a grasshopper!" Arthur did, however, register the point. "Times may have changed from when our Bert here was Jack the Lad, but men have always found it easier to spread themselves around. I guess when there is no woman to calm us down, we can be a bit like a child in a sweetshop."

"My old Mum got it right." John looked at the other men, taking in their surprise at him bringing his mother into this conversation. He nodded confidently.

"She was a very smart lady, well ahead of her time. I don't think she had ever actually been with anyone other than my Dad, but she had seen a lot of the world. She told me that the casual affairs – that would be Slack Alice for you, Bert – well, they are like a spoonful of sugar. They give you an instant rush but they're gone before you know it. And if that's all you eat, you'll get fat and have rotten teeth. The love of your life, now that is the roast beef, three veg and gravy; you can eat it every day of your life and it will sustain you for ever."

"The problem is though, John, most of us want that sweetness every now and again." Ben looked round at the three men. "And on the gay scene there's a sweetshop round every corner. Even though the cost of the sweets seems to go up with every year that passes."

Arthur wasn't at all sure he followed these food analogies. But Ben's last comment had told him what he needed to know.

"So young man, we've finally got to your dilemma. You think you have found the love of your life, but you can't help worrying about everything you are missing out on, and what's worse you feel the clock ticking. Even at your young age."

"He's got a sweet tooth, like Alice used to!"

Ben couldn't help but think Bert was right. They were both right. In fact the three old buffers weren't half as out of touch as Ben assumed they would be.

He nodded thoughtfully:

"The problem is that I know what is out there. And although it is insecure, by God is it a trip. I don't want to become one of those people who just settle down and start to live their lives through minor victories at work, a cooler car than my friends have and my kids' achievements. I want the excitement I've had in my life to continue. But I want Kelly as well. It's all irreconcilable. All the time I let that excitement pass me by it becomes harder to get back. I can feel my old life slipping away and I'm afraid the new one may be more secure, but it is just going to be a lot less fun."

There. He had admitted his innermost thoughts to them. It did sound rather self-indulgent, especially as Ben realised his was hardly one of life's sob stories, but it was how he felt.

Arthur gave the young American a long look.

"I have been a very lucky man in life. Fate and an overly polished floor brought my wonderful Cornisha to me, at a stage in my life when I had given up all hope of anyone ever being interested in this old carcass again. However, a long time before I was blessed by meeting Cornisha, I had an enduring and happy marriage."

Bert and John's faces switched into the appropriate reverential expression. This invariably settled upon their features whenever Arthur's first love was mentioned.

Arthur sighed.

"It took me a long time to find my Phyllis. John and Bert here already had a couple of kids and I was still playing the field, wondering why anyone would give up their youth voluntarily. And then I met this woman. She made me feel like I'd scored all the goals in 1966. I never had the doubts that you had, but then I suppose I wasn't wondering if I still fancied a big knob up my backside."

"That's a bit harsh, Arth!" John looked sympathetically over at a startled Ben. "I don't think it's just about what kind of sex you want. The boy's looking round at us and seeing his future and I don't think he likes it."

John laughed.

"On the face of it we don't really seem that exciting, do we!"

"What you have to realise, lad is this." Arthur looked seriously at the American. "You're so worried about your wonderful life fading away, when the only thing you need to care about is your imagination. Stay young inside and the outward signs of age mean nothing. The emotions I had all through my years with Phyllis knocked spots off all the flings I had with Ida and Connie and Doris and all the others. Nice girls all of them, but for me nothing compares to the thrill of being with the person you have loved for a long time, achieving things together, sharing the most important things in life with someone who really cares about you."

Arthur took a deep draft of his pint.

"Even at the end, when Phyllis' poor body was a pale shadow of the woman I had fallen in love with, all I saw was the sparkle of her personality. She was always twenty-three to me, no matter how many years had passed. And she made me feel like a young man too. You've got to work on yourself, lad, and not be dependent upon the outside world to fulfil your dreams."

"You certainly can't depend on the Hammers – that's a mug's game if ever there was one!" Bert grinned jovially.

The evening had turned out better than Ben had expected. As he said his goodbyes and headed off back to the familiarity of the tube and the Jubilee line back home, Ben thought again about his dilemma. It would not be easy to deal with, despite Arthur's words. Was security worth giving up the thrill of the chase for? Ben had always thought so. Indeed, society pretty much unanimously declared this to be the right course of action. But was it really right for him, right now? And more to the point, why did he have to bloody choose at all?

5

Showing the strip a clean pair of heels

How it had come to this, Harry could not fathom. It was three in the morning, and he was back in his hotel room nursing a black eye.

Despite it all, he smiled, then laughed. He was on his own. There was to be no profiteering from his marital freedom just yet. But what a night!

It had all started so promisingly at Eve's Garden. Harry had drunk his wine slowly, and observed the well-toned bodies gyrating. He allowed himself to relax. He was an old hand at this. You couldn't enjoy a show like this if you weren't relaxed. He sank into his cushioned banquette and wondered idly how much rouge had been applied to the ladies' nipples, and by whom. He hoped not much, as it was a bugger to get off white shirts. Actually, more recently, it was body make up that caused the problem. And mascara. And blusher. And sparkly... stuff. There was a great deal of sparkle – in powder, in body gel, in eyelashes and eyeshadows. Everywhere, except in the eyes.

But come, Harry chided himself. It doesn't do to go all doom and gloom about it all. It was true that not everyone loved their job – that was the case for this particular activity as much as any other. It was a job. A dancer's job. Not everyone is hung up about being naked for money. Some might say that it is cleaner than selling your soul. After all, what could be more revolting than a lawyer applying their intelligence to help an unworthy client?

We have strange social standards, thought Harry. Always have had, always will have. Living in fear of what others think keeps us all in our place. It keeps us grounded. Somehow people could be deliberately ignorant of what they enabled in an advisory capacity, yet allowed themselves to be outraged by personal sexual indulgences.

Harry smiled grimly. He had seen the worst of this in his work. He'd stood by while others were pressurised. He'd seen how strength or power were simply measured by how far you were prepared to go to make others bend to your will. When they didn't, you disposed of them. There was no assessment of quality. Mediocrity often won out, because mediocre people usually have the most to lose. In an unhappy situation, the gifted people leave, and the dim hang on by their nails, for as long as they can.

No wonder people got stressed. No one likes to be made to feel weak. But Harry had always taken the easy route, and simply not cared about quality or improvement in services. So long as he got paid, and had all the *signes exterieurs de richesse* that his lifestyle necessitated, he would not have cared if colleagues were being flayed alive in the next room.

Time flew in Eve's Garden. Harry watched the people coming and going, in so far as he could make them out in the dark room.

"Would you like a lap dance?"

Harry was impressed by what he saw. The woman in front of him was very pretty. She had an angelic face, and a lovely body in a very small bikini.

He knew the drill.

"May I buy you a glass of champagne first?"

"Yes," she said matter of factly, "that would be perfect."

She sat next to him.

"My name is Polina."

"Nice to meet you."

"I'm sorry to ask this, but I do have a favour I would like from you. It will be easy enough for you, and I promise that you will be doing the right thing."

Harry creased his forehead as he tried to remember whether this had ever been part of the drill before. No. No, it had definitely not been. This was novel.

She smiled.

"Can you look as if you are flirting with me – and enjoying yourself?"

She laughed coquettishly.

He remained puzzled.

"What?"

"Can you look as if you are flirting with me? Please smile."

Her voice was low and earnest, and she twirled her blonde hair as she spoke.

"Thank you. You look happier now. As I said, my name is Polina. I'm going to try to figure out how to walk out of here with your help. It needs to look natural."

Harry looked bemused.

"Please smile," she said again.

Harry grinned automatically.

"You can't walk out dressed like that," he said through creased cheeks.

"I know. I'd like to borrow your coat. The coat check girl is with me, and provided no one is looking she will give your coat to me in exchange for your coat tag. It is all as usual."

"Yes, due process there. What is this all about, Polina?"

"I will explain it all in good time. They are not holding me prisoner as such, but they have everything on me and they control me. I need your coat, some money, maybe a place to hide? I've been waiting for days for a decent looking man to come in and help me."

Despite himself, Harry felt a lift. Was she calling him *handsome*? Was he finally being given a compliment on his looks? It had been *ages* since the last one...

She looked him straight in the eyes.

"Most people do not look trustworthy. I can only hope that you are as you seem. I will cover your back, I promise, if your coat covers mine. You'll get everything back."

Harry was thinking. He suspected that he had to do the decent thing and help. There might be another compliment in it.

"I'll help you, but only if you keep my name out of it. I can give you some cash and the coat check ticket. My name is Harry Gumpert. I live in the Castle Lofts – it's an apartment complex on the South Bank. You can't go to my home. I'm divorcing my wife and I think a... dancer turning up may not help our mediation process. But the concierge of the building is a – well, *another* – decent chap, called Arthur Bilks. Please tell him that I sent you. There are some business cards in my coat pocket which will bear this out. He will host you until I can get there tomorrow, and we can work out what to do."

He told her the address, and got her to repeat it.

"There are cabs galore outside. Just grab one straight away."

That was when the fight had started at the next table. They were ludicrously burly men and they were hitting each other rather hard. The punches sounded like wet sand bags landing on a concrete pavement. Then someone threw a metal napkin holder, and it sailed past its intended target and hit Harry on the eyebrow.

He cried out. Meanwhile, the bouncers were charging in, and trying to figure out which bit of which person to grab. Polina saw her chance. Her eyes darted to the door. She got up and glided to the exit. No one was looking in her direction. Even Harry was more preoccupied with his face.

There was a flash of her blonde hair through the entrance door window, and then she was gone.

There was now quite a melee in Eve's Garden.

Harry observed all this with a degree of dismay. The champagne had been a real investment, with the expectation of immediate returns. He had been hoping for considerably more than this for his troubles.

The two bouncers had seized two men and were dragging them away, with some difficulty. There were four more still fighting. The bartender was keeping well away from the scene, but Harry sidled up to him and asked to pay.

The bartender looked downcast:

"It seems a bit unfair. I haven't got you your champagne yet."

Harry shrugged.

"I'd prefer to cancel the order, but I don't want any trouble."

The bartender nodded.

"Paying your way is the direction to a strong and healthy future."

"No doubt," agreed Harry.

And now here was Harry, back in his room, drunk as a lord, and alone. Why he hadn't simply sent Polina here was beyond him. He had switched into "decent" mode, like some strange machine, wired binary-style between unspeakable and its opposite. He regretted it, as he sensed that aged saviours weren't always first in line for blow jobs. But it had been fun, and his curiosity was tickled. He wondered what on earth Arthur and Cornisha would have made of it all.

Oh well. Time to sleep. There were a few more evenings to go before reality came knocking, and he sank into the fresh sheets like a footstep into delicate, white, powdery snow. This was some of the relief that he had been looking for.

Kasim put down his mascara wand and stared into the mirror at his newly volumised lashes.

Perfect.

Make up was a powerful tool. His skin was flawless. His hair haloed his head and cascaded onto his shoulders, gleaming and sleek, like a well-groomed wild animal. Kasim stepped back and smoothed his figure-hugging little black number. The overall effect would have the Fashion Police straining for superlatives.

He was preparing for a meeting in the City.

He still couldn't quite believe it. He was well accustomed to confusing people, and felt as if he now knew how they might feel. As it happened, few had met a Palestinian drag queen before.

Kasim was always curious to see what reaction he would provoke by his very being. There was always a reaction. It was often an awkward silence, followed by nervous laughter. He had experienced a number of versions of how things went from there – everything from being called a drag terrorist – which he rather liked – to having his hands seized by sensitive liberals whose eyes would well up with sympathetic tears for the plight of his people.

However, being invited to address a group of privileged young London lawyers on matters pertaining to sexuality in developing nations was another matter. This was one experience he hadn't anticipated. Like many good jokes, it had all stemmed from a chance encounter in a bar. His spontaneous joining into an earnest conversation had impressed upon the lawyers whose group he had crashed that there was something going on behind his deep green eyes. It seemed clear that the Palestinian could bring more than just colour to their deliberations. Thus he had been officially invited to address them, aiding these fine young minds in their goal of helping the sexually oppressed.

Kasim finished off the last of his Bombay and tonic, and blew himself a kiss. He ran through the points he was planning to make. He had prepared conscientiously for the occasion. He didn't want to forget anything, or crack under questioning. He discerned that there was something ambassadorial about the mission he had agreed to. He felt confident – he had dealt with far tougher crowds than a group of politically correct lawyers in some bland office. This should be fun. Things invariably were whenever he transformed himself into his drag alter ego.

Lady Gaza was ready to go.

There is something wonderful about incongruity. It is a source of joy and excitement. Children are at their most appealing when sharing with adults a new and fresh view of the world. They have the ability to remind adults that they once saw the world through a different lens. That sense of fun lingers. So it often is, too, when worlds collide. As Lady Gaza stepped into the foyer of Sagworth Turner Dickerhint, she could have been a visitor from another planet.

The atrium was large and gleaming. It housed a few sculptures that were dwarfed by the space – and the energy in the forms seemed to be straining to run away, crashing through the panes, and galloping down the dull grey streets, leaving pieces of glass glinting magically on the floor like diamonds in the pale City light. Lady Gaza's heels made a woodpecker noise on the cold shiny floor. The colour in her red jacket slashed through the discreet shades of the receptionists' uniforms.

They looked at her with undisguised surprise.

"Hello, darlings. I am here to see Ben Barlettano."

"Certainly. Your name is…?"

"Lady Gaza, darling."

There was a quick whisper but the receptionist printed

the visitor's badge with minimum fuss.

Lady Gaza held up the plastic square with its clumsy pin and thick plastic grip. It reminded her of NHS spectacles in days of yore. She had been told about these.

"Oh no," she sighed theatrically, "Must I really wear this? Hours to perfect this outfit and then seconds to ruin it with this horrible little piece of plastic."

The receptionist smiled:

"You don't have to put it on if you don't want to. Just have it on you at all times. There's information about the fire escapes on there."

Lady Gaza laughed.

"Make sure the really handsome firemen are told to search for me. I should be delighted to be rescued."

The receptionist giggled:

"If you take the elevator to the twelfth floor, someone will direct you to the meeting room."

"Thank you," said Lady Gaza, heading towards the lifts.

She felt eyes following her. She squared her shoulders – you either loved it, or you didn't.

"Onwards and upwards," she said.

There was a ripple of excitement in the meeting room, as Lady Gaza sat at the head of a large conference table, her fine legs crossed elegantly. Ben Barlettano smouldered next to her. Her femininity emphasised his classic good looks.

There was a crackle in the air. Individually, these two were, most likely, people who were actually having sex, and lots of it. The work-beaten LGBTQ group members were stirred. The pheromones made them feel like moths darting around a flame.

Ben smiled at the good turnout:

"Welcome to the inaugural meeting of the Sagworth Turner Dickerhint LGBTQ society."

He gave the group his warmest smile. This was his second inaugural speech. As a newly merged law firm, Sagworth Turner Dickerhint now hosted a much increased LGBTQ group. He met the eager eyes looking at him. The group definitely felt like something more effective, on numbers alone.

Ben was determined that the group would actually achieve something. He did not want this to be the window dressing that many of his heterosexual peers believed it to be. He was aware that some had asked why it was even necessary to have such a group, now that the body of legislation on the statute books extended to gay marriage. Ben believed that such confidence in the achievements of diversity initiatives was misplaced. Vigilance was vital. Rights were given, but they could then be ignored – or taken away. There was also the small matter of doing something for the majority of gays who were not fortunate enough to live in an open-minded society. Twenty-first century London was but one aspect of an often cruel and savage world.

"Ben, I have a question," ventured a woman from the other end of the table. "Have we added the Q for Questioning to the group's name to accommodate you and your reign over our little band of outcasts? You do seem to swing more than the doors into a restaurant kitchen."

Ben squirmed slightly. Lynne Glackett could always be relied upon to disrupt his efforts to impose dignity and calm efficiency upon proceedings.

It was common knowledge that Ben had arrived in London an apparently heterosexual jock. It didn't take him long to explore bisexuality and its glorious opportunities. It was fair to say that he had jumped around in his preferences. He gained membership of the Muscle Mary "A" List, and now he was somehow back in a strikingly conformist situation. On the face of it, he was in a monogamous relationship with a white American female. This was all impossible to deny.

Ben forced a grin:

"Well spotted, Lynne. I guess that I have journeyed through our group's alphabet more than some. I might struggle with claiming to be a lesbian, of course."

"I'm not so sure, Ben. Spend a bit of time with our Pam and you'll be swapping those shiny black shoes for orange Doc Martens faster than you can say halibuts in Hackney."

Pam Shank sighed noisily.

"*Really*, Lynne?"

Pam was rather good at public sighing. She had had many an occasion to practice in her years of being Lynne's best friend.

Pam hammered home her point.

"Just because our chairperson has been quite the flibbertigibbet, please do not make light of the issues facing the Questioning. We had to fight to win the right to be free to take the path of our choosing – but we should not forget those not yet sure which way their paths may lie."

Never one to wait before contributing to a debate, Caspar Steele leaned forward.

"Well said!" he declared.

He directed a pitying look at Ben:

"Although hovering at the crossroads was never going to be for me, it can be an agonising time of transition. And apparently it can last for many, many years."

This was not quite how Ben had envisaged launching the new group might go. His dream of being a strong respected leader, guiding members whose feelings ranged from respect to utter adoration, was yet again being flannelled out of the bathroom. Honestly. Didn't people want to be led by his dreamboat self? It was almost as if they had their own minds and ideas.

Maybe, Ben thought, he should just accept that in place of gravitas, the attainment of which he never quite seemed to achieve, his role was to get everyone relaxed by being the butt of a friendly joke or two. Even if he wasn't sure – ever – how friendly Caspar was actually being.

He looked straight at Casper:

"You may mock, but flexibility with regards to one's sexuality is nothing to sneeze at. It could be a useful tool, particularly in certain cultures which are hardly welcoming to the out-and-proud – which I think is a good segue into introducing our guest this evening."

Ben looked at the group with narrowed eyes, willing them into respecting both him and the occasion.

"Kasim Hourani was born and brought up in Palestine, and moved to the UK as a young adult, where he has had great success as an entertainer going by the name of Lady Gaza. It is as his alter ego Lady Gaza that he is here today. She is going to talk to us about her experiences of living as a gay man in a hostile environment – and what she thinks

Western groups like ours could do to help. Lady Gaza, thank you for coming – and welcome."

Lady Gaza stood up, and put her hands on her hips:

"It wasn't all hostility you know. You'd be surprised by just how much cock I got out there."

A ripple of laughter went round the table.

Lady Gaza put her hands together:

"When most opportunities to live a normal life, to strive to build a future, a meaningful career, a house or a business are taken away from you, human beings often fall back on the one thing that always remains with them. Biology."

Curious faces looked at her. The audience was attentive. She pressed on:

"Whatever happens, people build their families, or at least have as much sex as they possibly can. Sex reminds you that you are a sentient being. Your oppressor may take away material things, but they cannot remove what it is that defines you as a man or a woman, or to put it more appropriately, a sexual being. Sex is a driving force. In the heat of the moment everything else is blocked out and you are briefly master of your own destiny; in control, or willingly giving the control to your partner. The oppressor is vanquished, and you have had your victory. It's important to keep some focus on this simple point about human relationships. Otherwise one can quickly get lost in other aspects of the wider social issues. We are not here, for example, to talk of the injustice meted out to my people, but rather about the injustice that they and others like them serve up to people like me. It is this cascade of unfairness and bigotry that we have to tackle – because there is no injustice that should claim to be greater than any other. That is why we have laws – and very importantly, this is why laws must not be allowed to be ignored. I don't care if you are a Christian B&B owner wanting to have your own way. You cannot ignore the law of the land. None of us should. The minute you allow small transgressions in the name of personal beliefs, you are opening a bigger box that leads to terrible excess and persecution. It is really as serious as that."

Lady Gaza smiled. She raised her hands:

"So what can groups like yours do? Well, first you need to gain trust and acceptance. The way you do that is to unite behind a heart-warming, universal message of helping the downtrodden. We don't want to alienate anyone with our extreme political views, do we? You've got hard work ahead. Your very first hurdle is a tough issue to tackle. It is the attention span of the privileged few living in liberal societies. I mean, let's face it: cats in a box. Dogs doing tricks and looking cute. Those are the things that get the most likes on social media. Will that change anything? Anything at all? No. It will not. So you need to take your small steps, and persist. Develop awareness of who we are, what we do, our right to be different, our right to celebrate each other. Educate the young and the powerful, ignore the bigoted in between, and enforce the law. That's what you do best, and it is best that you do just that. You don't need change to operate the machinery that you already have in place, and that people are too lazy to work with. Be people that can be counted upon to do and say the right thing."

Lynne looked thoughtful. She put her hand up, and received a nod from Ben.

"You raise a number of very different and valid points. But when there is oppression all around, is it realistic to clatter on about the rights of a few queens in high heels? Can we ever expect justice for the minority, if even the majority feel nobody gives two hoots about them? And – indeed – is it even ethical to ignore the many, and focus on the few? Who is the more oppressed, at any one time?"

Ben looked pensive.

"The world is full of injustices, Lynne, and various groupings exist to support the victims of each one. Our group is the LGBTQ group, and as such we are primarily concerned with the fate of LGBTQ people. As an individual you are free to join the groups supporting any oppressed majority, but we have to concentrate on what we can do, in line with our mission statement. So, yes: *we* will focus on queens in heels, dykes in orange Doc Martens, and everyone who seems to covet genitalia that others would prefer that they do not."

Lynne acquiesced.

"Fair point, Ben. But whilst I can see bringing up the fate of oppressed people everywhere is somewhat pointless at a meeting of the local donkey sanctuary, we have to be cognisant of the political environment in which LGBTQ people live. Lady Gaza has a far better idea of what might actually be possible in her country than a bunch of woolly liberals like us trying to impose our values on people who have very different struggles to us."

Lynne looked enquiringly at Ben, wondering if he might disagree, which of course he didn't.

Lady Gaza thought she had been silent for long enough,

given a receptive and captive audience. It was time for her to exploit her podium further.

"My little lesbian friend is wise. *The past is a foreign country: they do things differently there.* Imagine if you had proposed gay marriage in England in 1947. You would have been met with utter incomprehension. In fact, it is some of those *traditional* values that you British have largely left behind, which are at the root of much of the oppression that we gays face in many countries where you once ruled. Section 377 is a queer-bashing gift that your Empire left behind when your country ran out of money and called the soldiers home. And before you Americans start looking too smug, some of your evangelical preachers are doing some *lovely* international work of their own right now in the present day."

Cornisha Burrows attended the LGBTQ meetings on sufferance. She was the token "T", knew it, and hated it. But this meeting was surprising her. It felt relevant, even for her. She would not have expected a speech from a drag queen to remind her of her own family. She raised her hand, and spoke softly when given the floor.

"Never forget your past, and still less what you did. Because those you did it to certainly won't. Why should you believe anyone now, even if they were to admit that they were wrong in the past?"

Pam felt that this went too far.

"Our forefathers did *not* speak for us, Cornisha. They were wrong, and we are right on this issue. It is one thing to understand history, it is quite another to be its prisoner."

"There are things which we can do," said Lady Gaza

decisively. "Although they tried to victimise me, I vowed that I would be myself, and that I would never be their victim. I will tell you though, it was no walk in the park. There were so many times when I felt that I was alone, and terrifyingly so. Loneliness is a curse that everyone understands. Where I have been, I didn't even have a phone support line to call when I was at my lowest. What is your group doing to support organisations like Al-Qaws? Have you even heard of it?"

Ben had done his research.

"Al-Qaws offers support to the Palestinian LGBTQ community. I sent them an email this week."

He had no more than that.

Caspar sniffed at this.

"Well, I bet that was a nice surprise for them. Did you find them on Gaydar or Manhunt? Oh no, silly me, you are not into that anymore."

Ben reminded himself not to react to baiting from a cocky junior. He knew Casper well enough by now to know that whenever the conversation became too serious, he could be counted on to provoke Ben. Almost as if he had no respect for authority, thought Ben grimly. The little sod.

Lady Gaza was nodding.

"You may joke, but the Internet is very important. It shows us we are not alone. But it is not enough. We all need role models closer to home. Seeing gay clubs in Brighton doesn't always help a man struggling in Baghdad. These groups are important. They are the beachheads. I hope you didn't just send Al-Qaws some of those photos that you left with my friend Zahoor, Ben."

"I have opened a dialogue to see what we could do to help."

The meeting had not exactly gone the way Ben had thought it would, but it was a start. In due course a motion was passed to select some LGBTQ groups across the world and reach out to forge links with them. Ben wondered though what on earth they would be able to achieve. Was he really able to give advice to people halfway across the globe, when he was struggling to master his own relationship? Did he even understand or relate to the issues facing gay people elsewhere?

At times, the world seemed a daunting place to get anything done.

Kelly was discussing her personal life with the intensity of the UN Security Council examining its own navel.

Rubens listened intently. He knew something was up. She had sworn him to secrecy, so the signs were there. Something was coming. He rose to the occasion and gasped dramatically as she confessed that she had once again leapt into bed with Morten, like a salmon off to the spawning ground.

"Oh Kelly! You're like a gay man with boobs!" said Rubens, wide-eyed at her revelation. The moment was spoiled, not unexpectedly, by his immediate recollection of the existence of Ben – lovely, reliable, handsome Ben.

"What were you *thinking*?" he asked, his hands flying to his face like a fifties actress.

Couples are a barmy concept, he thought ruefully. You can't enjoy the scandal when you love them both – then again, maybe one can only really enjoy such matters when one doesn't know or – frankly – much care about the protagonists. Was this another reason for celebrity obsession?

Kelly said nothing, but looked at him.

Rubens shook his head, half admiringly.

"All the time we have known each other it has been *me* with the fun stories of a latest conquest, and you talking about something *boring* like the functions offered by the new chair for your desk."

Kelly frowned.

"Oh yes," said Rubens, "You once spoke for half an hour about how that chair could swivel and bend. Don't deny it, lawyer girl. I *timed* you! But that was then. Look at us now! Here I am, more concerned about the off-road parking, proximity to local amenities, and room for a dining table in the kitchen in our possible new flat – because *we will want to entertain*. And here you are, making the beast with two backs with a man who makes me want to take drawing lessons, so handsome is he."

Rubens looked almost glum. The memory of the chase and the capture fell upon him like sudden rain. How much *fun* had it all been?

Kelly drained the last of her Phallus In Wonderland, the cocktail du jour at Outrageous Fortune. She looked happier already.

"You're right. This is wrong in every way – but isn't it wonderful, too? I do remember that chair you are talking about. That was pretty good but maybe it won't surprise you that this situation is quite engrossing, too. We all live vicariously sometimes. Maybe it is your turn. I did envy

144

your tales of the city. It's easy to feel left out when someone is having an exciting time. I didn't resent you but there was always a strong slug of envy that it wasn't me getting all that cock, to say nothing of the fabulous foreplay in all those clubs you used to go to."

"I used to go to," repeated Rubens softly. "Kelly, it's not that I don't want to have lovely dinner parties, and fuss over getting the right Teflon kitchenware to make the perfect feijoada, but it leaves me with a hole inside me thinking that I don't have my young life any more. Where has the old me gone? This was never supposed to happen to me."

"Dear Rubens, not even you can completely resist the passing of time. You remember when you used to tell me about that old guy who was always at Scream? You don't want to be him, do you? At some time you have to pass the baton on to the younger generations, love."

"The younger generations? Love? Do you really want to hurt me?" Rubens looked at Kelly like a dog that had just been unfairly blamed for stealing the smoked salmon when all along it had been the perfidious feline.

Kelly sighed:

"Rubens, you can still feel young without needing to repeat exactly what you have been doing for the past fifteen years. Ben and I have been quite frank about wanting to avoid the slippery slope to middle-aged crisis. We want each other, we want to build something together, but we don't want to stop having fun. Well, I know I don't. I am not sure if Ben has worked it all out yet."

She winced slightly. She knew she was somewhat arguing with herself.

"We have been discussing it," she continued, "I just don't think that he thought it would materialise just like this, and with the baggage of history behind it. But it is just so much better with people you know and like! You know that, I know that, and that's just the blatant inevitability of it all."

"If it's so inevitable, how come you're discussing it like a war crime?" asked Rubens triumphantly.

"Well," said Kelly, drawing out the word as only a Southerner could, "do I need to spell it out? Straight men can be emotional *basket-cases* at times. Ben is no exception. When it comes to Ben's emotions, his gay gene is *definitely* recessive."

She had a point, thought Rubens. Considering everything Ben had going for him, he had come close to ruining things on many occasions, with a drama worthy of Laurence Olivier. Maybe that was the same fight that he was currently having with himself? He shrugged. His own fights certainly all seemed to be with himself.

"Fun is vital, Kelly. I guess redefining the concept of fun is what happens to us all, as we move on in life. I do worry, though, when sex stops being part of the fun we have. You obviously feel that too, otherwise your Viking wouldn't have been balls deep in you the other night."

"Or I wouldn't have been sucking him in like a vampire squid," said Kelly thoughtfully. "Were you trying to shock me? It doesn't work, you know. I'm not ashamed of what I'm getting from Morten. He really ticks my boxes."

"It's all about technique," agreed Rubens.

He smiled brightly.

"Ok, Kelly, I know what to do. First, we have another

cocktail. Then, what say you to this: Tarquin has introduced me to domestic harmony and an unhealthy obsession with home furnishings. That's okay. But now it is time I introduced him to the cardigan-free zones where fun is really fun. I want to see him dance till he drops, his head explode with the beats, his eyes pop out at all the available candy on show, and then really appreciate what he has when he takes me home. I declare war on getting older, dear Kelly. I'm thinking… a foam party!"

The flash had returned to Rubens' eyes.

"What do you think?" he demanded, drawing himself up, "life in the handsome party boy, yet, no?"

This was much better. Kelly felt elated, as if she were in a new universe, despite not quite having the right visa.

"Rubens, please make me a drink of your choosing. Let's celebrate our rebirth, and raise a glass to vanquishing boredom as long as there is life left in our bones. I do have one question, though."

Kelly stopped, wondering how Rubens would react to the thought that had been titillating her for the past few days.

She decided the moment was right:

"I have a way forward. I have always wondered how Ben behaved when he was with a man. I have also wondered what it would feel like to have two men in my bed. Rubens, I want to have a threesome with Ben and Morten. And I need your help and support in making it happen."

6

Out of Africa, into the Elephant

Ben thought, as he often did, that there was something special about a city before it had drunk its first coffee of the day.

Like a morning shower that transforms dishevelled hair to squeaky clean and ready to go, the sanitary operatives were putting the finishing touches to the tidying up of Old Compton Street. The street glistened in the sunshine, seeming slightly unsure of its purpose in life. The day ahead had not started. It was as if it, too, was considering the prospect of facing work, as its morning alarm snatched it and other sleepers from the comfort of oblivion.

It had all been so different a few hours earlier. Soho had been brimming with energy, exuding all the unquestioning self-belief of a marketing executive unveiling the firm's new strategy. It had throbbed with energy, voices chatting, cheering, shouting, laughing – all manner of noises could be heard, above a background score of muffled music, escaping from venues failing to respect the neighbours their notices purported to care for.

Now the only noises breaking the silence were an

intermittent whirring followed by a clatter of glass as bins were hoisted up and emptied into the recycling trucks.

Ben loved central London before the tourists had emerged from their hotels. For a start, one could actually walk in a straight line. There weren't any groups of fifteen rucksack-wearing teenagers, aimlessly milling around the pavements as if they were waiting for a bus in the Piazza del Popolo. The spatially unaware irritated Ben almost as much as amateurs on the Tube. Although he had been the clueless arriviste once, he had embraced being a Londoner with all the zeal of the convert, and delighted always in the absence of inconvenient tourists as he walked to his favourite café.

As Kelly was busy that Saturday morning, Ben had decided to treat himself to one of his little pleasures in life: an English breakfast, with poached eggs and dry granary toast (virtue had its price) accompanied by plenty of coffee.

After a week of work surrounded by jabbering people, it really was heaven to be alone. Strong caffé latte and eggs with smoked bacon made a case for getting up early. Most of the other tables were occupied by single people like himself. The patrons divided their time between their victuals and their paper or electronic stimuli. The few groups talked in respectfully hushed tones, understanding that it was a time for quiet reflection.

In an attempt to stay relevant, Ben was reading the Economist. However, despite the interest this generated in the development of the gas fields of Turkmenistan, Ben's conversation with Arthur, and his own preoccupation with his relationship with Kelly kept drawing him away from the ably written article. As he stripped away the fat from the bacon, Ben wished that it were as easy to take a scalpel to the dull and destructive parts of his relationship. Ben guessed that he was just too much of a perfectionist.

Compromise was the key. Ben had to admit that the lingering jealousy that he still occasionally felt at the memory of Kelly's affair with that Scandinavian in Paris made her that little bit more exciting. If he were honest, knowing how desirable she was to others enhanced her appeal. It actually stimulated the excitement he experienced by being the one holding her. Oh, for an easier world where one could just switch these annoyingly contradictory feelings off, and simply be rational and happy at all times.

Someone familiar walked into the café.

Ben broke out a genuine smile.

"Hello, Alex! What on earth brings you here?"

Alex O'Connell, an owner of Outrageous Fortune, was a neighbour of Ben's in the Castle Lofts. He was one of Ben's oldest friends in London.

"Hey, Ben. What a coincidence. How are you? I'm meeting a visitor from Burkina Faso."

That was typical Alex. But then, Alex did have a finger in many pies. Or probably buns, thought Ben. As well as co-owning the bar, Alex ran a charitable organisation building wells and other small infrastructure in various African countries. He spent much of his time there. Alex also juggled a long-term relationship with Jamal Qureishi with a number of escapades as and when they presented themselves. Doubtless the acquaintance that Alex was meeting would be a tall, handsome man that he had met whilst leaning on a shovel or directing operations or whatever he actually did out there – besides cultivating attractive locals, that is.

Before Ben had time to ask Alex how he managed to seemingly have all his cakes at once and eat them with such gusto, a strikingly handsome blond man entered and called out a greeting.

"Doctor O'Connell, I presume?"

Alex grinned in recognition:

"You couldn't resist that, could you? Welcome to London!"

Alex held out a hand rather formally. The new arrival pushed it aside and gave Alex a bear hug, planting a smacker of a kiss on his right cheek.

Alex feigned a punch:

"It's good to see you, Morten. Welcome to London."

As Morten looked over at Ben, Alex pulled away from the big man's arms, and gestured over to the American.

"Morten, meet my good friend, Ben Barlettano. Ben, meet one of the finest doctors – and probably human beings – that I have the pleasure to know. Morten ran the clinic in one of the villages in Burkina where my charity works. We've also been working together on certain projects against the human trafficking trade."

Morten may not have been quite what Ben was expecting, but once again Alex had bagged himself a fine looking specimen. Ben felt a pang of envy. Morten looked as if he had a body to match his looks. It was emphasised by his close fitting Abercrombie shirt and skinny jeans. Thoughts of pipelines crossing the Caspian were now the furthest thing from Ben's mind as he folded up his magazine and concentrated on the Adonis who had barged in on his breakfast. He suddenly realised that he was staring, and hastily looked away to Alex, who had witnessed Ben's reaction and was utterly failing to suppress a smirk.

"Do you mind if we join you, Ben, or are you after some alone time?"

"Please, have a seat, I would be delighted!"

Ben blushed slightly as he realised just how keen he was sounding. He wanted to kick Alex, who was now grinning from ear to ear. Fortunately Morten seemed oblivious to the effect he was having on the American, and just sat down and picked up a menu.

"I'm starving. I need to eat."

Ben soon learned that Morten was originally from Karlstad in Sweden, had trained as a doctor in Stockholm, had spent the last two years working in West Africa, and was now in London working with a charity that cared for survivors of human trafficking.

"You have much more chance of achieving success if you do things on a small scale, and seek to replicate them if they work well in the field," said Morten.

Ben nodded, wondering if anyone in a law firm would ever be able to bring themselves to think small.

Although Ben had a healthy respect for anyone who abandoned the pursuit of career and material success for charity work, he had always had a sneaking suspicion that they were either privileged scions of the wealthy who could afford not to care about making a living, or hopelessly idealistic individuals who would never have made it in the cut-throat world of business. Yet listening to Morten quietly describing his successful career in medicine before deciding to set up the clinic with what sounded like a properly thought through business plan to put the project on a solid commercial footing, Ben was forced to reassess. Here was a clear-headed, capable professional who had made an active decision to give something back to society. Moreover, it was all presented in the unassuming way of one who felt what he was doing was completely normal and nothing to be remarked upon. Ben wondered if all Swedes were this modest. Ben could feel himself falling under the spell of the impressive doctor.

It had been a long time since anyone, man or woman, had inspired him this way.

"So, enough about me already, what about you, Ben?" Not even the small piece of spinach stuck to the side of his upper left canine could mar the perfect white smile that Morten directed to Ben, who was feeling increasingly like a teenage girl. He felt unable to escape the piercing gaze of the Swede's blue eyes.

"I'm a lawyer."

Ben didn't know what else to say. Describing anything he did at work would sound so utterly soulless after the talk on how the clinic was saving hundreds of lives a year. Besides, he wasn't sure that he could persuade Morten that lawyers did their jobs because of a deep-seated belief in the importance of justice.

"That was a conversation-killer," said Alex. "I'm afraid Morten's not the type to say *how interesting* if he doesn't mean it. Speaking of interesting, what are you up to whilst you are in London? Anyone I should know about?"

Morten took a drink of his mineral water, looking as if he were undecided how to reply to Alex's deceptively simple question.

"Actually, there is someone. I knew a girl in Paris before going out to Africa. It didn't end very well when I had to leave. Then I bumped into her again. It's nothing too serious yet, but we've decided to see each other again."

A girl!

Knowing Alex's reputation, Ben had blindly assumed that Morten and Alex had been shagging in Africa. Yet apart from the metrosexual body consciousness that had long ceased to be a reliable indicator of sexuality, it was true that there was nothing remotely gay about the Swede. Of course Morten was straight. What had Ben been thinking? He felt slightly ridiculous and not a little disappointed. He had spent the past half hour mentally undressing Morten, and wondering how he could get his number without Alex noticing. So obsessed was Ben now with living the excitement of the moment, he hadn't even had time to feel guilty about planning to play around. Whatever happened, he couldn't let Morten or Alex realise what he was thinking.

He tried to sound unconcerned:

"Yup. I can only imagine what my girlfriend would think if I said I was going to Africa for a couple of years."

Alex raised an eyebrow. Ben was not doing a good job in convincing him that the American was only interested in empathising with Morten. Ben grinned slightly inanely at them both, confirming Alex's suspicions as firmly as if Ben had invited the Swede for a rubdown at Spartacus Spa.

Morten smiled evenly:

"A person must do what his conscience tells him he must. I wasn't exactly happy about leaving her myself, but I had made a commitment. It would not have been right to put unreliable emotion before what I knew would achieve something important. It was a shame, but there was nothing to be done."

Although Ben thought there was something admirable about the Swede's uncompromising sense of duty, he did find the lack of even a hint of emotional conflict slightly chilling. Maybe Nordics had such a reputation for calm because they found it easier to control their emotions, at least outwardly. This had a certain logic to it. Emotions should be prevented from interfering with the good common sense that Northern climes had a reputation for. Ben wasn't sure that this approach would work for him in a relationship, even for a man as attractive as Morten was. It sounded as if this girl he had been seeing was a glutton for punishment. Perhaps she was a bit stupid, or desperate, if she was going to try and rekindle something with a man whose emotions were kept so firmly on ice.

Morten was used to people not really knowing how to react to such statements. He actually felt deeply about Kelly. Thoughts of her had never truly left him throughout his time in Africa, but this was a private matter. He smiled at Ben.

"I do have a heart. It's just that my head normally keeps it on a short leash. But when it slips it does so in style. Believe it or not, I can be extremely passionate."

He grinned.

"Or maybe that is a joke?"

As Morten stood up and walked over to the till to order another coffee, Ben's eyes couldn't help but take in the figure of the man again. His silhouette in those jeans, and the idle promise of discovering the passionate side to the Swede made him rather envious of the foolhardy woman. Ben wished it were him having a second bite at Morten's body.

Alex chuckled knowingly.

"Not sure you have much chance there, my friend. That butt you seem unable to take your eyes off is a one-way street. No offence, but if I couldn't worm my way in when the pickings were truly slim in Burkina, not sure how you will get his attention here in the city of a million single women."

Ben made a face at Alex. It was time to leave. They called for and paid the bill.

Ben stretched:

"I need the restroom."

Alex looked evenly at the American.

"Me too. Morten, we'll be out in a minute."

As he was standing slightly embarrassedly next to Alex at the urinal, Ben reflected on how he loved London's continued ability to throw unexpected pleasures in his way. The Swede was not someone he was going to forget in a hurry.

As he and Alex made their way out, he saw Morten embracing a woman with long brown hair outside. She certainly had an attractive shape. *Damn it!* He had been hoping that she would be a plain Jane. Even though the chances of him muscling in seemed all but non-existent, the spirit of competition was not so easily quashed. Ben's interest was piqued. He wondered what she looked like.

"Boys, come and meet the woman I have just been telling you about. This is the beautiful Kelly Danvers."

As Kelly swung round to greet them, the happy smile on her face froze, and then became an expression of horror that was mirrored in Ben's face.

There was silence.

Alex cleared his throat.

"Well, this is awkward."

Ben didn't register what Alex had said. Everything had suddenly fallen into place. The Scandinavian in Paris that had almost split Kelly and him up was Morten. This was *that* Morten. Ben felt numb.

Morten was confused. Ben and Kelly were staring at each other as if he had just introduced each of them to Pol Pot himself. He glanced at Alex, a puzzled look on his face. What was so awkward about introducing people in London? Anglos could be so complicated at times.

Ben knew he had to say something.

"We know each other, Morten. Actually, rather well."

Ben felt as if he had been kicked in the stomach. He and Kelly had talked about the *possibility* of an open relationship, but he didn't know she had already jumped in with both legs open. And with the man who was responsible for his broken heart two years earlier. *How could she?*

"Ben, I was going to tell you." As soon as the words were out, Kelly realised how great her mistake had been in not talking to Ben before embarking on her reprise with the Swede. It had seemed like innocent, biological joy – wholly in keeping with the spirit of her conversation with Ben about keeping their lives alive. For heaven's sake, she had even wondered if it would be possible to involve Ben. Yet her tardiness in coming clean and this chance meeting in Old Compton Street now risked everything. Her secret pleasures had turned into a poison that she could see in Ben's eyes. It was like acid. It had already started to corrode the nuts and bolts of their relationship from the inside out.

Ben was seething. No excuse or explanation could get Kelly out of this one. By open relationship he had meant the odd, random shag with a complete stranger, preferably when under the influence, and with the official other half nowhere in the vicinity. Morten broke just about every rule in the book of his open relationship guidelines. Not that he had written these down or even formulated them. However, in this very second, his rules were clear to him, even if to no one else.

"You were going to tell me?" Ben looked vituperatively at Kelly. "When exactly? When he decides to fuck off to West Africa again and you decide you should be honest with your poor schmuck of a boyfriend, as you will need him again?"

"Ben, it's not like that. I love you, I really do. Morten and I are just having a bit of fun."

As the truth dawned on him, Morten realised that Kelly had not exactly been honest with him either. He felt a little numb. This was quite a remarkable situation. And they both seemed so nice.

Ben noticed a couple of drag queens in daywear forming the nucleus of a small crowd gathering to watch the spectacle. He decided that he would not continue to put on a free show that morning. He had said his piece, red meat had been thrown to his inner furies, and calm started to return. He walked away from the group, turning to exclaim as he left.

"Fine, Kelly. It's just fine. Have fun today. I'm planning to."

Tarquin was in the front passenger seat of an estate agent's car, but it did not feel like much of a privilege. His lip had been curling like a Cheesy Wotsit ever since they had passed the Elephant & Castle. Rubens was leaning forward between the two front seats. He held a vantage point in the back of the cheerily emblazoned hatchback.

Rubens was taking action. He'd decided to interrupt the torrent of tosh coming from Tom, the agent, in the driver's seat, before Tarquin thought better of the whole escapade and asked the relentlessly upbeat agent to take them straight back to the Tube, and to make it snappy.

Rubens read Tarquin pretty well these days. He could tell from his boyfriend's demeanour that this was not what he had been dreaming of.

He clapped his hands:

"Gostoso, it's an up-and-coming area. It will be really handy for the Underground at Elephant – and for visiting Ben at the Castle Lofts. This place will be just like Islington's Upper Street in a few years."

Tarquin wanted to smile at Rubens for his *morning in*

Southwark sunny optimism, but he just wasn't feeling it. He had never been a particular fan of anywhere south of the river. It was also painful to admit the truth. The fact remained that he would have to conquer his sinking feelings. The realities of the London property market meant that he had not a snowball's chance in hell of acquiring anything remotely decent in an area he would actually like to live in. You had to be a celebrity chef or an oligarch on the run from Putin for that.

He sighed.

Tom capitalised on Rubens' opening.

"You're right, Rubens. This is a rapidly changing property hotspot down here right now, as evidenced by the extent of the regeneration area we've just passed. Awaiting regeneration, admittedly."

The estate agent was delighted to receive support from Rubens. Tom felt Tarquin hadn't been responding at all the way he had hoped. Tom was a good-looking, well-built man who consciously chose close-fitting clothes. He normally had gay couples eating out of his hand. He even flattered himself that this was his specialist demographic. With pink pounds fluttering in Tom's imagination like net curtains on a breezy day, it had taken him less time than he had supposed would have been necessary to be accustomed to another man running his eyes over his body. It still felt a little weird – almost as if he were a piece of meat? However, after reasoning that they only did to him what he did to most of the women he met, Tom had become rather hooked on the flattery.

He checked his hair in the rear view mirror. He still

looked good. He wondered whether it would be going too far to have a not-so-surreptitious pretend scratch at the bulge between his legs. That usually went down a treat with the gays. You had to have your individually developed tricks and techniques. This turned a salesman into a closer of deals. Tom made sure that he re-adjusted himself regularly during all his gay viewings. He doubted that it was classy to use his sex in this way; it certainly wasn't taught in the sales training courses he had attended, but then again, they encouraged lateral thinking. Anyway, his ego, and his bulge, thoroughly enjoyed the stroking. More importantly, Tom was convinced that it was excellent for business. He certainly didn't lack confidence. He thought it clear that the successful sale of a semi down a slightly shabby street in Tooting could wholly turn on his successful production of a semi down his slightly shiny, straining trousers.

Although loath to admit ever being attracted to anything in such cheap fabric, Tarquin did notice the man sitting beside him in *that* way. Tarquin had a documented weakness for the so-called piece of rough. The estate agent fitted that mould perfectly. Tarquin could make out Tom's thigh muscles through his nasty trousers every time he flexed to press a pedal. He also took in the unashamed tightness of Tom's white shirt, stretched over a well-muscled torso. It was all in deliciously poor taste. Such a shame the agent couldn't remain silent. Like Victorian children, Tom should be seen and not heard.

Sadly, that was unlikely to transpire.

"We're almost there now. It's really no distance from the Elephant." Tom slowed down to take a sharp left hand corner. "You see that, although the house itself nestles within a quiet enclave of period streets, it offers exceptionally easy access to all the local amenities."

Tarquin winced again. He decided that if he had to suffer the slings and arrows of Tom's outrageous clichés, then he could at least take arms against his sea of rubbish. Chloroform might work, at a pinch?

Tarquin tilted his head:

"It's a crying shame that one has only got ten fingernails, I don't know how I am going to manage to try out all those lovely shops on the Walworth Road. Maybe I will have to get my toenails painted as well. Do you think varnish looks good on a man, Tom?"

Tom had an estate agent's thick skin. Sarcasm bounced off him like an English footballer's attempts on goal. Nothing proffered by Tarquin was likely to pierce Tom to the quick. Instead, the estate agent was delighted. At last, the client was engaging with him. Maybe he could close this sale after all. And if he didn't, then it would not be for lack of flirting.

He squared his shoulders and glanced at his target, in what he trusted was a manly yet coquettish way.

"I think you could definitely pull it off, Tarquin."

He winked.

"I have pulled it off pretty well myself a few times."

For a moment Tom toyed with the idea of suggesting they could pull it off together in celebration if Tarquin and Rubens bought the house, but even he had to draw the line somewhere. He contented himself with Tarquin's tight smile.

"Quite the metrosexual, you are," said Tarquin – but his heart wasn't in it.

"… and here we are."

As the car pulled up outside an old but nondescript house, Rubens felt that he should be more excited. The estate agent's advertisement had assured them that this was a rare opportunity to acquire a highly individual residence in Kennington borders. He had felt little when the car swept into the eagerly sought-after cul-de-sac, except for thinking that only underpants should contain both a *cul* and a *sac*.

Rubens had never owned a house. Despite the underwhelming kerb appeal of the place, he couldn't help but feel a thrill as he followed Tarquin and Tom through the front door.

Sadly for the tingling, the first thing that greeted the three men was a poky little entrance hall, with faded floral wallpaper and an overly busy carpet that had long tired of being cheery.

They proceeded through a door on the right into an equally depressing sitting room.

Tom open his arms expansively and gesticulated with a tenor's conviction.

"As you can see, lads, there is tremendous scope to remodel here. You could really put your own stamp on this place, especially if you knocked through to the kitchen."

Tarquin felt that, rather like the house, Tom's sales pitch would benefit from some updating. But he had to concede a grudging admiration for the unflappable way in which the agent could find positive things to say about this least prepossessing of interiors.

"Why don't I take you... upstairs?" said Tom, deliberately. Tom ensured that he preceded the art dealer up the staircase, even stopping halfway up and pretending to check he still had his wallet in the back pocket of his trousers, ensuring that Tarquin had a perfect view of his firm behind, squeezed like two giant potatoes into trousers that threatened to split every time he took an exaggerated stride up a step.

Despite everything, Tarquin was beginning to enjoy himself. A salesman himself, he was silently ticking off Tom's tactics. They were a vulgar but entertaining copy of the skills and even charm that Tarquin would use on his own clients when trying to shift a lingering Old Master. It helped that, unlike the property, the man was certainly in tip-top condition.

Tom strode into the main bedroom like Genghis Khan into a smouldering village square.

"Here's where the magic happens. As you can see, it is a very generously proportioned master."

Tarquin held the estate agent's gaze, willing him to break into laughter at his own preposterous comment, but Tom was far too focussed on his commission. He moved to the window, as if dancing to stage directions.

"Now, gents, look at the lovely view of the garden. It is perfect for al fresco dining in the summer, and extremely easily maintained."

As Rubens peered out through the window he reflected that easy maintenance was obviously code for tiny. Thank goodness for rubbish English weather.

They completed the tour of the house. Tom pointed out many imaginary period features, and marvelled at how these kept warmth and tradition throughout the house. Rubens wasn't at all sure it was charm and character oozing from the walls. There was something about the avocado bathroom suite that pleaded *I'll be back in fashion soon*.

A tinny rendition of a generic club track started up. It was Tom's mobile phone, burbling into life.

Tom looked at it as if it were the second coming.

"I'm sorry, boys, do you mind if I take this?"

Tarquin acceded to the request with an aristocratic nod of the head. Tom trotted off downstairs, leaving Tarquin and Rubens alone.

Tarquin looked around with a keen gaze.

"So. Here we are. What do you think, Rubens? Could you see us making something of this? It's overpriced, of course. Bizarrely, though, beneath the sorry excuse of the last occupant's taste in interior design, I think this actually has potential. Could you see us settling down here? Could we make a life here?"

Rubens stood still. There it was again. Settling down. Was that what he wanted? It clearly must be. He was here, after all. But every time he heard them, the words resonated like the toll of a bell. He wanted this – but he wasn't quite ready to hang up his dancing shoes just yet.

Rubens sometimes feared that Tarquin had never found his party vibe in the first place. He sometimes wondered whether Tarquin had proceeded straight from kindergarten to gallery openings, with nary a pause for the night-lifeblood that had been the metronome of Rubens's life so far? The throb and pulsation of clubs had thudded successfully for Rubens for a long time now. Music beats were the backdrop to many of the highs of his time in London. If this house were to be purchased, where would it lead? Would Rubens ever see the inside of a club again? Or would everything become dinner parties with Fiona Grafton-Findlemere, barbecues with the Selby-Oakes and their substantial budget for minor Venetian artists, and endless quiet nights in? Rubens suddenly shivered. No one was walking on his grave – but was he digging it?

"Rubens?"

Tarquin saw the troubled look. It was a rare cloud – something was obviously wrong. He put an arm around his lover.

"Are you annoyed because the Bard of Barnet takes every opportunity to show me he goes to the gym? I can appreciate that he has the finest stash of double entendres this side of the Carry On films."

Rubens looked intently at Tarquin. His brown eyes widened as they always did when he had something serious to say. They were beautiful. It hit Tarquin every time.

Rubens spoke slowly.

"No. Not that. I like Tom actually. He's funny. A gay man would never flirt that badly. I was waiting for him to drop his pen in front of you and then have to bend over to pick it up."

He paused.

"I also know that whilst you enjoy looking at him parading his muscles about, you wouldn't make a move – even if he were on offer."

Rubens lowered his voice, a little melodramatically.

"And *that*, Tarquin – that, right there. That's what makes me worried."

Tarquin wasn't quite sure he had heard right.

"You're worried that I *don't* jump all over other men, Rubens? Wouldn't a normal jealous Latino appreciate that most about me?"

"It is a contradiction, Tarquin, but there is logic here. It may be Brazilian logic, but there is logic."

Rubens smiled at the man he loved. It was a nervous smile, unusually for him.

"It's the finality of it all. I do want you for me, and I do want to buy a house with you and I want to do all the things we have talked about, but that's not all I want. Question marks are exciting, Tarquin. I don't want my life mapped out for the next thirty years. I love the security you bring, but I am never going to be the man who buys a Volvo estate, Tarquin. Ever."

Rubens paused. Tarquin was still. He was not about to interrupt.

"I worry that you are in a very different place to me, Tarquin. You don't seem to have any desire for the wilder side of life. Even if Tom were gay and suggested a three-way upstairs, I think you would just tell him to stop being silly, and then ask him how much the council tax is. This scares me. I want to feel that there is still the chance of us doing crazy things together."

Rubens looked beseechingly into his partner's eyes. Tarquin held his gaze, considering how best to reply. A moment passed in silence, broken only by the distant sound of Tom on the telephone.

"Rubens, I know at times I may seem like a boring old fart… "

"I did not say that, Tarquin," interrupted Rubens.

Tarquin raised an eyebrow:

"Well, you came pretty close. In fairness, though, I do shut out an awful lot from my life. But you're right – I may be different in that respect. Most of the time I am delighted with my choices. Come on, Rubens. I don't think I would be a happier or more fulfilled person had I spent every Saturday night for the past fifteen years off my face on a dance-floor. Do you? Clubs, Rubens, are best left to members. It's almost impossible to talk, and the few conversations one manages to have are deathly dull, since almost everyone seems to hail from some alien culture that denies true individuality. Everything revolves around the physical – faces, bodies, how you dance, how you look, what you are wearing. It's just another uniform with less appealing braid. Why would I want to put myself out there, for all those strangers to judge me, on looks alone? It's not made any better by the fact that I could, no doubt, pass their strange and unpredictable tests. I'm perfectly happy to admit that, as far as I know, no one in a club has ever given a midget's toss about who I am. Knowing something properly substantive about me would not even occur as a concept to the average patron of a London club. Why, Rubens – why would I put myself through that mill? My currency, such as it is, is devalued whenever I enter a place like that. It's depressing feeling invisible simply because one has neither muscles, nor natural rhythm like you do.

It's even more depressing if one is liked for no reason whatsoever other than idle and unthinking *lust*."

Rubens heart sank. Tarquin could be stubborn at times.

Tarquin realised this was important for his lover.

At that inconvenient point, they heard footsteps on the stairs and the sound of Tom saying goodbye to someone. The rest of the conversation was going to have to wait awhile.

Tom came in beaming like a lighthouse.

"So what are your thoughts, me old muckers?"

Rubens thoughts raced. At this point, it felt as if he were making the biggest mistake of his life in buying a house with someone who was manifestly poles apart from him. Initially, he had adored Tarquin's avoidance of the gay scene. It had struck Rubens as confident – bold, and daring, and different. Rubens had himself gradually loosened his ties to his former life. He had rather adopted the mores of his beloved. Yet now, despite appreciating Tarquin for all his strength and qualities, Rubens was feeling startlingly caged in.

He stared glumly at Tom, unable to respond.

"What's the council tax here?" Tarquin asked neutrally.

"I've left the papers downstairs. I'll tell you when we go down," smiled Tom.

"Actually – would you mind getting the figure now, Tom? I would like to know."

The two men's eyes met in something close to a challenge, before Tom gave way and headed back downstairs. Rubens looked vacantly out of the window, wondering if Tarquin had deliberately asked about the tax just to spite him.

Rubens wanted to get out of the house as soon as he could.

"Hey, you."

Rubens turned round. Tarquin was smiling at him. He came over and wrapped his arms around the Brazilian, before stepping back and taking both his hands.

Touch can change a great deal. As they held each other close, the warmth calmed them. *We are not the same, but we are together. Together, we are stronger.*

Tarquin spoke earnestly:

"I am sure you can understand why I live my life the way I do. However, I freely admit that I have missed out on some things in life because of the choices I have made. Such as, for example, meeting you sooner."

Tarquin spoke quickly now, not wanting to be interrupted by Tom with his council tax numbers:

"I'm never going to be a club baby like you, Rubens, but that doesn't mean that I can't ever go out. I can see that I may need to. This is important to us. I can see that more than ever. I will try harder and be there for you. I can actually be rather mad when I want to be, and I'm not talking about the time when I accidentally had lemon *and* milk in my Earl Grey."

Rubens softened. He knew this. Some of the best moments with his boyfriend had involved Rubens gently corrupting Tarquin.

"Gostoso, I will help – and I must also accept that I am no longer a young chicken."

"A spring chicken."

"Are they older?"

Tarquin hurriedly let go of Rubens' hands as they heard

Tom's footsteps approaching again. He sank to a whisper.

"It's okay. I get it. I know this is a great deal to ask of you. So let's do both. We can do both. I will find my pretty, vacant side and polish it up. You can help me. With your help, I can kick this ass of mine into a little youthful misbehaviour. We can start today."

Tom arrived babbling about the monthly bills. Tarquin barely listened. It had only been a ruse to get Tom out of the way. He stepped in quickly.

"Tom, I think we are going to put in an offer. We like it."

The estate agent invisibly thumped the air, silently yelling *Get in!* to a group of imaginary supporters. How had he ever doubted his talents? He was a pink pound *magnet*, he was.

"Although the vendor is motivated to make a quick sale, I would recommend you stick close to the asking price," Tom smiled reassuringly, "you wouldn't want to miss out on an opportunity like this."

Tarquin smiled back properly for the first time at the estate agent, who was visibly delighted that he had turned this one around. Tarquin spoke with warmth in his voice.

"Tom, thank you so much for showing us this property."

Tarquin moved closer to the estate agent, put his hand on Tom's forearm, and looked engagingly at him.

"If we manage to secure the property, I insist that you come over and visit us when we've moved in. Rubens and I would love to have you over to sample that al-fresco dining. Maybe even a spit roast if you're feeling daring. What do you say? I'll bet it will be right up your alley."

Tarquin felt the muscles in Tom's forearm tense, as the

agent stuttered something whilst moving away, detaching himself from Tarquin's grip. Behind them Rubens was failing to suppress a shout of laughter.

Much to Tom's relief – to whom it now occurred that he should probably turn it down a notch next time he had the gays over – Tarquin and Rubens told him that they would walk back to the Tube on foot, better to explore the neighbourhood. After deciding that they did both want the house if it were available at the right price, they discussed what their opening offer would be. Tarquin turned over their conversation. If ever he were to savour the modern Bacchanalian delights of this world, it would surely be with Rubens. He had to make sure that this would happen. Losing Rubens was not an outcome he wished to contemplate, or allow.

Action was required.

He turned to Rubens:

"If our offer gets accepted, I think we should go out and celebrate. Dinner would be easy, but how about you take me somewhere this time? Somewhere I wouldn't necessarily want my clients knowing I had been to."

Tarquin grinned mischievously.

Rubens was armed. Jamal had told him only recently about a party that they really should go to at the weekend. The Brazilian had been wondering how the hell he would be able to go. It had all suddenly fallen into place.

"Have you ever been to a foam party, Tarquin?" Rubens didn't wait for the reply. "Well, that's where we will be going if the offer's accepted. It's Club Adam. Adam, as in the naked guy in the garden?"

Tarquin nodded gravely. He knew who Adam might be.

Rubens rubbed his hands in delight:

"Adam then. Just Adam. No Eve, of course – and a whole load of snakes."

Their offer was accepted that very same day.

Heading to the office wasn't exactly the kind of fun that Ben had had in mind when he had walked away from Kelly that morning, miserably threatening to enjoy himself.

Spending Saturday afternoon with his boss working on a deal was not a high point in Ben's life. It happened too often. It was usually productive. But it was quite the opposite of hedonism. Not even the prospect of Club Adam on Sunday afternoon dislodged Ben's feeling that others were having an infinitely nicer time than he was.

He walked in the all too familiar streets around the office. Caspar would be looking forward to a night of partying. Rubens would be at his sparkling best, moving seamlessly from brunch to afternoon cocktails. He would be the host everyone aspired to meet at Outrageous Fortune. As for Kelly, Ben preferred not to think of what she would be getting up to. It would probably involve Scandinavian fingers.

As if on cue, a group of laughing twenty-somethings clutching bottles and cans almost knocked him over as they exited from an off-licence. They were far too busy to even clock Ben's presence. London could be counted on to make it perfectly obvious how many distractions there were at hand. And yet, the city managed sometimes to keep them just out of reach, taunting the downtrodden with tantalising glimpses of what their life might be like. Ben moved out of the youngsters' way and gave in to turf envy.

What was Kelly thinking?

Ben wasn't even in the mood for revenge. That seemed so two years ago. This was all about jealousy, he decided. Privately, Ben could admit that he simply didn't like the idea of Kelly doing better out of their open relationship arrangement than he did – or perhaps even than he *could*?

As he glumly trudged along the street towards the office, he felt old. That feeling had been geyser-ing up quite a bit of late. His leaden step betrayed resignation to the fact that, quite possibly, and at a relatively young age, his best years were already behind him. Ben didn't even feel that he had any fight left inside him. Maybe discussing a deal with his boss on a Saturday was just what he should be doing. Was this now the highlight of his weekends?

London Bridge lightened his mood.

Ben always felt a thrill of pleasure when crossing any of London's bridges. The city opened up in a way that normally required the scaling of a skyscraper or the ascent to a ridiculously overpriced loft. Aside from the understated beauty of the river, for once bathed in sunshine, the array of buildings and monuments lining the banks of the Thames testified with dignity to the fact that, for a century or so, this was the centre of the world, the richest place on the planet, a city that knew its own importance, built to encourage every visitor to doff their cap in deference.

Ben had certainly himself felt impelled to get on his knees and worship on many occasions since arriving four years earlier. His mind flitted back to Club Adam and the stimulation a naked foam party promised.

He started to perk up. Sauntering over London Bridge on a bright, warm afternoon was pleasant. It was a change from facing down the hordes of determined commuters hustling him out of the way, focused on another personal best to Bank. This was a moment that Ben would not be enjoying, had Hartmut not summoned him that day.

Ben stopped, and leaned on the parapet, drinking in the view. During the week, this action would earn him looks of incomprehension, and even annoyance from the weekday hamster-wheel commuters. Ben let the Saturday feel wash through him. The scene around him was a pleasure to survey. He enjoyed being part of it, and fixing that instant of the city, with him in it.

London Bridge wasn't the finest looking of bridges, and even suffered the indignity of constantly having its name appropriated by that more illustrious of crossings, Tower Bridge. However, it did offer splendid views, particularly of its confusing neighbour. That, and HMS Belfast, which he had always fancied visiting but knew that he probably never would, were the sentinels of a glorious past. The Glass Testicle, as he happily called the Greater London Authority building, housed the sentinels of London's present in its rounded curves. The bulbous building was home to London's emasculated local politicians, busily planning bus lanes, cycle paths and maybe even a tube line extension, to be completed at a date that seemed so far away as to be almost fantasy-like. More power of course lay north of the river, in the Gherkin, the Cheese-Grater and the Walkie-Talkie. Ben wondered what nickname would befall the next skyscraper. All the silly names were enough to make an Old Lady weep.

A large, wet, skinny latte with an extra shot later, Ben was ensconced in his office at Sagworth Turner Dickerhint, waiting for Hartmut who was uncharacteristically delayed.

Hartmut swept in, a vision in a long black leather coat, eyes twinkling.

"I'm here, mein Freund! Ich bin da!"

He strode into his office, whipped off his highwayman's garb, and headed over to see Ben.

"Good morning, Ben. I do apologise for my tardiness. I got carried away with my writing and unforgivably lost track of time."

Ben looked up to see his boss framed by the office doorway. Hartmut was wearing his customary round wire-rimmed spectacles. He had opted today for a black turtleneck instead of a classic business shirt. Tight black leather trousers were adorned with a thick chain in place of a belt, and finished off with black workman-style boots, albeit with a suspiciously shiny steel toecap that glinted menacingly in the office lights.

Hartmut looked as if he were about to ascend the stage at the Moscone Center and launch the latest must-have device. Ben cocked his head as he thought this through. Hartmut would launch a device such as the iCuffs, serving his own particular niche. Not only would iCuffs serve their primary purpose of keeping a slave secure, but they would also measure the biological vitals of the subject, informing the Master's iControl app of the effect the spanking was having and whether pace, radius or strength should be modified for the optimum effect. A breakdown of calories burned would be immediately available, as slaves never seemed to favour the lardier Master or Mistress. Should the slave not prove worthy, then the iControl would scan the vicinity through a VIP membership of the social network, Thrashr, locating and messaging new slaves as required. Thanks to Bluetooth-enabled communication with a suite of add-ons, a mere flick of the eye could tighten the iClamps, or insert or extract the iPlug or iBrate.

Realising that he was staring fixedly at the rather phallic fastener on Hartmut's waist, Ben smothered his thoughts of what he would do with a remote controlled iBrate.

"No problem, Hartmut. I've been catching up on email."

The office inbox was the bane of Ben's life. Work was preoccupying enough, but then there was personal email and various OTT accounts, all calling determinedly for attention. It seemed utterly impossible to keep up with the flood of messages that came one's way. Evolution would need far more time than Ben had available to equip humanity with such ability. Ben remembered how, in his youth, his mother's face would light up with delight when a letter from a friend arrived by post. It was quite an event. Some were wonderful pieces of writing that had obviously taken some time and care to produce. Ben wondered if anyone would ever publish a book of someone's collected emails. It would happen, at some point. Someone would buy it. Probably quite a few, especially as it would probably be available in an e-version, too – perhaps completed with drunkenly posted videos. What would Jane Austen say?

Or for that matter, Hartmut, the latest budding author, who was staring at Ben with an amused grin.

"You seem rather distracted, Ben. Dreamy, I might say. Does this mean I am not going to get much work out of you today?"

"Don't worry, Hartmut," Ben replied, as he got up, picked up his laptop, and followed Hartmut into his office. "I was just thinking about your book. How is it going?"

"I am rather pleased with it. I am happy with my title Justizia. I also contemplated *Mastering the briefs*. That might have worked on many levels. On top of things, you see – a good place to be. Rather like I hope you will be today. But Justizia it is. Take a look at this."

As Ben opened the file Hartmut passed him, a smart rap came on the door.

"Gentlemen, great to see you in the Saturday saddle! Weekends are for wimps! You're firing on all cylinders, hey guys?"

The intruder stretched out his right arm, demonstratively shot two fingers at the folder, shouted *Bam!* and then holstered his hand.

Hartmut and Ben sighed, softly and simultaneously. Some people you wished would simply stay home and out of the way. Jacques Dorf was one of those people. He hung around the office like a moth infestation. He annoyed in many ways, sometimes in tiny ways, but with a consistency that would get him top marks in a gymnastics routine.

Jacques Dorf had a special line in special lines. These were always followed up by a wink and an annoying clicking sound. Jacques never waited for replies, as he wasn't remotely interested in what Hartmut and Ben were up to. However, Jacques did want to ensure that *they* were fully aware of the excellent work *he* was doing.

"Not sure if you know, guys, but I have been tasked with leading the group making sure we rip all the synergies from this monster of a merger – and I can tell you I'm really bench-pressing this one."

Jacques frowned, theatrically, and lowered his voice by an octave.

"Whether we like it or not, pigs are coming home to roost. We have a togetherness shortfall round here."

He nodded confidently, his smile returning.

"We need to raise morale round here, guys, and high five the future. It's up to me to lace some Nikes on this hippo, and make sure she hits the tape faster."

Jacques had never been one to worry about blank looks in response to his utterings. They only confirmed to him that mere mortals couldn't keep up with his lightning-fast brain. Jesus, these two were so old school. But he'd planted the seed. Time to beat a retreat and attack again later. He'd make sure of their support, however, with a clever little compliment. He winked again.

"Been popping thoughts into my fishbowl all day and I can tell you those bubbles have been blowing large and hard. Large and hard! Next step is to work out how we socialise these pearls through our thought leaders, you know. Hey guys – I think *I* know. Watch your inboxes!"

Jacques retreated blowing imaginary bubbles at his two interlocutors, like a puffer fish.

Hartmut and Ben stared at the empty doorway, unsure

quite how to follow Jacques' performance.

Hartmut broke the silence:

"I sometimes wonder if I will ever master the English language. I didn't really understand anything of what that young man uttered."

Ben wasn't at all sure he had fared any better than his boss.

"I wouldn't worry, Hartmut. Jacques has his own special line in business bullshit. I think he feels it makes him more modern. The reality of course is that he is just a linguistic criminal."

Hartmut looked evenly at the American.

"Indeed. I do find it intensely irritating when these new terms break free from the marketing and strategy departments, and start polluting our daily lives. Do you think they have any idea what we actually do – and what effect their ridiculous pronouncements have on our opinion of them and their attempts to make us do what they think we should be doing according to the latest consultant they have been slavishly listening to?"

Ben concurred. He mentally winced every time he was asked to take a deep dive into a subject, or to secure face time with someone, or to make sure he had all his ducks in a row before even thinking about opening his kimono.

"So your characters won't be running any ideas up the flagpole to see who salutes in Justizia, then?"

Hartmut looked thoughtfully at the grinning American.

"Although my work is concerned with a rather different analysis of how one's private life, when kept private, should not be held against one in one's public sphere, it would seem somewhat of a waste if I missed the opportunity to lampoon all this nonsensical doublespeak. However, given the proclivities of the characters involved, I would like to put a certain twist on things. I should give it a go. The idea is appealing. I am going to look through the glory hole and see what pokes out."

Ben chortled.

"Let's lube up, wander round the darkroom and see who accommodates." As soon as the words were out, the American wondered if he had gone too far. He needn't have worried.

"Quite," replied Hartmut. "I rather like that one. Let me make a note."

After carefully tapping on his iPhone, he turned to the American.

"I know you, along with certain others, feel that my writing project is an error."

Ben wondered whether to protest.

Hartmut paused, weighing his words.

"I do hold a different view to you all about this, and I quite accept that you may not see it this way. You see, I still feel that the hypocrisy that runs deep through our profession must be attacked in a full frontal manner. To misquote Edmund Burke: the only thing necessary for the triumph of duplicity is for honest men to say nothing. Although I enjoy a darkroom as much as you seem to, my dear, I aim to shine a pitiless light into the darker recesses of our profession. So many worse things are happening than my attempts at literature."

The German had a point. Ben had first-hand knowledge

of what the seemingly most respectable lawyers got up to behind the scenes. They seemed to think that so long as no one knew of their actions – of their profound conservatism, of their bullying and bigotry – it didn't count. They were for all the world like dieters awake and standing in front of the fridge at night, cramming in gluttonous leftovers, convinced that they could simply lie about why they weren't losing weight. It seemed that some parts of the law had been enjoying this twisted relationship with reality since Chaucer put pen to paper. But was the world ready to accept a practising insider exhibiting such honesty? Despite all Hartmut's best intentions, Ben still feared that, in time-honoured fashion, the legal community would close ranks, and Hartmut Glick would be cast into the wilderness. Hartmut, however, seemed utterly set on the idea, and did not fear the consequences.

Ben decided to keep his counsel.

"Well, you definitely have material for a chapter there. I admire you, Hartmut. Now, should we get on with the task in hand?"

As Ben ploughed through the documents that Hartmut had provided him with, his mind kept wandering back to Hartmut's project. Why did it seem so uncomfortable for people to admit that their work colleagues had a whole life set apart from the daily interactions round the coffee machine? Was it simply that the average individual found the thought of their co-workers actually having sex, or even discussing it, somewhat distasteful, rather like not wanting to see anyone naked? One's workaday interactions were remarkably antiseptic as a rule. Was this natural? Was this healthy and modern, or should one be far more aware of the foibles of the biological beings that shared one's immediate oxygen? Ben sighed. He certainly wouldn't find a solution to his concerns that afternoon. For his own part, he felt quite happy that he could pretend that the vast majority of unattractive, pudgy men that inhabited his working world were *always* fully clothed and wouldn't, couldn't and shouldn't emit bodily fluids ever, anywhere in his vicinity.

Sadly, it was not merely the biological that could offend Ben's delicate nature. Jacques was back.

"I can see our competitors are going to be crushed by the wheels of industry. Guys, I've been told I can't boil the ocean – but when you check the fruity little email I have just wopped over to you both, I think you are going to be impressed! The bull has been taken firmly by the horns and cheese has been made."

Jacques mimed wrestling a large object to the ground and then attempted what looked like churning to the nonplussed pair.

"Do we want to make waves with this merger? I say we do! Gentlemen, I announce the arrival of a tsunami. We are going to leave no survivors and steal their pillows to boot!"

Ben quickly clicked on his mail and speed read the cant that Jacques had sent over.

Unfortunately it would probably be necessary to embrace the new strategy. Office politics can be like that. However, it did not mean that he too would have to spout the new management chapter and verse. Ben would leave it to others to get tangled up in this.

"Jacques, this is fantastic. I cannot wait to action these points. Let's strap this big boy on and see who spreads."

Jacques Dorf paused. He knew of Ben's reputation as a rectum wrecker and wasn't sure he should be showing any enthusiasm in respect of what might be a veiled invite. Then again, it was important to galvanise support for his career-enhancing project, and if every straight man on TV seemed happy to flirt with other men, then maybe he should just go with the flow.

Jacques grabbed his crotch with one hand, and clawed the air with the other.

"Ben, you and me together? Well, I'd *like* to see who could resist. We will have them all! Hungry and dripping, Ben. Hungry and dripping."

7

Of minge and men

For the first time since arriving in England Polina felt a proper sense of warmth.

Arthur Bilks' cosy house made her feel at home.

Cornisha had made a hearty meat stew. It tasted wonderful. The meat had been properly prepared, trimmed, seasoned, and cooked slowly. It was tender and filling.

Home cooking is unparalleled in its ability to soothe the nerves. Polina had gobbled down her plateful as fast as politeness allowed. After gratefully accepting and consuming a second serving, she felt restored. More importantly, she felt safe.

Arthur had been largely silent on the drive home the night before, a fact Polina had also been grateful for. The dreams that had accompanied her on the trip from Poland had been so comprehensively shattered by the experiences of the past weeks that she had felt drained of any desire to communicate. She was glad of the chance to watch the world go by from a car window, to let her mind be empty of thought, and to just be.

When they had reached their destination, Cornisha had picked up on Polina's mood. The older woman had gently made small talk whilst she showed her unexpected guest the spare room, and explained the foibles of the temperamental shower.

Sitting next to the motherly figure on the velour sofa, Polina felt ready to tell these kind people what had happened.

Although Cornisha hadn't been at all sure that it was a good idea, Arthur had invited John and Bert around. They were generously contributing to the sense of male embarrassment in the living room. They looked anywhere except at Polina. This gave the gathering the feeling of a particularly distracted class.

Polina felt confident. This contrasted with the uncertainties and hesitations that had beset her these last few weeks. She sensed the men around her now were all a little nervous. She didn't want to make them uncomfortable, and yet it felt good to her that the women seemed to be in control for once.

She smiled, very faintly. It was time to say something.

She folded her hands in her lap:

"Thank you, Arthur and Cornisha, for all of this. I am sorry to be intruding in your life, but I am afraid I have got myself into trouble. I really did not know what to do, other than to first try to escape, and then work things out."

Polina paused. Cornisha reached over and pressed her hand. She smiled encouragingly. The three men looked, if anything, slightly more uncomfortable than before.

"I suppose I fell for a very old trick." Polina stopped,

and looked into the cheery fake flames of the gas fire in the hearth. She felt reluctant to besmirch this wholesome place with stories of the depravity she had witnessed. However, she knew, too, that if there was ever to be any justice meted out to those godless men who had betrayed her, then the path started with her telling her story. It could well be a long time before Janusz and Slava would be judged by their maker. They seemed to be rather adept at avoiding him.

Polina definitely wanted Janusz and Slava to pay for what they had done here on earth. She cast her mind back to the beginning:

"It's a bad story. One day in Warsaw – it was cold – after my boyfriend had let me down yet again, a man came and sat by me in a park. He was really charismatic. We started talking. With hindsight it was not really a chance meeting. Unfortunately, I realised this far too late. People like him look out for people like me."

Polina felt a surge of bitterness as she said this. When bad decisions are recounted, you really do re-live the stupidity and desperation that drove you to take them. Maybe this is one reason why victims of crime can find it so very hard to testify.

"He said I should follow my dreams and dance. He told me that there were jobs available in London. It seemed too good to be true – you know, that a stranger should happen to strike up conversation with me and that it should lead to the chance of a new job in another country. And of course it was. I keep blaming myself for being so naive, but at the time I just wanted something to happen to me, to pull me out of my life."

Polina's silent audience couldn't taste the bitterness that invaded her again. Said out loud, this all seemed inconceivably stupid. How could she have been so dismissive of her previous life? That life was pure. She would do anything to go back to Poland now, to turn back the clock and escape the nightmare that England had become.

She failed to stop a tear glistening down her cheek. Cornisha gently squeezed her hand again. Polina looked at her. Cornisha radiated sympathy, understanding and support. Although well meaning, it all had the opposite effect of that intended. Polina had been so unused to any kindness at all in the past few months that all her defences came crashing down.

To the utter discomfort of the men in the room, Polina started sobbing uncontrollably.

Cornisha hugged her tightly.

"It's okay, my dear, you let it out. Tears are funny things. They can make you fragile when you keep them in, but let them out and they sometimes make you stronger. Cry away, my dear. We've all been there."

Without letting go, Cornisha turned to the assembled embarrassed trio.

"Arthur, please make some more tea? John you'll easily find the milk, and Bert, the sugar. Oh, and a biscuit. There are Fruit Shortcakes and some Bourbon Creams in the tin. Take your time. I'll call you when we are ready."

The three men didn't need asking twice. In fact Bert scurried so fast into the kitchen that he almost pulled a muscle in his left thigh. Arthur and John followed promptly.

Arthur put the kettle on.

"I don't like seeing a woman cry. I never know what to say."

John opened the fridge.

"Almost as bad as seeing a grown man cry. Not right, that."

"And that, coming from a Hammers fan."

Bert grinned. Banter and a solid door between him and a crying woman was making him feel better already.

"You have a point there, Bert."

John located the milk, shaking his head over its fancy semi-skimmedness.

He bent over slowly to find a milk jug.

"These days, the one time it is just about acceptable to shed a tear is over a result. Winning or losing doesn't matter. Real men can cry over a football score."

"Just over football, mind." Bert was rooting round in the biscuit tin. "It wouldn't do to weep over Wimbledon would it? Bless them, but only those fairy fellas could shed a tear for Andy Murray, no matter how *emotional* Clare Balding says it all is."

Arthur thought that exceptions could probably be made, as a minimum for family tragedy, but on the whole he felt that his friends were right. When Arthur was a young man, he didn't remember ever seeing men cry – not even over West Ham and its perennial quest for trophies. Nowadays though, Paul Gascoigne and his ilk had opened the floodgates to teary displays both on and off the pitch, rather like Beckham had opened the legs of men everywhere to posing in pouches.

Progress was a funny thing. It went off in all directions, it seemed, like an unruly garden hose.

Despite this, there were limits – and crying over tennis would be an example of those.

Football teams were different. They went back a century or more. Most men had longer relationships with their teams than they had with either their wives or their children, so, in a sense, it was no wonder you got a bit cut up when things went wrong, or overexcited when the team excelled. No one felt as if they belonged to a golfer, a Grand Prix racer or Andy Murray in the same way. Somehow, your football team really was your community. In Arthur's generation, it was a link forged with your father, and perhaps his own father before him. The team populated your earliest memories and would carry on after you were cold in the ground. That was truly a relationship worthy of a tear or two.

"So what is the story with her anyway?" Bert was satisfied that he had now located enough biscuits.

Arthur shook his head.

"I don't really know. One of the gentlemen in the Lofts asked me if Cornisha and I could do him a large favour, and then this Polina turned up. I didn't really like to ask on the way here, as she seemed on edge. I think she's fallen in with a bad lot, if you get my drift."

John and Bert certainly did, and nodded. If there was one thing that was way worse than being in a room with a crying woman, then it was being in a car with one. Alone.

"Arthur, we're ready for you now." Although he loved the sound of Cornisha's voice, Arthur couldn't hold in a sigh of foreboding.

"I suppose that we're going to find out now what this is all about."

Mercifully, the tears had stopped when the three men trooped back in, and took their seats for act two.

Polina looked over at the biscuits. She hadn't had a biscuit for days. Cornisha filled the cups, the tea's stream cheerfully calming all around it.

"I apologise for my weakness some moments ago," said Polina quietly "I haven't cried since I arrived in this country. Do not worry, I will not be crying again. I am far too angry for that."

Polina's eyes showed signs of defiance. She gave the group a small but reassuring smile.

Cornisha reciprocated the smile in silent encouragement. The three men nodded.

"There was a friend who needed dancers. Janusz was telling the truth up to that point. His friend had a bar."

Polina shook her head. The three men held their breath.

"I met Slava, the man with the bar, straight away. If I had not been so excited to finally be here in London, I would have noticed there was something fishy about him. Janusz didn't show me the bar straight away. The first day, we went round London, stopping in cafes for drinks, seeing the tourist sites. It was almost like a holiday – especially the party that Slava and Janusz threw for me on the first night. I thought they were so kind, and I was so lucky. It was the night of the second day that they took me to the bar and showed me what I needed to do."

Polina paused again. Her attractive face twisted with

anger as she remembered what she had been told. The others kept quiet, all eyes now on her.

"I was expected to perform pole dances."

Bert had been very impressed with Polina's grasp of English, but he thought he should correct her slip.

"I think you mean Polish dances. I know it seems a bit old-fashioned, bringing foreigners here to London to entertain us with your traditional dancing, but, you know, there are worse jobs."

Polina looked at Bert. Arthur and John winced, as they willed themselves to melt into the velour. Cornisha, used to such pearls from Bert, rolled her eyes and took a sip of tea.

Polina stared at Bert:

"Polish dances? *Polish dances?* Excuse me, but that was not the job. The job that I was to do was to dance for the pleasure of men, nearly naked, like a prostitute."

Polina spat the last word out with a fair degree of venom. The room was transfixed. Bert was mortified. He was certainly not going to open his mouth again, save to gulp tea. Even that seemed too dangerous without an invitation to do so. Who knew what offence he might further cause the woman? He decided to keep quiet.

Thankfully Polina was not going to be put off her stride.

"Sorry. I know it's unexpected. I also know now that I have been very stupid. The job was to perform a sexual dance. Do you know twerking? Like that, but worse. I meant pole dancing, around a pole – not traditional dancing from Poland. I am a traditional girl, I could even have done that. I was expecting something in a troupe – classical, or modern dance. There is so much on in London, and dancers do get injured – maybe working as a stand in?"

Bert now recalled why he normally kept silent in – and preferably even hid from – conversations like this. He was as red as his skin allowed him to go.

"Oh, I'm sorry, I thought you were from Poland," he managed to mumble.

"Yes, I am. Is a Pole doing pole dancing confusing for you?"

Polina rolled her eyes, and turned to Cornisha for some intelligent support.

Cornisha patted Polina's knee.

"Go on, dear. He means well, really he does. He's very traditional like you are, and he's not used to such goings on. He got a bit confused, but he is on your side, as we all are here."

Polina took the older woman's hand and squeezed it.

"As soon as I saw the club I straight away told Janusz that I would not do that. The place was disgusting. It was full of men of all ages – businessmen in groups, older men on their own, young men on stag nights.. They're all paying money so that women would dance nearly naked for them. It was like something from Sodom and Gomorrah."

Polina looked pointedly at the three men in the room, as if to reprimand them for their guilt in sharing a gender with the men from the club.

"Eve's Garden is the name of the place," Polina continued. She shook her head.

"They had the bad taste to dirty the holy name of Eve with that den of wickedness. I asked Janusz to take me away immediately, but he told me that other Polish women worked there, in fact there were women from all over the world, and it was really all in order, and I should not be worried."

Although John had never bought into UKIP's scaremongering about Polish plumbers taking away local people's livelihoods, he couldn't help but imagine getting Kippers onto the subject of all these Polish pole dancers. *What about all our real, ordinary, decent, hardworking English pole dancers, their wages being undercut by EU floozies gyrating visa-free in girlie bars up and down the country? English minge for English men I say!* Definitely not a discussion for now, that much was clear. He concentrated on Polina again.

"After I threatened to make a scene, he took me to a private room in the back. It was there that he pulled out his iPad and he showed me a video." Polina swallowed. The tension in the room went up a notch – although Bert's concern was also for whether Polina might go for the last couple of Bourbon Creams. He quite fancied them for himself. Thankfully, biscuits were no longer on Polina's mind.

"The party that Slava and Janusz had so kindly thrown to celebrate my arrival was a trap. I do not drink very much, and yet there is a part of the night that I am missing. They told me I was dancing and having fun. In fact they had drugged me, and then they filmed me having sex: with both of them. This is what Slava showed me in that room. This is when he told me that I had no choice but to work there."

Bert had already been wishing that he had stayed at home to watch the snooker. Hell, he would have even preferred taking his wife to Westfield to buy her a new pair of shoes compared to this. Arthur trusted that Cornisha knew full well his role was to ferry the needy around in his car, and to provide the occasional physical support, so would not be looking to him to proffer emotional support.

John found a voice of decency on behalf of the men.

"That is illegal here, Polina. There have been quite a few cases on TV concerning men using date-rape drugs. You have had a terrible experience, and we're all very sorry. The only shame in that video is that of the disgusting cowards who took advantage of you. It's not even you in that video. It's your body – but the drugs they administered to you had robbed it of your personality, your being. You had no idea of what you were doing, unlike those bastards who knew exactly what they were up to. They must be stopped, Polina. We can help you."

It wasn't the first time that John had startled Arthur and Bert with his pitch perfect take on the modern world. For Cornisha it was a relief, and a pleasant surprise.

"John is right, my dear," Cornisha said calmly.

She looked intently at Polina, as she continued to hold her hand: "You have absolutely nothing to be ashamed of here. You are the victim, and we can do something about this. Maybe we can get some of the other girls to come forward as well."

The words of support were not having the effect that John and Cornisha had hoped for. Polina gave the others a forlorn look.

"I understand what you are saying, but Janusz threatened to send the video and photos to my mother and father back in Warsaw. My family is very religious and I think that the

195

shame would kill my poor grandmother. My parents might never speak to me again."

Cornisha nodded.

"I see. My dear, your parents must love you very much. Although they would be hurt and shocked, they would be on your side too. They would want to see the perpetrators brought to justice, exactly as we do."

Polina sighed.

"Cornisha, my mother and father do love me very much, but they are very traditional people. They would never forgive me for leaving Warsaw. You see, they told me – they warned me – that London would be a place full of danger. With so many people some will definitely be bad, they said. They told me it was risky. I ignored them. They will think that I brought it on myself because as a daughter I should have listened to what my father and mother said, and not just gone and followed my own silly, selfish desires to have a more exciting life."

Polina turned to face Cornisha. There was empathy in the older woman's eyes. It comforted her, because she suspected that, whatever assurances these good people were giving her, her overly principled mother would not find it so easy to forgive her, were she ever made aware of the issue. How to explain it to them? She would try.

"My parents said London would be full of drug addicts and criminals and paedophiles and homosexuals – and it is true. I have seen them. Janusz even took me to a bar that was full of homosexuals. It was *disgusting*. I saw them with my own eyes just parading their, well, homosexuality, about – as if it were nothing to be ashamed of. I have even seen men who thought they were women. It makes me sad for their souls, even if they are perverts... "

Polina had no idea what she had said, but the atmosphere in the room had changed. She blinked, a little unsure as to what had happened.

Cornisha smartly withdrew her hand from a surprised Polina's grasp, and pressed her lips together furiously. Arthur felt himself bristling. He was about to inform Polina that he would not allow her to speak like that under his roof, when he remembered how he had reacted when he first found out that Cornisha was a transsexual. Bert had no idea what planet Polina's parents were from, as he had always understood that it was Paris and all the European cities that were bursting at the seams with the real and dangerous perverts. Even John was momentarily stumped.

Thankfully at that moment the doorbell rang.

All three men jumped up like pet dogs, to run to the door. It was the perfect excuse to absent themselves from the conversation.

Arthur lifted a warning hand and stared down Bert and John.

"Very polite of you, but I think I can get my own front door. You two sit yourselves down."

Arthur was glad of the diversion. He suspected that it would be Harry Gumpert at the door. If it were the Jehovah's Witnesses he might actually ask them a question or two. The time out would do him good.

It was indeed Harry, expensively dressed, smiling slightly foolishly.

"Arthur, old chap, how can I thank you?"

Harry strode purposefully into the hall past Arthur, firmly grasping the handle to the door he assumed led to the lounge, and opened it to greet the ironing board and vacuum cleaner that were kept in the hallway cupboard.

Arthur blinked.

"It's through here, Mr Gumpert. Unless of course you're feeling concerned about the cleanliness of the carpet on the stairs there."

Harry backed out of the cupboard, and followed Arthur into the lounge. He continued to stride with purpose. It was always important to remind people who was the boss.

He was taken aback to see several faces greeting him, but his equanimity was restored when Bert jumped up and offered him his armchair.

Harry settled down and spoke a little too loudly, as if lecturing underlings.

"Arthur and Cornisha, I deeply appreciate what you are doing for this young woman. Needless to say, I would appreciate all of your discretion here, especially when it comes to Sagworth Turner Dickerhint. Polina, I trust that you feel safe here with these kind people?"

Harry smiled. Confidence and certainty would see him through this.

Polina found Harry's debonair attitude slightly creepy. This was not a social occasion. Harry's assumed authority made her nervous. After all, he was just another punter to her. She reminded herself that it was thanks to him that she was here at all. Without him consenting to help in her escape from Eve's Garden, she would still be there – although admittedly she had not left him too much choice in the matter. Gratitude had to be a grey area, though. Ultimately, Harry and his money were the root cause of a considerable amount of misery. She decided that she should remain wary of him, as he was a certified sinner – albeit one she remained glad to have met.

She tucked a strand of hair behind one ear.

"Thank you for saving me from that bad place and the things they were making me do. I was going crazy there. I don't know how much longer I could have carried on. This is the first time in this country that I have felt safe, surrounded by respectable people who are like me."

She gave Cornisha her most heartfelt smile, which Cornisha struggled manfully to return. Polina did not notice. She was preoccupied.

"I fear, though, that they will come looking for me, and threaten me, maybe through my parents. I know this is not over yet. Some of the other girls in the club have tried to escape but Slava always found a way to keep them under his control. The man is a monster. Janusz is little better. I think they are dangerous people who are used to getting their way, and they will not be happy that I have run away. It isn't over."

Cornisha nodded.

"I think we all need more tea and biscuits."

Her suggestion was met with approval around the room. Polina looked perplexed. She had spent too little time in the British Isles to know that upon the occurring of a crisis, a Briton's natural reaction is to make tea. In all the history of mankind, tea had never made anything worse than it already was.

*

Almost as comforting as a good brew was the sanctuary of the kitchen to which John, Bert and Arthur repaired. All three had remained on best behaviour, despite Bert's faux pas. They were itching to catch up on what they had heard. Not that they were indulging in gossip, mind. Men don't gossip. Men debate and discuss. This applied on this occasion. They were simply sharing views, endeavouring to understand matters more profoundly, in order to take a reasoned course of action.

Bert emitted a low whistle.

"Well, blow me over. So, Arthur, was your Mr Gumpert in that Eve's Garden place when he met Polina?"

They all concurred that there was no other version of events that would make sense.

Bert's eyes widened.

"What do we think he was doing there?"

He looked at John and Arthur, and shook his head. Arthur opened a cupboard door on the hunt for a packet of Custard Creams.

"I know he is a customer of yours, Arthur, in a certain sense," said John, as he filled the kettle, "but he's certainly giving himself some airs and graces, considering he's been caught red-handed in a girlie bar. He may think himself all heroic – and fair play to him on helping a dancing damsel in distress – but I doubt he'd be so high-and-mighty if his wife were here with us."

Arthur sighed.

"He likes to think himself quite the card, our Harry Gumpert. Once upon a time I daresay he was."

It was a curious situation for Arthur to find himself in. Most of the residents of the Castle Lofts treated Arthur and his concierge colleagues as if they were half men, half desk. For certain residents, they were akin to inanimate objects – to be ignored, on the whole, unless a specific task was required of them. Yet Arthur observed the people who came and went, and knew far more about them than they could ever imagine. He knew about the affair Harry had had with Monique, and that it was over, and also that Harry's wife, Sarah, increasingly seemed to have the upper hand in their relationship. He had observed how Sarah had seemed to grow in confidence over the past few months, whereas Harry seemed smaller and older. Maybe this trip to Eve's Garden was just part of Harry's mid-life crisis. Arthur would watch out for a new motorbike or sports car being driven in. None of it surprised Arthur, though. None of it was new.

He shook his head at the obviousness of people.

"I suppose helping poor Polina made Harry feel like the big man again. It's good to play the knight in shining armour."

"Good analogy," replied John, "as Sir Gumpert through there seems to have delegated all the real work to his squire, the loyal Arthur. Now you and Cornisha are left holding the baby, and a very – er – *traditional* baby it is. I saw poor Cornisha's reaction."

Arthur sighed again. He couldn't find it in himself to be especially offended by Polina's remarks. They were run of the mill bigotry. It wasn't so long ago that he found *alternative lifestyles* pretty upsetting himself. And yet, he didn't want to stay silent when situations affected Cornisha.

"Despite all the talk of justice round here, I reckon this is a very tricky situation and we should get Polina on the first flight back to Warsaw," Bert said firmly. "She could be in danger, and she doesn't exactly fit in here either. Let's get her out of here before any more trouble happens."

The three men looked at each other. Arthur reflected that there didn't seem to be a better plan on offer. But he didn't like to just take the views of two men on the matter. He would see what Cornisha thought, before he could recommend any action at all.

Although not party to the kitchen conversation, Harry Gumpert would have agreed wholeheartedly with Bert. It wasn't that Harry regretted helping Polina. He had thrilled to the surge of power he had felt as he got one over on the bloodsucking crooks who ran Eve's Garden. That would teach them to price a beer at over a tenner.

Now, though, her presence was manifestly a danger to his position. Harry sensed that he had done the right thing, the honourable thing. However, it was such an unfamiliar feeling not to have pursued the most self-serving course of action that he was now unsure how to react. His moral compass – ancient and rusty as it was – was spinning wildly. This would not do. He decided to bank the virtuous moment, ignore the inconvenient compass, and revert to looking after number one.

He looked deep into Polina's eyes.

"Polina, I think we should get you on a flight back home as soon as possible. Don't worry, I will pay for your ticket.

It's the least I can do to show you that not everyone is awful here in London. I can see that you could think we all are. Present company excepted, of course," he added quickly, including Cornisha in his generous smile.

Neither of the two women reacted to Harry's munificence in the way Harry considered they should have.

Polina's gaze turned steely.

"Harry, that is kind of you, but I need to get myself together before I am ready to face my parents. I need to talk about what has happened, maybe with another woman who can give me some advice. I also want those monsters to face justice for what they have done, what they are still doing. How many more people are they going to make suffer in this way?"

Although upset by the views of the younger woman on modern London life, Cornisha knew that there was a bigger picture. One way or another, there was a mess to untangle here.

Cornisha pursed her lips:

"Polina, you're safe here. Why don't you stay here for a couple of days, so that we can think, and discuss your next move?"

Cornisha looked hard at Harry, daring him to interrupt her, which of course he didn't. She pressed her finger tips together.

"I can see that there is also the small matter of whether these people should be allowed to get away with drugging someone, raping them, blackmailing them, illegal trafficking both them and other people, and running an establishment with forced labour. As a legal expert, Harry, no doubt all this must also be exercising your conscience as much as it does mine."

A hundred thoughts raced through Harry's mind. It sounded as if Cornisha wanted to fight for justice for the young Pole. This was very bad indeed. Justice meant shining a light into the activities at Eve's Garden – and that meant shining a light on Harry's visit to the club. In Harry's experience, openness and transparency were rarely the best course of action. He certainly didn't want the details of his private life to ever be made public.

Harry ignored the muffled murmurs of the remains of his conscience. He summoned his most ingratiating smile.

"Well, now, let's think about this very carefully indeed. Cornisha, I fully understand your desire to avoid precipitate action. If you can cope with Polina staying here a couple of days, then I think that is a superb idea. It gives us all time to plan what to do next."

Harry studiously avoided the thorny topic of taking action against the owners of Eve's Garden. Good heavens, he had been hoping to return there in the coming days to enjoy some more feminine attention. That certainly seemed like a vain hope now.

Cornisha knew that this was playing for time. Lawyers did this, almost fanatically. No decision could ever be made unless it had been kicked down the road several times. Whether this was to allow someone else to eventually claim credit for the idea, or simply because no one wanted ever to shoulder something as arduous as responsibility – who could tell? The net effect remained that the evolution of business mores was slowed, with issues passed from generation to generation. Change would happen – if indeed it ever did – in a far off future, with someone else's head above the parapet, or on the block.

But Polina needed time, and at least Harry's passing of the buck gave her that. Polina probably needed to have a conversation with people who could really help to sort out this situation: people who had the sensitivity to grasp the full picture and possible outcomes. This situation needed people who would cater for Polina's particular position, but who also, unlike Harry, had the courage to do the right thing, even when difficult.

Cornisha would make a call to Kelly. She and Ben were exactly the kind of ballsy lawyers the situation needed right now.

8

Bubble, bubble, no toil, some trouble

Ben hated plastic shower curtains.

No matter how hard he tried to keep his body away from the infernal hanging ghoul, it always contrived to stick to his shoulders and back, chilling and disgusting him in equal measure with its clammy embrace. The one attacking him now was an old curtain, way past its best. The faint traces of mould that he suspected had returned at its foot certainly didn't help, but the very concept of plastic sheeting vexed him. No matter whether such devices were adorned with cheery seascapes, reproductions of Van Gogh or even jaunty Tottenham Hotspur logos, a shower curtain's very existence downgraded the whole bathroom experience.

Money would buy a proper shower cubicle with a door. Ben hankered for a door – a door that did not flap like a thing possessed, as if it were terrified, for all the world as if Anthony Perkins were about to drop in and stab someone to death through it.

Ben roughly drew the curtain to one side and stepped in front of the mirror to towel off. He surveyed the physique that would shortly be on show at Club Adam's foam fiesta.

Ben was satisfied with what he saw – just. The extra hours spent at his desk recently had translated to fewer gym sessions and a resulting loss of tone and volume. It remained all too apparent to his critical eyes. Others may still be kind to him, but Ben could tell that he wasn't quite as fit as he had been when he arrived in London.

"At least I know I'm a Grohe, not a show-er," he said aloud. The pun didn't quite work, but it pleased him anyway.

He applied moisturiser. It had become a routine recently. He used to shy away from such products. They seemed unfit for purpose to an oily-skinned teen. Ben's skin had now, however, decided to act its age. It needed assistance. He had been told that moisturising often and thoroughly really would keep the wrinkles at bay. He wasn't sure he bought it, but it afforded some guilt-free time staring at himself in the mirror, just to make sure he hadn't missed a bit.

Given the new beauty routine, he enjoyed post-workout sessions at the gym. He wasn't quite exhibitionist enough to slather himself in full view, in the buff. However, standing in his pants in the male locker room massaging his freshly pumped muscles brought him looks of attention and desire. He still craved these. He had decided to fight it no longer, and merely accept that most men who devoted hours of their week to sculpting their bodies had more than a streak of the peacock in them.

Ben enjoyed displaying.

What to wear? It seemed somewhat pointless

spending ages picking out an outfit that, once arrived at the destination, would be unceremoniously dumped in a bin liner. However, there was the journey to think of and potentially a queue to get in. The patrons of Club Adam's naked extravaganzas may be free and easy inside the venue, but they remained gay men, who would fashion a sarcastic comment for any sartorial faux pas, even glimpsed momentarily whilst paying to get in. Ben settled on a safe pair of jeans and neutral T-Shirt and pulled on an old pair of sneakers. It took great skill to look as if one hadn't spent a moment thinking about what one was wearing.

It was time to head downstairs for the customary pre-party vodkas with Alex and Jamal. If he was going to take full advantage of what Club Adam had to offer, Ben knew he should ensure that he was well lubricated, inside and out.

Across town, Tarquin Henderson-Smythe was having second thoughts. It had seemed a good idea to agree to Rubens' party suggestion. Clearly, a naked foam party was a fitting way to celebrate buying a house. If this didn't reassert one's fun side, what would? It wasn't so much killing two birds with one stone, as downing a whole flock, with bubbles.

That was what Tarquin had thought then. Today, however, in the cold light of a London Sunday afternoon, he was regretting his decision.

He was searching for an escape route – the plug hole out.

He held his temple for effect, and smiled winningly at his love.

"I think I've got one of my heads coming on, Rubens. Would you be *really* upset if we didn't go? We could rent that Angelina Jolie movie you've been wanting to see. It's got great reviews."

Rubens stared at his partner, incredulous.

"Gostoso. Please."

He folded his arms in mock exasperation.

"If you're going to lie to me, then you need to become a lot better at it. Second, do not involve Angelina in your deception. Veramente. *No*."

Tarquin had to admit that a headache was hardly original stuff. Could he cut himself quite badly shaving and then plead hygiene? Maybe a slip too far: self-harm was no joking matter. Claiming he had nothing to wear wasn't going to help either.

"Rubens, I know I said what I said – but I *really* don't want to go. It's just not me. I may be gay, but that doesn't mean that I have to swan about like some performing pony – especially not in the nude with hundreds of drunken, undiscriminating men covered in foam and ready for a gangbang. I mean, call me precious – but it makes me feel uncomfortable just thinking about it. Dirty, even."

"Gostoso, if there is one thing it is impossible to feel after a foam party, it is dirty. You come out and it's as if you've gone through the extra long cycle in the washing machine. Even old trainers smell as if they are made of spring flowers. It's really very handy."

Tarquin did have a rather nice old pair of Reebok's he was awfully fond of but couldn't quite seem to shift the gym smell from. Could he possibly justify going to a voyeuristic orgy to see if it would perform a cleansing miracle on his favourite running shoes?

"Take this," said Rubens, coming back from the kitchen with two chunky glasses in hand, ice clinking like tiny bells. He gave one to Tarquin. It had a delightful picture of a Cheshire Cat upon it, and bore the words *drink me*. A fat slice of lemon swam lazily amongst the ice, like a Liberal Democrat seal. Tarquin rarely needed any persuasion to down a gin and tonic, but Rubens was taking no chances.

He raised his glass:

"Let's toast doing things we don't normally do. I've made it strong, so it will hopefully shrink your reservations. Then we can finish getting ready and go."

Rubens had a steely look in his eyes. Tarquin was getting to know this look. Easy-going, flexible Rubens was not going to give way. Whether he wanted to or not, Tarquin would be falling down the rabbit hole this afternoon. He drained his glass – it *was* delicious – and sighed momentously.

"Well lace me up and call me Alice. Let's get a move on. We wouldn't want to be late for the tea party, would we?"

A different negotiation was going on in a flat in Hackney.

Janusz was making things clear to Milo.

"I do not often go to places like this, so I hope this *Club Adam* of yours is going to be... mind blowing. If I want a man then I can charm him if I have time, or pay him if I don't. I can also do both if he is particularly good. Like you."

Janusz raised his glass. He gave Milo a sea-deep smile that drowned the Serb's hesitations.

Janusz was addictive – deeply attractive on a primitive, irresistible level. Milo knew that he would be having sex with Janusz even without being paid to do so. The exchange of money, however, underscored all too clearly that this was a short-term, transactional affair, and that Janusz liked to be captain of his own boat.

Milo didn't suppose for a minute that a man like Janusz was likely to be tied down – tied up, possibly, but that was it. In any event, despite Janusz's energetic enthusiasm for sex and effortless ability to cope with all that Milo had to offer, Milo retained a sneaky feeling that, ultimately, Janusz swung towards the heterosexual end of the bisexual spectrum.

No, this was clearly a short-term bit of fun – nothing more. It may be enriching in a pecuniary sense, but Milo would be unlikely to be making any deposits in the bank of spiritual fulfilment on the back of it.

Milo reflected gloomily that he was a grown man who appreciated all this. Yet here he was, like a teenager, what with the heart flutterings and the feelings.

He squared his shoulders, and smiled mechanically at his lover-come-client.

"Don't worry, Janusz, I am sure you are going to like the club. I think there is a good chance you will bump into some of my friends as well, who I think you will also appreciate."

Apart from the somewhat miserable Polina, Milo had only ever met one of Janusz's friends, and that only briefly, after he and Janusz had spent a night in this very same Hackney flat. Milo hadn't quite been able to put his finger on it, but the expensive contents of the premises didn't match the modesty of the building. Things seemed even odder when the next day Slava turned up in a yellow Maserati, accompanied by a blonde with meanly covered, generous breasts.

Milo had not warmed to Slava. Slava had glanced at Milo as if he were automatically assessing his value. Amber – for it was she – had not even looked at Milo. She lavished a smacker on Janusz, whose hands wandered over her bottom, eliciting a purr of pleasure from the woman rather than the slap Milo thought it merited. The greeting between the three friends was complicit. There was clearly history here, and of a sort that Milo thought it was better for him to know as little of as possible. Milo knew all too well the dangers of history.

Still, that was yesterday. Today was supposed to be a fun time.

"Well, any friend of yours, as they say… " Janusz replied.

His change in tone signified that Milo was about to get an instruction, an instruction that would be underpinned by the exchange of banknotes. Milo knew that these banknotes held the relationship together, and would also ensure its ultimate demise.

"I am most delighted to meet your friends, Milo, but if I am going to this Adam place, then what I am really after is an *experience*. So, my handsome friend, I want you to be on full display when the time comes. You will reel in all the best lookers to our corner so that we may enjoy them together. Not that I cannot pull in the boys myself, you know, but I imagine that, in a place like this one, witty conversation is somewhat underappreciated, and it's too wet to be flashing my fifty pound notes. Besides, why have a dog and bark yourself? Not that I consider you a dog, of course. Now come here and lie down. Look at these notes – so useful at all times. I can tickle your stomach with the Queen's face."

Caspar had read the Club Adam webpage ten times now. He now knew that he should definitely leave his suede designer mules at home. The biggest issue, however, was that he thought he should really be leaving himself at home with the mules, too.

Saturday night had promised much. During the day, post gym, Caspar had picked up a new T-shirt and a pair of jeans in Oxford Street. He had been feeling on top of the world – as if he were a catch, ready to glitter in the constellation of London's nightlife. The conversation flowed over drinks with friends, his jokes had hit the spot and he enjoyed the flirtation that had been directed his way. He was ready to move in for the kill on the dancefloor.

Last night's club, however, had not fulfilled expectations. He had settled on one prospect, then another, and then another but for whatever reason – boyfriends, he expected, for what else could stand in the way of his magnetism – nothing had come to fruition.

The dregs of the group had decided to try Scream, the after hours *du moment* that was *de rigueur* for the gay clubber who was not prepared for the day of rest to commence. Caspar had been sure that, fuelled up as he was, with standards commensurately relaxed, there was *no way* that he would be returning home alone.

And yet, as regular people were just starting to contemplate a lazy Sunday lunch, Caspar found himself lying alone in his bed, with only Grindr and Manhunt for company. Even they were failing to impress that morning. He had planned nothing other than spending the morning with the guy he was sure that he would have picked up, and then happily wasting the rest of the day in the pleasant haze of post-coital well being.

This gnawing dissatisfaction inside was not part of the plan. Caspar's unflappable confidence was shaken, but not damaged beyond repair. Caspar was merely annoyed with the unreliability of London. This had led him to browse through the *Musts & Maybes* for Sunday – and hence, to find Club Adam.

Caspar considered sex clubs to be either for the old'n'ugly, or the terminally perverted. Saunas were just as bad, unless of course they were attached to a five star hotel or had contextual validation, such as those in Budapest, or Istanbul. He remained determined, though, that the weekend would not scotch his plans without him fighting back. Club Adam, at least, had the foam party. Foam was fun. Foam was young. Foam was fine.

Caspar managed to convince himself that it sounded more like Ibiza hedonism than a Vauxhall slut drop. He was still feeling pretty high. That was a good enough excuse in itself. Caspar decided that the prospect of anonymous sex at a Sunday afternoon club in south London was an improvement on the certainty of anonymous solitude in his central London studio.

He tossed his mules into the back of the wardrobe and scrabbled about for his oldest trainers.

Alex raised friendly eyebrows at Ben.

"Hey, Ben, come on in. How are you doing?"

Ben hadn't seen Alex since the *Morten-gatan* episode of

the day before. His presence at that scene had not been entirely welcome. Alex was one of those people whom Ben wanted to think well of him. Ben felt that he had somewhat blotted his copy book in that respect – what with the domestic quarrelling in the street, and the spontaneous exposé of sexual mishaps. Alex's otherwise innocuous greeting now seemed pregnant with concern that Ben was going to have another meltdown.

It was too much to be considered such a *loser*.

Ben gritted his teeth.

"Alex, I suffered enough last time we went through all this. To unkind eyes it might seem that I have a knee-jerk reaction, every time I find my girlfriend is shagging a Scandinavian, to ask immediately where the nearest sex party is. But it *is* different this time."

Alex kept a calm and interested look on his face.

Ben added defensively.

"We had already planned to go to this club *long* before yesterday's turn of events."

"And Kelly?" prompted Alex, kindly.

Ben lowered his voice to sound more mature.

"I am avoiding her calls, true – but that is just to work some things through in my mind. This could be a positive development. What's sauce for the goose is sauce for the gander."

Jamal wandered over.

"Hey, Ben."

"Hey" Ben replied automatically.

Ben looked at his friends. He attempted to compose his features into an appropriate, weighty expression. Gravitas would be too much to hope for, especially given the topic – but he had watched the speeches, he had a dream, and he wanted to be judged by the content of his character rather than the supposed thickness of his skin.

Jamal grinned at Alex.

"What's a gander? Is it code for a hung top? Are there going to be some at the party this afternoon? I'll make sure I cover them with my sauce."

Alex smiled.

"Ignore my beautiful, facetious and, er, slightly crude husband. So, Ben, are you saying that you want to have an open relationship with Kelly or... what?"

Alex seemed to be playing the role of concerned parent rather than the complicit friend Ben wanted.

He sighed.

"Truth be told I'm not at all sure what I want – but I do know this. I'll get something from a damned good shag this afternoon, and a damned strong drink right now. How am I supposed to know what I think? I love her – but she's taking liberties. I'm not sure what to do about it. But I'll worry about tomorrow when tomorrow comes. Today I am just going to have the most fun – including sex – that I can have and stay healthy and legal."

Ben looked at the two men.

"So, now that my state of mind has been assessed, do you think I might possibly get that drink?"

"Sorry, Ben. No more questions. Or advice." Alex smiled at his friend. "Now, we have a fantastic new vodka that is perfect with Red Bull. Straight from Sweden – Absolut Lingonberry. Just kidding, Ben! Just kidding."

Caspar had prepared himself to be naked in front of a few hundred random strangers, but the absence of a queue outside the club had completely thrown him.

What to do?

He felt he should avoid any London club other people did not feel it worth queuing to enter. He wondered if it was too late to think better of the idea. He hardly wanted to be seen shilly-shallying in front of the doors of a sex party on a Sunday afternoon, so he whipped out his phone and marched smartly past the unsuspecting doormen.

He needed to buy some time.

He pretended to be tweeting, emailing, instagramming, pinteresting, snapchatting – whatever social media dictated to him, all while keeping the entrance to Club Adam under surveillance from a discreet distance.

The punters started to trickle in. Caspar sized them up as they disappeared inside.

Minger. Even with clothes on, Caspar could tell that he could never drink until *that* particular ogre was attractive.

Too old. Caspar firmly believed that old people – namely anyone over the age of forty – should never subject others to the sight of their unclothed bodies. He found it disgusting when they insisted on flaunting all that aged flesh. What did they think they were? Hung steaks? People like that had ruined his couple of attempts at a sauna experience.

Too flabby. Bracketed with the over-forties. So far, it was not looking good, as Caspar continued to spy on the entrance from a safe distance.

Wait a minute. A couple of men were approaching the door with a lazy stride, quite unlike the slightly hurried *what am I missing?* mincing of the previous three. He couldn't quite make out the shorter one, but the guy nearer him was handsome. Caspar felt a slight stirring and forgot to pretend to look at his phone every so often as he fixed the pair.

Maybe he should go in after all.

As Caspar dithered, the handsome man's companion removed his baseball cap. It was that cute barman, with the famous donkey schlong, from Outrageous Fortune! Who would have thought? Caspar was definitely going to go in now.

Just as he was finally pocketing his phone, someone tapped him on the shoulder.

"MI6 is on the other side of the street, Caspar."

Crikey. It was Ben Barlettano. Ben looked at Caspar with a grin that was struggling not to become a smirk. Two other men stood behind Ben. Both were handsome – one dark and well built, one tall and blond. Caspar panicked for a moment. Sad old Ben could never find out that he was feeling desperate enough to go into a sex club, and certainly not when he was in such attractive company. How did Ben get to know men like this anyhow?

"I'm waiting for... Wallace."

Caspar needed a cover, and names were always useful. A bus had just passed advertising a plumber with that name. Wallace it was.

Caspar went for it:

"He lost his phone last night as he was in such a mess, and then we had an argument. He's not at his flat. Long story."

Ben looked evenly at the young queen. It sounded plausible, but lawyers were paid to make the preposterous sound plausible every day, so that probably meant Caspar was lying.

"As you are obviously casing the joint, Caspar, you'd better come into Club Adam with us to see if this Wallace is covered in six feet of foam somewhere."

"He could be covered in something else," added Jamal helpfully.

Caspar nodded at Jamal half-heartedly. His will to resist being dragged in to the club by Ben was fading fast. He still thought Ben was a lame example of an older gay man, but Ben's friends were hot, and he had just seen a proper, appropriately-endowed stripper walk through the doors. *The stripper.* He had momentarily forgotten the stripper.

Caspar shrugged:

"Yeah, good point. Wallace has mentioned this place before, and I would like to find him."

Alex looked intently at Caspar, at his face, then up and down his body as if he were a lamb at auction.

"Tell us what he looks like, and we'll go find him for you, and send him out. That way you won't ruin those lovely trainers of yours in all that foam."

Alex had noticed that Caspar was impeccably dressed, save for an incongruously scruffy pair of sneakers. It was as if Meryl Streep had somehow worn her gardening gloves to the Oscars.

No! Caspar really wanted to experience the inside of Adam now. Maybe this Alex was flirting with him. In any case he wasn't going to thwart Caspar Steele.

"He's really rather nondescript, I'm afraid, especially in the dark. Average height, slim, brown hair... I'd better come in with you and look for him myself."

"Well, of course you should. I mean, why should he be having all the fun?"

Alex smirked in amusement at Caspar's inexpert attempt at concealing his desperation for dick. He took Caspar's arm.

"Adam is practically a religion, you know, for us gay boys. And it is Sunday after all. The day of the Lord-knows-what-might-happen. You'll soon be on your knees and worshipping all the miraculous sights that come your way."

Alex refrained from finishing off with a chorus of hallelujahs.

Tarquin Henderson-Smythe tended to regard Vauxhall as a giant junction rather than a destination in itself.

Dominated by the railway tracks and a monstrous new build on the river, it reeked of transience. Unprepossessing though the environment might be, Tarquin was going to try to have fun – or at least pretend to – in this Adam place. Looking around him, he did rather wonder why Rubens had somehow persuaded him to spend his precious Sunday afternoon at what seemed to be a take-away in a bus station.

Tarquin sighed, quietly, not wanting Rubens to see he really did not want to be there at all.

Rubens was busily looking at the new stores that had recently opened in the arches. He called Tarquin over.

"Ooh, gostoso, we could come here and get some

inspiration for the new place. It might even still be open after the party."

Rubens smiled at his partner, his face full of childlike enthusiasm, as he gesticulated at the wares in the kitchen and bathroom store situated a couple of doors up from the sex club.

Tarquin was about to retort that he was aiming to escape Vauxhall without picking up anything unpleasant, when a gorgeous white minimalist kitchen in the window of the shop caught his eye. He had to stop.

Tarquin had always disliked clutter. It was unsightly and made cleaning the counter tops take an age. The smooth-topped vision in front of him looked fabulous. It had everything a modern family required. There was of course the full range of built-in appliances, but also neat touches such as specialised drawers with dedicated breadboxes and cutlery trays. Was that a pull-out trash can and recycling bin combo, attractively camouflaged with a cabinet front? He marvelled at the slide-out broom cupboard for unsightly mops. The toe-kick drawers were perfect for the serving platters and baking trays that Tarquin had never quite been able to fit into normal, standard kitchen cupboards. It even advertised an up-to-date appliance garage with lift-up pocket door. Tarquin had no idea what that was, but he felt instinctively that he and Rubens needed one. This place was close to heaven!

Rubens recorded all the details diligently.

"They do bathrooms here as well, and then there is a nice tile and natural stone shop round the corner. It's very handy really."

Tarquin nodded eagerly.

"Well, if we're not too long in the club, maybe we might go in."

He smiled at Rubens, thinking that the afternoon may yet be salvaged.

"Oh, look at that suite back there!"

Rubens was pleased that Tarquin seemed happier, but he didn't really want to curtail his afternoon's hedonism so he could go and choose a sink. Time may well come when he would get more excited over driving to an out-of-town garden superstore for some new petunias and discounted compost rather than meeting Jamal for an all-night bender – but that time had not arrived today. Rubens would resist its arrival for as long as possible.

"Good idea, gostoso." Rubens took Tarquin's arm and gently drew him away from the shop window.

Amber Bluett had a decision to make.

She surveyed the scene in front of her, sipping the flute of champagne that Slava had insisted she have. Welcome to Eve's Garden, she thought.

She rather liked the place. The décor was dark, but surprisingly sumptuous.

Of course, punters were far more likely to part with ridiculous amounts of money for very little if they felt somewhat overawed by the ambience. It was rather like the clever pricing of afternoon tea at one of the swankier London hotels, where a suite for the night could cost as much as a small car. The punter felt almost privileged to be given access. They therefore thought nothing of paying the price of organic steak for a miserly crust free sandwich, and some tired cake that could not decide if it were too sticky or too sweet, as it crouched sulkily on a small china stack.

Never mind tea, thought Amber – try pricing tits instead. Her lip curled. Oh yes. Add in the promise of sex, and men could be persuaded to splash out quite unfeasibly large amounts of money. Generations of jewellers might attest to this.

In Eve's Garden Amber was at liberty to truly be herself. She could never get away with six-inch heeled leather boots at Sagworth Turner Dickerhint, and certainly not the bustier that was distracting every man in her orbit. Her breasts were like enormous white planets, bulging roundly from the top of the laced-up garment. She chuckled to herself. In Slava's establishment, diversity meant offering women of many different looks, sizes, colours and creeds, primed up to strip as much money as possible from the men ravenously ogling them. Strippers by name, strippers by nature. Better still, it was all so gloriously heterosexual. With the exception of a little light lesbianism – the show must go on – this was a place where LGBTQ was given no Q for quarter.

Amber sneered again. If they were *ever* to have a sideline to strip pounds from the pink pervs, then that would be strictly behind closed doors, with all the attendant tacit shame she wished they had the *decency* to remember. Pride? Really? *Not on her watch.*

Whether it was wise to give up on Sagworth Turner Dickerhint and devote her time to Eve's Garden was another matter altogether. Exasperated as she may be by the corporate nancies who minced around any difficult issues, with their sham respect for the individual, and empty kowtowing to best practice, Amber had discovered that there were ways around the rules if one applied oneself, or just had a natural flair for being mean. Nicholas Casterway was living proof that the art of professional belittling was thriving in the legal sector. Sagworth Turner Dickerhint was a stable behemoth which would be paying her for as many years as she cared to deceive it. Amber was acutely aware of the benefits of her present situation.

By contrast, although she felt delightfully free at Eve's Garden, Amber sensed that its future was inherently precarious. Then again, as she took another sip of champagne, she did feel as though she was born to do this. What to do? She accepted another flute of champagne from the indisputably attentive barman as she contemplated her dilemma. Appealing as it was to think of wielding a sword to slice through the pros and cons of career change, Amber decided that she would leave this particular Gordian knot alone for now, and ride both horses until matters became clearer.

"Who are *you*?"

Amber was disturbed from her musings by a woman with short, bleached blonde hair. Her pale skin stretched tightly over a decent bone structure, and her pursed, thin lips spelt trouble. The woman's green eyes offered a clear challenge to authority. This was something that none of the other girls Amber had met thus far had dared show.

Amber needed to deal firmly with this woman's insolence.

"I am the new manager here, and so, I suspect, your boss. I hope we are not going to have a problem."

Amber held the woman's gaze, narrowing her eyes ever so slightly in the way that usually sent her colleagues at Sagworth Turner Dickerhint scurrying away with a mumbled apology.

The blonde woman, however, was made of sterner stuff than the paper tigers in the office. They were generally incapable of responding to full-frontal aggression. This woman was not so easily tamed.

"Well that depends on you, sweetie." A lazy grin slashed the woman's mouth. "Stay out of my way, and I will stay out of yours. The name's Merima. The last manager learnt how to behave round me and we got on just fine. I hope you are smart enough to do the same. See you around, sweetie."

The grin flickered again, as Merima turned on her heel and made to walk away. Amber had other ideas:

"I did not dismiss you, Merima."

Amber pronounced the woman's name slowly and deliberately. She made sure her stance underlined her intent:

"Sit yourself down a moment, and let's get a couple of things clear."

Merima swivelled back and directed a mocking stare at Amber. This was irritating. But Amber knew about being irritating in turn.

"I am your manager and as such you will do what I say. Otherwise I will make your life very unpleasant. Sweetie."

Amber's tone was hard. She was used to being obeyed.

Merima looked surprised. She clutched the chain

around her neck, threw back her head and laughed, before leaning in until her face was just a few inches from Amber's.

"Am I supposed to be intimidated? Please! You're going to have to try a bit harder than that."

She drew back, scowling, holding Amber's gaze.

Amber resisted the temptation to slap Merima smartly across the cheek. It would send the wrong message to the customers, and besides, Merima looked more than ready and capable of fighting back. Yet this woman could not be allowed to get away with such disrespect, otherwise Amber would have lost the battle before she had properly begun.

Reluctantly, she decided she had to play along – for now. She forced a smile, her eyes resolutely refusing to participate in the fake emotion.

"The only thing that is trying is this conversation. Merima, we should start again. Let's be quite clear that we need a chain of command here. I want to run a tight ship, but there is no reason why we cannot each play our part here without there being any unpleasantness. My aim is to keep our patron out of the day-to-day, as we both know life will be far better for you girls if we limit his participation to the occasional drink and breaking in the new girls. But I can only make sure Slava is all smiles here if I am personally satisfied with everyone's attitude and contribution."

Merima didn't respond immediately. She stared at Amber trying to weigh up exactly who she was dealing with, and whether it was worth making an effort.

Amber continued:

"I may even need someone round here to keep an eye on things – to let me know how the girls are, if you get my drift."

Merima raised an eyebrow.

"So you want me to be a spy for you? Not really my style. At least you have realised that Polina running off like that has changed things. I am not so stupid as to challenge Slava but, honey, none of us have seen any consequences for her actions. What's to stop any of us deciding that the magician is really all smoke and mirrors and following the yellow brick road out of here?"

Amber could feel her blood pressure rise. As soon as she had heard of Polina's escape she had known that action had to be taken. It was clearly as serious as she had thought. She needed to speak to Slava. A challenge had been set. Amber was a woman of action. She now knew that she had a job to do at Eve's Garden.

She looked grimly at Merima.

"I wouldn't get any ideas if I were you. I would not want to be in Polina's shoes right now. You will hear soon enough what happens to a girl who crosses us. Now, delightful as this conversation is, I think it is time you went and earned us some money. But we will talk again. Soon."

Club Adam's doormen had been friendly, far more so than Tarquin remembered from his previous experiences. Tarquin associated gay clubs with stuck-up and uninterested attitude horrors.

Club Adam seemed different.

Tarquin had admittedly been stripped of more money than he had expected, and then all of his clothes to boot, yet it had been done with a smile and an explanation of how everything worked. It was as if the staff working there actually cared that he enjoyed himself. This was quite a novel concept for a London venue.

The first room was still empty. There was a large bar along one side of it. A few foamy trainers and patches on the floor attested to the bubbles beyond.

It had seemed awfully strange initially, standing there completely naked save for his sneakers and a can of Red Stripe. The feeling was compounded when Rubens' friends had turned up. Tarquin knew Ben, of course, and had met Alex and Jamal, but he hadn't yet been introduced to their penises and was not too sure of the correct etiquette in such situations. He was of course interested in what they were packing, but it did seem rather nouveau to peek, and so he kept matters entirely at eye-level despite the temptation. He allowed himself to admire their well-exercised bottoms, when they decided to go off "exploring". Tarquin had told Rubens he felt he needed another drink before he was able to peel himself away from what had become his comfort zone in the club.

"Well this certainly makes a change from Old Bond Street."

The voice sounded familiar. Tarquin turned round to see Rory Ramsey-Hall grinning at him. It took a moment to recognise him, as it was the first time Tarquin had seen Rory without his tweed jacket and a Barbour.

Tarquin wondered if he still had his brogues on.

Rory smiled pleasantly at him:

"I didn't think this would be your scene, old boy."

"Well it is my first time, actually. I'm not quite sure what to make of it, to be perfectly honest."

"Oh, it's really rather jolly. It's one of the friendliest places in London. I suppose that it all makes sense, really. It's awfully difficult to have an attitude when we're all here in the altogether."

Rory paused, and drank from his beer can.

"Polite society gets in such a tizzy over public nudity. It's all natural to me."

It was still a challenge to know where to look, but Tarquin was surprised at how normal it was becoming to be standing there, in the buff, chatting away as if they were weighing up whether to put an offer in on a piece.

Rory was a highly respected art dealer. He was a man whose opinion Tarquin had actively sought on more than one occasion. Clearly, the place attracted all types. If one could get over the strangeness of being unclad in public, there was actually something down-to-earth about the experience. Maybe Tarquin could actually enjoy himself. Why had he worried so about the seediness and unpleasantness of it all?

"I'm just going to the loo, I'll be back in a moment, gostoso."

Rubens flashed Tarquin a smile and squeezed his arm as he walked off.

"Is that chap in the business as well? Did I see him in Maastricht this year?"

Tarquin had completely forgotten to introduce his partner to Rory. He paused, realising that he had never actually told Rory that he was gay. Then he remembered where he was. *Relax and stop feeling so out of sorts* he told himself.

"Rubens is my partner, actually. We've just bought a house together. Odd as it may sound, we're here celebrating our future domestic bliss. Rubens has finally convinced me to step out of my comfort zone and try something new."

Tarquin smiled confidently, proud that he was making substantial progress.

"Well, congratulations, old boy! Spiffing news!" Rory clapped Tarquin on the back, looking genuinely pleased to be sharing in the glad tidings. "I believe a toast is in order."

They bumped cans of beer. Tarquin took a deep draught, feeling the beer flow through his body. Things were looking up. He took another gulp, thinking that he might even allow himself to get a little tipsy. He should just relax and go with the flow. Why get so hung up about nakedness? –Heck, he was even starting to think he should go for a tour around the club when Rubens returned. He was so glad to have bumped into Rory. He made a mental note that he and Rubens should invite him over for dinner.

He spoke up.

"When Rubens comes back, why don't we go for a little walk round the club? I can't stay stuck to this bar all night like a wallflower, can I?"

Tarquin felt he was exuding warmth and bonhomie. Life felt good. Why had he been holed up in his own little world for so long? He needed to relax.

Rory picked up on Tarquin's lightening of mood, as he put his arm around his waist and gave him a friendly squeeze.

"Excellent plan, dear friend!"

Rory turned and looked Tarquin straight in the eye.

"I can show you all the nooks and crannies this place has to offer. There's a fun little room upstairs at the back that I particularly savour. Now, tell me, my dear, would you be open to giving me a good fisting?"

Tarquin froze. Rory took hold of his hand and examined his knuckles.

"Jolly good. It looks like you have excellent attributes. I have quite the capacity, you know, and all the goodies are down my rugger socks. Slip slidin' away. You'll fit in fine with the regulars. Why, you'll be able to Chekhov the three fisters."

Rory chuckled convivially.

Tarquin was staggered. Thankfully, Rubens returned. Although he hadn't heard the conversation, he could immediately see that Tarquin seemed spooked. He certainly didn't appear to be enjoying having his hand fondled by the lardy gentleman by his side.

Rubens didn't appreciate the hungry look in the man's eyes.

He squared up.

"Excuse me. I need to steal my boyfriend away. Catch you later, old boy!"

No words were needed as Tarquin gladly let himself be dragged away from a suddenly scary Rory at the bar.

Tarquin grabbed Rubens' arm:

"Thank you, darling. Look after me. I need you tonight."

Despite the plethora of possibilities unfolding around him, Ben was wrestling with a particularly horny dilemma.

Having sex with a work colleague seemed a bad idea.

The very perception that he might be taking advantage of a junior member of staff was damning. And yet, there was no denying it – he felt a powerful urge to give that pert-bottomed Caspar such a right royal rogering that he would never show him insolence again.

Caspar, for his part, had no such qualms, not since a chance encounter in a New York bath house with desperately dull Don from accounts had led to a secret affair. That had been the best sex Caspar had had in forever. Caspar obviously concealed the relationship from his friends, barely even admitting to knowing who the man was. He did not need the judgement which came with shagging such a bore.

In present circumstances, Caspar had greedily taken in Ben's body. He was now quite prepared to allow Ben entry into his pantheon of secret guilty pleasures and hidden embarrassing crushes. As with dull Don, the key lay in preventing Ben from talking whilst they played. Never mind reality. Casper simply willed himself to picture the personality he would have preferred in what was undeniably a splendid physical specimen.

In a busy and time-starved life, if you can't get the perfect mind in the perfect body (which even Caspar knew was nigh on impossible), you just patchworked it all together, using alcohol or stimulants as neat stitches.

This wasn't about love or affection. It was a sensory experience, like stuffing your face with a giant cream bun.

So an unexpected game was on.

Ben nodded at Caspar.

"Do you want a hand in finding that friend of yours?"

Ben didn't believe in the existence of Wallace for one moment, but pretending to search for him meant going into dark corners. Dark corners exuded opportunity.

Caspar nodded curtly.

"Okay. Let's try through there."

The double doors at the end of the bar led to a wide corridor. The foam was ankle deep at one end and approaching knee height at the other. Beyond that, men stepped into the main dance floor of the club. Ben was momentarily distracted from his goal of seeing to Caspar by the sight of a few hundred naked men, and more foam than he had ever thought possible.

It poured out of a massive pipe in the middle of the room. People delightedly submerged themselves underneath the heaving white mass, and then staggered away, like seven-foot snowmen, desperately trying to rediscover features and breathing holes after the exhilaration of being at the centre of it all. It seemed like a gargantuan washing machine with all one's dirty washing scrambled together, legs and arms protruding in unlikely directions. It was quite a sight.

As Caspar led him across the almost invisible floor, Ben was jostled pleasantly by the enthusiastic dancers, feeling squeaky-clean flesh slipping past him. It was sensual, so much so, that he couldn't resist grabbing Caspar and pulling him back towards him.

"Whoah, Ben – you almost knocked me over."

Caspar glanced at his companion. He made sure that he had a good grope of Ben's stiffening penis under the foam as he did so. "Let's go over... there. I think I can see someone in that huddle of people who looks like Wallace."

As the only thing that could be made out in the direction Caspar was pointing was an amorphous mass of foam and shadows slightly separated off from the main room, Ben realised that was probably a cue. He followed his prey with a slippery grin on his face.

The corner was indeed being well utilised. There was plenty of action going on. The crowd was two deep around the epicentre, trying to get a closer look, or maybe even to join in. Unrequested audience participation was a common hazard at Club Adam.

Of course Caspar couldn't make out his imaginary friend, Wallace, but he did notice the stripper in the middle of it all, heavily involved with the sexy older man he had arrived with, along with Ben's two attractive friends.

This was what Caspar had been desperately seeking all weekend. He grabbed Ben's arm, not bothering to pretend any longer and barged through the crowd positioning himself neatly between Ben and Milo.

Although somewhat disconcerted at the presence of Alex and Jamal, an unwritten rule of Ben's being to avoid proximity to the erect penis of anyone he knew and did not want to have sex with, his misgivings were overpowered when Caspar bent ninety degrees, thrust his bottom towards Milo's groin and firmly took control of Ben's cock with expert lips.

Ben's brain started to dissolve. All became foamy pleasure as the group coalesced into one, the rhythmic thrustings aligning perfectly with the beat of the music. Caspar was particularly talented orally, and Ben's excitement was only sharpened by the action going on around him. The cares of the weekend disappeared as he worked towards the only goal that seemed to matter in his entire life. Career, relationships, friends and family seemed as nothing compared to the driving urgency to reach orgasm.

His objective was attained too soon. It felt good, but it was also over. It literally was just sex – the famed no-strings-attached sex that some could never manage even if they understood it in principle. Ben could handle this now. He knew how to walk away. He became aware of the grasping hands around him, and roughly detached himself from the morass. He headed off to the bathroom, leaving the remainder of the group to fade from his mind, as if they had been tuned out of the world.

Some distance away, Tarquin Henderson-Smythe had finally allowed the stimulation of the club to overcome his unsettling experience at the bar. He was not remotely desirous of actually making contact with the seething mass of bodies nearby, but the voyeur in him appreciated the artistry of some of the manoeuvres. There were clearly quite a few old masters in the group. Politely swatting away the odd digit that dared to try to touch them, he and Rubens did what they did best; a monogamous physical affair that permitted the brain to run riot with external stimuli whilst their bodies worshipped each other.

The group later congregated at the bar. Caspar had decided, in time-honoured fashion, that his guilty pleasure now felt a bit pathetic, and he was now busily working on Alex and Jamal. He was satiated for the moment, but the weekend was not over, and there were many more to come. At very least he needed a phone number, just in case the older couple didn't have the stamina that he had.

Tarquin was talking to Janusz about the art galleries of Warsaw. He was impressed that Club Adam attracted some thoughtful types, even if he was praying that Janusz would remain thoughtful, and not bring up the subject of fisting.

Ben found himself with Rubens and Milo.

"So, how are you doing, anyway, gostoso?"

Rubens' gentle smile reminded Ben that life was full of small moments of joy, despite everything that conspired to complicate things. He weighed up his answer. He had done the jealous, broken-hearted boyfriend to death when he and Rubens had dated a couple of years earlier, and he was starting to bore himself with his Scandinavian obsession. Ultimately, although he was not entirely at ease with Kelly's lack of candour, and the bruising of his ego, he had missed being a free agent. Could there possibly be a way of having Kelly's cakes and eating someone else's too?

"I'm OK, Rubens. Really, I am. Let's not talk about me. I think we've all had enough drama where my love life is concerned."

Ben turned, and grinned at the Serb standing with them.

"Milo, apart from continuing to be the brightest star in our galaxy, what's up with you?"

Milo was not much of a talker. He didn't need to be. Ben obviously wanted to direct the conversation away from himself.

Milo looked evenly at Ben, took a draught of his beer,

and then looked with some deliberation over at Janusz. He shrugged.

"A lot is good. Janusz is attractive, interesting and generous. And I like him. It's a pity that he makes me feel like a toy that he is fascinated with right now, but still a toy, that I know he will get tired of and move on from. He'll leave me like an abandoned Rubik's Cube or a broken Tamagochi. So it is. I am enjoying his money, his attention, his kindnesses even, but I can hear the clock ticking. I don't want it to end, but I know it will."

For all the time Ben had known the bartender, Milo had never come across as an upbeat, joyous character. Milo specialised in a more serious vein of thought. This little speech struck Ben as particularly poignant. Ben nodded empathetically.

Milo sighed.

"I'm really not bothered about being pimped out. I mean, he doesn't just have sex with me. He uses me to attract other guys he wishes to have to sex with. I really have no problem with that." Milo suddenly grabbed his own penis.

"I figure God gave me this as compensation for a crappy family and being brought up in a war zone, and I have used it extremely well ever since. This is the only friend I can truly rely on, the friend who always brings me money, who makes me smile, and will never stab me in the back, although he is very good at stabbing, you know."

Milo attempted a grin. Ben realised Milo was attempting a joke and smiled back. He briefly contemplated the penis that Milo was proffering as proof of the inherent untrustworthiness of others.

"I think it makes you more popular as well," offered Rubens helpfully. "Everyone likes a large penis. Even for those few who are not size queens, it generally inspires respect."

Ben had to agree. His own endowment had certainly filled the holes his stumbling personality may have occasionally left unattended. Thank goodness that in amongst his other challenges in life he had at least never had to struggle with the unbearable lightness of penis.

Milo was staring over at Janusz again.

"But, there is something funny going on. He stays in this flat in Hackney which I think belongs to this Ukrainian friend of his. Slava – the friend – drives a very flash car, and yet the flat is one of those council ones. He wears a Rolex. I found a box of fifty-pound notes when I was nosing through his bathroom cabinet."

Although trained to be suspicious of everyone, Ben was naturally uncomfortable in rushing to judgement, especially of people he had not met.

"Come on, Milo, maybe Slava is just a hard-working businessman who prefers cars to a nice house."

Milo looked evenly at Ben.

"Maybe. But there is something between Janusz and this Slava, something that all my instincts tell me I do not want to know anything about. I don't think their business involves selling organic, vegetarian pasties to nice respectable families. I can sense something wrong there. And then there was the woman. Not that I should be the judge here, but she looked like a prostitute when she got out of Slava's Maserati – all blonde hair and big tits. The weird thing was, she looked strangely familiar. I have seen her before."

Milo paused, and narrowed his eyes. It was obvious that he was trying to force unruly memory to bend to his will.

A faint, but satisfied smile came to his lips.

"I have seen this woman before. I am sure I saw her with you, Ben."

Ben started. What would he have been doing with a prostitute?

Milo must be mistaken. He shook his head:

"I don't think so. I don't usually hang out with hookers, Milo – well, not the female sort."

Ben blushed, momentarily concerned that Milo might be offended.

"Sorry. You know what I mean. Maybe she just reminds you of a lawyer? Anyhow, lovely though this is, this talk of large breasts reminds me that I have had enough of staring at cock today – not that the Penis de Milo isn't one of the better ones, of course. It's time I sent myself home."

Ben knew that he would not be able to face the washing up that evening.

9

Wine, women and all gone wrong

"Well, I never thought I would be doing this, and certainly never thought I'd like it!" Kelly smiled over her glass of wine at Cornisha. "Who knew England could actually produce a respectable red, or for that matter any wine at all?"

Wine after work was a regular ritual for Kelly and Cornisha. There were few work colleagues that one would wish to hang around with a second more than was necessary. But Kelly and Cornisha barely saw each other at work, and these sessions were better than therapy.

"They need to work harder on naming these wines," said Cornisha, pensively. "They're up against our Anglophone conviction that anything that sounds Latin will be intrinsically tastier and more romantic than what comes from England or America. That's nothing, however, that a bit of good marketing couldn't solve."

"Do you think the marketing could work on the men from round these parts, too?" Kelly smirked and took another sip.

Cornisha shrugged.

"I think even the Gods of marketing would struggle to make Englishmen as outwardly romantic as the Continentals. But we should be thankful for small mercies: at least you know where you are with the British male, once you get over the fact they find it hard to express any personal emotions at all, and feel most comfortable hiding behind a generous dollop of humour. My Arthur may not be one to make grand romantic gestures, but I know that when he does something, he means it. There's substance to it."

Cornisha took another drink.

"Rather like this wine. Have you ever been here before, by the way?"

"I haven't actually. Thank you for introducing me to yet another wine bar. You can't have too many to call on in the recurring hour of need."

"I love this place," Cornisha replied. "This is one of the very few things I do that my father might actually approve of, God rest his bitter soul. He could have come here and got pleasantly plastered on entirely English wines and spirits, not having to buy anything from Johnny Foreigner. That was of course before my mother drove him home in the Volvo, sat him on the sofa they picked up in Tuscany, and ate Boeuf Bourgignon whilst watching a repeat of an American sitcom on their Sony television. Ach, mein Papa. He was such a little Englander."

Cornisha raised her glass.

Kelly nodded:

"Jingoists. They should call a fragrance after them. They do crop up at the most unexpected moments. Like any martyr to conviction, they will never change their minds. Everything that happens to them abroad merely confirms their own worst suspicions. You know that they attract trouble. If there is one dubious waiter in the whole of a foreign capital, they will find him, get served by him, get ripped off, and dine out on the incident for the next forty years. They read tabloids that confirm every twisted prejudice that they develop. Those papers. It's a scandal what they get away with – the poison they feed to addicted eyes. They seem to be constantly moaning about everything. No one's safe. Not even the royals, whom of course the press treats with cloying adoration in the abstract, whilst masterfully and self-righteously condemning individuals, should one of them stray from the hallowed road to Queen Motherdom."

"So true," agreed Cornisha. "I'm no royalist, but I remember reading a dreadful little piece when Charles and Camilla re-opened a market a few years ago. They swung between showing how in touch the couple were buying builder's tea with milk and sugar from Maria's Market Café, but then implied privileged extravagance by Camilla's purchase of a fourteen-pound bottle of olive oil to make up for Charles' rudeness to the stallholder."

"In fairness, it is rather a lot of money for oil, no matter how organic and fair trade it might be. You could probably pick up most of the stall for fourteen pounds down Elephant & Castle's East Street Market."

Cornisha smiled approvingly:

"Now that's a real market as I remember them. Lovely fresh vegetables and meat at low prices, cheek by jowl with plastic tat that you wonder who on earth buys."

Cornisha mulled over her wine.

"I adore Borough Market, but it's about as representative of British markets as London Bridge's Shard is of English railway station architecture. Parts of Borough Market remind me of Harrods Food Hall these days, and with prices to match. Still, they have managed to turn a market in London into a tourist attraction. It's a rare British success and it gets visitors enthusiastic about our food."

"Yes – our food. Like raclette!"

As Kelly laughed, Cornisha thought of the visitor who had wolfed down *her* British food.

"There is an issue that I would very much like to get your views on, Kelly. Last night, Arthur brought home a young woman and told me that she would be living with us."

Kelly's eyes widened. This sounded unorthodox.

She frowned.

"Either my ears or the wine appear to be playing tricks on me."

"Yes, I can hear how that might have sounded." Cornisha smiled. "But it's all too real. It's quite a delicate situation, actually. It may need quite a bit of attention."

Kelly leaned in.

"Go on."

Cornisha sighed.

"The young woman's name is Polina, and she is in trouble. I think we need your help."

As Cornisha related the story to her, Kelly's first thought was to talk to Morten. This was familiar territory for him.

Morten had been involved for some time in the fight against trafficking, albeit out of Africa. But the principles and patterns were probably familiar to him. He would have the right experience – he'd know where to start. He would know people; he could offer practical advice.

And yet, before going to him, there was someone she needed to speak to first. Someone whose opinion mattered as much to her, and to whom she always instinctively raced when trouble arrived. Although it would be a difficult call, and as despicably selfish as it sounded, this poor Polina had come into the picture at the right time to make Kelly realise what she needed to do.

Kelly pulled out her phone and called Ben.

Cornisha silently applauded. Everything was going as she had hoped that it would.

Like a vampire entering a convention of virgins, Nicholas sauntered into the conference room where Hartmut was working.

Hartmut looked up, surprised.

"I've been waiting a long time to have it out with you, Hartmut."

Hartmut put his pen down and looked over his glasses at the tall slender man who was interrupting his peace.

Nicholas assumed a superior, slight world weary air. It was important to have the upper hand. His words betrayed him, though. Words do that. As he had said them, he had been conscious that he sounded tinny, pulp fictiony – like a cartoon villain. It irritated the knickers off him.

Hartmut looked at Nicholas with equanimity.

He was used to dealing with gluttons for punishment. He knew though that it was the day-in, day-out inevitability of encounters with the office nemesis that could truly bring a person down. Nicholas remained one of Hartmut's least favourite people. Hartmut had long lost any vestiges of respect for the man.

Hartmut had no intention of backing down.

He pressed his hands lightly together. Control was important.

"Nicholas, you do not like confrontation. So it comes as no surprise to me that you have done all you could to avoid it."

Nicholas held Hartmut's gaze levelly.

"Confrontation is not pleasant. However, one rule, Hartmut, in civil society, is that you do not get your own way at all times."

Hartmut moved a little closer.

"That rule is meaningless, expressed as a generality. It's a perception. What does "getting one's own way" mean? Does it mean not conforming to your world views, Mr Casterway? Am I beholden to you in some way that you cannot explain, that you might impose your views upon me?"

Nicholas stood his ground, like some dogged red neck who wasn't quite sure what the relevant legal test for standing one's ground actually was.

"Civil society is bigger than you or I, Hartmut," he said loftily.

"Than you or *me*," corrected Hartmut.

Nicholas did not waver:

"Both could be correct. What *you* don't appreciate is precisely that there is something bigger than you or... me. The firm, Hartmut. The industries that we serve. The *clients*."

His voice dipped reverentially on the last words.

Hartmut looked at him.

"What exactly are you driving at, Nicholas?"

"It has come to my attention that you are... ah... writing a book."

"Are you referring to the new edition of *Glick on Golden Handcuffs and Restraint of Trade*?"

"No I am not!" exploded Nicholas, "your moderately successful textbook is the least of my concerns!"

He jabbed a finger at his partner:

"You have written... fiction!"

Hartmut shrugged:

"And?"

Nicholas breathed deeply. It was difficult for him to articulate his views about the matter. What screamed inside him was the wrong of it all, the wrong that Hartmut was committing, the terrible insanity of a person not complying with the stereotype that they ought to fit by virtue of their occupation and/or position. Nicholas positively winced with frustration:

"Hartmut, do not play games with me. What we are discussing is the... subject matter."

"The subject matter?"

"The subject matter."

"What subject matter?"

"The. One. You. Write. About."

Hartmut looked at Nicholas:

"I really am not following this. Say it. Express yourself, Nicholas."

"No games, Hartmut. This is my question to you. Why would you throw away a brilliant career on such abominations?"

Unexpectedly, Hartmut chuckled. This really was all too ridiculous for words. Nicholas was a fanatic. Hartmut knew he would never convince him, but it would be fun to have a go.

"I am grateful for your tardy appreciation of my brilliant career. I will therefore try to explain this, Nicholas – really I will. I am however sceptical that I will succeed in getting through to you. The very language you use, your inability to articulate exactly what it is that you object to, the defensive positioning of your body all tell me that your mind is already made up. I'm not going to be able to convince you. Unlike in a commercial difference of opinion, where we could skulk around until we reached some tawdry agreement and part, not remotely abashed at the necessary compromise that we had agreed upon, this is all too public – all too polarised. You do not like my predilections. You do not own a swing, or a paddle, or a pair of handcuffs. More worryingly, you despise and are even disgusted by my dearly beloved homosexual friends."

Hartmut stopped briefly, and looked at Nicholas with pity.

"The world offers varied and diverse people. We have freedoms, here, where we are greatly fortunate to live and breathe. These freedoms have been hard fought for, hard won. They are not permanent gifts. In a situation where you raise my writing fiction on a theme that displeases you as a source of professional concern, then I can simply say this to you. You are a slave to convention, and I am free. This is more important than that glib statement might sound. The secret I would share with you is this: there is not much... cop... to convention. You're not going to have much fun with narrow-minded people. Mainstream culture has never really been where it is at, Nicholas. Fun often streams from the avant garde. If it takes me to wave a little counter-cultural flag around the arid slopes of this monolith, then – mein Gott – I shall do it!"

Hartmut squared his shoulders.

"For most kindly, well meaning, helpful people who do not believe that the struggle for freedoms continues, or who think that history is over, then what I have said so far would be enough. For you Nicholas, there is an additional point. That point is: fuck you."

Nicholas recoiled.

Hartmut continued in measured tones.

"Yes, fuck you, with your hypocrisy and your mediocrity – with your assertion of superiority about moral values, with your joining ranks with other herded animals who follow set paths, docile oxen going around in circles, tied to a pump. You do not have to like me or anything that I do – but you are not one to tell me that it is wrong, or even cause for concern."

Nicholas squared up in turn and stilled his shaking hands.

"Those who swear have already lost the argument,

Hartmut! What you say makes no sense. You do not understand decency and propriety. You have no place amongst us. You are a *deviant*. Let me tell you this: this is not over. I am off to the Pan Pacific conference so do not have the time to deal with this more fully at present, but I will return. When I return, Hartmut, you will hear a great deal more about this."

Hartmut waved ironically:

"Gute Nacht, Nicholas. When you return I shall still be here. I am not going to leave because of you."

"We'll see about that. I'll whip you into shape, rest assured of that."

"I thought you'd never offer, mein klein partnerial pal."

After Club Adam, Milo had been surprised to receive a call from Janusz.

Milo knew that when he was being treated like a sex toy, interest usually faded as fast as it had surged. Not that anyone seemed to care in the slightest, but Milo was also in possession of a functioning brain, which he occasionally enjoyed using.

Although he liked the mysterious Polish man, Milo had ruminated over the situation at length. He had concluded that he would be neither the man's trophy nor his toy. He had therefore declined the latest invitation to drinks. It always hurt to end a relationship with a person that you wished could change just enough to become relationship material, but in his heart Milo knew that it was for the best. Janusz was simply the latest in a line of men who had never really shown any interest in Milo beyond the obvious.

Milo wondered if blondes with enormous boobs felt the same way about their endowments as he did about his. It was both a blessing, and his greatest curse. He was defined by his dick, measured by his member, coveted for his cock, even paid for the penis that made him a minor celebrity on the London scene.

In turn he had come to lean on it, like the third leg people likened it to. Milo was self-reliant. He had come through far tougher episodes in life than the London dating scene. However, when it came to meeting men, he had lost confidence in his ability to be appreciated for himself. Apart from Janusz, pretty much all the men that made advances to him already knew him from his work. Milo couldn't help feeling that he had just become the "I shagged the stripper" boast of the morning after.

He had almost given up trying to escape his role. He mostly went through with his partners' fantasies. Not that he didn't enjoy the sex: in fact he had started to take pleasure in really giving it hard to the men who had made it so obvious what they really were interested in. *If you think you can take it, then…*

Janusz had seemed different. There had been a genuine spark between them. The Pole had seemed to pick up on Milo's simmering sexuality, always on the point of boiling over with just the right touch of heat. After Milo had told Janusz bluntly that it was over on the telephone, Janusz simply turned up at Outrageous Fortune, alone.

This reignited the old flame – just enough. There was Janusz, insolent and confident, looking straight at Milo. Whatever the future may bring, Milo thought, one more night, one last night with Janusz, would be a fitting end to the rollercoaster ride.

Janusz gestured lazily at Milo.

"Take care with the hot water in the shower, you remember what it is like here. That boiler is on the blink. I keep telling Slava to fix his damn heating system, so we can have reliable services to go with all of this luxury, but does he listen to his old friend?"

Lying on the bed, Janusz exuded confidence in his nakedness.

Milo shook his head sadly. Janusz seemed more attractive after they had had sex than before. Milo recognised the danger sign flashing red, but now allowed himself to dream. It had been a long time since anyone had made him feel this way, and perhaps Milo *could* put up with the mystery, the shady surroundings of this too cool council flat, and even the foibles of the water heater that made taking a shower seem like bathing in Llandudno in January with the occasional kettle of scalding water thrown over you. He felt he would put up with all of this as long as Janusz made him feel the way that he did in that moment.

Milo wished he had pulled on more than his underwear when he bumped into Slava, who was exiting the bathroom.

Slava was wrapped in a towel, having just finished the trauma Milo was about to face.

"Go in, my friend, the water is lovely. I don't know why Amber never wants to take a shower here."

Slava flashed a grin at Milo, who although he disliked and distrusted the Ukrainian, couldn't help but track the tattoos around Slava's muscled physique. He could see why Amber was so keen to get it on with him.

Slava noticed the younger man looking at him. He laughed. He clapped Milo on the shoulder, stared intently into his eyes, and put his free hand down to his towel.

"I think you want to see where this ink finishes, right?"

Slava started to undo his towel revealing another couple of inches of flesh. He then abruptly withdrew his hand from Milo's shoulder and stepped back, doing up his towel as he did so.

"I am only teasing you, my friend. Unlike Janusz, I am not at all attracted by the cock, no matter how big and beautiful it might be."

Slava glanced at the swollen goods in Milo's underpants.

"Although, speaking as a businessman, you are quite a proposition, Milo."

Usually, when a man was eying Milo's groin, the Serb felt a surge of power. It was a familiar occurrence. Men fell under Milo's spell.

With Slava, however, he felt no such thing. The older man's threatening grin made Milo uneasy. Slava looked like a farmer working out how to maximise the return from a young bull, that he may or may not turn into steaks.

Milo felt more than a little vulnerable under Slava's hard gaze.

Slava gestured.

"Show me that cock of yours. And please don't be shy, I know what you have just been doing with it."

Milo generally reacted badly to orders like that, and yet he mechanically dropped his underwear. He was afraid of Slava, and felt uncharacteristically powerless to resist. He felt stupid, almost violated, standing there naked being surveyed like property – and yet he meekly complied, not wanting to make an enemy of the Ukrainian. There were some people one really should not pick a fight with. Milo was acutely aware that Slava would make a very bad enemy indeed.

"Huh. I think you are wasted in that bar."

Slava was all smiles again, the businessman's cold assessment now replaced by the hiring manager's charm.

"I could find a much better use for your talents in one of my businesses. I am sure we could both make some good money. However, go wash that thing of yours, you smell of sex. We can talk business another time; I need to bury my face in Amber's breasts again."

Milo had the briefest of showers. The water heater had a worse attitude than its owner. In any case he would never be able to feel clean with Slava present in that flat. Milo wrapped himself up in a towel and headed back to the relative safety of the bedroom.

Slava had beaten him to it. He was talking to Janusz.

"I think we should use this Milo of yours. There is always a market for men with assets like his. I have been thinking about how to diversify for some time."

Milo pricked up his ears when he heard his name.

He loitered outside the door, keen to hear how Janusz would respond, unsure about interrupting.

Janusz spoke up.

"He should certainly be making more money than he does in that bar. And that means that we could also turn a profit on him."

Milo's heart sank as he heard Janusz describe him in such terms. So, he had been right all along: the Pole was just using him and would not think twice at selling him to the highest bidder. It was time to get out.

Janusz continued.

"Milo has a strong personality. The lights are on behind his eyes. He is intelligent, and interesting – worth getting to know. I think he is tired of being seen as a stripper and wants to be appreciated for his mind. I have become quite fond of him, actually."

Milo's heart leapt. He smiled in the dark to himself. Maybe there was hope after all.

From inside the bedroom, Janusz continued.

"But regardless of any personal attachment I may have to Milo, he would make a difficult employee for you. He may act like a deer in the headlights when you catch him nearly naked, but that is just his smart telling him not to piss you off in your domain. If you try to control him, try to make him do things he does not want to do, that Serb will rebel. Milo and his large cannon is good, very good – but Milo the loose cannon would cause a lot of damage. We would not want another Polina situation on our hands, would we?"

Milo's brows knitted. Wasn't Polina the name of that girl who came to the bar with Janusz, the first time he had met him?

Slava spoke again, aggression seething in every word.

"That bitch will regret challenging me. I will leave her in a state that no one will be able to look at her, never mind think of paying the whore."

Milo shivered in his towel. His instinct had served him well. He pitied that poor girl Polina. Milo had no doubt that Slava would follow up words with actions. Milo felt frozen to the spot, unable to move. It seemed impossible to now pretend that he had just arrived from the bathroom.

Slava continued.

"I also fired the manager of Eve's Garden. He was lucky I did not break his legs. Amber will do a much better job. I have persuaded her to take the role. She already has some interesting ideas about how we can track Polina down. At some point Polina will call or visit her parents. Amber wants to meet her. And I like Warsaw – especially at this time of year."

Milo had forgotten about Amber. He turned from the door of Janusz' room to peer down the corridor to where he supposed Amber and her large breasts were awaiting Slava's return. Unfortunately for Milo, they had got tired of waiting and had been standing silently next to him, watching as he eavesdropped upon the conversation. Amber walked up to Milo and pushed open the bedroom door, ushering him in like a farm dog directing a delinquent sheep.

"Milo has been simply *fascinated* by all you had to say about Polina. He couldn't tear himself away from your conversation."

Amber had a delicately venomous tone to her voice, which made Milo shudder. She was a great match for Slava. She looked with some contempt at the men on the bed.

"Whilst I am pleased you like my ideas for revenge on our little runaway, I do think you could be a little more careful in what you say, when there are such impressionable young ears around here."

Milo's eyes were fixed on Slava. The tattooed, muscular torso, which, under different circumstances, would have been quite a turn-on for Milo, now served to underline the scale of the threat this man could pose. Slava had nothing of the *Look-at-me-Barbie-Show* of an Ibiza gay beach in August, and everything of the menacing gang member who backed up evil intent with brute force. Amber pushed Milo further into the room, demonstrating surprising strength herself.

"Get in there, you. Oh, and you won't be needing *that*."

Amber smartly stripped the towel from around him, leaving Milo standing naked.

She closed the door behind her.

"My," said Amber, surveying Milo in the same forensic way Slava had. "Maybe we could find a place for him somewhere."

She turned to Janusz: "Who knew you were a size queen?"

No one laughed.

Standing naked in front of an audience normally made Milo feel powerful, proud and validated. It was strange how things turned out. Tonight he had never felt more humiliated.

Slava looked at him.

"I know I should be more original, Milo, but quite simply, if you talk about this to anyone I will cut your cock off. Then you will be no use to anyone, certainly not my partner here."

Janusz was still lying, almost naked, on the bed, seemingly immune to both the tension and the threats.

"Milo, Milo. You now need to think very carefully about how you will answer, and also how you will behave."

There was no threatening tone to Janusz's words.

He shrugged.

"In my younger, more romantic days, I might have leapt to your defence, but we both know that is not going to happen if you misbehave."

"Whatever happened to Baby Janusz?" Amber allowed herself a smirk. "I think it is time you called your toy boy a taxi."

She walked over to Milo and got hold of him by the chin, forcing him to look at her.

"But before you go, Milo, don't imagine for one instant that Slava's is an empty threat. If we hear one rumour about this, then we will come after you – and we know where to find you."

She paused, a look of delighted sadism glinting in her eyes, as she reached down and took Milo's shivering genitals in her hand, applying just enough pressure to make Milo take a sharp intake of breath:

"Never mind slicing it off. I've always wondered what it would be like to crush a man's testicles under my high heels. And I don't mean in some S&M pleasurable pain way."

Milo started involuntarily as Amber increased the pressure.

"So, my dear boy, you whisper a word of this to anyone, and, one way or another, you will be working as a eunuch for us for the rest of your natural days."

Amber released her grip, but not before giving one last hard squeeze, just to make sure Milo would be sore for some time and would not forget.

Slava had been watching the scene with approval. Amber was going to make an excellent madam. She had the right qualifications – glamour, smartness and ruthlessness, combined with a twist of pleasure at inflicting pain. There should be no more Polinas on her watch. The girls would be too frightened of her to dare to disobey.

It was time to cut the boy some slack. Give him some hope. Slava was not used to playing the good cop, but after Amber's performance, he needed to restore the balance.

"But none of this has to happen, Milo."

He handed him his towel with a broad smile. "We should not be enemies. I truly believe that you could have a great career with us, and you could earn some good money. Janusz has got exceptional taste in men *and* women. We will leave you two to finish off, and I will be in touch with you. In a few months' time we will all be laughing over this night as we drink champagne and celebrate our success together. Or so I hope," he added darkly.

It would not have done to be too much of a good cop.

Slava needn't have worried. Milo had had enough experience of dangerous situations to know when people were serious or not.

He would keep his mouth shut tight. Poor Polina.

Monique and Jake sat quietly in the still evening.

A copy of Sizzle! magazine lay between them, like a

sword between two lovers.

If only it were anything as noble as that, thought Monique. Maybe it'd be better styled as a blunt knife, which could still hurt deeply when used with enough force, and with no where near the finery and slickness of a Seppuku blade.

The photos were unmistakeable. They did not look good.

Monique was calm.

"So. They said you went out with her."

Jake nodded.

"They are right. Seven of us met up. Her boyfriend was there."

Monique grimaced.

"He's not in this photograph. And… you're kissing her."

"It's a trick of the light. I'm giving her a damned good public hug. I'm not kissing her any differently than I would kiss my mother."

"Oedipus-tastic," said Monique evenly. "Are you saying that they have cropped this photo to isolate you?"

"Of course – this is the oldest trick in publication – and you know it as well as I do. They cut the one the day before to show just me and her exiting a restaurant. Come on, there's a video clip of that. You can see how manipulated the photo was. Her boyfriend was literally just next to her. One careful re-centering of the shot, and it looks like a date between her and me."

"Why are they doing this?"

Jake looked puzzled.

"You know why. You see it all the time, with others.

It's crisis creation. It is more interesting for them than us being happy."

They both paused and looked over the grainy photographs, feeling as if the cheap tabloid ink might stain their fingers.

Monique wrapped her arms around herself.

"It's the *pity* that I can't stand. People will now look at me, you know? It's as if they imagine that I don't know what is going on, or what is being said."

"The world – if this represents anything like the world – would like nothing better than for us not to be getting along."

"Is that any different to the world wishing us ill?"

"It's no difference at all. But really – you have to learn to live with it. People will always talk. People will project onto you. It's sport to them. They don't care, really – and to be perfectly honest, why should they? The world does wish us ill. Our unhappiness would make people feel better about their own lot. In some ways, it's our gift to this world audience. We must shut out that world. They know nothing."

Monique remained quiet.

Jake knelt in front of her.

"We know what this is like. We've been here before."

"It doesn't really help to know that. It is upsetting. It's not only the inaccuracy. It's the clumsy meanness of it all – as if my feelings were worthless."

"Feelings are among the top things that psychopaths don't understand. A journalist is not looking to accommodate feelings at the best of times. A tabloid journalist is positively out to get reactions. And you get those by tweaking the tiger's tail."

"Kelly says successful corporate lawyers are psychopaths. If journalists are too, are there any nice people left?"

"Yes, but it's hard to be nice and to get on in life. Ultimately everyone wants their fifteen minutes of fame. Everyone's jostling for attention. Most of us want to be noticed by our childhood heroes, and don't care overly much about who we stamp on in the process. We're just a bit too childish around attention. We crave that. We crave relevance. You and I are closer to fame than most others. We perhaps have to pay for the attention and relevance – such as it is – somehow."

"Well, you are close to fame – so close you're snogging it. I'm a hanger on."

"You're *my* hanger on. I'm lucky to have a decent one – a beautiful and brilliant one."

Monique looked again at the photographs.

"It feels like an attack."

"I know. But you know the reality of it."

"What about the truth?"

"The truth is very hard to communicate at the best of times."

Monique looked closely at the woman in the photographs.

"I resent her, that's for sure. Why is she not defending this? She hasn't debunked the position at all."

Jake laughed softly:

"I think – and I know you won't like this – that she is flattered. It's just possible that she may imagine that this is helping her. You know better than me that you need to stay in the fickle public eye. So there needs to be news about you, if you're playing that game. You've got to continue to be a known known. This exposure may be making her more glamorous by association. A possibility of a fling with me is more newsworthy than whatever the position is with her current squeeze. Look, I don't condone it – but emerging from the mass of wannabes is a tough call. She's invested a lot in this – taken risks. Why would she rush to deny something that – frankly – makes her more interesting?"

"Because it upsets me?"

"You count for very little in her calculations. For that matter, so do I. Don't let it get to you. Never mistake people who are using you with friends. When you are being used with the appropriate amount of charm and financial reward, you find yourself living with it. It's a job."

"No wonder people despise fame."

"Yes, no wonder. Especially those who wanted it and never quite got there."

"Some people genuinely don't aspire to be famous."

"I think to reject it properly you need to have experienced it. But I can well understand those who do flee it. It's as exposed as a desert out there these days. Wander out without taking precautions and you'll end up one of those sun-scorched skeletons – with your jaw seized in a permanent scream."

Monique smiled sadly:

"The glare of the limelight leaves precious little room for subtlety. You're right. It *is* like heading out in the baking sun and realising a little too late that in only a short while you will be roasted alive. Yet the sunshine seems so inviting from the edge, from the shadows. And the people in the sun seem so pretty, and happy, and blessed."

"No more, no less than anyone else. There are advantages to fame, too – no doubt about it."

They sat quietly, heads together. Love was hard enough when there were fewer choices. It was harder still when choices abounded.

Perhaps cutting off the world was the only way to manage?

"Sometimes I want to lock you in a room and keep you to myself," said Monique.

"Sometimes I would be happy to head right in there. Be brave. We'll try to plot a course through all this. Please stay on the road with me."

Milo had lived through far worse than being humiliated and threatened by a pimp and his moll. All the same, his experience at Slava's Hackney pad had left him with a sense of disquiet.

Maybe it was only when a menace appeared on the horizon that he realised how peaceful and secure his life in London was. All the problems and issues that the British and their media endlessly droned on about, such as misery caused by a tube strike, really were first world problems.

Milo had experienced proper misery, which was somewhat more serious than *a nightmare bus journey*. For the first time since London had become his sanctuary, Milo was waking up with an uneasy feeling.

He felt he should do something, but he was afraid to do it.

As he stepped off the bus at Elephant & Castle, Milo wondered why Rubens wanted to see him outside of work. The bar seemed to be working well, no money had gone missing, and so he wasn't expecting to be admonished about anything.

It couldn't be that. After all, they were meeting at Ben's flat which was hardly the place for a dressing down. The idea was to go out for a drink. Apparently Tarquin was away in New York or some such art-selling place, and so Rubens was free.

Milo would have liked a garden. If Janusz had not been such a criminal and a terrible human being, it might just have been possible.

Milo sighed. The chances of him ever achieving what Rubens had were pretty slim. He was grateful to his new home for many things, but London was hardly the easiest place to find a good partner and an affordable place to live that a hamster wouldn't dismiss as too bijou.

"Evening, Milo."

Milo liked Arthur Bilks. He didn't waste words, and always seemed even-tempered. He wished he had a father more like Arthur, and less like the bad excuse of a parent that his real father had been. Milo greeted Arthur warmly and thanked him for the directions, efficiently given, to Ben's flat.

He couldn't decide whether he liked the Castle Lofts or not. The modern block of flats was one of a number of ugly buildings built by a financially constrained council. It could have been a straight transplant from the communist bloc. And yet, now that Elephant & Castle was finally, really, changing with all its ultra-modern blocks and skyscrapers, the Castle Lofts were acquiring a semi-historical air. It wasn't quite Hampton Court Palace, but it represented an epoch that Milo thought worthy of preservation.

"Milo, come in!"

Ben opened the door wide, and gave Milo a hug as he walked in. Milo liked Ben, but it felt awkward. Milo was not into such displays, and he didn't really think Ben was, either. Rubens' greeting was of course far more natural. Even Milo felt a touch Carioca after an embrace from the man from Rio.

Ben was effusive.

"So, how are things, Milo? What's new with that mysterious man of yours?"

Ben had a twinge as he remembered the scene at Club Adam, wishing for a moment that Rubens wasn't there and he could have an inappropriate private session with Milo.

"I think it has run its course, I am afraid." Milo hesitated. He wanted to tell Rubens and Ben about what had happened. However, although he felt stronger now he was away from that place, his instinct still told him to avoid poking bears unless he had a very large stick indeed.

"Oh, that's a pity," lied Ben, as he wondered if there might now be a chance. If Kelly was able to enjoy a whole smorgasbord of delights, well why couldn't he at least fantasise about a taste of Serbian sausage?

"He was weird, Milo," said Rubens. "I do not think it is a pity at all. I think you are well out of that. We've all been there. You had your fun, and that is it."

Rubens was far more direct than Ben could ever be. Ben

wondered how Rubens could know how Milo was feeling. Maybe Milo was really hurt.

Milo was actually thinking that Rubens had understood the situation better than he realised. The Brazilian could be a shrewd judge of character. Rubens had exhibited a tough streak before, when being wrongly accused of theft had once almost got him fired. Milo narrowed his eyes. He really wanted to share his burden with Rubens. But he couldn't.

Rubens gesticulated confidently.

"Never mind all that. On a much more positive note, I have a proposal for you, Milo. I need a deputy manager in the bar. I have discussed this with Jamal and Alex, and we would like you to take that position. It's more work, but more money too. What do you say?"

The last time Rubens had talked to Milo about his future in the bar, it was to tell him that he did not have one. How things changed. Did this mean that someone was actually going to give him responsibility that went beyond tantalising customers?

"That is amazing, Rubens. Yes. Yes."

Milo smiled weakly, feeling slightly dazed. Had he really heard right? What a time to be promoted.

Ben clapped his hands.

"Do please look a little more excited. It's another thing we might drink to tonight."

Ben hated it when he fancied someone. He seemed incapable then of communicating without sounding slightly idiotic. Or clapping. Who clapped, these days?

For the first time since the episode with Slava in Hackney,

Milo smiled properly. Rubens had always been on his side. Milo had been working as Rubens' unofficial right hand man recently. Milo knew he could do the job. He didn't get distracted by all the fluff around him. Rubens' offer was real. It made complete sense.

"Rubens, thank you. I am happy to be given the chance to prove myself."

He embraced Rubens. The two men shared similar backgrounds, bonds forged in difficult times. They had built trust between them.

As Milo sat down again, he felt tearful.

Milo never cried. Never. Not through the horrors he had witnessed when his country fell apart in the nineties. Strangely little when his parents were killed. Certainly never over work. He couldn't actually remember the last time he had felt even close to tears. Yet, after the shaking of his security by Slava and Janusz, the evidence that there remained true relationships in his life, people who cared for him, knew him and would push him forward, finally pierced him.

Maybe because it had been such a long time coming, Milo was shedding tears, to Rubens' surprise and Ben's utter discomfort.

"Hey, Milo, we didn't put anything in the drink. It's just vodka. What's wrong?"

Milo looked at Rubens, his eyes glistening. He breathed in. Enough was enough now.

"I also have something to say to you."

Suddenly Milo wondered why he had ever thought it was a good idea keeping the threat to himself. Of course he should tell Rubens. He should have told him right away. And Ben too. He remembered the part Ben had played a couple of years earlier in saving his reputation.

"I really did like Janusz. As you both know I also accepted money from him."

Milo stopped. He wondered if Ben judged him for still moonlighting as a gigolo, despite now having a regular job in Outrageous Fortune.

Ben's face betrayed no hint of judgement. Who was he to judge anyone? He had fallen into this role himself once, years earlier. It was also easy to judge when you had plenty of other good money-making options bequeathed to you by a fine education and documents from the right country. Besides, lawyers sold more than their bodies to their clients. They frequently sold their consciences. Ben remembered one loud lawyer who openly mocked medical claimants while acting for a tobacco company. Attempting to settle the definition of what is disgusting can lead to an interesting conversation.

But Ben was not as virtuous as some of his thoughts were. Ultimately, Ben was in predator mode. He wondered if his prey was hurt, and open to the possibility of someone, like himself, kissing it all better, and making it all feel alright – at least for a while.

Milo continued.

"It's a strange thing when money mixes with sex."

He paused again. He decided to direct his comments at Ben. He wanted to ask Rubens if he had felt the same way – but wasn't sure how much Ben knew. The last thing he wanted was to embarrass his boss. Some kind of explanation might smooth the way.

"So you know, Ben, I got used to the quick jobs with the ugly or old men, even if it was weird. I told myself that I was their only option for sex with someone they actually fancied. In turn, they were my only option if I wanted to stay in this city and actually experience something of the golden life I saw around me."

Milo was fully aware that the vast majority of new Londoners performed a whole array of menial tasks to make ends meet without resorting to what he did. Doubtless most of them had higher moral standards than he did, but at least he wasn't hurting anyone. He was just providing a service for which there had been demand since human history began.

"Even the repeat customers I could cope with. I would always treat them respectfully, provided they did the same to me, which the majority did. Then there were the customers who really didn't need to pay. The ones who, with a bit of effort, could have taken themselves to the nearest bar or club or sauna and picked up for free."

Milo realised he had neglected his vodka. He remedied the situation. Alcohol seemed the right bedfellow for this conversation.

"I think some wanted the thrill of the forbidden, and some were just too damn lazy to try. With some of them I used to really enjoy myself. These were guys who I would have had sex with for free – and then at the end I am a hundred pounds richer. That was easy."

Milo took a deep breath.

"And then there are the ones like Janusz who want their

convenience, but most of all are addicted to the power of being able to buy pretty much anything they want. Even more than sex, they are trying to buy control."

Like the professional barman that he was, Rubens had ably refilled Milo's glass without interfering with the flow of the conversation.

Milo sipped again and continued.

"Whichever type of customer I get, because I consider that the guys give me money to give them a good time, well, I try to be nice to them. Of course, some of them seem to think that I really like them. They seem to forget that I am only there because a commercial transaction is occurring. I used to think they were so stupid."

Ben reflected that it wasn't that different for him. He had plenty of clients with whom he had spent merry evenings over dinner and drinks, whom he found crashing bores. Thank God sex had never been on the menu. Milo carried on, interrupting Ben's musings.

"And yet, every so often, I do have a client that I could really imagine being something more. Janusz was one of these. That is why I now feel stupid myself."

Milo felt a pang of sadness as he remembered the nights during his relationship with the Pole when Janusz wouldn't call him, when he had had to coldly remind himself that it was just a sale and purchase agreement. Thoughts were the worst ever companions to unexpected feelings. They were like weapons that Milo turned upon himself, spewing the shrapnel of reality, shredding his fragile dreams.

Although, for Rubens, there was nothing particularly surprising, or new in what Milo said, other than the fact that Milo was teetering dangerously close to admitting he could feel love, he sensed that the Serb was leading them somewhere.

Milo was in control of his emotions. Most of them, anyway. When his humiliation had occurred, he had been intimidated by Slava. This, combined with his crush on Janusz, had suppressed any fury. He now felt anger well up inside him:

"I really felt something for Janusz. I really hoped that he could see me as something more than just a pizza delivered to his door to satisfy a momentary craving. But that was never going to happen. If I needed proof of that, then it happened a few days ago."

Milo took a deep breath. Rubens sensed that he had got to the important bit. He leaned forward.

"I should have told you straight away. I overheard a conversation between Janusz and Slava that I should not have. Worse, I got found out. They then threatened to cut my dick off if I talked."

Rubens stared at Milo open-mouthed.

Ben reached for his drink, and spoke slowly but firmly.

"Well, now, that's not funny. Milo, start from the beginning. We need details."

Ben's mind was racing as Milo recounted the night's happenings. The only information that Milo had was the first names of the people involved, and the address of the flat in Hackney. It wasn't really enough to launch a case or get the police involved. This Polina had seemingly disappeared off the face of the earth, leaving just the threat to investigate. It would then be Milo's word against that of

Slava, Janusz and Amber – if indeed these were even their real names.

Hang on, hold your horses, thought Ben. There was something in Milo's description of Amber that sounded uncannily like his nemesis at work. Amber was not a common name.

"Milo, let's go over something again. Is it correct that you said that this Amber woman was blonde, good-looking, slim but with very generous breasts, which she liked to show to their best advantage? Also that she turned from being a coquettish girlfriend into a snarling viper who seemed to enjoy the threats even more than the men did?"

Milo nodded. He was angry. He had fought so many years to let go of his innate desire for revenge when wronged, but now he wanted to give full flow to it.

Ben rummaged for his phone, and started flicking through photos.

"Just a minute, Milo."

Eventually he found what he was looking for. It was a rather awkward group photo of the Sagworth Turner Dickerhint LGBTQ committee posing with the HR department.

Amber Bluett was in business attire, but Milo still recognised her.

"You *know* this woman? Do not tell me she is a friend of yours?"

Milo's eyes were flashing fire. Ben hurriedly assured Milo that Amber Bluett was in no way a friend of his. The very thought, he assured him, was ludicrous. The woman was a menace and of course firmly ensconced in his law firm. No one ever seemed to mind that she was a fearful bully. She was allowed to sail on through. Sadistic morons needed jobs too – that was the only way, Ben explained, that he could rationalise it for himself.

Notwithstanding the evidence, Ben was having trouble processing all these facts. How did this even begin to make sense? Was Amber Bluett involved in human trafficking? How on earth had she progressed into this? Was there some sort of manual on how to penetrate the Kingdom of Evil that he had failed to spot in the firm's policy documents?

He needed to talk this through with someone. If he was going to take down Amber once for all then he knew exactly who he wanted by his side. Despite his irritation with her recent sexploits, his mind raced to Kelly.

Just then Ben's telephone rang.

He stared at the phone, shook his head at the coincidence, and answered:

"Hi, Kelly. This is funny. I was just about to call you. I think you'll be properly taken aback by this."

10

The road to hell

United by something greater than themselves, and focusing on the neck up for a change, Ben and Kelly agreed to meet at Ben's flat the next day.

Ben eyed the bottles on his kitchen worktop.

His bar had never been so well-stocked. It had evolved over time, like a child growing up.

Ben recalled with a shudder the start of the collection: cheap bottles of spirits, and wine to strip paint with – an alcoholic kaleidoscope of weird, wonderful and downright bizarre offerings. As Ben spread his wings and travelled more, he added to the display. He bought intriguing liquors from overseas that somehow never got drunk, and curdled in their corners like old people in a nursing home.

Now, he bought better stuff, a little absent-mindedly, often ending up with six bottles of vodka and just the one of gin. Ben's wine had also moved up several rungs on the quality scale. It was distinctly more palatable now. Alcohol offered straightforward pleasures, but Ben also appreciated it as a crutch in times of need.

Today he eyed his bar gratefully. It would help to

smooth out the situation ahead.

Kelly was on her way over to discuss recent events, and she had insisted on bringing Morten with her. Ben had frowned on the suggestion. Kelly had pointed out that Morten had specific experience of what they were discussing. He had expertise. This was valuable: Ben could not disagree with that.

He liked Morten, despite the obvious inconvenience of his entanglement with Kelly. Life and likes could be undesirably confusing in that way.

He tapped his fingers nervously. Would it be rude to start before his guests? Could he plead a medicinal need? It was quite a stressful situation, and the visitors were late.

Just then the intercom sounded. *Please be Kelly!*

"Hello, is that Ben? It's Morten here."

Crap!

"Hi Morten. Come in. Lifts are past reception. It's the top floor."

Ben had a few minutes. He skipped to the bathroom like an insecure teenager, and eyed himself in the mirror. The polo shirt was tight enough to show the definition of his chest, but loose enough to imply that this was unintentional. The jeans were decidedly skinny, but then it seemed that every man under the age of forty put his pins on display these days. Ben was fortunate to have good legs. In skinny jeans, his did not look like awkwardly joined sausages.

This was a small but significant mercy for the world at large. If only others could be as considerate.

Ben quickly sprayed some cologne on, and then wished that he hadn't.

There was a soft knock. He opened the door, and greeted Morten, who seemed perfectly relaxed, looking cool and handsome in a pair of khaki Bermuda shorts and a fitted white T-shirt.

Ben gave him what he considered to be a manly smile and invited him into the flat with a slightly extravagant wave. Needless to say, his overfamiliar next door neighbour walked past. Seeing Morten walk in, he gave Ben an exaggerated wink and both thumbs up.

Ben managed to avoid rolling his eyes, failed to return an empathic grin, and quickly shut the door.

"Can I get you a drink?" asked Ben, pointing at the bottles, and hoping that Morten wouldn't ask him to use the kettle. Thankfully, Morten asked for his vodka to be strong with just a splash of tonic.

Ben smiled with relief as he cracked a tray of ice cubes.

"I am so glad not to be drinking alone. I did wonder if you might be tee-total. You know, being a doctor, and off in Africa saving lives most of the time."

"Good God, no. You don't know many doctors, do you? I wouldn't get by without a few drinks every so often. Sometimes it's only the thought of a large stiff one at the end of the day that keeps me going."

"Hear, hear," smirked Ben.

He wondered if Morten was oblivious to the double entendre, or if it was the quirky, understated Swedish sense of humour coming out. It wasn't easy to tell.

The intercom buzzed again. Kelly's ascent was covered by talk of the merits of vodka brands and the success of designer gin. The medium of alcohol was wafting Ben through yet another potentially awkward moment. Praise be to spirits galore.

"Hi Ben. Oh, hello Morten. You got here before me."

For a moment Kelly hovered in the doorway, wondering whether she should give the men a kiss. She decided to keep things business-like and strode in, not touching either of them.

Ben poured her a glass of wine which she clutched gratefully.

Where to sit? Ben had an armchair and a sofa in his lounge. Without waiting to be invited, Kelly bagged the armchair. Sitting next to either man with the other present would have felt odd.

It felt good to be with Kelly again, thought Ben. It was nice to see her. It was enormously peculiar that the cause of Ben's negative feelings was sitting next to him. Meanwhile, Morten continued to seem very much at home. Ben was flummoxed. Then again, it probably stood to reason that if Morten was used to educating people, dealing with red tape and treating the sick in field hospitals in various African countries, a love triangle in the safety of London held little concern for him. Ben wished he could be as calm and unperturbed.

He thought they should get on with the matter.

"So where do we begin? It sounds like we have stories to share. Show me yours and I'll show you mine," he added with a diffident smile.

Kelly thought Ben's clumsy attempts at humour were rather endearing. Despite his physical stature, he retained elements of adolescent awkwardness which lent him, to

Kelly's eyes at least, a delicious vulnerability. And yet it was that same lack of assurance in Ben that had made Morten's self confidence so attractive to her. It was a conundrum. Was it so greedy of her, so terribly wrong, to think that she needed them both, in order to knit together the perfect man? She would have to get back to herself on that one. The rules of attraction were impossible to reconcile with ordinary moral standards.

Be that as it may, for the time being, they needed to concoct a plan regarding Polina.

Kelly nodded. It was time to get to the point, so she launched in.

"I've already touched on this with Morten when I asked him to come today – but in a nutshell we're here because Cornisha has an unexpected lodger. She is a Polish woman who was sold a story of a job in London, only to be drugged, raped and then blackmailed into having to work as a pole dancer. After a while she says that she decided to take her chances and escape with the help of Harry Gumpert – yes, I know: what was he doing there? He's a partner at Sagworth Turner Dickerhint, Morten – can you believe it? Let's park that: I think it's the least of the issues, though we'd all like to know the answer. More pressingly, our private dancer is scared that the criminals running the show will come after her or her parents in Warsaw."

Ben stared at Kelly, thunderstruck. Surely this couldn't be a coincidence. Ben spoke slowly.

"Is her name Polina?"

It was Kelly's turn to look amazed. Ben quickly filled his guests in about the conversation he had had with Milo.

Kelly spoke excitedly.

"So now we have witnesses. It's no longer just Polina's word against the others. And we know the name of the place – although I probably could have just asked Harry. I think we may have enough to make a case and get the police involved."

Ben smiled. There was one piece of information that he had not yet shared.

"There's something else. And you are not going to believe this."

He paused theatrically.

"This Slava has a girlfriend, who is also the new manager at Eve's Garden after they sacked the one who let Polina escape."

Kelly felt let down.

"I hardly see how that's relevant, Ben, as she wasn't even around when Polina ran away."

"True," admitted Ben, "but she did threaten Milo in no uncertain terms."

"Milo's word against hers. Where would this get us? I think we should ignore her and concentrate on the bigger fish."

Kelly was slightly irritated by the way that Ben was smiling at her. Surely he realised how serious this was.

Morten stayed silent, listening attentively.

"Well, we can ignore her if you want. Although we do have a name." Ben paused again, amused by the look of growing exasperation on Kelly's face. He knew she wanted to get down to action and plan what to do next. Ben was rather enjoying himself.

"So? Who is she?" Kelly was ready to slap Ben if he didn't stop behaving like a silly schoolgirl.

Ben decided he had strung Kelly along enough.

"You are *not* going to believe this, Kelly, but Slava's girlfriend is none other than our dear old friend, Amber Bluett. Milo remembered her name. He instantly recognised a photo of her."

Kelly wasn't often speechless.

She gawped like a goldfish. Then she felt angry.

What *was* it with some people, some people like Amber, who *always* seemed to get away with bad behaviour? Amber was a criminally-minded harpy, a rehabilitation-proof bigot who only ever thought of herself.

Kelly could not think of anyone who deserved a comeuppance more. After all this time, Amber still seemed to be getting away with it.

Anger was soon overtaken by a thrill of excitement.

This time, at long last, they might just have enough to take the woman down.

Kelly spoke animatedly.

"This is good, Ben. Well, not good, but, well, you know what I mean. I reckon we should be able to tie her into the trafficking of those poor women, and we can certainly get her sacked from Sagworth Turner Dickerhint."

Kelly's eyes flashed at the thought of finally meting out justice to the woman who had tried to ruin her life.

Ben felt much the same way.

"All true enough, but we need to plan this carefully. We don't want to screw anything up so she wriggles free again. The focus should remain on Polina's difficulties."

Ben wondered for a moment if he had done well to tell Kelly about Amber. Suddenly justice for Polina seemed to have faded from his girlfriend's mind, eclipsed by thoughts of revenge on their nemesis.

Kelly nodded.

"You're quite right, Ben. This is why Morten is here."

Ben had almost forgotten the man sitting silently next to him. Glancing at him, Ben too lost focus on Polina and was plunged back into the emotions of the past few days. The thought of Morten and Kelly together had lacerated him with burning jealousy, and yet the fact that Ben himself had been undeniably attracted to Morten that day in Soho with Alex meant the pain was now tinged with desire.

This pain and pleasure cocktail was intriguing, annoying and not a little frustrating. Ben wondered whether he had spent too much time with Hartmut, so that his boss's predilection for S&M had somehow rubbed off on him. Was the ether of their office impregnated with it? It would explain why they both stayed in law. In any case, Morten had experienced something that Ben had experienced too. Sharing a bedfellow binds people in strange ways. For Ben, it meant that he had an undisputed connection with the handsome Swede.

Morten probably never gave it a moment's thought.

"Ben?"

Kelly was looking at him questioningly. Ben had been silent, gazing into space for longer than he realised.

Ben ordered his emotions, a smile curling awkwardly round his lips.

"Sorry, I was just thinking about the weirdness of the

situation. Not just with Polina and Amber, I mean."

Kelly frowned.

Ben looked at her:

"Yes, Kelly. You know – the three of us? Together in one place? Discussing serious matters? Bit strange. That's all."

Morten spoke up, slowly and seriously.

"I am really sorry about what happened, Ben – particularly as you are such a great guy. I really enjoyed meeting you with Alex, and in a parallel universe you are just the kind of man I would be delighted to count amongst my friends."

Where did that come from? And what did it mean?

Ben stared at Morten, as Kelly shuffled uncomfortably in her armchair. Ben felt released from his perennial desire to say what others wanted to hear. For once, he was just going to say what was on his mind and let the others work it out as they wished.

He turned to Morten. He really was strikingly good looking.

"Do you know that when we met with Alex that day in Soho, I was convinced that you were gay. I was actually really attracted to you."

Ben glanced at an increasingly mortified Kelly, before snickering.

"That was the best thing about the whole sorry affair. At least I haven't been played for a minger!"

Morten's calm was in stark contrast to Kelly's embarrassment.

"Well, you're not the first to think that, Ben. You are not totally barking up the wrong tree, either. Although it's now a long time ago, I did experiment when I was a young man. I think sexuality is a continuum, even if most of us are pretty close to one end or the other, and tend to get more set in our ways as we mature. And for the record, I can see why Kelly is so into you."

Kelly was appalled. Casting guilt to one side, she experienced a rush of wholly unreasonable panic. Although Morten was a card-carrying paragon of modern man, she had never thought that he could ever be remotely interested in cock. What was this damned play? Had she really managed to bounce from one bisexual to another? What was she: some sort of bifurcated sexuality lightning rod? Worst of all, the men seemed to like each other. When she had idly considered that together Ben and Morten would make her perfect man, she hadn't actually thought of the possibility of them *being* together.

Ben wasn't at all sure how to react. But then he saw the look on Kelly's face, and suddenly it all seemed so ridiculous that he couldn't stop himself from sniggering some more.

He tried to contain it by taking a drink, but this just amplified his chuckling. As Ben's merriment grew, it defused the emotions that had overcome them from their different sides of the affair.

Kelly smiled, too. There *was* a ridiculous, funny side to all of this. She joined Ben in the now somewhat unhinged laughter echoing around the room.

Morten smiled politely, safe in the knowledge that Anglos regularly hid behind humour in order to avoid expressing their emotions. They would get there in their own sweet time.

After a few minutes of smiling along, Morten decided they should get back to business.

"So. The police are probably already aware of the nature of business at Eve's Garden. Second hand stories will not help them build any sort of case, or get them to take action they have not already done. We would need Polina and Milo to give statements. Will they do that, do you think?"

Given how frightened Milo was of Slava, Ben suddenly felt less confident.

"I don't think Milo has a great relationship with authority. I would have to talk to him."

Kelly was slightly more confident.

"Polina seems to want to get justice. I think she will, given time."

"She does know that should this go to trial, their lawyers will make her out to be a drug-addled prostitute with the morals of a corrupt politician."

Morten looked coolly at Kelly, not a hint of emotion troubling his challenge.

"She will be ripped apart and she needs to be prepared," he pointed out. "Unfortunately, in cases like these, getting to the truth is often a lot easier than getting proof of the matter. It is vulnerable people, often on the margins of societies, who get taken advantage of – almost by definition. Giving the victims confidence and then establishing their credibility is hard. But – obviously – it can be done."

"We need to speak to Milo and Polina," responded Ben. He had a nasty nagging feeling that Eve's Garden had probably seen situations like this before, and had survived them. It was just as well they had a dispassionate

Scandinavian advising them. This was a situation that needed a calm and settled mind.

Kelly narrowed her eyes.

"Well, at least we can push ahead with getting Amber fired from Sagworth Turner Dickerhint. Not having to watch her lord it round the corridors at work would make me feel better already. Exposing her as a conspirator in sex trafficking is exactly the sort of result I've been aspiring to."

Ben frowned.

"We could, but I'm not sure that would be a good idea if there is an investigation of the club underway. Knowing Amber, it would be better not to alert her to the danger. Besides, we can't very well waltz up to the partners and say we have reason to believe your Human Resources director is moonlighting as a madam, and here's a male stripper who recognises her. I can't see them liking that one bit."

Kelly stared rather glumly at Ben. He had a point. With all their history, and without clear proof, it could smack of petty revenge against a reformed character. Sagworth Turner Dickerhint HR were unlikely to send an investigative team to a lap-dancing club, with all the potential for public embarrassment that might cause. Knowing Amber, she would probably even have a story of how she had been on a mission of mercy at Eve's Garden, using her experience in prison to empathise with the women, and her HR knowledge to ensure they knew their rights. She would probably come out of the whole affair smelling of roses.

What was it about law firms? Why did partners find it so challenging to detect proper bastards? Was it because their antennae were carefully tuned towards rewarding them, as a rule?

They would have to tread carefully.

"I think we should bring it to the partners attention, without alerting Amber," said Kelly decisively.

Ben shrugged.

"To be honest, why not? We have nothing to lose."

Morten decided that they had gone as far as they could for one day. They had the beginning of a plan.

"Guys, it's a start. We're not certain it will work, but we know what we need to do. In the meantime, there is no point assuming we are going to fail. Let's drop the long faces. There is a well-stocked bar over there. What say we have a few drinks, put Amber Bluett et al out of our minds for a while, and get to know each other a little better? We're going to have to work as a team on this, after all."

In East London, the lights were low.

Polina arrived back at Arthur and Cornisha's house. She had been to the cinema.

Cornisha had sent her to see a film club showing of "Breakfast on Pluto". Polina was mildly puzzled. She'd been marched off two days running to the silver screen, to see "The Dallas Buyers Club" and "Priscilla: Queen of the Desert". Meanwhile, the video was recording "La Cage aux Folles".

"Thank you for the ticket, Cornisha."

"Did you enjoy it?"

Cornisha sounded uncharacteristically brusque.

Polina nodded. "These are good films. Amazing performances."

She was wondering what was going on. She wanted to

please Cornisha, who could not have been more supportive of her in her ordeal.

There seemed to be something up.

Cornisha sighed.

"Hmmm. There is "The Danish Girl", too. But we may not have enough time. I think we can have a little chat now."

"Sure," said Polina.

They sat on the sofa, as so often before.

Cornisha reflected that Polina had spent considerable time on her sofa discussing important issues. It was a veritable Parliament of discovery for the young Pole.

Cornisha straightened her back determinedly.

"I'm pretty sure that you would not want to upset me, Polina. I think we get on well, and Arthur and I have been happy to help you in a manifest time of need."

Polina blinked uncomprehendingly.

"Of course I would not want to upset you. I don't even know what would have happened by now without your help. You have been like angels to me. Have I upset you? Is there something wrong?"

"There is nothing wrong. At least, nothing wrong as far as I am concerned – nothing that can't be put right. But I do have a big favour to ask of you. I am going to ask you to reconsider your views about something which is very important, which matters hugely to me, and which I think you may never have yet really thought about, even though you have strong opinions about it. Will you see what you can do? I know there can be no promises in advance."

Polina's eyes widened.

"There *can* be promises in advance. I am so surprised

that you have to ask me this after what you have done for me! I will consider anything. Is it something that you need me to do for you?"

Cornisha sighed.

"Please listen. That is all I can ask at this stage. Let's start with the easy bit. You know what your parents said about London being full of homosexuals?"

Polina nodded.

"Yes. They did warn me."

"Well, London is not full of homosexuals. London is full of everybody. We do have a diversity of people here, and the majority of people here – with the law on our side – are happy about that. We think that sexuality is a personal choice and one that should be respected. I can't believe I'm saying this in this way, but some of my best friends are homosexual. This includes lesbians."

"Unbelievable," said Polina "Quite unbelievable. You do know what they do, don't you?"

"What do you mean?"

"Well... you know. In bed. They are not like you and me."

"Does it bother you? I mean, why would it matter?"

Polina was silent. She thought about it.

Cornisha persisted.

"If I were to ask you to simply accept that not everyone is like you, would you at least consider that a fair statement – and be able to live with it?"

Polina nodded solemnly.

"I can accept that, if it matters to you."

"It really, really matters to me," said Cornisha grimly.

"In life, you see, the one tough thing every generation has to face is understanding that their parents may not have been right about everything. It is truly important to question matters, and form your own opinions. In forming any opinion about any matter, the first step is to discuss the matter with someone who has expertise on the subject. You, my dear, need to meet some gays."

Polina took a deep breath.

"Some English gays?"

"We could find other nationalities to throw into the mix."

Polina stood up.

"May I make you a cup of tea?"

"Yes. Yes, indeed." said Cornisha, "this is absolutely on that level of importance. And we have one more big thing to talk about."

She clicked her teeth.

"Of course. The Crying Game."

"Eh?" said Polina.

"The Crying Game. Excellent film by Neil Jordan. That too, you must watch."

"Is it that important?"

"No, that's just an aside. I want you to see things that may help you understand. Look at me, Polina. What do you see?"

Polina cleared her throat nervously.

"I see an English lady. Dressed in green. A kind English lady. You work in a law firm. You like biscuits."

"I certainly like tea. Do please make some, there's a dear. Come back soon."

Polina took her time.

"So," she asked, putting two mugs in front of them, "what is your news?"

"Polina, I was not always as I am now."

"This is true for all of us, Cornisha. I was very different myself… "

"I was a man."

"You were… a man?"

"Yes. Technically, I was a man. But I was in the wrong body. I am a woman now."

Polina was shocked, visibly so.

"Are you making fun of me?"

Cornisha looked cross.

"How would there be any fun in this? Look, Polina. I know that you seem to despise anyone who is not completely within median societal norms. I can see that you are already feeling uncomfortable and shocked. How do you think that makes me feel? How do you think I felt when you called people who aren't like you disgusting? Polina, how can you use such words for people like me – when you have actually met people who do properly deserve such labels?"

Polina bowed her head.

"I do feel dizzy. It is a huge surprise. I really, really don't know what to say."

"That's quite alright. I am going to tell you a few things. I suspect that I can guess what you are thinking. It's not the first discussion I've had on the topic. So: please listen."

Polina blinked.

Cornisha spoke quietly.

"I was born a boy. I knew very early on that something was not right. First point: I was not traumatised, or conditioned, or changed. I have always been what I am. I simply am a woman. Second point: I don't think I could ever claim to know everything that biological women go through. But I don't see that as critical. I am just a person. Ultimately, as with everyone, I am only an expert on me. Third point: the surgery was successful. I have a female body. Fourth point: there is no threat to others through me being who I am. I am not a freak. I am not a weirdo. There is alternative sexuality, and there is crime. We have an age of consent. We have rules about how we live our lives. Nothing is unlawful about being part of the LGBTQ community. Fifth point: Arthur and I are very, very happy together. But he dumped me when he found out. So nothing is easy, and I don't expect you to accept this wholeheartedly, straight away. But I want you to try to empathise. Sex and gender is not just a straight person's game."

Polina was silent.

The two women sat there, musing on their differences.

Cornisha sighed.

"It's a lot to take in. As I said, you need to meet people and hear directly from them. We demonise what we are not, or what we don't know. We form views based on incomplete information. We have prejudice built into us, like poorly written code. Just remember, though Polina – we're all just people. You can't like everyone, and you don't have to. But don't attack people merely because they are different. If they mean you no harm, leave them be."

*

Ben and Kelly stepped into the conference room.

It was brimming with partners. A plankton of partners, mused Ben, as he watched the important people come in and mingle like amoeba in a petri dish. Lord, there were many of them. There were partners there whom no one ever usually saw. They were probably from the property department.

The turnout was very good. There was awareness that this was something to do with sex. Partners in law firms can react like Mary Whitehouse on speed. Anything slightly disreputable had to be examined thoroughly, discussed at length, reviewed from every angle, before judgment was passed. In the case of a book, of course, they wouldn't actually read it. That would be taking thoroughness too far. Just knowing sex was involved would be enough. Judging was important, but so was time.

Of course, anything to do with homosexuality was especially troublesome. That should just be buried. Being gay was just too awful. Being anything other than straight was frightening, unsettling, and just plain wrong. Also forbidden. Also: had to be stopped. Discreetly, though. There was a lot of tosh about discrimination about. It was a mine field. This is why the meeting was as packed as a hipster's skinny trousers. There was much to avoid saying, and much to avoid discussing. There was safety in numbers.

That being said, the gathered throng knew that this probably concerned ordinary, vanilla sex. This was because Amber was somehow involved. Amber was a hero – satisfyingly anti-gay, anti-employee, and very much into sex – sex used as a weapon, or at very least as a persuasive tool. She had plenty of tools to persuade, that much was clear. Amber was the sort of support staff one could actually rely upon to do one's dirty business for one – an indispensable operator, with breasts that Canova would have spent hours mapping, before coaxing the likeness of their beauteousness from cold hard marble. You had to give it to Amber. She had carved herself a niche and a half. The partners revered her.

They didn't understand Ben. He was good looking, which made them nervous. He also seemed to be one of the team, through sheer determination, if nothing else. But he wasn't somehow quite the right *sort*. Christ, he led the LGBT group. He'd even added other letters to it, Qs and Is, and goodness knows what else. All very X rated, that was certain. Kelly frightened them, as any woman with an opinion would. She was vocal and opinionated, all right. They gave her leeway, as she was after all American, and probably couldn't help herself. Nonetheless, these attendees made for an alarming meeting: one at which something non-anticipated might be said. This was all the more peculiar as there was no Amber to hide behind.

Amber and sex – no wonder the partners were quivering.

Kelly rose to speak, and looked around the room.

Peregrine Thornton was stroking his numerous chins. Harry Gumpert was smiling in a corner. David "Dangerous" Milner had just arrived breathlessly, like an out of shape milk tray man who had either lost, or more likely eaten, the box of chocolates, and felt the urge to apologise. Hartmut was looking at Kelly encouragingly, while Bartlett de Vere made coffee far too loudly. Had he never made a coffee before? The clinking and crashing was operatic in volume. Peregrine helped himself to his third biscuit. Kelly shook her head, half in admiration. That was characteristic of Peregrine – no secret eating. It was all very open, like his permanently filled mouth. Tim Bindman looked as if a parent had died. His face was a mask of suffering, like one of the foxes he so loved to set dogs on.

Kelly surveyed them all. She felt prepared, but reminded herself that she had rarely heard of a partners' meeting that had changed the direction of matters. This, though, surely would be different.

"Thank you for coming along," she said, "It's important to have a number of you here. I've set out some facts in this memo... " Kelly went around the room, handing out sheets of paper. "This is so we have everything straight."

Heads bent over paper, foreheads furrowed slightly.

Kelly put her hands together, like a politician.

"We've unfortunately established that Sagworth Turner Dickerhint's Head of Human Resources is moonlighting as the manager of a stripper club. She has also been connected to human trafficking. We're sorry to bring this to your attention, but felt that we had no alternative."

Oh, you had an alternative, thought Nicholas Casterway. You meddling little...

"Are we sure about this?" asked Tim Bindman, "I mean, Amber is a model employee."

Hartmut Glick raised an eyebrow.

"It's certainly serious. If it's true – and there is nothing suggesting that it isn't – we must act."

"Hold on," said Dangerous Dave, "shouldn't Amber be

294

here to address these issues?"

Ben stared at him.

"It's a criminal matter. So with respect that might not be the best approach. The police are dealing with this. We wanted you to be informed so that the firm can handle any fall out as best it can."

Dangerous Dave looked distinctly unhappy.

"Oh. Who involved the police?"

"A specialist trafficking charity," said Kelly smoothly. She could see how this was shaping up. Lawyers hated attention being drawn to unlawful practices. Things could be tolerated – and frequently were – so long as they did not attract attention. A bit of crime was best kept under wraps, like a breastfeeding mum. Theft, bestiality, stalking, bullying – all very much best kept in the family.

Harry Gumpert was nervous.

"This all sounds very bad. Is there any way the police could be persuaded to minimise the involvement of Sagworth Turner Dickerhint's good name in this fiasco? Could we... avoid any attention? Do we even need to act?"

"Well," said Kelly reasonably, nudging Ben so he shut his open mouth, "you'd probably want to terminate Amber's employment for gross misconduct. That's obviously something the firm should do sooner rather than later."

Ben nodded.

"Something like this needs to be detached from the firm."

He felt that he was finally mastering the art of British understatement.

Bartlett de Vere wobbled.

"What if she is innocent?"

Ben and Kelly looked equally surprised.

Ben took up the challenge:

"She's admitted to running the strip club – see page two of the memo."

Bartlett did not touch the memo, but pursed his lips.

"Well, of course that's not great – but… "

Ben leaned forward.

"But what? She's been moonlighting. That alone is enough. Frankly, if she got off on these other charges it would be a miscarriage of justice. The point is that she is highly likely to have been knowingly trafficking women. It's not a great notch on our diversity belt."

The partners grimaced and rhubarbed. Ben shot an incredulous look at Kelly.

Tim Bindman tried to look intelligent.

"What if we did nothing?" he offered.

Ben kept his temper with some difficulty.

"Do nothing? Where would that take the firm?"

Tim attempted to compose his features into those of a strategic thinker.

"Well, if we do nothing, it sort of… takes care of itself, doesn't it? She gets taken away, charged and banged up. If she's innocent, we haven't prejudged it. Isn't that easier?"

"Doing nothing is always easier," said Kelly. She wasn't even being ironic. She found the meeting was fulfilling her every expectation.

Hartmut looked at Harry. Harry was keeping still. He was debating whether to pretend to have received an urgent call.

Hartmut turned to Nicholas.

"What do you think, Nicholas?"

Nicholas looked intrigued.

"I'm not sure what to think, Hartmut. I don't judge my fellow human beings in the abstract. I'd like to hear from Amber before taking this any further."

"You cannot be serious, Mr Casterway," said Ben quietly.

Nicholas looked at Ben.

"You will always find me very serious when it involves the reputation of the firm."

The room went quite still.

Tim Bindman knew the rota.

"Well," he said, with a fair pretence at cheerfulness, "why don't we review the memo, take matters under advisement, and reconvene in a couple of weeks? There is nothing that needs doing straight away, and things may be clearer by then."

Tim knew that kicking the problem down the road was his strongest suit. He also knew that he would be on holiday in a couple of weeks.

After some further whitterings on largely irrelevant and even unrelated matters, the meeting disbanded, more abruptly than expected.

Ben and Kelly were left looking at each other, genuinely gobsmacked.

"Did that just happen?" asked Ben, almost in awe.

Hartmut stopped on his way out.

"Don't worry. She will be fired. It'll take a while. Things take a while around here."

"Why?" asked Ben.

"Why indeed," said Hartmut. "Why, indeed.".

11

Karma and chameleons

"May I speak to the manager, please?"

Rubens turned to face the rather serious-looking customer, whom he did not recognise. A practised smile came to his face. He prepared himself for service. He would no doubt have to defuse the situation and assure the customer that the manager would be with him in a moment. Then he remembered that he *was* the manager. Rubens still had to pinch himself at times to remind himself that things had turned out as they had.

He squared his shoulders.

"You're speaking to him."

Although Rubens had never really been particularly focused on status, it did feel good to say that.

"How can I help?"

Rubens hoped that Dorota hadn't given the customer attitude. As customers went, he looked as if he could be a demanding one.

"Ah, splendid," replied the man. "It's my first time in this bar. I just wanted to say that I think you are doing something *very* right here. Top notch dirty martinis, friendly and prompt service – and my boyfriend and I love the décor. I'll be posting on Trip Advisor, but I wanted to pay my compliments in person. I enjoy posting damning comments on social media when service underwhelms, but I do feel one should appreciate a good job well done. Restore the balance, so to speak. Now, might we have a couple more of those excellent martinis?"

Rubens smiled warmly, and graciously thanked the man. Balance, indeed. Despite difficult customers, fractious staff, badly behaved pets, the endless demand for more revenues and cost control, there were also moments like this. They made Rubens feel that it was all worthwhile. Maybe he now knew what he was doing.

He had moved smartly on.

Rubens glanced at his watch.

Time waited indeed for no person. It was time: an Outrageous Fortune board meeting was starting imminently. He told the bar staff to give him a call if things got hectic, and headed through to the back where the others were waiting.

It wasn't the most salubrious of spaces. It was a simple storeroom with a small space allocated for the drag queens' dressing room. Various other performers could also fight over this turf, if they were feeling brave. It was a room with no view, but a room where transformation was welcome, and artistic skills were given the oxygen of exposure. A city needs many things, but venues for the arts, all sorts of arts, are its white cells.

Lady Gaza had assumed her rightful position on the most comfortable chair, with her back to the theatre mirror.

Jamal and Alex were sitting on uncomfortable little metal chairs either side of her. Milo had sensibly opted to perch on the cases of bottled beers stacked by the opposite wall. Although one of the inhospitable little chairs was still available, Rubens also opted for the cases of beer, and carefully sat down next to Milo.

No, it certainly wasn't the kind of boardroom that Ben or Tarquin would identify with. It was not thronged with sumptuous leather chairs and a long table designed to impress and intimidate. Yet, for all that, over the years the backroom at Outrageous Fortune had seen a few power struggles – and quite a few powder struggles besides. Seeds of innovation had sprouted, generously watered by supplies from the bar. Plans had been hatched, ideas had taken wing, successes celebrated and setbacks digested. Like the mythical Silicon Valley garage that Rubens felt sure had nasty little metal chair equivalents of its own, the backroom at Outrageous Fortune knew that it could be destined for greater things.

In fact, as it happened, greater things were on the agenda today.

Alex cleared his throat:

"We want to go through all the details for Friday. As you know, we're opening a new bar. I know you all – and in particular our glamourous new manager Lady Gaza – have been working hard to make sure that the launch party at Outrageous Fortune Boudoir will go with a bang. However, as the old adage goes, you don't get a second chance to make a first impression. We have a reputation to uphold. So let's keep an eye on the details."

Alex looked at Lady Gaza, who smiled graciously at him, as if to a courtier. She was as calm as a cat whose greatest decision in life was whether to go back to snoozing on the radiator, or to try her luck at finding a lap to lodge on. She dealt well with stress. This may have been the first bar in London that she was entrusted with managing, but Lady Gaza had had experience galore back home. In her former employment, she was never sure if supplies would arrive, or when the premises might be closed down for some spurious reason. By contrast, London played largely by the rules, and she knew she could make a success of it.

She spoke confidently.

"Staff training is complete, stock is in, and we have already had a dry run with friends. It all works like clockwork. The acts are booked. I know them all. We can depend on them. The ads are out and social media is abuzz, darlings. I've even found time to post and tweet like a demon. I have not been a Lazy Gaza. Everyone is going to be there, and they are going to love us."

Alex was pleased that everything seemed under control, but Lady Gaza's certainty was slightly disconcerting. After all, something always went wrong on launch night.

He frowned.

"Are you sure that all the acts are going to turn up on time? I don't mean to be rude, but our type of performer is not always the most reliable, and we want this to be perfect."

Lady Gaza controlled a look of feline contempt for a canine that would never get it.

"Darling, are you referring to the drag queens? Dear

boy, when you have been struggling with your identity all of your life, then one can quite understand that arriving on time may not seem the life and death scenario that society tries to drill into you. However, all my girls understand that they will have quite an audience on Friday, and that they could be on to rather a good gig if they play their cards right. Alex, please do not worry your pretty little head. They will be there. Besides, you are in a rather fortunate position. Should there happen to be any problems, your glamorous new manager is more than capable of filling any gaps."

She blew Alex a kiss.

"I know you want this to be perfect. I do too, with all my heart. Of course, something unexpected will occur, but we have plans B galore. We have friendly DJs on the guest list. They'll be ready if needed. As for go go boys – well, the problem will be keeping them *off* the stage, darling. If anyone fails to show, then we will handle it."

Milo half smiled.

"This brings back memories, Gaza. That's how I got started here in London. I had just landed, and a friend and I had managed to scrape together enough money to go for a drink in a bar in Bermondsey. It was not the most salubrious place. We had nursed our beers for ever it seemed, waiting for the promised stripper to arrive. I had never seen a stripper in the flesh before and so, believe it or not, it was quite exciting for me."

"That's hard to swallow," said Rubens.

Lady Gaza nodded.

"I think of most strippers as Amazons who swallow," she said.

Milo shook his head, reliving the memory of who he used to be, thinking back to what London had seemed to be only a few years earlier. He smiled.

"It's true, you know. Anyhow, just as we thought we couldn't possibly spend any more time nursing the last of the beer, an announcement was made. Apparently the stripper had let them down. They had some not very nice things to say about the guy, and then asked if there was anyone in the audience who would like to earn a hundred pounds and drinks on the house to boot. It took one look of encouragement from my friend, a quick check that I had clean underwear on, and a new star was born. That was the first money I ever earned in this city. I should thank that stripper, Long John Swiveller – he opened a back door into survival for me."

"I'm sure that wasn't the only back door he opened up," remarked Jamal. "Good story, though. We must all play our parts on Friday too, whether or not we have anyone letting us down. We are each and every one a key part of Outrageous Fortune. It's a people business, and the reputation we have built up for style, quality drinks, and friendly but professional customer service has been hard fought for. We must all be on point all evening, and then we need to get the surprise number just right. It will be the first time that the five of us are on stage together. Although you will be leading, Mistress Gaza, we all need to know our parts."

"Don't worry, Jamal," said Rubens soothingly. "We have rehearsed the number enough times, and even Alex knows the moves. After the speech he gives thanking everyone, no one will expect what comes next. It will go down a storm."

"You're right to make the point, though, Jamal." Alex looked at his partner. "Despite propagating an image that fabulous just *happens* at Outrageous Fortune, we all know that there is a ton of work that goes into anything successful. I have been practising all week, both in and out of the shower."

Rubens nodded in agreement. Alex was right. Rubens had been working very hard indeed to maintain the impression that everything in Outrageous Fortune happened effortlessly. London crowds gave short shrift to anyone unrehearsed.

"I have another idea I want to propose to you." Lady Gaza glanced around the room. "It is something that matters to me, so please do bear with me. Given the experiences of everyone in this room, I hope you will support me."

She smiled at Milo.

"I am of course not the only one to have come to this country with nothing, and then worried about whether or not I would be able to make it. Like many others, I have felt intimidated by all the people around me who seemed rooted and stable, when I felt I could be blown away by the next storm."

The four men looked intently at her. They knew that behind her serene appearance, Lady Gaza aimed to make her mark through far more than her dexterity with a mascara wand. She continued, speaking slowly and carefully, weighing her words.

"I am very grateful that I have been able to attain a certain stability in our society. It is in great part, though I say it myself, down to a willingness to accept the culture that has given me a new home, and being prepared to work hard towards a goal. However, I would never have been able to do it without the help of certain people whose kindness I shall never forget. All of us need a helping hand every so often."

She paused to take a sip of the tonic water by her side.

"Now I think it is time that I started to give back. I also want, in my own tiny way, to make a stand for the tolerance that this country has stood for for so long. As I keep saying to anyone who will listen, it is a delicate flower. Without constant care and vigilance, it would so easily wither and die. We all need to quietly reinforce the better side of society's nature in whatever way we can. In my case, I want to do it through humour, style, and showing people a good time."

Lady Gaza looked earnestly at the men, wanting reassurance that she had not lost them. She needn't have worried.

"My proposal is this. Once a month, we put on a show at the Boudoir, featuring performers who came to London as immigrants, as refugees. Let's showcase those of us who were once wholly dependent upon the generosity of this country to help them start over. It matters to me that we do this. I want these shows to be a spectacle, the highlight of the month, where our customers can see exactly what we refugees can achieve, enriching the society that has helped us, just like generations have done in the past. I want us to consider this as part of our corporate responsibility. We should donate part of the profits from these evenings to charities that work with new refugees, helping them adapt to the UK, so that they too can become contributing members of this society. For this too is key: just as the British have shown tolerance and acceptance to us, we immigrants must embrace the culture of this country, otherwise why are we here? Certainly not for the weather. Nor, in most part, for the food."

The Outrageous Fortune directors were silent for a moment. Lady Gaza wondered if she had misjudged the mood. After all, they were gathered to discuss the launch of a commercial venture, not to try to save the world. Then Alex leaned over and gave her a kiss on the cheek.

"I love the idea. You need to make sure that whoever you engage is as amazing as you are, otherwise it could rather backfire. But if we do this right, then I think not only will it be a lovely gesture, it won't do us any harm commercially either. I am proud of you, Kasim."

Alex, in common with most of Lady Gaza's friends, only used her real name exceedingly rarely. Kasim blushed under the make-up.

Jamal smiled.

"Then it's settled. I too think it is an excellent idea."

"I would only ask that we call the night "From Croydon with love", as we have all passed through those godforsaken hallways on the search for salvation."

Rubens and Milo both smirked. The immigration office in Croydon was very much a rite of passage, of which most native Londoners were blissfully unaware.

Alex made a couple of notes and checked the agenda.

"It seems that we are ready for Friday. However, before we close the meeting and go for a well-deserved drink, Jamal and I have got some more exciting news. Jamal?"

Jamal tried to affect cool. He leant back on his little metal chair, but quickly decided he valued his spine more than that. He stood up instead, and grinned widely, rubbing his hands.

"Alex and I have found a perfect location in Peckham for our *third* venue." He heavily emphasised the ordinal. "Yes, people, you heard right. It needs work, as you would expect – but the price is good, we have arranged the funding, and if you like it when we go to see it again next week, Rubens, we want to sign the paperwork this month. As we want you to set it up, we would especially value having you on board with this."

Rubens wasn't sure how to react. This was big news.

Jamal continued.

"Our builders have quoted. The timing works very well for them. We thought that it would take a couple of months to do the work on the new place, by which time the Boudoir should be up and running. Our first ideas are to implement a more industrial feel down in Peckham. We'll obviously still be outrageously chic, of course – but achieve a grittier feel than this bar's cousins north of the river."

"Wonderful, habibie!" purred Lady Gaza. "What is this place like? The space, I mean."

"It's on two floors, on the main road near the Overground," responded Alex. "It's a decent size ground floor bar, but the really cool thing is a large basement which is currently used as an oversized storeroom. We think we could get a licence for a club on weekends."

Rubens was starting to get excited.

"You want to open a club?"

Jamal nodded enthusiastically.

"Why not? Between us we have decades of clubbing experience, and, with a few honourable exceptions, we have been bitching about other people's venues, bad attitudes on the door, inept organisation and manufactured DJs for *years*. Isn't it about time that we did something about it? Or at least give everyone else a chance to bitch about us?"

Lady Gaza nodded excitedly.

"We open the bar first, get that going and launched, whilst we finish off the space below, and get the license. This means that, when we are ready to launch our first dance nights, we should already have some business coming through the bar. The guys at the Dalston Superstore have made it work, and apparently Peckham is the new Shoreditch."

"I love it! Maybe we can call it Outrageous Fortune Underground. People will think it is just for the style of the bar, and then, bang! We open the basement club." Rubens was now almost bouncing with anticipation. He couldn't wait to go and see the venue.

The meeting closed. The feelings knitted by the twin needles of action and progress were hard to beat.

Later that evening, as Rubens gazed at his colleagues, he felt that luck was truly smiling at him and his friends. Luck had frankly been a bit of a bitch at times, especially to poor Milo. It seemed, though, that Alex may be right in what he said about sooner or later balance being restored.

Now Milo would take over as manager at Outrageous Fortune, Rubens would open and run Outrageous Fortune Underground, and Lady Gaza would reign at Outrageous Fortune Boudoir. It all fitted. Milo could now put Janusz, Slava and Amber out of his head. Milo trusted that karma would get them in the end, on some future, dismal day.

Rubens felt good. Things were looking positive all

round. A happy equilibrium was being achieved. He was allowed boys nights out with Jamal, so long as he respected boundaries. Tarquin may even join them on occasion, so long as he could keep his clothes on. Things were looking up.

Not that Tarquin hadn't been traumatised, of course. Rubens was currently unable to take Tarquin's hands, or even joke about fisting. What was the world coming to? For the time being at least, the slightest hint of anything knuckle-related sent Tarquin scurrying for refuge, scarred as he was by the offer of generous accommodation from Rory Ramsey-Hall.

Rubens smiled genially. This would pass. It was a small price to pay for being able to go out dancing with the man he loved.

Obrigado, Londres.

Kelly was furious.

"I can't believe it! Is this what decision making is like? Is this how these tossers run the firm? The mind boggling stupidity of it all! The amorality! The... big boys club, with no proper big boys!"

Ben was less heated.

"Don't get too upset. We've gone over this until we were blue in the face. Apathy rules in large organisations. Craven people seem to do well. No one wants to put their head above the parapet to point out the incongruities of any process or system in any meaningful way. You just ignore them. Don't do as they ask, and ignore them. Do as they do to you. Above all: don't expect them to play by your rules."

"How ridiculously inefficient."

"Yes. Nope," said Ben, "you've just got to do what you've got to do. I take it you still want to do something?"

She nodded.

"Well," said Ben, "I have a plan."

Polina looked at them as if they were stark staring mad.

"You do know you are not dealing with nice people here?"

Ben leaned forward.

"We have to stop them."

Polina blew out her cheeks.

"Well, yes, I can see that. But it sounds as if in all this, I am going to be very exposed. I am to be some sort of bait. I'm really not sure about this."

"Not just any bait," said Ben, "you're the key to our master plan. The master bait."

Kelly clasped her hands.

"We have got to get them, Polina. Remember, they are threatening your family and your own peace of mind."

Polina looked pained.

"I know that. I'm finally auditioning for dancing roles – and getting somewhere. I have a recall for proper employment, did I tell you that? I'm buried in LGBT films. I'm truly challenging myself. But this is downright dangerous. I don't want to die."

Kelly snorted.

"No one does. Not really. Not unless you've been lied to about what to expect on the other side. But everything you do is a death risk. We're all just sacks of water and bits, wandering around waiting to be punctured – maybe by something as trivial as a mosquito. Surely you only get a few chances in life to be a heroine – a real one. This is your chance."

Polina rolled her eyes.

"It certainly is my life at stake. As for the waitressing part... how much of a cliché?"

"We've all done it at some time," said Kelly stoutly, "come on, Polina! It's pay back time!"

Ben had to admit that Kelly could be oddly persuasive at times. Who would have bought those arguments? But, like a well manipulated electorate, Polina obligingly did.

Polina looked rather nice in the Sagworth waitressing get up. The black shirt set off her blonde hair prettily, with a lovely contemporary fascist feel. The catering manager, who was doing a favour for Kelly, thought privately that this was the easiest favour she had ever granted. The new recruit was perfect.

What a shame that this was on a temporary basis.

Amber turned as purple as an aubergine when she realised what had transpired.

"What is that woman doing here?"

"Oh, don't get all UKIP on my arse," said the catering manager tartly. She, much like the support staff as a whole, had very little time for Amber.

"Polina is very dedicated and we're lucky to have her filling in. Unless you would like to step in yourself, and serve our clients their Very Important Person lunch?"

"You've got a bad attitude," said Amber sourly. She

knew she could not take matters much further at this point.

The catering manager sniffed.

"I wouldn't worry about it. I don't. I'm good at my job, and I know it. You stay in your territory, Bluett. You stick with making the lawyers' lives a misery. I cheer them up here with some half-decent wine."

"I can cheer up lawyers too," snarled Amber. "A lot more efficiently than you," she added pompously.

"Whatever," the catering manager waved dismissively, "I don't even want to know. Now scoot. We have canapés to serve."

Amber retreated to her office, fuming.

Of course, once she had calmed down, ideas flowed. Amber saw exactly what a fine opportunity this development presented,

Slava was not in a good mood. Sometimes life just gets to you. Some days, you're tired, and flat, and can't raise a decent guffaw. Human trafficking just brings you down, especially when loose ends abound.

Amber marched into the room as if she owned it.

"Where's Janusz?"

"Here."

Janusz was lying listlessly on the sofa, playing Candy Crush. Slava's mood had got to him.

Slava felt better, for some reason, after glancing at Amber.

"You look as if you've just fired somebody. What's up?"

"It's better than that, lads. You can thank me later. I've found Polina."

Slava stood up.

"What? Where?"

Amber cackled like a pantomime witch.

"You won't believe it. She's working at Sagworth. She's waitressing!"

"That is incredible," said Slava, "what a waste of potential."

"I know what's on the menu for her," said Janusz.

"I think I do too," said Slava. He turned to Amber.

"What do we do?"

Amber narrowed her eyes.

"I thought you'd ask. I've been thinking. As it turns out, it's simple. Sagworth's executive lift takes you straight from the lower ground car park to the executive floor, where Polina is working."

"How do you use it?" asked Janusz.

Amber rounded on him.

"Really?"

"You're not an executive," Janusz pointed out.

Amber folded her arms.

"Let's just say that I have access, shall we. If you haven't figured that out by now, I'm not sure I can help you. Anyway, where were we? The car park. Let's not complicate things. I'll bring her down to the car park, using the lift. You, my friends, will be in the car park."

Janusz turned to Slava.

"What message will we be sending?"

Slava looked intent.

"No one must ever think we are a soft touch. The business depends on it. So we go in hard."

"When?" asked Janusz simply.

Amber looked at the men.

"She's only there on a temporary basis. The sooner, the better. Her next shift is lunchtime – day after tomorrow."

"That is lucky. I am free then," said Slava, "are you free, Janusz?"

"Most fortunately enough, I am."

Polina expected the worst, but was still wholly wrongfooted when Amber press ganged her into the executive lift.

"What are you doing?" she asked weakly, her throat closing up.

"I want a word with you," said Amber, pressing the car park button.

"What do you think you're doing?" asked Polina. She wasn't trying too hard to resist, but felt genuinely terrified. Ignoring both her fight and her flee instincts was making her heart pound.

Amber was strong. Polina realised very quickly that she was in way above her head.

"We need to talk," said Amber.

"You're a bad conversationalist at the best of times," said Polina. "I have nothing to say to you."

"I'm sure we'll find something to talk about."

The lift was modern. You barely felt it move. Before any more could be said, the lift doors opened and Amber pushed Polina out into the concrete gloom.

Polina felt very frightened.

"Are you there?" she cried, despite herself.

"Who, my little fugitive? Me?"

Slava stood there. In the dimly lit bunker he seemed bigger. His gloves gave him the air of a practised assassin.

"What do you want?" asked Polina.

"We had a deal," Slava said smoothly, "I'm afraid that there are consequences when you breach a contract. I'm sure your tedious lawyer friends will have filled you in on this."

He took a step to the side.

Polina looked wildly around, and now saw Janusz. He looked relaxed.

"You don't have to do this," she said in a quivering voice.

"I do," said Janusz. He moved forward.

"I agree with my colleague," said Slava, "We cannot let you get away with disrespecting us in the manner that you have. You know this. You knew it at the time that you left the club. I'm here to make sure that you are punished, so that others don't get ideas above themselves. Actions have consequences, and I'm afraid you won't like these consequences. I am going to disfigure you."

"Not so fast."

Ben and Kelly emerged from behind Harry Gumpert's car.

Harry Gumpert's car was a textbook illustration of the need for the congestion charge to be increased twice or thrice immediately. It was a huge gas guzzling object which Harry persisted in driving to and from the office. This although not only were public transport links excellent, but he could virtually walk to work from the Elephant and Castle.

Harry should of course have been doing that – if only to prevent him slowly growing that massive square behind that businessmen acquire after years of ramming their posteriors into conference room seats.

But, for now, as a small contribution towards society at large, Gumpert's car had provided a perfect place to conceal white knights.

Slava looked a tad nonplussed.

"What?" he asked, not unreasonably, looking Kelly up and down.

"I suggest that you leave this woman alone," said Kelly.

"This is none of your business," asserted Janusz.

"I've made it my business. Both personally and professionally," replied Kelly.

"We're here to arrest you. We're protecting Polina from your planned assault," added Ben.

Amber was furious.

"Oh yeah? You and whose army?"

"Well. There is me."

A huge security guard stepped out of the car park shadows. He looked very official indeed.

Amber recognised him. She had often given him grief over his timekeeping while he was nursing his sick wife.

"And there is me."

A wiry man who worked in the post room emerged. He was known throughout the firm for his strength, gained both by determined training and by lugging paper packs around all day.

"We're all here, too."

More emerged – the firm's driver, whom Amber had unsuccessfully fought to put on a zero hours contract, the print room boys, a solid core of couriers, some surprisingly buff IT specialists, a large selection of security personnel, and several secretaries who had a close interest in martial arts.

"Last but not least, I'm here."

This was the smallest security guard, who had a feasorme reputation quite belied by his stature: "I used to be in the South African police, you know."

Everyone nodded. They had heard that before.

There were at least fifty of them.

Amber, Janusz and Slava were surrounded.

Police sirens sounded, quite close now.

"You reap what you sow," said Kelly to Amber.

"You should take heed of that yourself," snapped Amber, her face contorted.

Kelly stared at her.

"To be honest, I do, Amber. But you're a really nasty piece of work. It's best that someone stands up to you. And if it has to be us, so be it."

The police made quick work of arresting the three traffickers.

Ben shook a number of hands.

"Thank you all. That went remarkably well. It was never guaranteed."

"Now you tell me," said Polina grimly. She shuddered.

"Together we were something else," said Kelly enthusiastically. "Woo hoo!"

"It's a shame we didn't get to rough 'em up," said a passing staff member, reflectively.

"What matters is that we could have if we had wanted to – but chose not too," said Kelly. "That surely is the best philosophy."

"You may be right. Anyway, glad to be of help. That Amber was a liability. The partners never listened – just because she sucked up to them. You've both done something you can be proud of. It's ended up making life easier for all of us here, as well as supporting that nice young woman."

He grinned, and headed back to work.

After providing names, contact details and video evidence of the incident to the police, everyone melted back to their posts.

Only the catering manager was left fuming, as she ran around the excutive level far above their heads, wondering where on earth her newest recruit had disappeared to, leaving overfed visitors in the lurch like large besuited baby birds, calling desperately for more stuffing.

This was, at long last, a happy day, decided Kelly. Polina's call back had been successful. She had now invited her friends to the recording of a prime time television show.

"She referred to us as her saviours, you know. It's big. I've given her to understand that some of us may feel uncomfortable with the religious undertones," said Kelly to Ben and Morten, who had been content to tag along, still experimenting with their new friendship.

Morten grinned wryly.

"We have saved her ass. And now she gets to shake it on TV. Progress is a beautiful thing."

It was a very different world to visit.

TV is its own universe, thought Kelly. Everywhere she turned, loud, confident people strode, brashly greeting each other. What struck her most – and perhaps it was an unfair perception – was just how self-absorbed everyone seemed. The impression could not have been stronger if they were all wearing T-shirts stating: "It *is* all about me."

Kelly smiled. One sliver of gratitude she felt for her legal training was that it made her question things. She thought about matters, whether she wanted to or not. She tested pros and cons as an automatic reflex, on an ongoing basis. Sometimes, she changed her views – and knew why. The time she spent considering things meant, though, that, once formed, her opinions sometimes shot out like bullets, hard, steely and targeted, not softened by the context of her prior work on the facts.

That was one downside to thinking.

Kelly smiled grimly, as she considered how she could properly claim – with some merit – to be occasionally misunderstood. Maybe it was unavoidable. It was after all a waste of time to engage with anyone who didn't apply the same thoroughness to appraising events and issues. The problem remained, as far as Kelly could judge, that she encountered, with alarming frequency, individuals (well, men) who did not value an opinion formed by a woman – or were incapable of appreciating that one might be cleverer than them.

Few of these people on TV seemed to have queried anything in their lives. They were important. They believed it unquestioningly, like cult members clutching their own self published book of rules. Self publication? Only rubbish could come from that.

Kelly nudged Ben.

"This all makes a law firm seem positively monastic."

"Yeah. Monastic. Including those orgies between monks and nuns." said Ben, whose interest in medieval mores was limited, but precise.

"I'm not sure a law firm has the gumption to come up with the parameters for an orgy," mused Kelly, "We know they indulge in the odd extra curricular shag once in a while. I rather think that's the extent of their repertoire. This little lot, though – why, you'd imagine that if you crammed them into a dressing room, it'd be heaving buttocks within seconds."

"Maybe," said Morten, "maybe not."

Ben shrugged.

"I think you might be right – but they'd all be staring into the mirrors as they heaved. What a bore that would be."

Polina's invitation had provoked curiosity among the three friends. Being a backing dancer in an over-hyped talent show was not quite artist nirvana – but Polina was obviously ecstatic about it, and proud. It was everything that she could possibly have hoped for. Whatever misgivings her English acquaintances might have had, it still felt like the beginning of a success story.

This was only the fourth time that Polina was appearing on television. She had procured invitations for all her rescuers. Not all had accepted. Polina had decided against inviting Harry. Cornisha had declined, shuddering discreetly, citing an alternative commitment that Kelly suspected was probably staying in with a good book.

The studio stage seemed much smaller than it appeared

on the TV screen. The crowd on the other hand was more overwhelming – a giant herd of shiny and over-excited people, being whipped into a frenzied mass, like a sort of human Angel Delight. Being present amongst them all was an experience in itself. Kelly was enjoying it, although, if she were perfectly honest, what she was enjoying most was being seated between Morten and Ben.

On one side, Morten stretched his long legs, his thigh connecting with hers, the subtle warmth turning her on like a thermostat. On the other side, Ben's leg felt strong and muscular. She rather liked the feel of that, too. Kelly was conscious that there was a real and present danger of her splaying her legs like a starfish in order to enjoy both sensations. She reluctantly adjusted her seating position. The dignity of public positionings did not sit well with the athletic positionings of sex. Yet again, the gap between the public and private yawned, like a badly crafted economic matrix.

She glanced at Morten, who looked down at her with desire. She could see it in his eyes. She had his attention. She waited a beat before looking at Ben. Ben's glance was no less intense. It was funny how Ben sometimes caught her mood so perfectly, when he was not obsessing about his own insecurities. His dark, brooding Italian good looks struck her most when they were out and about. Kelly was conscious that both men were getting a fair amount of attention. She, too, sensed that other men in turn were trying to work out if she was attached to one or the other of her companions. It gave her a thrill to think that she could have answered truthfully that she was involved with both.

The brightly-lit fake theatre did not matter much. The false party and the hyping of mediocrity were simply the back drop to a wonderful feeling of achievement.

"I wanted this," thought Kelly, "I wanted it and I have got it."

The show marched determinedly on.

Polina had told them to wait for her.

"The mob will leave. Just come down to the front and I'll come out to see you."

"Won't we be pressed to leave?" asked Ben.

Polina laughed.

"Just look confident! I know you can do it."

Kelly nodded.

"Okay. We'll assume the implacable sense of entitlement of a clipboard holder. They never get questioned. They always stand firm."

This went to plan. Polina skipped out, dazzling in a sequined head piece and a cinch-waisted blue and silver costume. Her eyelashes were as long as an elephant's trunk. Despite the gaudy get up, she looked surprisingly pretty. Happiness twinkled out of her, like sunlight on a pond.

"How do you dance in those shoes?" asked Kelly admiringly.

Polina laughed.

"They are as solid as silver hooves! You should get a pair."

"They'd be good for kicking butt," said Kelly.

Ben kissed Polina.

"Well done! Not a foot wrong. I can't believe it. I could not follow those routines like that."

Polina smiled.

"Thank you."

Morten nodded.

"I think I'd be left making it up as I went along. That's the way I tend to roll."

Polina was looking over their heads and waved shyly.

Kelly spotted him first: a tall, burly cameraman, who looked as if his feet might be devoured by the snakes of cables around him. *Where were Health and Safety when you needed them?* He looked… shy?

Oh Lord. Polina had an admirer!

Kelly could not stop giggling as they left the studio, even when their breath was snatched away by the cold London evening air.

"Isn't this glorious?" she said, "what a result! We've completely sorted her life out!"

She hugged Ben, then hugged Morten. Her exhilaration was infectious. The men grinned.

"Where to now?"

They wandered back to Ben's flat, which was closest, and fell on the sofa.

"Ben. It's very hot in your flat," said Kelly, after several vodkas.

"Mmmmmm," said Ben non-committedly.

Morten stripped off his jumper. It was like hitting a pause button – just one moment, but very clear, and stark, and obvious. His silhouette was taut and dramatically beautiful. His blond hair fell playfully over his forehead, and his eyes glittered like a belly dancer's navel.

It was happening.

Kelly wanted Ben and Morten.

Ben wanted Morten and Kelly.

Morten had no idea of the strength of everyone's desires, but he was Scandinavian. He fancied a shag.

Whether it happened now, whether it happened soon, it felt like an inevitability. They were drifting like tectonic plates, and the crash would happen in very slow motion. It felt good. They were understanding the signs, establishing the connections. The guidance of their feelings was being accepted, and comfort gained with each casual touch. It was like adults being given explanations about the characteristics, differences and similarities between classical artists. As each little fact dropped, there was a hit.

What a glow, what a feeling of connection, of reassurance as one slaked one's thirst for knowledge – the past, the present and the future somehow forming a pattern that made sense. The map emerging could be related to and digested – this is who I am, this is what I will do – like a favourite meal with a little fancy wine. It may or may not have applied to ordinary crowd scenes – to the instant, heady fix of a TV studio – but whatever mass is being manipulated, from one's own body to a heaving crowd, the trick is in the comfort levels being there.

Kelly, Ben and Morten were in a moment. They were connected. They knew they belonged, they existed, and this was about them. Others may never know what they had, or begin to understand it.

It only concerned them. It only mattered to them. The world at large was going to keep on spinning – and should spin, and leave them in peace, as they pondered their next moves.

12

Flights of fantasy

Nicholas Casterway glared balefully around. He forged ahead, determined to make his way to the lounge at Gatwick as quickly as possible.

His trip to the Pan Pacific conference had not started well. Roadworks on the M23 had meant that he had had to take the train to the airport, with all the unwanted contact with the hoi polloi that *that* entailed. He had of course sought refuge in the first class carriage, and yet, even there, he detected a number of people whom he did not really consider worthy of occupying the space. Some of them looked as if they were thoroughly enjoying the treat of being able to afford a little luxury, talking in hushed tones and smiling contentedly as they stretched out in the somewhat less uncomfortable seats. Nicholas considered them all to be irredeemably common. The prices were simply far too accessible these days.

Far worse was to come when he disembarked at the windswept platform. He was caught up in a baying throng which offended his senses with loud, grating voices and premature beachwear. Why on earth airports didn't have a fully dedicated, proper first class service was beyond him. There seemed to be no escape from the herds of holidaymakers. They were barring his way to the sanctuary which he now so desperately sought. Nobody seemed to know where they were going, permanently distracted by the duty free shopping or indulging in arguments about which of the unpleasant eateries they should try. The lavatory facilities also seemed to be a source of uncertainty and tension, particularly in the extended family groups. There was always a snotty little nipper or an infirm elderly relative who could be relied upon to decide at a moment's notice that they needed to use the loo. Whiny voices and much tugging at sleeves ensued. It was simply all too much.

After far too long spent being reminded that the vast majority of humanity would be better off crawling back into the primordial soup from whence it emerged, Nicholas' ordeal was finally over. He found a place in the lounge. He clutched his gin and tonic and reclined in a leather armchair.

He relaxed, allowing his eye to wander over to a young, blonde woman, tastefully dressed, but whose generous natural endowments were impossible to conceal. While it certainly wasn't Nicholas' style to make any attempt at approaching the woman – this despite the fact that she seemed to be travelling alone – she would function most admirably as a canvas upon which he could project a salacious fantasy or two. Maybe she would be on the same plane. Maybe she would be sitting next to him.

Nicholas' flight of fancy made him think of the heady hours spent with Amber Bluett when she would indulge

Nicholas' penchant for role play to its cold, carnal climax. If only the buxom blonde currently helping herself to another glass of wine were really Amber in disguise. He could join the mile high club with Amber's oversized breasts pretending to belong to some spoilt heiress. Putting Amber in her place in the first class bathroom would bring a delicious combination of licentious luxury and tawdry toilet sex which, in Nicholas' eyes, defined the woman perfectly. Corrupting the cabin crew to allow them to do so would be icing on his praetorian cake. Nicholas savoured the idea. Amber would have boasted a suitably ridiculous pseudonym such as Princess Pandora of Porkmenistan, and he would have to writhe on the horns of the dilemma of whether or not to open her box.

Needless to say, the box would be opened and thoroughly explored. The evils therein had already flown that particular coop and were lurking in whichever environment Amber happened to inhabit. Nicholas had already noted how the atmosphere around Amber in the office had become more fearful, with small episodes of everyday bullying and intimidation being a regular occurrence. Stories were subtly twisted, like misunderstood whispers, designed to set erstwhile allies against each other. Nicholas' spies reported that, wherever a partnerial falling out occurred, Amber's touch was often detected. Nicholas hadn't yet worked out whether she had a master plan for her own self-advancement or if it were just for the sheer fun of seeing the human relations around her become ones based upon suspicion and mistrust, with all the opportunity for further mischief that this afforded her.

He wondered how it was that his colleagues were too dim to see what the woman was doing. Amber did always deploy just the right amount of cleavage to adhere to the dress code whilst ensuring that the male partners' eyes adhered to her breasts. She blinded her interlocutors to the webs of lies that she would spin, while they were spellbound by her tastefully jiggling orbs. The disdain Nicholas reserved for the vast majority of his colleagues was truly well-deserved, if, as lawyers, they allowed themselves to be hoodwinked by that meretricious ex-jailbird from Essex. Vile bodies, buxom as they might be, were there to be enjoyed – and discarded. They were certainly not to be held in esteem, or to be feared, as if they had actual power. A bead of cold, irate sweat formed on Nicholas' brow at the very idea that Amber might be amassing power.

Paradoxically, Nicholas was attracted to and loathed Amber in equal measure. He still did. It was an essential part of how she made him feel – notably, in that she made him feel something at all. Having sex with her was like screwing a coarser, more common version of himself, with the notable compensation of those delectable breasts. The woman had made him feel alive, in sharp contrast to most of humanity, whom Nicholas considered to be bovine, ovine, or worse.

Did he miss her? It was a question that Nicholas never thought he would ever ask himself of any woman. He imagined her wielding a cattle prod, as she cleared a path through the bleating masses of Gatwick Airport. He loved how she sought revenge on those who crossed her, however innocently, employing devious manoeuvres and pure, full-frontal aggression. He imagined her smile of satisfaction as bodies fell writhing to the ground around her, clutching the prodded part in pain as she stepped over – and occasionally on – them, wearing her six-inch stilettos.

Yes. If Amber were here, it would have been a little easier. After some extended foreplay and champagne in the lounge, they would board the plane together. Amber would most certainly have delighted in having sex with him. He shivered as he thought of her cheap fragrance, and her poor grammar. The combination of her cruel, vindictive accomplishments, melded with her council estate past (and no doubt future), would transport Nicholas through contempt and copulation, to a chillingly climactic coitus.

Oh, how he loved to desire yet despise the vile creature.

Was Amber Bluett his S&M? Nicholas suddenly wondered if he had more in common with Hartmut Glick than he cared to admit. He discarded that idea immediately. Some facts were irrefutable: one was that there were many *essential* differences between himself and Hartmut. He, Nicholas, had the common decency and good manners to conceal, and if necessary deny to the death, all the deviant behaviours that he so thrilled to. His discretion was assured almost as much as his indulgences were. Nicholas was not yet sure what he would get up to at the conference – it might be some adventure derived from a passing mutual attraction. Or he might simply purchase sex – vanilla or dress-up, man or woman. Through it all, one thing of course was certain. Whatever happened at the Pan Pacific Conference would stay at the Pan Pacific Conference. It would not make its way back to London, would not be paraded about in some diversity society, and would most certainly not be glorified in a smutty book.

Nicholas needed another gin to calm himself down. Why did Hartmut have to ruin what was a perfectly respectable career by flaunting his perversions in this way? Grudgingly, Nicholas had to admit that the German was not totally devoid of talent, a fact which immediately lifted Hartmut some way above the medley of legal mediocrity that both men listened to daily at Sagworth Turner Dickerhint, like a very bad joke of a radio show. But, mused Nicholas, did Hartmut seriously think that, just because he wasn't a complete fool, and it was the twenty-first century, that he could get away with such a stunt? What sort of optimist would he have to be to believe such tripe?

Nicholas had been forced to leave matters unresolved because of the trip. However, he would deal with the German as soon as he returned. It would be the usual rallying around of the fearful and faithful. Bartlett DeVere could always be relied upon to be scandalised at the slightest hint of modernity. He would be a steadfast ally and perfect pawn. Bartlett would no doubt be apoplectic when Nicholas informed him of the depths of depravity to which Hartmut had not only sunk, but had also documented, in detail, in writings that were about to be published. Nicholas pictured Bartlett, puce with all the self-righteous outrage of a tabloid article which had just discovered EU plans to give asylum-seeking lesbian mothers preferential access to the NHS. With the right stimulus, Bartlett would be rhapsodising at the earliest opportunity as to why such behaviour not only ill-behoved the German, but made his existing relationship with Sagworth Turner Dickerhint simply untenable. Nicholas should check that Bartlett had his inhaler handy, as such intense huffing and puffing would surely bring on one of his wheezing episodes.

Publicly, Nicholas would play the reasonable peace-maker, positioning himself neatly between the more implacably conservative partners who could not countenance Hartmut's continued presence amongst them, and the German's band of more liberal-minded supporters. Privately, Nicholas would ensure the fire remained stoked by getting his hands on a copy of the offending manuscript and leaking choice extracts to the Bartletts of the building. Nicholas had found that leaving stray pages on the printer was a most effective method of communication. Everyone knew how temperamental printers could be, sometimes whirring obediently into action, other times spitefully swallowing print commands never to be seen again, or spitting these offerings out later, either on the original machine at some random point over the next twenty-four hours, or mysteriously from another printer entirely.

As Nicholas plotted how he could finally get IT to work for him, he began to relax. He finished his drink just as his flight was called.

Although there had been no Amber lookalike on board, Nicholas had otherwise been hard pressed to fault the trip so far.

He had slept well, eaten well, and been treated with appropriate servility by the clearly homosexual steward. This underling had been instantly cowed into submission with Nicholas' very first threatening glare. Other passengers may have appreciated the female cabin crew of a certain age, with their silky manners, mastery of their craft, and their easy sense of humour which generally charmed all around them, but Nicholas could not abide the sense of equality that such interaction subtly implied. He did not appreciate it, either, when the pilots strayed from the merely informative into gentle irony. After all, they were mere airborne chauffeurs. It was just about bearable given that they were keeping him safely in the air – but when such familiarity came from serving staff, Nicholas really felt that Britain had irreversibly and irrefutably gone to the dogs.

Thank heavens for this male steward, who, in addition to fulfilling his role quite admirably, could also serve as another one of Nicholas' fantasies. Nicholas pursed his lips. That man was bursting for the most delicious humiliation, all in the service of rendering Nicholas' trip that little bit more special.

Whilst contemplating the possible subjugation of the disposable being who had kept him well supplied on the journey, Nicholas had decided that, as a distraction, and in case the expulsion of Glick became somewhat intense, he might rekindle the relationship with Amber. Nicholas had assembled a number of new role play characters that would delight and stimulate most satisfactorily. Encounters could potentially be even sweeter should Amber not initially be willing to participate. Nicholas' spies had kept him well informed of the latest rumours which were swirling around the Essex blonde. Personally Nicholas felt quite titillated by the fact that she was moonlighting as a madam. However, in order to get what he wanted, he would thoroughly enjoy feigning horror, and then subtly threatening her with the repercussions of her failure to cooperate. How splendid it would all be! More manoeuvring, and cleverness, and cockiness, and power!

Nicholas was awoken from his ruthless reveries by a deafening bang and a blinding white light.

Screams echoed round the cabin. Something had changed in the comforting hum of the plane's engines. He peered out of the window and to his horror saw a plume of smoke coming from the engine on his side of the plane. At that moment the pilot's voice came over the intercom. It mostly succeeding in sounding reassuring.

"Ladies and gentlemen, there is no need to be alarmed. The right hand engine has taken a direct lightning hit and it is out of action. The good news is that the other engine is fine, and is more than capable of getting us to the nearest airport. We will thus be making an unscheduled landing. However, you are in no danger."

Although Nicholas noticed nervous looks from seasoned passengers, the cabin crew seemed to be bustling about as normal. As he gratefully sipped his umpteenth gin and tonic, he glanced at the in-flight map. They were over the Arafura Sea, close to the coast of New Guinea. Nicholas wondered whether the pilot would be heading to the nearest airport in Australia. He wasn't at all sure of how many suitable places there would be to land in New Guinea. Port Moresby was the other side of the island, and he didn't fancy it in any case. He associated that whole godforsaken land with the cannibal stories he had read as a child. It was not the way that he had planned on going at all.

Until now, Nicholas hadn't even registered the storm before the strike that had taken out the right hand engine. Now he, and everyone else on board, seemed to be acutely aware of every rumbling which reverberated around the sky. Nicholas found himself monitoring the intensity of the rain on the window. He was now slightly less pleased with the servile steward. He had a little bit too much of the panic-stricken bullock being led to the slaughter in his eyes, even though his training was thankfully robust enough for it all to be kept in. Thank heavens for small mercies, thought Nicholas. He really would have lost his rag had that one started blubbing.

Little by little, as the plane started to clear the storm, calm returned to the aircraft. Passengers were talking in normal tones again, if tinged with relief. The female crew's sense of humour was back in action. Drinks had been gulped, and there was beginning to be an almost party-like atmosphere on board. Everyone was happy to have got through the episode, and just felt positive about being alive.

How Nicholas detested it. Thankfully the pilot's voice returned and announced they were to commence descending towards Daru Airport shortly. It reminded everyone that they still had to make a landing with one engine, and then suffer heavens alone knows how long a delay in New Guinea. Although irritating to Nicholas, he was grateful for the dampener this awareness inflicted on the other passengers. It returned them to a subdued mood.

This was infinitely preferable to their former vexating gaiety.

As was customary for him, Nicholas decided it was time to go and freshen up and change, so as to arrive relatively fresh. After all, they could be in Daru for some time, and he was not at all sure whether hotel facilities would be either forthcoming or even available. They were over land now. All Nicholas could see was endless forest, broken only by some mountains in the distance and the odd lake. It seemed rather hopeful to expect a Shangri La or Conrad to miraculously appear upon landing.

As Nicholas was about to enter the washroom, armed with his toilet bag and spare clothes, the submissive steward appeared and brushed past him rather deliberately. The steward's bottom rubbed slowly and firmly against Nicholas' groin. Nicholas felt the anger well inside him at such outrageous behaviour. He was about to play merry hell, when he realised that it wasn't just anger that had welled up. The steward, too, immediately noticed the disturbance down below. He was emboldened enough to whisper to Nicholas that he would knock on the door in a couple of minutes. He then rushed off with the first smile on his face since the lightning strike.

Nicholas had not felt this incensed in quite some time. What were things coming to when a steward felt it was acceptable to not only overstep the bounds of propriety, but then actively proposition him, a customer, whilst still on the plane? Lightning strikes and thoughts of one's own mortality would only excuse so much. This *behaviour* was well beyond what Nicholas could possibly countenance.

He would ensure that the man was sacked as soon as he got home to the UK.

Nicholas thought happily about how he might end the man's career, as he slowly and deliberately undressed – lower half first, followed by a methodical freshen up with wet wipes. Nicholas' personal habits all seemed completely run of the mill to him. He never gave them a second thought. He was preparing to slip on fresh smalls. There was nothing more to it. However, as he gingerly cleaned his privates, like some giant adult pandering to his own small baby, he was reminded of his earlier mile high fantasy with an Amber lookalike.

Nicholas had never had a problem with his own flexible sexuality. The offer seemed to be there on a plate. It wasn't a blonde woman from Essex – but it was a servant of sorts. Why not take advantage of the young man, in the way Nicholas desired? Even better, why not then complain about him anyway? With his old college chum on the BA board, there would be no doubt as to who would be believed. Nicholas silently praised his own genius. Who dares, wins.

The knock duly came.

Nicholas opened the door a crack and peered out with an aggrieved look on his face. It was indeed the steward. Oh, he was eagerness personified. Nicholas allowed him to push the folding door open, then pulled him in, shutting and bolting the door behind him, and sinking the man immediately to his knees by firm pressure on his slightly sloping shoulders.

Nicholas was determined that everything would be

done his way. Regardless of this being a sexual encounter, the steward would at all times retain his role of airborne servant. Nicholas was merely adding a few extra duties to the flight manual.

Despite Nicholas' most devious planning, he had reckoned without the storm. Just as he was starting to enjoy himself, in a delightfully twisted if somewhat cramped way, there was a repeat of the sickening bang that had taken out the right hand engine.

The lights went out.

The steward, along with most of the passengers, screamed. He was specific in his concern.

"I don't want to die in a toilet!"

Although Nicholas was rather rattled by the noise himself, he was more petrified at the thought of being stuck in a confined space with a screaming queen. He therefore unlocked the door and pushed the steward out. The steward sprawled forward into darkness. Nicholas didn't give it a moment's thought. He briskly shut himself inside once again. He needed to locate his clean underwear in the dark. It was no matter that he could hear all sorts of noises now coming from outside the cubicle, and the plane was lurching about in a most alarming fashion. Standards were standards. Nicholas was determined to get to wherever it was he was destined, arrival gates or pearly gates, in a clean, decent and presentable state.

As he fumbled around to try to find clothing for his lower half in the dark, he wondered if this was what Hartmut got up to of a weekend. He tensed with anger again at the thought of the German and his disgustingly open attitude to perversion. Wasn't the whole point of perversion to enjoy something in secret that one knew one's acquaintances would be scandalised by? Wasn't the secret part the most important one? Which fool didn't realise this?

The thought that he had to get back to London in one piece so that he could ensure Hartmut Glick got his come-uppance was the last one which went through Nicholas' mind, as a particularly violent lurch caused him to lose his footing and bang his head hard against the door. He blacked out, a gaggle of grinning Hartmuts the last image printed upon his brain.

Nicholas woke up with a throbbing pain in his left arm. Actually, he ached all over.

He peered round through the bright sunlight. He appeared to be on the beach of a small island on the shore of an idyllic sea, with thick forest behind him.

He looked around more carefully. Pieces of aeroplane debris were scattered around.

It was worse. Lifeless bodies and body parts were intermingled with the wreckage. Matter was mingled, everything was both pierced and twisted in almost unrecognisable ways. It brought to mind a modern version of a Hieronymus Bosch triptych, albeit one in which the artist had taken inspiration from a particularly ghastly journey on a budget airline, and had wished to get revenge on the uncomfortable seats, nasty colour schemes and lack of sartorial sense of one's fellow passengers.

Nicholas stood up, wincing at the pain in his arm.

He stepped carefully along the beach. Where were the other survivors? He still intended to get the steward fired, if he had survived, although it would now be cold comfort given the level of inconvenience the airline had put him to.

Where in hell had they come down? Why were there no emergency services around? Nicholas had left his phone in his seat pocket, but surely one of the crew or other passengers should have called assistance by now.

After a few minutes walking along the beach, Nicholas came to an unpleasant realisation. He appeared to be the only person alive. Had he been saved by being in the toilet? The bathroom pod was half-submerged, and broken in pieces not far from where he had woken up on the beach. Maybe they had landed in the water and the bathroom pod had been the last piece of the aircraft to break up, cushioning him from the impact. His shirt had been ripped, the left sleeve shredded and soaked in the blood that had come from the cut on his arm. Other than that he was intact – though naked below the waist. There was no sign of his clothes.

So was this it? He was a knickerless castaway. He had no means of communication and he was in the middle of nowhere in New Guinea. Goodness knows how many cannibalistic tribes of wild men were currently beating a path to where the great metal bird had plummeted into the lake.

It was at that moment that Nicholas heard the drums in the distance. He stood transfixed, not knowing whether to be relieved or worried, as a couple of canoes rounded the headland. They were close enough to make out the occupants faces. They did not look friendly, but then he had never found bones used as clothing or jewellery particularly reassuring.

A moment later he knew he should be worried. Very worried. He recoiled in horror as one of the men stood up, took a bow and then aimed an arrow at him, which narrowly missed his head. Nicholas turned tail and ran as fast as his bony, bare white buttocks could carry him.

"These days," Jake liked to say, "I *prefer* using the back entrance." He may as well say it first. It vaguely entertained his band mates. They were extremely easily amused. He found it better to get his point across before the crass jokes followed. To ribald ribbing about using the tradesmen entrance, back passages and other rear references, Jake these days had to sneak into most venues through their lesser frequented entrances. The courtyards, the kitchens, the back streets. The unsmiling faces of edifices, with few lights or signs.

Although initially finding it a tad degrading, Monique had become resigned to the new inevitability of finding different ways into venues. She found the secrecy of it all interesting. Avoiding attention was harder than at first it might appear. Jake and Monique would sometimes dress up, with a fair degree of imagination. Sometimes they felt unrecogniseable, even to each other. All this just to avoid the press.

Tonight, though, they had walked in, heads high, through the front door. The launch of Outrageous Fortune Boudoir was an event that they were glad to support.

Monique appreciated that there might have been something strangely appropriate about sneaking in and out the back door of a boudoir – but, paparazzi be damned, they were going to make an entrance, exactly as they should. Jake had resisted at first, not wanting to turn the night into a media scrum, before he had had the idea to enlist the assistance of Jacqui. Jacqui La Jones. She was his drag alter ego.

Jake liked dressing up. He was comfortable in a dress. He made a beautiful woman. He was comfortable with that, too.

The bar was filling up as they made their way to a table at the back of the room. Cornisha, Kelly and Ben were doing an excellent job of convincing a bottle of cava that it was every bit as good as champagne. The cava was nice. It wasn't champagne, but it had no pretensions of being so. It was crisp and citrussy, as good gossip should be.

"Oh my giddy aunt! I would never have recognised you, my dear."

Cornisha's mouth hung open slightly inelegantly for a second, as she saw Jake looking like a teenage girl – albeit one who had followed a make-up tutorial to the letter, perhaps on the subject of face contouring. The trowelling and layering that had taken place put to shame that that took place on a major infrastructure project.

The result was – er- impactful.

Cornisha quickly recovered her poise.

"Jacqui is rather popular, even if I do say so myself. Hello, hello, hello."

Jake airkissed Cornisha and Kelly before clapping Ben on the back. "It's funny, I'm used to gay men coming on to me, because it's kind of a rite of passage for any passably attractive popstar to do the gay clubs these days, and, you know, you don't go there to be all old school, do you? But when straight men come on to Jacqui, I actually feel rather vulnerable." He shuddered delicately.

Cornisha sniffed.

"My dear, the worst your gay fans would do to you would be to subject you to some protracted shrieking."

She raised a knowing eyebrow: "As Jacqui, however, you have exchanged the power of fame and masculinity, for the relative vulnerability of an anonymous female, with cheekbones to die for. It is a sad fact that you will attract some unwelcome attention from undesirable sorts of a far less easily dissuaded sort – as well as, one would hope, the respectful looks of admiration that you may be seeking."

"Welcome to our world, Jake," said Kelly.

Jake felt a little slightly guilty. He had been to parties, many of them, where women were considered fair game. Society expected young women wanting to look attractive to display skin as if it were territory for others to roam on. He imagined that he felt some of the same pressure, sometimes. To sense that undercurrent of chauvinism lurking in the recesses of the modern world that he supposed he inhabited was food for thought.

"Well at least if any undesirable does get overfriendly, they are going to be in for a bit of a shock," offered Ben.

"Quite a big shock, actually," said Monique, crisply. "For goodness sake don't get frisky tonight, Jake, otherwise that tuck isn't going to hold."

"Too much information, my dear."

Cornisha glanced at Jake's crotch. She lapsed into laughter.

"Sorry, I'm just picturing your preparations. Now, are we going to be hearing you sing, dear? If that is so, we're going to need more drinks."

Hartmut and Caroline rarely, if ever, felt vulnerable, no matter what their attire. They carried off their classic black leather look that evening with practised poise, with just the faintest of sartorial nods to the evening in store, with large diamanté buckles on their studded belts. They slipped with feline grace through the effervescent throng of the built and the bejewelled to the sanctuary of their friends.

"Hartmut!" Ben jumped up as he saw his boss approach, and gave him a bear hug. Hartmut suppressed an urge to flinch and move away from such unaccustomed proximity. He reciprocated gingerly, circling Ben's shoulders with his leather clad arms. Thankfully it was all over quickly.

Ben embraced Caroline, and then stepped back to allow an orgy of cheek kissing in the group.

As people settled in, Ben took his boss aside:

"Is there any word regarding Nicholas' whereabouts, Hartmut?" he enquired. He was unsure as to which answer he wanted to the question.

"It does not look good. There is no trace of him, but his wallet has been found amongst the debris," replied Hartmut sombrely.

Hartmut was in fact deeply saddened. He had never liked Nicholas Casterway, but this was not an end he would have wished on anyone.

Ben, too, had been numbed by the tragedy that had unfurled, and yet he could not help but feel relief that Nicholas would no longer be casting his malevolent shadow over his life.

"How awful," muttered Ben. He frowned: he hated sounding so unconvincing, speaking thus about Nicholas.

"Indeed," responded Hartmut neutrally.

The two men stood in silence for a moment, their grave demeanour at odds with the levity around them.

Hartmut's pragmatism eventually kicked in.

"Of course, with Nicholas gone, the question of my book has now assumed its rightfully insignificant place in the partners' minds. Indeed, on a number of points, I think we can safely say that Sagworth Turner Dickerhint has a reasonable chance of becoming a better environment in which to work. It is an ill wind that is blowing us some good, Ben."

Hartmut kept an appropriately tombstone-like expression, but both men knew that the disappearance of Nicholas Casterway should have a positive effect on human happiness in their law firm, way beyond their own quarrels with the man. Scruples at having to square this with the tragedy of the loss of life of the other passengers could be worked through another time.

"Do you mind if I interrupt?"

Kelly's dazzling smile banished Ben and Hartmut's moral struggle, for a moment, at least.

"I take it you have heard, Hartmut, about Amber?"

Hartmut nodded. The night was supposed to be one of celebration of new beginnings, of success built on hard work and talent, and of pure unadulterated fun. And yet death and arrests cast a long shadow, even when they took horrible people. Perhaps because, like all demons, their disappearance could only signal that others would soon be there to take their place.

One concern vanishing did not mean that all others would retreat tidily. In any event, Amber and Nicholas already seemed to be lurking in the shadows, threatening and caustic from beyond the grave and from the depths of prison.

Hartmut sighed. Oh, scruples be damned. It was time to slay those thoughts and move on:

"After all the agonising about how we could use the force of the law to ensure the woman was stopped, she was ultimately outsmarted by all those she was unkind to. Next time someone tried to throw their weight around, we shall have to cite the tragic example of our former HR manager."

Kelly sniffed.

"At the speed at which action was going to be taken, we'd have still be agonising over the correct procedure to boot her out come our retirements."

With regard to Nicholas, Kelly regretted any premature loss of life, but she also felt angry that somehow the man had managed to avoid a proper reckoning. Death may seem the ultimate reckoning, but not when you still had things to say.

The party was heating up. The buzz helped to bring Hartmut, Ben and Kelly back to the here and now.

They were soon pounced upon by a hipster beardy pair. The two looked familiar.

"Do you know, I never bought all that dildo empowerment crap you spouted, Pam, until I stuck one down the front of my trousers. I think I might start wearing one to the office. I'd love to accidentally rub up against Bartlett DeVere's bottom in the lift. Imagine how pleased he'd be. Hello everyone!"

Lynne Glackett beamed as Pam Shank glowered at her. It was a familiar routine. They were dressed as drag kings, another trend to hit London's unflappable watering holes.

Pam was pursing her lips.

"That's not what I said, Lynne. And for goodness sake don't let's start on sausage jokes this evening. Is there nothing obvious that you wouldn't stoop to? You really are the most rubbish feminist I have ever clapped eyes on. Your lack of consistency is disheartening. You can't condemn sexual harassment, woman, then indulge in it yourself."

Pam glowered. She was capable of holding a glare for an entire evening when the mood was right. It was made easy for her, as there was so very much that was so very infuriating about the world.

"Oh, and pleased to meat you too! Get it?" laughed Lynne.

Lynne was her very own captive audience, and it made her very happy.

The bar owners showed up next in what had become the impromptu VIP area of the bar. No one complained about that. Tarquin and Alex moved with feline grace through the crowd, at ease in expensive suits. Rubens and Jamal, on the other hand, seemed to be somewhat constricted by their tight-fitting suits, as if they had not quite got used to what felt like fancy dress.

"Boys! You certainly are a sight for sore eyes." Kelly twinkled at the latest arrivals.

"Well, if we can't make an effort for our grand opening, when would we? It's all in support of our dear Kasim. And here she is!"

Lady Gaza glittered from tiara-clad-head to Louboutin-toe.

"I am certainly glad you could make it, gentlemen. You are most decorative. Thank you. For a moment I wondered if our dancing troupe were going to let us down. But we can pack up those worries in our fashionable kit bag. We've scored. Jacqui La Jones here will be performing with her band, who for one evening only will be named the Fondant Fancies. I hope you have a sweet tooth, boys. In anticipation of all that candy fluff, we have whipped up a suitably half-baked, warm-up band of drag queens. Behold the Angel Delights."

Lady Gaza smiled and theatrically indicated the brightly coloured drag queens trailing in her wake.

"I present to you Cherry Slice, Sue Flay, Victoria Sponge, and – in homage to our dangerous liaison of Louisiana lovely and Italian American – the finger-licking Tara May Sue."

Four drag queens in a coordinated curtsey is something perhaps only the Queen of England herself might properly appreciate.

Caspar stood in a queue three-deep at the bar, waiting to be served. He generally preferred table service, but he had offered to buy a round anyway. The friends he had brought that evening couldn't stop telling him how cool Outrageous Fortune was. They had spotted Ben early, and were waxing lyrical about how gorgeous he was, and how lucky Caspar was to work in close proximity to such a stud.

Caspar had smiled with all the sincerity and naturalness of an over-Botoxed TV presenter feigning enthusiasm for a reality star's latest literary venture. He suggested they needed more alcohol. He certainly did.

It was so frustrating. Caspar still perceived Ben as an embarrassing shag who had somehow reached heights and places that seemed utterly unattainable to the more conventionally attractive younger models that Caspar liked to be seen around with. Caspar called them his designer purses, as their main purpose was to look great on his arm, and engender envy in others. Yet now these friends of his were telling him that Ben was actually the finest thing he could be seen out with after all, and he just *couldn't* bring himself to tell them that Ben and he had actually had sex. Not after all the barriers that Caspar had so carefully erected. Caspar realised with a start that he was dying to see his acquaintances' jealous looks as he described how Ben had taken him, and what a stud indeed he really was. Oh, life could be so unfair at times.

As Caspar was pondering the injustice of it all, he absent-mindedly knocked into a woman carrying a glass of wine back from the bar, with the result that half of the glass ended up on the floor.

Caspar was mortified.

"Oh gosh, I am so dreadfully sorry. Please, let me buy

you another drink to make up for my clumsiness. Thank goodness it didn't go on your dress. Oh, how stupid of me."

Caspar detested it when buffoons spilt his drink. This is what thinking about Ben led to – spillage and chaos.

He looked at the woman, feeling unexpectedly sheepish. The woman looked familiar.

Before she could respond, Caspar realised how he knew her:

"Oh my. I recognise you. OMG, you're a dancer on TV, aren't you? Oh, you are fabulous! I love your routines, and that attitude is fierce. I can't believe I've spilt your drink! Oh, please let me buy you a drink? This is amazing. We should have champagne!"

It was the first time that Polina had been recognised in public by a complete stranger. Caspar seemed a harmless sort of dolt. She blushed with pleasure and a hint of embarrassment. At least the first time being accosted by a fan would be hard to forget.

Polina had an automatic reflex of saying yes to surprisingly generous offers. Some people. They never learn. But at least this was relatively harmless.

"That is very kind of you, I would love some champagne. My name is Polina, by the way."

They chatted quite happily about banal things. Sometimes a good untaxing conversation is a welcome respite. All Caspar's thoughts of Ben were eclipsed by his delight at meeting his new celebrity friend. The attraction, purely platonic, seemed mutual.

Polina had been more than a little worried about her first trip to a gay bar. Cornisha persuaded her that the time had come to take the plunge. Polina felt an odd uneasiness. She had butterflies in her stomach. It was a perturbing to see all these men all over each other. However, people seemed kind, and… normal. There were many very attractive men too.

She wouldn't go to far as to say she was truly comfortable, but she did relax slowly.

She scrutinised her young admirer. Caspar was evidently homosexual, but he seemed sophisticated. He paid her many compliments. He made her laugh and feel as if she were the only girl in the world. He was always singularily unlikely to sell her to a friend for sexual purposes. This wasn't a bad starter for ten, where friendship was concerned.

Polina was soon sitting with Caspar and his friends. Being treated like a proper star felt delightful, and – like many women before her – she wished that she had acquired gay friends earlier. This joyous, if predictable, outcome was interrupted when music swelled and boomed.

The loudspeakers crackled.

"Ladies, gentlemen, and any other denomination of welcome guests, I am here to welcome you to… Outrageous Fortune Boudoir!"

Lady Gaza made a dramatic entrance onto the stage and paused.

A huge chorus of cheers and applause echoed round the room. Lady Gaza had changed and now appeared as a bridal couple, her left side kitted out in a wedding dress, tiara and train, while her right side presented as Kasim in a dinner jacket, complete with facial hair and dramatic gelled black hair.

She allowed the uproar to subside slightly.

"Now, gorgeous friends, we have a very special treat for you this evening. In a representation evoking both sweetness and light, one of the best-known London bands has dropped in – and in a new guise. Here, to give us an exclusive live performance of their new song "Thong bird", please welcome the Fondant Furies – known for this night only as the Fondant Fancies! Yes! I certainly fancy them. Please put your hands together for the fabulous Jacqui La Jones and her band, together with the Boudoir residents, our very own Angel Delights. Oh, and here come a few handsome male dancers for you trashy queens out there, too. We like a full stage."

Jake suffered nerves when he took to the stage in front of his legions of fans, but this felt different – more intimate, more exposed, like cabaret. His nervousness was on a whole new scale. He headed onto stage to thunderous applause. Was performing as Jacqui really a good idea? With a brand new song at that? Cameras flashed. Phones were aloft. There was no going back. He squared his shoulders, and went for it.

Soon, everyone seemed to be on their feet, dancing. Jake had no more qualms. He even winked lasciviously as Rubens, down to a pair of hot pants, slut dropped in front of him. Jake was soon in his element. He strutted round the stage, posing for the cameras, duetting with Tara May Sue, and luxuriating in an entire room focussing on him. The grand finale came with Jamal and Alex hoisting him skywards in a fireman's lift. He raised an arm, and held it aloft triumphantly.

Outrageous Fortune Boudoir indulged him. The crowd cheered and screamed. Such acclaim, especially in a confined space, produces a unique energy. The journalists present captured every minute. The Twittersphere obediently produced trends: #Jacqui and #OutrageousFortuneBoudoir.

Lady Gaza drank in the success. In the midst of a world where there were many things which she could not be happy about, she and her friends had struck out for what they believed in. They were a hit.

An uneventful week had passed. Kelly had invited Morten and Ben over, with ulterior motives stacked up like planes at Heathrow.

She was in full preparation mode.

"Rubens! Rubens – I need help with this."

Rubens smiled at Kelly.

"No no no… you don't! You look gorgeous. If you needed help with your hair, I should have brought Gaza with me. I can only do a shaved head. Unless… you fancy that?""

Kelly ignored the irrelevances. She frowned theatrically.

"Gorgeous won't cut it. I'm trying to find *irresistible*. Properly addictive, and necessary. I need to be utterly intoxicating tonight. Come on. This is it, Rubens. This is my chance."

Rubens glanced around Kelly's flat. He looked puzzled.

"I don't get it. This is looking beautiful. You've got delicious snacks and delicacies laid out. You've prepared fountains of drinks of which we have consumed more than a bucket as we speak. Well done us, incidentally, for this makes us more fun and witty. There is soft but sexy music playing – good rhythm, good vibrations. The playlist will go for *hours* – hopefully just like you guys. There are cushions on the floor, for goodness sake. There are *candles*."

Kelly looked at him.

"Rubens. We're talking about Ben here."

"Ah," said Rubens. "I do see your point. Although even Ben isn't a spoilsport."

Kelly nodded.

"I know. But he is prone to breaking into conversations about politics at the strangest moments."

Rubens scoffed.

"He never did that with me!"

"I'll ignore that. I could say something mean about the audience, but I'll ignore it. The problem is, Rubens, if you'll take my advice about men… "

Rubens threw up his hands.

"Now I have heard it all! Kelly Danvers. What goes through your head? Oh, do tell me what you know about men, for I am sure that I have no idea whatsoever about those mysterious creatures."

He perched on a chair with his hands under his chin, pausing only to drink a slug of margarita.

"Don't be such a man-child, you Brazilian-waxed doll. This is a terrible secret and you must not repeat it. But what I am about to tell you can be a phenomenal disappointment for those who do not realise it. *Men are actually not as easy as they advertise themselves to be*."

Rubens waved his arms.

"Cannot compute. No, seriously Kelly, can-not

com-pute. What *are* you talking about?"

Kelly smiled knowingly.

"Just because it doesn't apply to you, doesn't mean it's not true. Men can be discerning, you know. Or scared. Or just not up for it. So this, tonight – well, it's not a done deal."

Rubens creased his forehead.

"Kelly, the three of you have been prancing around like show ponies for the last many weeks. You have, every last Jack Russell of you, been sniffing around like dogs in dog club. You can cut the sexual anticipation with a knife. Morten is up for it. Ben will find his mojo in the experience. You have prepared a veritable cave of lubricious delights, and you do look gorgeous. If this threesome is not on, I'll eat carbohydrates after seven for a week."

"I'm telling you. All this sex, sex, sex – and then sometimes they pass."

"I've never heard of it, but I'm sure you're right. In some other universe."

"Anyway, what do you think?"

Rubens did like what he saw.

Kelly had chosen a red silk dress that wrapped around her, and should unwrap around her very easily. It showed off alluring cleavage and flattered her legs. Her hair was loose and she wore small sparkling jewellery that would not get in the way.

"Very nice," said Rubens. "For two pins I'd join in myself."

"Much as I love and appreciate you, you're not invited. Now, see this: I've got hold ups on. They don't last when you walk around in them – but they are quite sexy for staying in, don't you think?"

Rubens nodded.

"Very erotic. I like the shoes, too."

"I need to get them quite drunk and off their heads – but not so off their heads that they can't enjoy it."

"Dear me, this is very choreographed. But I agree. Look. You want my advice, so I'll provide it. First things first – get on with it quickly. Don't give them the chance to back out. Then watch something a little racy and try again. Also: be generous. It won't be all about you."

"Well, you *say* that… "

In the event, Kelly need not have worried, because every little thing was going to be alright.

Morten strode into the mood-lit room, and set a couple of bottles of champagne down like chess pieces on the kitchen counter. He turned to grab Ben.

"Ben! My friend."

He held Ben by the shoulders and leaned in to kiss him. It was decisive. It was straightforward. Before anyone felt obliged to react, Morten reached out for Kelly and kissed her too.

Kelly seized a bottle and deftly sprang it open. She looked at the men and drank from it deeply.

"Good temperature," she said, "care for some? Glasses not required."

"I see a couple of margarita pitchers ready to go, too," said Ben calmly. He turned the music up.

Drunk enough, already. You didn't need much – just something to take the edge off. Kelly felt distinctly happy, warm and excited. She was now kissing Ben – and Morten was kissing her too. Her dress was falling open, and she was reclining, and it was all that she could have wished for.

Was it so wrong that alcohol played such a part, she wondered drowsily? Alcohol, humanity's happy companion for so long. It was doomed and condemned, no doubt rightly sometimes – but it deserved praise, too, for its vital roles – as a social lubricant, a courage-inciting brew, an inhibitor-relaxant. Like almost every other consumable that one could think of, it had its limits. It had its place. But limits and intolerances do not deprive alcohol of significance or, put at its most simple, of the joys that it brings.

Kelly was grateful for its warm embrace, as it brought her to more pleasure than she had thought possible. Her head was finally cleared of mice-like scurrying thoughts. Her whole being was surrendered.

Everything was alright.

As she came to, spent, exhausted, throbbing and tingling, she reflected drowsily on the nature of experiences. They were but the passing of seconds and hours and days. We are, all of us, so insignificant in the universe. Our convictions are simply to be expressed and communicated – they may live on, but we ourselves will disappear like snow in spring. Does it ever matter what anyone thinks? Be true to yourself, she decided, and dare to be different, if that works for you.

She looked at the men as they settled down to sleep. She thought they would be asleep long before she was. In the event, they all went out like lights in the 1970s.

Interestingly, when Kelly woke up the next day, she could remember very little. She watched Morten stroll around the flat preparing breakfast, a naked Greek statue without the ludicrous fig leafery. Meanwhile, Ben was blearily making coffee for them all.

They were very at ease with each other now.

Ben saw her emerging. He looked at his watch.

"You know I need to run now. I've got tickets to a rugby match."

"Sure," yawned Kelly, "More strange shaped balls for you."

Ben smiled as he brought her a coffee, just as she liked it.

"It feels okay, doesn't it? Of course, Morten is disappearing off again next week."

She smiled at him.

"He'll never be ours. But he is pretty good to have around."

"I think I actually agree," said Ben.

"Enjoy your day," said Kelly, her dressing gown falling open, "oh Gawd, sorry."

Ben threw his head back and laughed.

"Seriously? Seriously? That is surely the most inappropriate apology ever. Have a great day. See you later tonight."

He pointed at her dishevelled front:

"As for all this. As for all this… what can I say?"

He smiled a dazzling, confident smile.

"It's just tits. See ya!"

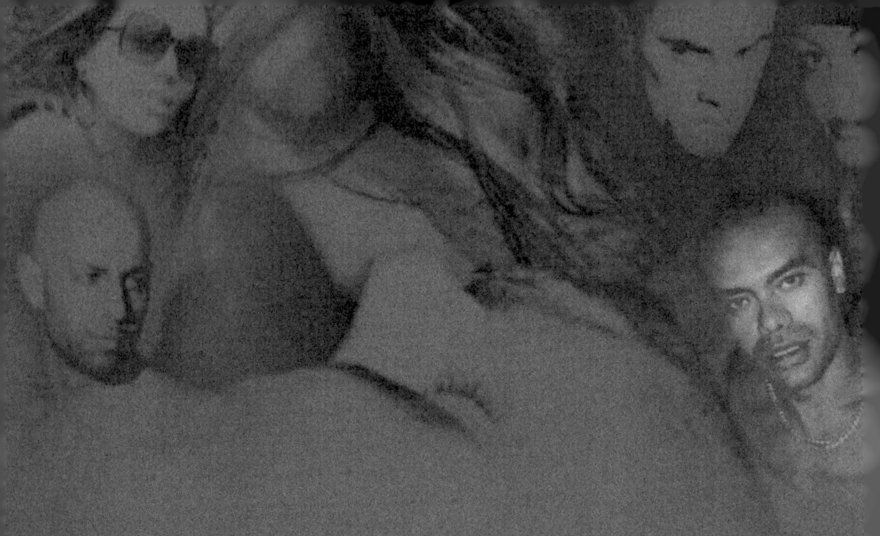

TIM BRADY & MELANIE WILLEM

BIG BEN

LAW AND DISORDER

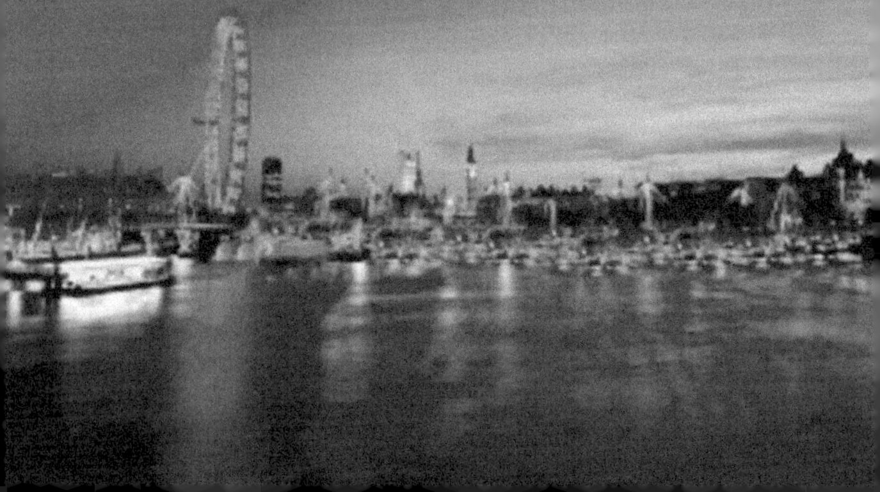

London, England. Ben Barlettano, a successful, highly-sexed yet still wet behind the ears 26-year old New York lawyer lands in the Elephant & Castle.

Through a chain of unexpected experiences, Ben discovers his new life. Exciting, sometimes harsh, occasionally extreme, but never dull. Ben meets a number of people, each with stories and secrets. There is the respectable senior partner who is addicted to bondage clubs; the serenely efficient office manager who cannot bring herself to tell her boyfriend she, too, used to have a penis; the statuesque gym instructor hiding his emotions under a perennial smile; and of course the woman Ben falls for, almost on day one, who seems afraid of nothing – until she gets scared.

Uncomfortable encounters in Turkish baths, moonlighting as an escort for charity, violent arguments with a neighbour and thoroughly mismanaging a ménage-à-trois are just some of the things that Ben is utterly unprepared for.

Will Ben survive what London throws at him, or will he end up scuttling back to his Italian mamma in New York?

TIM BRADY & MELANIE WILLEM

BEAUX, BELLES

GRIND AND PUNISHMENT

London, England. Ben Barlettano is a successful lawyer in the new firm created by the merger between Beaux Aspen and Dickerhint Strudel. So far, so dull – but the past rears up, in the shape of Amber Bluett, ex-convict, now a cynical Human Resources Manager bent on revenge.

Juggling leadership of the LGBT group, a long-distance relationship with Kelly, his Paris-based girlfriend from Louisiana, and the problems behind the scenes at Outrageous Fortune, the gay bar managed by his ex-boyfriend, Ben has his hands full.

Will Ben retain the confidence of his bondage-loving boss, survive the humiliation of his mother dating a toy boy, navigate the shoals of relationship challenges, and keep his career alive in the face of hard partying?

Turn again, Ben. A lot can happen within earshot of the bells of St-Mary-le-Bow.

Contact us:
Facebook (melandtimbooks)
Twitter (melandtimbooks)